SILVER WINGS, IRON CROSS

TOM YOUNG

SILVER WINGS, IRON CROSS

KENSINGTON BOOKS
www.kensingtonbooks.com

KENSINGTON BOOKS are published by

Kensington Publishing Corp.
119 West 40th Street
New York, NY 10018

All Kensington titles, imprints, and distributed lines are available at special quantity discounts for bulk purchases for sales promotion, premiums, fundraising, educational, or institutional use. Special book excerpts or customized printings can also be created to fit specific needs. For details, write or phone the office of the Kensington Special Sales Manager: Attn. Special Sales Department. Kensington Publishing Corp., 119 West 40th Street, New York, NY 10018. Phone: 1-800-221-2647.

Library of Congress Card Catalogue Number: 2019953651

Kensington and the K logo Reg. U.S. Pat. & TM Off.

ISBN-13: 978-1-4967-3043-5
ISBN-10: 1-4967-3043-7
First Kensington Hardcover Edition: June 2020

ISBN-13: 978-1-4967-3045-9 (ebook)
ISBN-10: 1-4967-3045-3 (ebook)

10 9 8 7 6 5 4 3 2 1

Printed in the United States of America

In memory of Brigadier General V. Wayne "Speedy" Lloyd

PART I

1

Your Target for Today . . .

In the 94th Bomb Group's briefing room, at the ungodly hour of 0400, Lieutenant Karl Hagan watched the S-2 officer reveal the map for the day's mission. A length of red yarn depicted the planned flight. The yarn stretched from the 94th's base at Rougham Field in Bury St Edmunds, England, across the English Channel, and into Germany. Pins stuck in the map at turn points angled the yarn through course changes en route to the primary target: Bremen. Karl felt ice form in his chest.

On this, Karl's last assigned mission, the U.S. Eighth Air Force was ordering him to bomb his family. Although his parents had lived in Pennsylvania since leaving Germany at the end of the Great War, Karl still had relatives who worked in the factories and shipyards of Bremen, turning out aircraft and U-boats for the Third Reich. Those relatives included Karl's uncle Rainer and aunt Federica.

As pilot and aircraft commander of a B-17 Flying Fortress, Karl had always known this could happen. But for thirty-four missions, he and his crew had struck targets far from any Hagan home: the submarine pens at Saint-Nazaire, the former automobile plants at Antwerp, the airfield at Beaumont-le-Roger. All the while, Karl hoped the war would end before his crew opened a bomb bay anywhere near his extended family.

Karl eyed the framed photographs on the wall in the briefing room: President Franklin D. Roosevelt, Secretary of War Henry Stimson, Supreme Allied Commander Dwight Eisenhower. The S-2's words sounded distant and hollow; Karl could barely listen. This war presented so many ways to make people suffer, to force them to do unspeakable things, to face impossible decisions. Thus far, Karl had focused single-mindedly on his duty. *If I do that,* he figured, *I can't go wrong.* Duty had become the magnetic north on his moral compass.

But now the compass spun, showed no direction.

I cannot do this, Karl thought. *But I have to do this.*

The S-2 stood with his hands on his hips, the very picture of military bearing in his Ike jacket and tie. "Your target for today, gentlemen," he said, "is the Focke-Wulf aircraft factory in Bremen. I don't need to tell you how the Focke-Wulfs and Messerschmitts have taken a toll on us. Your alternate target is the submarine facility on the River Weser. As you know, German U-boats have played hell with our merchant fleet. Whichever target you hit, now's your chance to get payback."

None of the two hundred men in the Nissen hut hooted or growled in bravado, and Karl knew why. Yes, payback was sweet, but the aircraft plant and sub pens would be heavily defended. This mission was no milk run to an easy target in occupied France. On this mission, German fighter planes and flak gunners would exact a toll. Statistics promised that some of the men sitting to Karl's left and right, dressed in their leather A-2 jackets and flying coveralls, would not come back.

"They're gonna make us pay for our ticket home," Adrian whispered, sitting next to Karl.

Adrian Baum had flown as Karl's copilot for his entire tour. Son of a Bronx rabbi, Adrian fought and flew as if the survival of his people depended on him. He seldom went to London on pass. Instead, he spent most of his free time studying flight manuals, poring over aircraft performance charts, reviewing training films, and writing his parents. He spoke often of New York's attractions, and he'd promised to show Karl the sights when they got home.

For Karl, Adrian, and the rest of their crew, this—their thirty-fifth mission—would end their war one way or another. Eighth Air Force regs said fliers who completed thirty-five bombing raids could go home for permanent Stateside duty. Crews reaching that goal joined "The Lucky Bastard Club," and they celebrated with a send-off party, usually soaked with English ale and Scotch whisky. They received unofficial certificates with these words under their names:

> . . . *who on this date achieved the remarkable record of having sallied forth, and returned, no fewer than 35 risky times, bearing tons and tons of H.E. Goodwill to the Fuehrer and would-be Fuehrers, thru the courtesy of Eighth Bomber Command, who sponsors these programs in the interest of government "of the people, by the people, and for the people."*

Karl looked forward to joining the Lucky Bastard Club as much as anyone. But why did his price of membership have to be a raid on Bremen? He despised what Adolf Hitler had done to his parents' homeland and took pride in his small role fighting Nazism. But dropping bombs on Bremen could mean dropping bombs on uncles and cousins, some of whom did not support National Socialism. Letters from Bremen had stopped coming, but Karl knew his uncle Rainer had been fired from his job at Bremer Vulkan AG for political reasons. Karl did not know the details, but Adrian had told him there were rumors of slave labor at German factories.

"If your uncle is the mensch you say he is," Adrian had said, "maybe he got into trouble speaking out against forced labor at his company."

A good guess, Karl supposed. He appreciated Adrian's analytical mind and cool competence, both on the ground and in the air. Karl's copilot was his right-hand man, quite literally.

As the briefing continued, the S-2 discussed mission details: formation type, assembly point, route, initial point, bombing altitude. He displayed a reconnaissance photo of the Focke-Wulf plant and surrounding area.

When the S-2 finished, the weather officer took the podium. "You can expect good VFR for takeoff and over your target," the weatherman said. "Forecast for this morning here at Rougham is scattered clouds at five thousand feet, light and variable winds. CAVU for northern Germany—ceiling and visibility unlimited."

Not good, Karl thought. *If we can see the target, the flak gunners can see us.*

To the left of the weather charts, another board listed the aircraft and crews on today's mission, arranged by their places in the formation. A tail number and an aircraft commander's name represented each airplane. Karl found HAGAN 632 at the number-five position in the low squadron. Call sign, Fireball Able. At least he had a good ship to fly: 632 meant *Hellstorm,* an F-model with a reputation for luck.

Hellstorm had taken more than her share of battle damage, but none of her crew members had ever been seriously hurt. She had undergone five engine changes, and the sheet metal guys had given her an entirely new rudder and vertical stabilizer. All the maintenance work reminded Karl of the old joke about the hundred-year-old ax: It's had only two new heads and five new handles. But *Hellstorm* was still *Hellstorm;* you just felt it in the way she flew. Airplanes might not have souls, but they sure had personalities.

"Stations time is 0615," the S-2 announced. "Aircraft commanders, take charge of your crews."

With a scraping of chairs, the men stood up and set about their tasks. Karl's waist gunners, Sergeants Chris Ryan and Thomas Firth, along with tail gunner Morgan Anders, checked with the armament shack to make sure *Hellstorm* had a full supply of .50-caliber ammunition. The gunners then joined Karl and the rest of the crew to wait in line for personal flight equipment. The men stood outside in the early-morning darkness, arms folded over their chests against a chilly breeze. As they talked, their breath became visible in the cool November air.

The crew consisted of ten men. In addition to the two pilots, two waist gunners, and the tail gunner, Karl's team included navigator Richard Conrad, bombardier Billy Pell, ball turret gunner Dick "The Kid" Russo, flight engineer and top turret gunner Joe Fairburn, and radio operator Steven Baker. At nineteen, Russo was the youngest. Twenty-eight-year-old Fairburn was the oldest. Karl and Adrian were twenty-three.

They emerged from the flight equipment shop loaded with leather flying helmets, throat microphones, goggles, Mae West flotation devices, and parachute harnesses. Karl wore a standard-issue .45 pistol, Colt model M1911, under his jacket. A pouch in a lower leg pocket of his flight suit contained an escape kit with a silk map, candy and gum, razor blades, water purification tablets, and parachute cord. By the time the men clambered aboard jeeps and trucks to ride out to the hardstands, the first rays of sunrise painted blood-colored streaks across the east.

The bustle of activity—the rumble of the fuel trucks, the flutter of the wind sock, the mechanics pinning engine cowlings—refreshed Karl like a tonic. He felt he played a role in something vastly bigger than himself, that even if he made an utter mess of the rest of his life, he had already justified his presence on the planet, established a right to the air he breathed.

And yet . . . he could not forget his kin, across the English Channel, across lines on a map. If not for his father's choices, Karl might live in Germany now. Would he have joined the *Luftwaffe*? Would he have become a hapless draftee in the army? Perhaps he would have remained in the civilian labor force. On this very morning, he might have risen for work at a factory, unaware that his workplace had finally made the target list.

The dawn illuminated scores of bombers bristling with guns and propellers, their lines sharp and hard and lethal despite the whimsical names and topless girls painted on their noses: *Bouncin' Annie, Lush Thrush, Passionate Witch.* Underneath the names, swastikas represented German fighters downed by gunners, and orange bombs stood for completed missions.

Hellstorm's nose bore four swastikas and twenty bombs. Another marking read: *U.S. ARMY B-17-F, AIR FORCES SERIAL NO. 42-24632, SERVICE THIS AIRPLANE WITH 100 OCTANE FUEL.* The truck groaned to a stop in front of *Hellstorm*'s left wing, and Karl jumped off the tailgate, inhaled the cold morning air and fumes of gas and oil. His crew disembarked behind him. The men lined up, and Karl inspected them for proper gear. After he found everything in order, he tried to think of stirring words for them—something along the lines of the St. Crispin's Day speech, or perhaps the poem "Invictus." He did the best he could, but he felt he came up short.

"We've gone to hell thirty-four times," Karl said. "We've had each other's back for every mile and every bullet and every bomb."

He paused, too distracted to think of something better. "One more time, fellas," he said finally. "One more time." The men cheered, clapped, and turned to their duties.

"Let's get it done," Pell, the bombardier, said.

Karl hoisted his parachute bag from the truck and set it down at the B-17's forward access hatch, under the nose of the aircraft.

"Pell," he said, gloved fingers spread wide for emphasis, "I need you to drop 'em right down the pickle barrel this time."

"You know I always do," Pell said. "Anything special about today?"

Karl hesitated, considered what to tell the bombardier. "Ah, well, no," he said. "I just want our last one perfect."

"You got it, boss."

Not as easy as Pell made it sound, Karl knew. The Norden bombsight, a highly classified gyroscopic instrument that could be coupled to the airplane's autopilot, allowed bombing with greater precision than the old vector sights. Flight tests showed a much smaller circular error with bombs dropped by Norden-equipped airplanes. But in combat, that circle widened. Flak-rattled crews, smoke over the target, and shifting winds aloft created more variables than a bombardier could crank into the adjustment knobs. Technology could not clear the fog of war.

Karl did a walk-around inspection as his crew boarded the B-17. Normally, the walk-around fell to Adrian and the ground crew chief, but Karl did it occasionally, and today he had a special motivation. Part of him hoped to find something wrong—some reason *Hellstorm* couldn't fly, some excuse to sit this one out. Yes, Karl knew, that Focke-Wulf plant needed to go. So did the shipyards and submarine pens in the area. To think civilians wouldn't die was self-delusion. Bombs had to fall on Bremen in this autumn of 1944; there was no getting around it. *But,* he asked himself, *do they have to fall from* my *airplane?*

He checked the tires: no cuts in the treads, no leaks from the brake lines. Good pressure on the gear struts: Both showed an inch and a half of the shiny silver inner cylinder. Karl spun the supercharger wheels on all four engines, checked the linkage on the wastegates. The Wright R-1820 engines showed normal oil seepage, but no bad leaks. Props looked good; there were no dings or cracks. At the trailing edge of the left wing, Karl found just the right amount of play in the aileron trim tab. Nothing about *Hellstorm* looked even remotely out of sorts.

Karl made his way back to the forward crew access hatch and shoved his parachute bag inside. Then he reached up to the sides of the hatch and pulled himself through. The hatch offered no steps or boarding stairs: The Flying Fortress was built for agile young men.

Inside the Fort, a familiar smell filled Karl's nostrils: that oil-and-gunmetal odor of a military aircraft. He climbed into the cockpit and settled into the left seat. Adrian was already strapping himself into the right seat. From down below in the Plexiglas-tipped nose section, Karl heard the bombardier and navigator take their positions.

Through the windscreen, Karl saw other crews manning their ships. A weapons carrier with a load of bombs rolled past, splashing through oily pools of water on the taxiway. Atop the cubical control tower, the cups of the anemometer spun in the light breeze. Officers lined the tower's iron-railed balcony, observing the 94th gird for battle. Karl checked his watch: almost time for engine start.

"You guys ready?" he asked.

"Born ready," Adrian said.

"Yes, sir," said Fairburn, the flight engineer. Fairburn stood behind the pilots' seats to monitor gauges during engine start. He handed Karl the maintenance document, Form 1-A. Karl checked the fuel and bomb loads, noted the status mark—a red diagonal. That symbol meant the aircraft had only minor maintenance write-ups, nothing to prevent flight. Karl signed the form and passed it back to Fairburn.

"Let's get the checklist started," Karl said.

Adrian reached for a checklist stored in a plastic sheet protector. "Gyros," he said.

Karl checked the artificial horizon and the heading indicator. "Uncaged," he replied.

"Fuel shutoff switches."

"Open."

"Landing gear switch."

"Neutral."

"Mixture levers."

"Idle cutoff."

The singsong routine of checklist procedures had always comforted Karl. It put him in mind of a train rolling along a track, rails locking the wheels onto proper course. Each crew member became a moving part in a greater machine aimed at a common purpose. Nearly all aviators found reassurance in teamwork. Karl knew a navigator in his squadron who walked behind the airplane and threw up before every mission. But once you got him on headset and talking, he did okay.

Today, however, routine brought Karl no comfort. Now the train thundered toward a place he did not want to go. He could find no justification to stop the process: Nothing was wrong with the airplane. He flipped on the master and ignition switches. Checked batteries one, two, and three separately, then turned on all of them. Switched on the inverters, and the instruments hummed to life.

To save the batteries, Karl signaled for a ground crewman to connect external power: He put both arms out the left window and clamped his left hand over his right fist. The ground crewman plugged an electrical cord into the side of *Hellstorm*. The cord snaked from a portable generator, which growled like a lawn mower when started.

Another ground crewman stood fireguard with an extinguisher. Karl motioned with his index finger: Stand by to start number one. The crewman positioned himself behind the outboard engine on the left wing. Karl cracked the throttles open about half an inch.

"Start number one," Karl ordered.

With one hand, Adrian held the start switch for the number-one engine. With the other hand, he pumped the hand primer to force air out of the fuel line. After a few seconds, he pressed the mesh switch. The number-one prop began turning, and the nine-cylinder engine coughed and fired.

Karl set the throttle for 1000 RPM and watched the oil pressure rise. He glanced through the windscreen and saw the number-one props turning on a dozen ships. The tang of exhaust smoke seasoned the air.

"Number two," Karl said. He held two fingers out the window, repeated the start procedure.

A few minutes later, all four engines hummed at idle, and *Hellstorm* vibrated with life and power, a beast awakened. The ground crew unplugged external power. Across the airfield, the props of the other bombers blew a man-made gale, sweeping dust and exhaust smoke above the trees. Karl and Adrian, along with Fairburn standing behind them, buckled on their throat mikes and put on their headsets so they could talk over the interphone.

"Crew, check in on headset," Karl ordered.

"Copilot's up," Adrian said. He raised his fist above the throttles, and Karl bumped it with his own fist. Ready to go.

"Engineer," Fairburn responded, still standing behind the pilots.

"Bombardier."

"Navigator."

"Radio."

"Ball turret."

"Left waist gunner."

"Right waist."

"Tail gunner."

Karl knew the tone and timbre of their voices as if each man were a brother. They didn't need to call out crew positions; they could have said anything, and in one word, Karl would have known who was checking in. Back in the radio room, Baker was clearly at work: Pops and hums sounded in Karl's headset as the radios warmed up and came alive. On the command set, tower gave the lead ship clearance to taxi.

At the far end of the taxiway, B-17s began to roll out of their hardstands and onto the perimeter track. Karl nudged the throttles up to 1500 RPM to exercise the turbos. One by one, he eased back the prop control levers and watched for an RPM drop to make sure the propeller governors were working. Everything checked good; *Hellstorm* gave him no release from the dilemma splitting his heart in two. Good hydraulic pressure, good suction, good voltages. Good Lord.

Maybe something else would cause a mission scrub. Perhaps the weather forecast had worsened. Wouldn't be the first time Karl had seen raids called off at the last minute.

When his turn came, Karl released brakes, taxied out of the hardstand, and joined the procession of bombers lumbering for takeoff. The lead ship, piloted by the group commander, stopped at the runway hold-short line. Prop blast rippled the stubbled remains of a wheat field next to the runway.

The control tower's Aldis lamp flashed green.

The mission was a go.

2

Predators Become Prey

O berleutnant Wilhelm Albrecht balanced himself by pure instinct as the German submarine *U-351* pitched and rolled on the surface of a choppy sea. The boat's diesels turned twin screws that propelled the sixty-seven-meter boat at fourteen knots. Sissing froth spilled over the hull. Spray flecked Wilhelm's beard as he stood on the bridge: Shaving was not permitted on U-boats because it wasted fresh water. The Milky Way sparkled overhead in silver glory. Warrant Officer Heidrich stood next to Wilhelm, bracing himself against the swells.

"A fine night for hunting, sir," Heidrich remarked.

Wilhelm, the twenty-five-year-old executive officer and second in command of this Type VII *Kriegsmarine* U-boat, grunted in response. The fine nights for hunting were more than two years past, a period U-boat men called "The Happy Time." In 1942 alone, German subs, then the terror of merchantmen, had sent more than a thousand Allied ships to the bottom.

The *U-351* had done her share. From a distance, a convoy would appear as insects dotting the surface of a pond. Closer, the funnels and mastheads would materialize in the periscope, plump targets with holds full of ammunition, trucks, fuel, and food. This was a war of machines, of entire economies. Victory or disaster might depend on whether U.S. supplies and parts wound up in Churchill's ports or on the ocean floor.

The skipper would select a victim, maybe even two or three. Wilhelm would calculate target values, adjust speed and course, order tubes opened, and fire. The torpedoes would launch with a hiss of compressed air, the submarine shuddering with each shot. Tense seconds followed for the U-boat crew, short heartbeats, shallow breaths.

Then the ocean would erupt in fire. Billowing flames, towering smoke. Flares and star shells arcing into the sky as stricken vessels signaled for help. The U-boat would make a crash dive as destroyer escorts came seeking vengeance. A quick escape, then on to more hunting. Happy times, indeed, but now those days seemed from another life.

The next time Heidrich spoke, it was not idle chatter about the weather: "Shadow bearing two-one-zero."

Wilhelm turned to see a dark patch on the horizon, stars blanked out in the shape of a ship. From this angle, he couldn't say with certainty what type of vessel. But definitely not a tanker. Perhaps something more dangerous.

"We have a target," Wilhelm shouted through the bridge hatch. "Call the skipper."

Captain Brauer climbed the tower ladder and sent Heidrich to the control room. Wilhelm swung the Target Bearing Transmitter toward the shadow. Boots clanged on the deck plates below as men rushed to battle stations.

Brauer shouted orders into the voice tube: "Left full rudder, steer two-zero-zero. Engines full ahead."

The captain was stalking, maneuvering carefully for a good shot—the way a wolf might angle around prey before tearing in for the kill. Wilhelm knew why Brauer was being careful. This target could be a destroyer, and U-boats did not normally attack warships. The subs saved their torpedoes for merchantmen carrying enemy supplies and equipment. But targets had proved scarce during this patrol. *We'll get only one chance to fire,* Wilhelm thought, *and God help us if we miss.*

For an hour, the *U-351* closed on her target. Plenty of darkness remained. The captain ordered two minor course changes and bided his time. Then came the moment when Brauer's posture changed; his stance grew straighter. Wilhelm recognized the body language: The skipper was ready to fire.

Heidrich, now in position in the control room, called from below: "Target speed fifteen knots, course one-eight-zero."

"Prepare tubes two and three," Brauer ordered. "Surface attack."

Wilhelm's pulse quickened. He forgot about the chill of his damp navy-issued sweater and the seawater that splashed into his boots. These moments pushed to the back of his mind all the discomforts of submarine life: the cramped spaces, the rotten food, the condensation and mold, the stench of urine and oil. Now he felt only the thrill of the hunt.

"Tubes two and three ready," Heidrich called.

Wilhelm needed to keep the Target Bearing Transmitter aimed at the shadow. For the last several minutes, that task had required little movement. But now he had to swing the TBT several degrees. Then several more. The vessel was taking evasive action.

"She's turning fast!" Heidrich shouted.

The target's maneuver was no precautionary course change by a sleepy helmsman in the wheelhouse of a freighter. This was almost certainly an Allied destroyer coming hard about. Somehow, the *U-351* had been detected. And the target's evasive turn placed the U-boat out of position to shoot.

"Alaaarm!" Brauer cried. *"Verdammt."*

Wilhelm and Brauer leaped for the bridge hatch. Wilhelm scrambled down the tower ladder first; whenever the skipper was on the bridge and ordered a crash dive, he always waited to make sure everyone else was safely below. Brauer followed Wilhelm, slammed the hatch closed, and locked it.

"Dive to one-sixty meters," Brauer ordered. "Now, now, now."

Sailors yanked valve handles and turned handwheels. The ballast tanks opened and began to fill with salt water. The rush of water and the hiss of escaping air combined into a roar that reminded Wilhelm of an avalanche he'd witnessed during a ski trip in the Alps—back before the war, an eternity ago. He felt the boat tilt and descend at an angle. The depth gauge needle began dropping: thirty meters, forty meters, fifty.

The destroyer surged overhead, engines turning its screws at high

RPM. Sound traveled four times faster in water than in air, and the U-boat men could hear their enemy in pursuit. Loud pings struck the *U-351:* Asdic impulses sent from a U.S. vessel trying to pinpoint the sub's location. To Wilhelm, they felt like needles piercing his eardrums. The pings grew louder, the pain unbearable. The chugging of pistons joined the pings. Above all the noise came three distinct splashes.

Depth charges.

"Right full rudder," Brauer ordered. "Keep her coming down."

Wilhelm felt the U-boat turn: With her course and depth constantly changing, she became a more difficult target. The destroyer's engines grew fainter. Each man held his breath. The depth gauge read ninety meters and dropping.

Thunder rocked the ocean.

The explosion shook the boat, flickered the lights. Two seconds later, a closer blast pushed the *U-351* deeper into the water. Anything not bolted down went flying. Pencils, charts, and canned food clattered against decks and pipes. Glass faces of gauges cracked. Wilhelm fell against the edge of a chart table so hard, he cracked the table. Pain seared through his hip bone. Men cursed and shouted in fear and anger.

Another detonation put out the lights altogether. Despite Wilhelm's tightest grip on a valve handle, he got thrown into that damned table again. Someone fell against him. A loud cry came from somewhere aft. Wilhelm felt the boat moving. Was she sinking? Had the hull ruptured? He braced for an icy rush of seawater and the chest-rending agony of drowning.

Brauer clicked on a flashlight. "Emergency lighting," he ordered. Someone found switches and flipped them.

The dim light revealed water pouring, dripping, or spraying from dozens of ruptured gaskets. As exec, Wilhelm's duties included helping the skipper with damage control, and he considered ordering bilge pumps turned on. He decided to wait. The pumps' hammering would tell the enemy that the *U-351* was not quite dead.

Wilhelm glanced at the depth gauge. Mein Gott, *two hundred meters.* Crush depth was 230.

"Blow tanks two and three," Brauer called.

The hiss of compressed air reverberated through the hull. Wilhelm felt the deck angle shifting; the bow rose, then dropped again. Steel groaned. Hydraulic fluid dripped from unsealed valves. The depth needle slowed but kept moving. Two hundred ten meters.

"Blow one and four," the skipper ordered.

Another shot of compressed air forced seawater out of the tanks. With four ballast tanks now empty, the boat should have started an ascent. But still she fell. Two hundred twenty meters.

"Exec," Brauer said, "we're taking in water somewhere. Better find it if you ever want to see the sun again."

"Aye, sir," Wilhelm said.

A call from an aft compartment confirmed the skipper's suspicions: "Engine room's flooded!"

"Bilge pumps on," Wilhelm ordered. The boat had to purge that water whether the enemy heard the pumps or not. He wasn't even sure if the pumps would work at this depth against the enormous pressure of outside water. He should have turned them on earlier.

Wilhelm grabbed a flashlight and headed aft. Stumbled over the body of a machinist lying on the deck, the side of his head broken open with brain matter exposed. Probst, the fisherman's son from Rostock. Wilhelm hated to step across his body, as if it were so much flotsam, but he had no time for grief. The hull continued to groan. Was the boat still descending?

The farther aft Wilhelm moved, the deeper the water splashed over his boots. It had seeped inside from frigid black depths, and he began to shiver. In the engine room, in knee-deep brine, Wilhelm and a petty officer found the offending valve. Water gurgled from the ruptured valve like a fountain. Wilhelm kneeled and grabbed the submerged valve wheel. The wheel turned freely in both directions, but did not close the valve—because the wheel was attached to a broken spindle.

"Get the schematics," Wilhelm ordered. "See if there's an upstream valve."

A sailor flipped open a soggy engineering manual. Another held a flashlight. The men flipped pages, looked along the maze of plumbing.

"There," Petty Officer Wuerth said, pointing.

A sailor turned the valve wheel. The gurgling ended. The fatal leak stopped.

Wilhelm reported the news to the control room, then asked, "What's our depth, sir?"

"Two hundred thirty-five meters."

The men in the engine room looked at one another, then at the steel that surrounded them. According to the books, the hull should have collapsed by now. German craftsmanship, and perhaps Neptune's mercy, had granted a few extra meters. But one more centimeter, one more minute, could bring a fury of rending metal, bone-crushing pressure, cold blackness, and death.

Liter by liter, the bilge pumps emptied water from inside the hull. Meter by meter, the *U-351* began to rise. At 180 meters, Brauer told Wilhelm to stop the pumps.

The depth stabilized. No longer in danger of collapsing like a crushed tin can, the boat hung motionless in the water. This depth still offered protection from charges dropped by enemy warships. Submariners didn't normally control their buoyancy by starting and stopping bilge pumps, but for the moment, the technique had worked.

Sailors went to work on less serious leaks, and Wilhelm surveyed the damage. He found a bent shaft on one of the diesel engines, ten tripped relays, and cracked cells on battery number two. An electrician, Petty Officer Zeiser, went to work with a spool of copper wire to jump the bad cells.

The bent shaft meant the end of the patrol. A U-boat hobbling along on one engine could hardly maneuver for attack. When Brauer heard the news, he snatched off his white navy cap and threw it to the deck plates. His stream of profanity bordered on art.

Wilhelm understood his skipper's frustration: The U-boat fleet had taken so many losses in recent months, and U-boat victories were becoming scarce. Sometimes it seemed the Allies could read the coded messages from U-boat headquarters. The skipper had hoped this patrol would bring better luck.

Brauer placed his thumb and forefinger on the bridge of his nose, closed his eyes, and said, "Tell me when the battery is fixed. We'll run deep on the electric motors and get the hell out of here."

Hours later, the *U-351* surfaced. Up top, she could run on her remaining diesel engine, recharge her batteries, and let her crew breathe fresh air. Wilhelm climbed the tower ladder and opened the hatch. Residual pressure nearly threw him onto the bridge, and he caught himself with both hands on the hatch rim. The air smelled wonderful.

Dawn had broken gray. A solid overcast covered the sky, the same color as the U-boat. Rain slanted down in nettles. The *U-351* rode heaving swells.

From the bridge, Wilhelm saw more damage. The deck gun's barrel was bent and the feed mechanism blown off. The antiaircraft gun looked intact, though. That was good: The boat had a long way to get home, and she might need to defend herself.

Communication became easier on the surface, and radiograms flooded into the radio room. The decoded messages read like an obituary page:

ATTACKED BY AIRCRAFT. SINKING. *U-459*.

ATTACKED BY DESTROYER. SINKING. *U-327*.

SUNDERLAND AIRCRAFT. BOMBS. SINKING. *U-534*.

DISABLED AT GRID SQUARE BF 38. BOTH DIESELS OUT. BATTERIES DEAD. *U-635*.

Wilhelm knew men on each of those boats.

The *U-351*'s radio room sent out its own message: SEVERELY DAMAGED AT GRID SQUARE AF 52. ONE DIESEL OUT. BREAKING OFF PATROL.

Three weeks later, the *U-351* rode the surface of the North Sea near the German coast, her hull a gray dagger slicing through black water. Along the sides of the U-boat, Allied depth charges had burned away some of the gray paint to reveal streaks of protective red primer. Explosives had also creased the hull.

In the control room, Wilhelm plotted a course for home. He felt hopeless, but he kept his feelings to himself. The crewmen around him worked in near silence, undoubtedly mindful of those missing from their ranks. Three had been buried at sea. First, they'd said farewell to Probst, who'd died in the depth charge attack. Then, on the long slog back to Germany, a Spitfire had caught *U-351* on the surface and slashed down from the sky with guns blazing. Petty Officer Radisch had returned fire with the antiaircraft gun and paid with his life; he'd kept firing until riddled by strafing. Then the damaged battery had acted up again, emitting fumes that killed electrician Zeiser.

The survivors—forty-seven men, counting Captain Brauer—worked amid a maze of pipes and hatches, gauges and handwheels. Oil and grime darkened their faces and sleep deprivation hollowed their eyes. At the beginning of this patrol, they had sailed from Kiel in a wolf pack of five boats. Only the *U-351* limped home, and that by the grace of God.

The events of the past weeks seemed to fill a lifetime, as if all of Wilhelm's land-based existence had happened to someone else. Now, heading toward the sub pens at Bremen, Wilhelm began to think his shipmates and naval college classmates had died in vain. The Reich was shrinking from all sides; enemies had entered the Fatherland itself, something the Führer had called impossible. In the east, the Soviets had rolled into Nemmersdorf and massacred civilians. In the west, the town of Aachen had fallen to the Americans.

In better times, the *U-351* could have sailed into submarine bases in France—at Lorient or Saint-Nazaire—for repairs. The trip would have been shorter, and during refit, the crew would have enjoyed the fine food, wine, and women of Brittany.

Once when he'd had a few days off, he'd taken the train into Paris. "The City of Light" hummed along, almost as if no war existed. Vegetables grew in formerly ornamental gardens, and sometimes Wilhelm's uniform with the eagle on the right breast drew glares. But people strolled the Champs-Élysées and gathered in restaurants in a state of normalcy that Wilhelm found surreal—and in stark contrast to battles raging elsewhere.

In one of the restaurants, Wilhelm indulged in the luxury of good, hot food. After months of moldy bread and putrid sausages that tasted like oil, even a warm poached egg seemed opulent. But Wilhelm started with a bottle of Chablis and a plate of mussels. He pried open the shellfish as if each one were a gift from heaven—and to his navy palate, they were. Then he ordered pan-seared steak *au poivre* and a bottle of Cabernet Sauvignon. A woman rose from the bar and came over to his table.

"That's a lot of wine," she said, "even for a sailor. Do you need some help drinking it?"

Her name was Fia. Dark, flowing hair, red lips, and red nails. Said she worked for her country's diplomatic corps. She could have worked for the French Resistance, for all Wilhelm knew or cared. Didn't matter. He told her nothing she couldn't have read in the papers, spent two blissful nights with her, and returned for more hunting.

But now the Allies had taken France, and U-boats were on the run. Radar, sonar, aircraft, and new tactics by American and British destroyers had turned predators into prey. The future offered little but death. To survive another patrol, the men of the *U-351* would have to beat long, long odds.

3

Aerial Armada

As Karl taxied, music flowed into his headset. He recognized the tune: "Only Forever" by Bing Crosby. At first, he wondered if Baker was screwing around with the radios; Karl started to press his talk switch to order Baker to stop that nonsense. Then he remembered the last time he'd barked at his radio operator for playing music. Baker had explained with offended pride that he tuned only official frequencies—but sometimes civilian channels managed to bleed through. Especially on the ground.

The line of bombers halted momentarily on the taxiway, and Karl held his toe brakes. Bing continued crooning.

When did I last hear that song?

Oh, yeah, he thought. *Not a good memory.*

"Only Forever" had been playing on the radio the night Karl's cousin Gerhard tried to talk him out of joining the army. They'd been sitting in the bar of the Hotel Bethlehem, a favorite watering hole for Bethlehem Steel execs. Karl's and Gerhard's fathers both worked for Beth Steel—but not as executives. Karl respected his dad's rough job as a Pennsylvania steelworker. Steel would build a modern America, raise skyscrapers, put a car in every driveway. However, Karl had completed a year of business studies at Penn State, and he dreamed of a leather chair and a window office, of becoming a captain of industry. He wanted to work with his mind instead of his back, and his father approved.

"It iss de American dream," Dad said in his thick German accent. "The father vorks the blast furnace in coveralls. The son vorks the office in suit and tie."

But when it became clear war was coming, Karl decided to get ahead of the draft board. Volunteer now and maybe get to fly, he figured, or wait for the draft notice and carry a rifle through the mud. The family hated to see him leave school, but his logic made sense to everyone. Except Gerhard.

"Don't do this, Karl," Gerhard said over his stein of Rolling Rock. "This isn't our fight."

"What are you talking about?" Karl asked. "It's our fight if we get drafted. And we're gonna get drafted. Just a matter of time."

Gerhard took a sip of beer. Set down his stein and wiped foam from his upper lip. He picked up his pack of Luckies from the bar, shook out a cigarette, slipped it into his mouth. Looked around as if worried about strangers listening. Struck a match and lit the cigarette. Gerhard exhaled a long plume of smoke, held the Lucky between two fingers, and spoke in a low voice.

"Listen," Gerhard said. "That Jew Roosevelt just wants to help his Communist buddy Stalin. You are a full-blooded German. You and your parents speak German at the dinner table. You have no business fighting your fellow Aryans."

The bartender locked eyes with Gerhard, went over to the Philco radio, and turned up the volume on old Bing. Almost as if to cover the conversation.

Do those two know each other?

Karl didn't know what to say. If he had heard such nonsense from anyone else, he'd have gotten up and left. Or told the guy to mind his own damned business. Or told him to go back to Germany if it was so great there.

But this was Gerhard. Karl had grown up with him. They had played baseball together and caught trout in Pennsylvania's limestone streams flowing clear as tap water. Maybe Gerhard didn't really mean it. Maybe he was drunk. Sometimes he said crazy things. Karl knew people who hated Roosevelt so much, they couldn't think straight. Maybe Gerhard had been listening to them.

"Gerhard," Karl said, "anybody can print anything on some silly pamphlet. You can't believe everything you read."

Gerhard took another drag on his cigarette. The bartender lifted a glass from the sink and began drying it. The men down the bar talked of baseball scores and stock prices.

"I'm not going to be Roosevelt's cannon fodder," Gerhard said, "and you don't need to be, either. If you want to stay out of this draft, I know people who can help."

When Gerhard said that, the bartender looked over at Karl. "Only Forever" faded, and the bartender twisted a knob on the Philco to change stations. The radio blipped and crackled until the needle stopped. An announcer intoned: "You can be sure, with Pure. And now, Pure Oil proudly presents America's most distinguished commentator, H.V. Kaltenborn."

Karl ignored the broadcast, but Gerhard listened intently. After a minute or so, Gerhard said, "I don't know what's wrong with that man. He ought to be on our side."

"Whose side is that?" Karl asked.

Gerhard spread his arms as if amazed by such a dumb question. Blue smoke curled from the Lucky between the fingers of his left hand.

"I gotta go, Gerhard," Karl said. "Don't worry about me. I'll be fine."

Gerhard shook his head. Karl drained the last of his beer and left a quarter on the bar. As he left, an attractive couple entered the hotel. The woman wore a fox-fur wrap around her neck and a blue dress that hugged her waist. Normally, Karl would have paid more attention to the woman, but the man wore a navy officer's uniform with the gold wings of an aviator. The man looked happy.

I'd be happy, too, Karl thought, *with that girl on my arm and those wings on my chest.*

That had been just a few years ago. Seemed a lifetime had passed since then. Now Karl had the wings, at least, though they were army silver instead of navy gold. And he had one more mission to fly.

The lead ship thundered into the air, climbed away as its landing gear retracted. The second aircraft took off thirty seconds later. The 94th was contributing twenty aircraft to the hundred-bomber formation; the rest would come from the 100th, 96th, and 95th Bomb Groups at bases elsewhere in England. With planes lifting off at thirty-second intervals, it would take ten minutes just to get the 94th airborne. Then the formation of all the groups needed to assemble at altitude. The process could take more than an hour.

Finally, *Hellstorm* reached the hold-short line near the departure end of the runway. The ship ahead of *Hellstorm* began its takeoff roll. Black exhaust roiled from its engines. Adrian looked at his watch and said, "Hack." Karl taxied into the takeoff position. After half a minute ticked by, Adrian said, "Go."

With his feet on the brakes, Karl shoved the throttles forward. The whole aircraft vibrated with the power of the R-1820s, and the needles inside the instruments began to shudder. When the manifold pressure gauges showed twenty-five inches of pressure, Karl released the brakes. *Hellstorm* began to accelerate, and Karl pushed the throttles up to forty-six inches.

"All right, boys," he said, "she wants to fly."

Black tire marks along the pavement slid under the nose. As the aircraft gathered speed, the tire marks melded into a long black streak. When the airspeed indicator reached one hundred miles per hour, Karl eased back on the yoke, and *Hellstorm* lifted into the air. He tapped the brakes to stop the wheels from rotating, then said, "Gear up."

"Gear up," Adrian said. The copilot reached for the gear handle, and the wheels retracted and locked in the up position.

Below, the English countryside spread in late-autumn glory. Though past peak color, trees still splashed gold and burgundy along roadways and fence lines. Sheep grazed in a pasture—white dots sprinkled across a green carpet. Haystacks studded fields. Church spires anchored villages. A mule and cart plodded along a dirt path; the farmer looked up and waved.

Karl could not enjoy the view. The job of forming up required as much concentration as the bomb run over the target. Scores of bombers droning around in close proximity presented a constant danger of collision; more than one crew had died that way. Sweat moistened Karl's back as he started the assembly procedure.

He pulled back the power to thirty-five inches and pitched for 150 miles per hour. Rolled into a left turn and climbed at exactly three hundred feet per minute. *Hellstorm* followed her sister bombers ascending a spiral staircase through the sky.

With constant glances at the needle of his radio compass, Karl kept the airfield beacon off his left wing as he made several climbing revolutions. Above him, aircraft began to level off.

"Anybody got the lead ship?" Karl asked on interphone.

"Two o'clock high," Pell called from the bombardier's seat in the nose.

"There he is," Adrian said, pointing up and to the right.

Karl looked where Adrian was pointing. Sure enough, one of the B-17s, tiny at this distance, was firing flares. The flares meant *form up on me.* Incandescent dots of fire trailed arcs of smoke until the flares burned out and disappeared.

At ten thousand feet, Karl rolled out of his climbing turn and flew straight and level for a few minutes. "Everybody on oxygen," he ordered. He clipped on his mask, watched the blinker on his oxygen regulator change from black to white each time he inhaled. Through the interphone, each crew member checked in to confirm he was on oxygen, too.

Six-plane squadrons formed the basic elements of a combat formation. A formation consisted of lead groups, high groups, and low groups, with each group made up of lead, high, and low squadrons. The aircraft maintained assigned positions to provide mutually supporting fire from their guns. A good tight formation, flown with discipline and precision, made it harder for enemy fighters to attack without getting shot. Many got through, anyway.

A few miles of straight and level flight gave Karl a breather, but not for long. At a specified bearing on his radio compass, he turned again to continue droning around the beacon. All the while, he watched the location of other aircraft. Fortresses swarmed the English sky, ten lives aboard each machine. One by one, the bombers assembled into squadrons, and squadrons assembled into groups.

"A lot of steel in the air," Karl said.

"Do you suppose your dad poured some of it?" Adrian asked.

"I'm sure he did. Beth Steel makes most of the military's airplane cylinder forgings."

"Hey, your manifold pressure's low on engine two." Adrian pointed to the engine instruments, which were on the copilot's side of the panel. Karl had just set his power for twenty-eight inches of pressure. He placed his hand on the throttles; they all lined up evenly. But, sure enough, pressure on engine two had crept down to twenty-five inches. Typical of Adrian to catch that; the guy never missed a thing. From all his studying, he knew the airplane almost as well as Fairburn, the flight engineer.

"Engineer," Karl called on interphone. "Can you take a look at something for me?"

"Yes, sir." Joe Fairburn climbed down from the top gun turret and stood behind Karl and Adrian. The engineer had already donned his heavy leather B-3 jacket against the cold temperatures of altitude.

"Number two's running a little weak," Karl said.

"Yeah, I heard." Fairburn peered at the instrument panel. "Let's see, you got all your mixtures in auto lean. You got all your cowl flaps closed. Fuel pressure looks good, too."

"So it's not anything we're doing wrong?" Adrian asked.

Fairburn shook his head. "I don't think so, sir. The wastegate could be sticking, or maybe the pressure relief valve's dicked up."

"Is it gonna get worse as we climb?" Karl said.

"Probably."

"All right," Karl said. "Stay right there for a minute. Let me join up, here."

At the controls of a heavy bomber, Karl did not have the luxury of focusing on one problem at a time. An aircraft commander constantly prioritized, and Karl's instructors had drilled into him the top priorities: *aviate, navigate, communicate.* In that order. Right now, he had to focus on flying the airplane. Assigned to the low squadron's position number five, he needed to slide in just aft and to the right of ship number four.

"I think this gaggle's starting to come together," Adrian said.

Ahead, the three nearest bombers had formed up on one another. Aircraft number two flew behind and right of the squadron lead ship, with number three behind and to the left. Though ungainly on the ground, in the air the Fortresses took on an aura of majesty. Guns jutted from the turrets, and fuselages sloped smoothly upward into the vertical stabilizers of the tails. Wings wide like avenging angels, with four whirring propellers that appeared as translucent discs.

The tail of aircraft number four drew Karl's attention now. Like all ships of the 94th Bomb Group, it carried a square A on the vertical stabilizer. Karl had a technique for keeping in position: Put that A just behind the forward edge of his side window.

"Fireball Able Four," Adrian called on the radio, "Fireball Able Five's ready to join on you."

"You're cleared in, Five."

Karl goosed his throttles for a little more speed. All the manifold pressure needles moved up, with number two still lagging. Fairburn groaned his disapproval at the engine's performance.

Suddenly *Hellstorm* began to bounce and rattle. The ride went from silky smooth to that of a pickup truck on a washboard dirt road. Karl felt himself thrown against his harness straps. Standing behind the pilots' seats, Fairburn nearly fell. The flight engineer cursed and gripped the seat backs with both hands.

"There's the wake turbulence," Adrian said.

Yep, Karl thought. *It's probably from the lead ship or from number two.* In formation flying, prop wash and wingtip vortices presented an ever-present hassle. Karl pulled back on the yoke slightly, using only his fingertips. *Hellstorm* climbed forty feet. Enough to smooth out the ride.

"Thanks, boss." The Southern-accented voice of Morgan Anders, back at the tail gun. In rough air, the tail gunner had it worst.

Karl fine-tuned his position as best he could. Descended just a hair and cracked the throttles. The A on Four's tail slid into its proper place in Karl's window. He flew close enough that he could see the faces of Four's tail gunner and right waist gunner. The tail gunner waved.

"All right, Adrian," Karl said, "take the plane for me."

"Copilot's aircraft," Adrian said. He placed one hand on his yoke and the other on the throttles.

"Talk to me about this engine, Joe," Karl said.

"It's running good, sir. It's just not making full power. No way to know more until the grease monkeys tear into it."

That stubborn number-two manifold pressure needle stayed about three inches lower than the other engines. Karl had a decision to make. Some malfunctions gave you no choice: a runaway prop, a leaking oxygen system, a jammed gun. You never flew into combat with one of those. But this problem fell into a gray area. Worst case, the engine would fail. The Fort could still fly on three engines, but you didn't want to lose an engine in enemy airspace.

Some crews had turned back for less—but that was no way to win a war. And you never, ever wanted the other guys to think you were yellow. Still, Karl did not want to fly to Bremen today.

He looked through the windscreen at the aerial armada gathering around him. Bombers stacked themselves above and below him; he counted thirty airplanes, and those were just the ones he could see. Seventy others would make up this formation: a hundred airplanes and a thousand men, representing the height of American technology and industrial power. Who was he to put his own desires first?

"Okay, guys, you heard us talking about the engine problem," Karl said. "Anybody got any input?" The decision was Karl's alone, but he sought advice from his men whenever possible, if only to gauge their mood.

"I'd hate to waste these bombs," Pell called.

The bombardier had a point. If *Hellstorm* aborted the mission, it could not land back at base with live bombs on board. Karl would have to fly to the jettison area and drop the bombs in the English Channel.

"We get this thing done," navigator Conrad said, "our war ends today."

"Y'all gon' make my fiancée real mad if you keep me here too long," Anders said. "I got a wedding date. In six weeks."

"I got a date, too," Fairburn said, "in less time than that."

Karl knew about Fairburn's date. His wife was expecting a baby. Other crew members had calendars marked, too. The ball turret gunner, Dick Russo, had been accepted for the next term at Seton Hall. Russo was known as the Kid because he was nineteen and looked about twelve. The bombardier, Pell, was so eager to get back to the States that he'd already started packing. Everybody had begun planning for life after the military. In their minds, they were halfway home already.

That damned manifold pressure needle stayed low—but not dangerously low. Karl almost wished the engine would fail altogether and make his call easy. The interphone grew quiet; the crew waited for his decision. He had plenty of reasons to hate the Nazis, and now he had one more: for forcing him to make a stark choice between family and duty.

He glanced over at the number-four ship. *Crescent City Maiden* was her name; the aircraft commander came from New Orleans. The nose art depicted a woman with impossibly large breasts in a gauzy red gown, lounging with a cocktail glass in her hand. The *A* on *Maiden*'s vertical stabilizer stayed locked in Karl's window; Adrian was doing a good job of holding position. Karl noted the aircraft's other markings, especially the white star on the fuselage.

That white star represented the U.S. Army Air Forces, everyone in the Air Forces, and everybody back home. How many hardworking women had riveted these airplanes together? How many hardworking taxpayers had paid for them? Each airplane cost more than two hundred thousand dollars, more money than Karl could imagine.

Hell, he thought, *this ain't about me and what I want. And I've flown with worse glitches than this. Damn it, damn it, damn it.*

"All right, boys," he said finally. "We're going."

Hoots and cheers sounded from behind and below the cockpit.

Yeah, Karl thought, *you fellas want to go home, and so do I. But this is Bremen, a major city of the Reich, not some half-defended French target. Don't start celebrating yet.*

4

Suicide Order

As the wounded *U-351* entered the mouth of the River Weser, Wilhelm mounted the ladder to join Captain Brauer on the bridge. Air, cool and clean, filled Wilhelm's lungs; he could practically taste it. Respiration required no more conscious thought than heartbeat, but Wilhelm thought about it this morning. Something taken for granted now seemed a luxury: a life-giving breath in the sunlight, instead of a final chestful of water and diesel fuel in cold and complete darkness.

A minesweeper lay at anchor near the Weser's east bank, and beyond the warship, Wilhelm saw the port city of Bremerhaven. The port's devastation became evident from a couple kilometers away. The docks should have displayed a line of eleven loading cranes, but only three stood intact. The rest had toppled under Allied bombs. The gaps made Wilhelm think of a prizefighter with most of his teeth knocked out. He thought he remembered a fuel storage facility near the dock, but now there was only twisted debris.

"I hope Bremen has fared better," Brauer said.

Bremen lay farther upstream, but recent wireless reports had given no reason to think Bremen—or any other industrial city in Germany—had fared better.

"We do our jobs," Wilhelm said. "Why can't Göring do his?"

Luftwaffe chief Hermann Göring had once promised Allied warplanes would never penetrate German airspace. Now they did so routinely.

"Don't let the wrong person hear you talk like that, Exec," Brauer said.

Wilhelm knew his skipper meant only to keep him out of trouble, but the friendly advice darkened his mood. *Why is it,* Wilhelm wondered, *that I can fight so hard and risk such an awful death—yet some fat-ass landlubber Nazi with an honorary commission in the SS can overhear me speak truth in a beer hall, put on his black uniform, and turn me in? And then go back to his safe office job.*

Every time Wilhelm placed his feet back on dry land, things seemed worse than before.

The last time he'd gone ashore, he'd had time to take the train to Berlin, where his parents lived. In the Reich's capital, bombing had devastated entire blocks. Multistory apartment buildings stood with walls sheared off, their rooms exposed like dollhouses. A kitchen here, a bedroom there, opened to the weather. Staircases leading to nowhere.

Newly drafted infantrymen, barely old enough to shave, milled about the train station. Their belt buckles read: GOTT MIT UNS. *If they're headed to the Russian front,* Wilhelm thought, *they'll need all the divine intervention they can get.* But when he considered the increasing losses of U-boats, he realized even these young greenhorn soldiers probably stood a better chance of surviving than he did.

From the station, Wilhelm had tried to telephone his parents. The operator could not make a connection. Wilhelm fought panic. Were they dead under a mound of blasted bricks? No, no, the telephone system was unreliable. He hired a car that took him home to the Tiergarten district.

For generations, the Albrecht family had owned a comfortable three-story house in one of Berlin's finer neighborhoods. Wilhelm's father worked as an attorney for Daimler-Benz AG—fittingly, a company that built engines for submarines. The job did not bring fabulous wealth, but it kept the family firmly in the upper class. Father might have risen higher in the company if he'd been a Party member, but he stayed out of politics and advised Wilhelm to do the same.

Wilhelm found his home intact, quiet, dark, and locked. Where had everyone gone? He recalled that his parents had talked of evacuating to the countryside. Distant kin lived in Sembach, a farming village in the rolling hills of Rheinland-Pfalz. Wilhelm fumbled with his keys, found the one for the front door. At first, he had trouble inserting the key, and he wondered if the lock had been changed. But eventually the key worked; the lock had not been turned in some time and needed graphite lubrication.

Inside the house, sheets covered furniture and rugs. Dust coated the hardwood floors. Closets stood empty. Each footfall echoed loneliness. The air hung stale and musty. This home had always been such a place of warmth, life, and permanence. To see it abandoned meant a world spun out of control.

Wilhelm came to the century-old staircase. Placed his hand on the bannister and climbed slowly. Every step sounded its familiar groan or creak. Once upstairs, Wilhelm entered his old room. It looked the same and still smelled of the resins in ancient wood. Longing and nostalgia flooded Wilhelm as if some emotional hull had cracked.

The sea had always fascinated him, and his room contained mementoes of days when he thought the ocean meant adventure, not death. On the mantel: a model of the SMS *Ostfriesland,* one of the great battleships of the Imperial German Navy. On the bedside table: the hat from his old Sea Cadet uniform. On the wall: an oar from his boyhood rowing team. Wilhelm's parents had left all his things behind when they fled to the countryside. Had they given up hope of his return? Had they given up hope in the war itself?

Defeat appeared even more certain now as the *U-351* slid past Bremerhaven. To Wilhelm, Germany was the center of the universe, a place of absolute security. How could it be so violated? How could so many men fight so hard, follow the orders of their leaders, and still see things come to this?

When the U-boat reached Bremen, there would be no girls and no brass band, as there had been in previous homecomings. Now there would be just grim-faced dockworkers and exhausted machinists to

survey the boat's damage and work minimum fixes to make her seaworthy again.

Wilhelm's grandparents lived in Bremen, but would he find their
home deserted, too? He doubted he'd even have time to look. The
navy would certainly send him right back out on another patrol.

Official broadcasts promised new superweapons that would hurl
the Allies back into the sea. Missiles tipped with bombs that could
destroy an entire city. Jet-powered aircraft in enough numbers to
wipe the Brits and Yanks from the skies.

But if anybody had superweapons, it was the enemy. Their damnable radar alone made submariners miserable. Practically every time
the *U-351* tried to surface to gasp for air and recharge her batteries,
the radar detection operator would sing out a warning. An aircraft
would appear in the distance—a Sunderland or perhaps a Liberator—and the *U-351* would dive for her life. Another plunge into the
depths as a spread of bombs detonated behind her.

A call from the control room interrupted Wilhelm's dark thoughts:
"Sir, a new message from headquarters. You'll want to look at
this."

"You have the boat, Exec," Captain Brauer said. "I'll check it out."

Brauer disappeared down the bridge hatch. A few minutes later
he returned, pale-faced and expressionless.

"Our orders for the next patrol," the skipper said.

Brauer handed Wilhelm the decoded message: WHEN TORPE-
DOES ARE EXPENDED, ATTACK AND SINK ENEMY SHIPS BY RAMMING.

A suicide order. The *U-351* would propel itself into a freighter,
most likely breaching the hulls of both vessels, and the two would
sink together to a common grave. Berlin wanted Wilhelm and his
crew to trade their lives for a single Allied ship. A single freighter that
the roaring production of American shipyards would replace within
days. Wilhelm fought the urge to wad up the message and throw it
overboard. He kept his naval bearing. Handed the strip of paper back
to the skipper without a word.

And why must we die this way? Wilhelm asked himself. *Because a
handful of fanatics managed to spread their ideas widely enough
to succeed in politics.*

Their ideas included the notion that God had made mistakes and the Thousand-Year Reich would correct them. How had the nation that produced Martin Luther, Bach, and Goethe come to this? Politics.

At that moment, on the calm surface of the River Weser in the autumn of 1944, *Oberleutnant* Wilhelm Albrecht decided he would not help lead a crew of dedicated professional submariners to a pointless death. Wilhelm was done with war.

5

Cruel to Be Kind

Over the English Channel, frost edged Karl's windscreen. Through the glass, he watched the coastline of continental Europe define itself. White breakers crashed onto beaches of light-colored sand, and beyond the coastal dunes lay a patchwork quilt of farm fields. Karl's altimeter read 21,000 feet. From this altitude, the land ahead looked deceptively peaceful. No hint of the darkness that had fallen across the continent with Nazi occupation, nor of the desperate combat since the Allies had stormed ashore at Normandy.

Now that they were en route to their target, the bombers had organized into two "combat boxes." One box contained the standard number of fifty-four planes, and the other made do with forty-six. According to theory, in a combat box the B-17s' guns created interlocking fields of fire so withering that the formation could manage without fighter protection. That theory had become one of the air war's first casualties: German pilots found ways of stabbing into formations at high speed, firing on a lumbering bomber, then peeling away. As a remedy, friendly fighters now escorted bomber formations deep into Germany, thanks to fuel tank modifications to the P-51 Mustang. But even the best fighter pilots couldn't be everywhere at once. A dogfight to the formation's left might leave Forts exposed to the right, and some bombers would have to fend for themselves.

"Go ahead and test your guns, boys," Karl ordered.

Rapid-fire blasts sounded from over Karl's head—Fairburn, firing from the top turret: *wham wham wham!* The whole airframe shook with the recoil. Karl thought he caught a whiff of burned gunpowder from the Browning .50-caliber machine guns, but with his oxygen mask on, maybe that was just his imagination?

Russo's guns followed from the ball turret, underneath the aircraft. Pell and Conrad squeezed off shots from the cheek guns in the nose. Farther back, waist gunners Ryan and Firth opened up; Karl saw the tracers through the corner of his eye. More bangs and rattles followed when Baker fired his gun in the radio room and Anders blasted from the tail.

They weren't shooting for fun. In the subzero temperatures of high altitude, metal contracted and lubricant gummed up. A cold-soaked, uncharged weapon might not even chamber a round. The crews of the Eighth Air Force had learned a lot of things the hard way since their first combat mission in 1942—and another of those hard lessons concerned hypoxia. That was the reason for the next call on the interphone.

"Oxygen check," Conrad said.

"Pilot okay," Karl said.

"Copilot," Adrian said.

"Bombardier's good," Pell said.

The rest of the crew responded in turn, each one checking in to confirm he was conscious and breathing pure oxygen. Conrad would repeat the call every fifteen minutes. In the cold, thin air of high altitude, a leak or a loose fitting could cause someone to pass out. This modern war of technology and machines put the human body under unprecedented kinds of stress.

Far over *Hellstorm*, horsetail cirrus clouds fanned across the sky. Sunlight backlit the clouds and illuminated them with rainbow colors.

"Damn, that's pretty," Adrian said.

"Yeah, it is," Karl said, but the sight just made him sad. Somewhere God—if there was a god—was still making rainbows and clouds. But the whole world was at war, killing on an industrial scale. And for Karl, forcing him to bomb family. He asked himself: *Did I make the right decision? Can I still find a way to back out, a reason to abort?*

Don't be a Hamlet, Karl resolved. From high school, he remembered Shakespeare's Danish prince, who couldn't make up his mind about whether to avenge his father's death. Appropriate lines from *Hamlet* came to him now: *"I must be cruel only to be kind; Thus bad begins, and worse remains behind."*

Cruel to be kind, Karl thought. *Dear God.*

Back when he was a teenager in English class, he never imagined how that play's themes would return to haunt him. Hell, this mission would even take him within sight of Denmark: The egress route called for a left turn after hitting the target, which would take the bombers out over the North Sea, west of the Danish coast.

Karl began to shiver. No amount of fleece and leather could keep a man comfortable at this altitude. Some guys used those powder-blue electrical suits you could plug into the airplane, but Karl found the suits more trouble than they were worth. The wires would short-circuit, and you'd wind up with one leg too hot and everything else freezing. The Stanley bottle of hot tea Karl had brought could offer relief, but he wanted to save that for later. If he drank it too early, he'd spend much of the day needing to urinate, and he didn't like using the relief tube.

The formation flew tightly now; ships floated close, left and right, above and below. The planes at the top of the combat box, in the coldest air, began to leave condensation trails: Scores of long white stripes marked the sky. The scene might have awed an observer on the ground, but it just gave Karl more cause for worry. Contrails made it that much easier for enemy flak gunners to spot the formation and gauge its speed. But maybe it didn't matter. Radar probably gave the Germans the same information. And even without radar and contrails, it was hard to miss a hundred heavy bombers droning along in broad daylight.

Just a few nights ago, Karl had heard "Lord Haw Haw" taunting the Eighth Air Force via shortwave on that very subject:

"Germany calling, Germany calling. Good evening to my misguided American friends, especially those of the

U.S. Army Air Forces. Terribly sorry about those losses you've been taking. Sometimes it does seem rather un-sportsmanlike of our antiaircraft gunners and fighter pilots to take down so many of your bombers. But my goodness, you make it so easy. Our intelligence agents tell us you call it 'daylight precision bombing.' We call it madness, and so should you. Your British cousins don't dare fly over the Reich during the sunlight hours. That's why they send their Lancasters at night. They've long ago abandoned your suicidal tactics. Why should you lose your young lives doing something for the British that they won't do for themselves?"

"I'd like to drop a bomb in his lap and shut him up for good," Pell had said that night in the officers' club.

"He sure knows how to hit us with a low blow," Conrad said. "Sometimes I wonder about our tactics, myself."

"Yeah, but our tactics must have 'em worried," Karl said. "Why else would they talk about it?"

Everybody nodded, and Karl hoped his remark blunted Lord Haw Haw's impact on the men's morale. Karl had never considered himself much of a leader; he just wanted to fly airplanes. But along with the shiny new airplanes came the responsibilities of command. That meant more than barking orders. It meant looking after your guys, knowing their frame of mind. Ultimately it meant making them *want* to do the right thing.

Down below, the Dutch coast passed under the wings. The waters of the Zuider Zee lay calm, the surface like a sheet of iron. Above, the cirrus clouds began to join into a high overcast, and the colors drained from the sky. *Hellstorm* now flew in hostile airspace, and Karl thought of the dangers ahead.

"Adrian," Karl said, "can you take the airplane for a while?"

"Copilot's airplane," Adrian said.

Karl took his hands from the yoke and pulled off his left glove. That gave him enough dexterity to reach into a lower leg pocket and pull out a sheaf of charts and documents. From the handful of paper, he selected what he needed: an Army Air Forces Target Chart, an AAF

Plotting Chart, and an AAF World Aeronautical Chart. A single WAC chart didn't cover the entire world; the one Karl held now depicted just this part of Europe, on a 1:1,000,000 scale. He'd marked the WAC chart and the plotting chart with known flak concentrations. *Hellstorm* was not near any of the permanent antiaircraft batteries yet, but Karl decided to take no chances. The Germans could move mobile guns on flatbed train cars. They could also send up fighters at any time.

"Go ahead and put on your flak jackets, boys," Karl ordered, shoving his fingers back into the glove. "Just in case the Krauts surprise us."

Adrian cut his eyes over at Karl. The copilot's oxygen mask covered his mouth, but the lines around his eyes showed he was smiling. *Yeah, I know what you're thinking,* Karl mused. *I'm calling 'em "Krauts" and I'm one myself.*

Karl hoisted his flak jacket, built of nylon pockets containing steel inserts. Heavy and uncomfortable, but it could keep you among the living. He donned it over his other flying clothes, then took the yoke long enough for Adrian to put on his own flak jacket. Just as Karl transferred control back to Adrian, the first hint of danger came from the group commander in the lead ship:

"Fireball squadrons, look alive. We got bandits coming up from eleven o'clock low."

Despite the cold, Karl's palms sweated inside his gloves, and he felt a strange heat through his legs. He'd noticed that sensation before when close to the enemy's guns; Karl wondered if it came from somewhere primal. Maybe it was the circulatory system's automatic preparation to survive a grievous wound? A question for another day. Right now, he concentrated on scanning for enemy fighters. He focused on small chunks of the sky and ground; he shifted his eyes and scanned again. At first, he saw nothing.

"I got 'em," Russo called from the ball turret. "Right on the horizon, maybe ten miles out."

There. Karl caught movement along the line where the sky met the earth. A swarm of a dozen bees rose toward the formation. At a closing speed of maybe four hundred miles per hour, the bees quickly took the shapes of Messerschmitt Bf-109s.

From the corner of his eye, Karl saw friendly fighters—four Mustangs—maneuvering to intercept the 109s. Welcome assistance, but not enough to stop all the enemy planes at once.

"Gunners," Karl said, "we got Messerschmitts coming up. Remember—short bursts."

The 109s ripped into the lead squadron. They bored in on the Fortresses from dead ahead, twenty-millimeter cannons blazing. The fighters held what appeared to be a collision course—but at the last second, they banked hard and scattered among the bombers. From this distance, Karl could see no immediate damage to any of the Forts. The radios erupted with warning calls:

"Two of 'em coming up at the high squadron."

"Fireball Charlie, watch your nine o'clock."

"He's coming back around."

A German plane dived from somewhere above and rolled in for a pass at *Hellstorm*. Guns aboard neighboring B-17s opened up. Karl couldn't tell if they scored hits. The Messerschmitt veered up to fly over the top of *Hellstorm*.

"Top turret," Karl said, "coming your way."

Fairburn started firing before Karl finished talking. Expended brass clattered down from the turret. The 109 flashed so close, Karl could see oil stains underneath its engine cowling. An instant later, *Hellstorm*'s left waist gun opened up. One quick burst.

"Anybody hit him?" Karl asked.

"Not sure," Firth said from his waist gunner's position.

"Couldn't tell," Russo said.

"You guys got him," Anders called from the tail. "When he came by me, he was burning."

"Good work," Karl said. "Keep your eyes open."

Most of the enemy fighters concentrated their attack on the lead squadron. The 109s banked and turned, fired and dived, set up for additional passes. A Mustang dived behind one of the Messerschmitts and opened fire. The Messerschmitt spiraled to the ground, flaming.

Karl scanned to see if any Fortresses were damaged. The high squadron's number-two ship had taken hits; it started smoking from its left outboard engine. Then the left inboard began trailing smoke, too. The aircraft began a slow descent. Parachutes began to open underneath the bomber.

"One, two, three," Adrian said. He eventually counted chutes from all ten crewmen.

Karl eyed the cluster of descending parachutes. His attention in their direction, he found himself caught by surprise when the high squadron's number-four ship, *Knockout Punch,* exploded.

No distress call. No parachutes. Just a flaming gash in the sky where an airplane used to be.

Ten men gone in half a second.

6

Landfall

Wilhelm's decision to leave the war left him feeling ripped out from the inside. Giving up on his duty meant giving up everything. But duty to what? And to whom? The fanatics who had brought down such destruction on Germany? During the summer, a group of army officers had tried and failed to assassinate the Führer. Had they felt the way Wilhelm felt now?

Maybe, he thought, *but I can't compare myself to them*. They were trying to save the country. Wilhelm could only save his crew. The loss of their executive officer might delay their next patrol long enough for the war to end. Or at least long enough for someone to rescind this insane suicide order. Wilhelm had to find a way to desert before the *U-351* went to sea again. Repairs would take a few weeks at most. He would need to act fast.

Does this make me a coward? Wilhelm wondered.

No, he decided. Cowards don't brave ocean storms, depth charges, and aerial bombs. Cowards don't last a day on a U-boat.

Ahead, Bremen's concrete submarine bunkers came into view. The structures seemed to rise like mountains of stone heaved up from underground. With ceilings seven meters thick, they shielded boats from air raids. But the bunkers would do the *U-351* no good; Wilhelm had radioed ahead and learned that all bays were filled with wounded boats under repair. His sub would have to tie up at an exposed pier until space became available.

One of the facilities—U-boat Bunker Valentin—was still under construction. Plans called for Valentin to serve as an assembly plant for a new ultramodern submarine. *How can we build a revolutionary super U-boat,* Wilhelm wondered, *when we can barely supply parts for the Type VIIs? More crazy promises of miracle weapons.*

"I'd love to see the boats that will come out of that plant," Captain Brauer said.

"Yes, sir," Wilhelm said. As noncommittal a response as he could make. He knew what the skipper was really thinking: *The* U-351's *crew would not live to see new boats come out of Valentin.*

"I hear they're pushing hard to complete it," Brauer said. "Making the most of prison labor."

"We are all pushing hard," Wilhelm said. He did not say aloud his next thought: *But* why?

"Engine half ahead," Brauer ordered into the voice tube. He gave engine commands in the singular because battle damage had left only one diesel in running condition. The boat slowed as it approached its mooring. A few hundred meters in the distance, dockworkers stood on the pier, holding lines thick as a man's wrist.

The commands for mooring deepened Wilhelm's sense of loss. Never again would he help lead such a team of professionals; never again would he know the camaraderie of sailors at sea. He had devoted everything to his naval career, and he considered himself a good officer and mariner. If anyone needed proof, they needed only to look at his Iron Cross, First Class.

At the naval college, he'd found the life for which he was born. He'd thrown himself into his studies, loved every page of the books on navigation, oceanography, and naval architecture. He and his classmates honed their minds with study and their bodies with rowing, boxing, and running. The pounding of the surf, the luff of a sail, and the growl of a diesel engine stirred his soul. But his dedication had led him to this: an order to destroy a seaworthy U-boat and kill its finely tuned crew.

When the boat came alongside the pier, Brauer ordered the engine idled. A few minutes later, the skipper gave the order to shut down. Wilhelm could have sworn he heard the *U-351* sigh like a tired and wounded beast finally granted rest—though he knew the sound came from her exhaust air fan. She rocked in the black river water as dockhands and sailors tossed lines and draped loops around bollards.

Wilhelm lingered for a moment on the bridge, fingers hooked over the rail. From this station, he'd plotted attacks, ridden mountain-sized waves, watched great ships burn in the night, seen the destiny of nations play out across the seas. Never again would he wield such power.

With the boat firmly moored, the crew brought out their personal belongings. Men with bearded and grimy faces carried small seabags up the tower ladder. After most of the crew had emerged from the boat for the last time, Wilhelm stepped through the bridge hatch and climbed down to retrieve his things.

The odor inside the U-boat nearly made him retch. He'd spent the last few hours outside, up on the bridge in fresh air. The *U-351* stank of a long patrol: unwashed bodies, urine, oil and fuel, stale food. Despite the smell, Wilhelm took a long last look at the instruments, the chart table, the radio compartment—all the tools of a trade that had meant so much to him. He placed his hand over the Luger holstered on his belt, a weapon he had never fired in anger. Already these things seemed like museum pieces, mementoes of someone else's life.

A black thought pierced his nostalgia: If he couldn't stop the next patrol, this space would go dark and fill with seawater, and good men would drown for a cause unworthy of their lives.

By the time Wilhelm hauled his bag up the ladder and emerged onto the bridge, a fresh-faced ensign in clean fatigues had appeared on the dock.

"Sir," the ensign told Captain Brauer, "the flotilla commander sends his greetings. He asked me to tell you we have not yet found quarters for all your men. We expect to have the problem worked out before nightfall. In the meantime, I can offer you a tour of the new facility we're building."

Disappointment darkened the faces of Wilhelm's crewmates. They all wanted the same thing he did: a shower, a shave, and a long sleep. The skipper, ever a good officer of the Reich, did his best to maintain a good front.

"Thank you," Brauer said. "I'll go have a look." Then he addressed his crew. "You men can rest here if you like, or you can go with me. I know you all want to get cleaned up and into bed, and you deserve it."

Most of the sailors sat down on the pier. A few pulled packs of Gitanes from their pockets and lit up; they had bought the French cigarettes during better days in Brest or Lorient. Several men stretched out on their backs and quickly fell asleep. For appearances' sake, Wilhelm elected to take the tour. He did not yet know when he would make his escape, but until he left the base, he wanted to look like the dedicated officer he'd always been.

Three petty officers joined Wilhelm and the skipper for the tour of U-boat Bunker Valentin. The fresh-faced ensign led the way down the docks toward a mass of new concrete walls. Many of the submarine bays and associated workshops in the new facility had been completed, and beyond the completed portion, earthmovers crawled and cement mixers rotated. Civilian engineers and architects conferred over blueprints spread across boards laid over sawhorses. Construction cranes angled above the site like monstrous insects. Concrete slabs dangled from the cranes' cables.

"Here, we will assemble the Type XXI submarine," the ensign said. "I know you gentlemen look forward to sailing the new state of the art."

Wilhelm glanced at Brauer, who maintained expressionless military bearing. Hard to care about the new state of the art when your boat has been given a death sentence—with you in it.

The ensign slid open a steel door. Only darkness lay behind it, and in Wilhelm's current mood, the door looked more like an entrance to a crypt than to a modern *Kriegsmarine* base. The smell of moldering concrete rolled through the doorway. The ensign bade the men to enter, so enthusiastic that he practically chirped his words. "This will be the birthplace of the Reich's newest weapon, gentlemen," he said. "But for now, we are using it as a repair facility."

The ensign flipped a row of switches, and one by one, overhead lights flickered on. The glow revealed a row of U-boats in their protected slips. Other boats sat in dry dock on raised platforms. The cavern-like structure, with water lapping at walls that never saw the sun, looked like the final stop on a journey down the River Styx.

To Wilhelm's eyes, this was not a scene of progress and technology; it was a scene of ruin. Most of the U-boats had suffered severe battle damage. Like the *U-351,* they had made it back to port only by miracles. On the *U-201,* a depth charge had blown away much of the bridge structure. The *U-423* had a crease in her hull. Mud oozed from every hatch on the *U-374;* she'd been raised from the bottom after sinking in a training accident.

The boats in dry dock portended even worse things. They showed no battle damage—because they had not seen battle. They were not even Type VIIs. They were hopelessly outdated models previously used only for training. Now they were being outfitted for combat.

Captain Brauer leaned over and whispered to Wilhelm, "When a Liberator's radar picks them up, they'll last about ten minutes."

The men's footsteps echoed as they strode down a catwalk past the damaged boats. The ensign slid open another steel door and showed off a row of offices, a machine shop, and a parts warehouse. Wilhelm squinted when the young officer opened a door to the outside. Daylight seared Wilhelm's eyes as he stepped through the doorway. When his pupils adjusted, he found himself amid construction in progress. Scaffolding and partially built concrete walls towered over pools of mud. Foremen and civilian workers milled around the site. An adjacent fenced yard contained stacks of steel I beams and rebar.

"We hope to have this portion completed by the end of the year," the ensign said.

A large Opel truck with a covered bed pulled up near the fenced yard. Something about the truck seemed to make the ensign nervous.

"Ah, gentlemen," the ensign said, "perhaps we should leave these men to their work. Let's go back to your boat, and I will go see if your quarters are ready."

Wilhelm shaded his eyes with his palm. Two SS sergeants emerged from the truck, one pointing a machine pistol. The other pulled open the flap at the back of the vehicle and shouted, "*Juden.* Out of the truck."

One by one, emaciated men wearing black-and-white striped pajamas dropped from the tailgate. Their clothing hung from sticklike limbs. The men peered at the construction site through sunken, hollow eyes. Their heads were shaved, but dark stubble sprouted from their cheeks. Even from a distance of several meters, the truck smelled like a U-boat at the end of a long patrol. One of the men who jumped from the tailgate stumbled and fell into the mud. The guard with the machine pistol kicked him in the stomach. The man clutched his abdomen, and the guard kicked him again, this time in the face. The man staggered to his feet, clothing streaked with mud. Blood streamed from his mouth. He spat out something, probably a tooth.

"Prison labor?" Captain Brauer asked.

"Ah, yes," the ensign said. "They are early today. So much the better."

Slave *labor,* Wilhelm realized. *Is the navy I love, the country I love, built on the backs of these poor creatures?*

Wilhelm had heard talk of prisoners worked to death in factories and mines. Jews, as well as Russian, Polish, and French POWs. But over the past three years, he'd had neither the time nor the inclination to give it much thought. Now, however, he felt morally adrift, as if he had surfaced to take a bearing on a lighthouse and found the light extinguished.

The ensign began walking back toward the completed portion of the bunker, but Wilhelm and his crewmates did not follow. They watched the SS guards march the prisoners into the fenced yard, where the guards began to bark orders.

"Who are these men?" one of the petty officers asked, gesturing toward the prisoners.

"They are the *eisenkommandos,*" the ensign said. "The iron-moving detachments."

The prisoners formed two lines, one at either end of the stacked I beams. They lifted the I beams, one by one, and began carrying them into the construction site. Foremen pointed to show them where to place the I beams.

"Gentlemen," the ensign said, "we really must move along."

The U-boat men ignored him. Wilhelm watched the prisoners struggle through the mud with their heavy lengths of steel. After just one trip from the steel yard, the men were soaked in mud to the waist. Many of them coughed as they worked—the hacking, wet jags of pneumonia or influenza.

After two trips, some began to falter and sink to their knees in the mud. At the guards' shouts and curses, the prisoners raised themselves to their feet again, strain evident on their pinched faces. One of the slave workers dropped his end of an I beam; Wilhelm recognized him as the man the guard had kicked earlier. The same guard strode over to the man and began shouting.

"Up, you malingering dog," the guard yelled.

The man bent over and placed his fingers around the I beam again. He tried to lift with his back, and he groaned in pain. The beam slipped from his mud-slickened fingers. It dropped into the muck and splashed mud onto the SS guard's uniform.

The guard pointed his machine pistol at the prisoner's chest and fired a three-round burst. Blood sprayed from the man's exit wounds, and he dropped into the muck.

Wilhelm gaped. He opened his mouth to speak but could find no words to express his disgust. Why couldn't the prisoner have rested for ten minutes? Even if one thought in the coldest terms, after a moment of rest, the man might have given another day's work to the cause. For a second, Wilhelm fought the urge to draw his Luger and shoot the guard.

"I think we've seen enough," Captain Brauer said.

The skipper turned and followed the ensign back into the completed portion of the bunker. Wilhelm and the petty officers trailed close behind. Wilhelm's crewmates remained expressionless. None showed any revulsion over the murder, nor did they display the smirks one might expect of ardent Party men.

Inside the bunker, the group walked in silence. *Thank God,* Wilhelm thought, *that chirpy ensign has finally shut up.* Each of Wilhelm's footfalls felt odd; at the end of every patrol, he needed to get used to walking on land again. The firmness of the concrete under his feet made no sense: Didn't every surface pitch and roll?

But another strange sensation pulsed through the soles of his boots. Intermittent vibrations, almost like a U-boat's electric motors on the fritz. Some sort of construction equipment pounding outside, Wilhelm supposed.

When he emerged from the other end of the bunker, he saw the rest of the *U-351*'s crew on the pier beside their boat. But they were no longer lounging and smoking. Every man was on his feet, pointing into the sky and scanning.

With every vibration, Wilhelm now heard a distant rumble. The rumbles turned into distinct booms.

The Yanks had returned for another bombing raid.

"We need to get your men inside," the ensign said.

That's the first intelligent thing you've said today, Wilhelm thought.

7

Bomb Run

Black puffs filled the sky around *Hellstorm*. When those dark blossoms of smoke appeared, it meant the flak gunners had found you. The formation staggered through a stained sky. Karl reminded himself that the bursts he could see were already spent. They had already thrown jagged, hot metal either harmlessly into thin air, or through the metal skin of a B-17—perhaps into an engine, a fuel line, or a flier's flesh and bones. If one of those bursts took his life today, it would be the one he never saw.

In Karl's experience, flak had brought down more bombers than the German fighter planes. Sometimes a battery of guns would use calculated lead and open up together in Continuously Pointed Fire—which the Krauts appeared to be using now.

The key was to make yourself a difficult target. Screw up their firing solution by changing course or altitude, or both. The instructors said twenty-degree course changes at least every thirty seconds could make the difference between escaping the barrage or going down in a ball of fire. That was all well and good when you were en route to the target. But during the bomb run, amid the heaviest flak, you could take no evasive action. For bombing accuracy, you had to fly straight and level, just sit there and take it, for up to ninety eternal seconds.

Shrapnel struck *Hellstorm*'s underside. Sounded like gravel thrown against the fenders of a truck speeding down a dirt road. An instant later, black smoke bloomed just below the aircraft off the left wing. Karl's first worry centered on the ball turret gunner, suspended beneath the fuselage in what some guys called "the morgue."

"Hey, Kid, you all right?" Karl asked on interphone.

"I'm good, sir," Russo answered. "But I'm gonna need to change my shorts when we get back."

Karl appreciated the attempt at humor, but he had just seen friends blown from the sky. He could think of no good reply to Russo, so he scanned the flight instruments again, trying to tamp down his emotions. He wished he could turn off his feelings the way he could isolate electrical trouble in an airplane by pulling a circuit breaker.

Adrian was flying now, and he was changing course again to make *Hellstorm* a more difficult target. Only timing, navigation, and flak told the crew they had crossed into the Third Reich. The land below looked all the same: patches of fields and forests, silver ribbons of rivers, slate roof clusters of villages.

Up ahead, the first B-17s from the formation neared the target. Those ships had flown in the lead combat box. In a few minutes, the squadrons of the second combat box—including Karl's squadron in the low position—would peel out of formation and move into line at the initial point. They could maneuver to avoid flak for a few more minutes, and then they'd have to hold steady through the bombing run—no matter what came up at them.

"I liked it better when the fighters were coming after us," Pell said on interphone.

"You and me both," Anders replied from the tail gun. "At least then we could shoot back."

The Messerschmitts had vanished before the bombers came into range of the flak guns. The fighters wanted to give a clear field of fire to their compatriots manning the antiaircraft artillery batteries on the ground.

Except for those damned flak bursts, the sky ahead looked perfectly blue, just as forecast. The aircraft had offered no excuse to abort the mission, and the weather wouldn't, either. The number-two engine still showed weak manifold pressure, but it wasn't getting any worse. *Let's just get this over with,* Karl thought. *Let's just get it done, and pray to God that Pell—and all the other bombardiers— do their best work today.*

Adrian rolled out of his turn and held a steady course. All around *Hellstorm,* the other ships in the formation did the same. The flak bursts drifted off to the left; at least for a moment, the evasive action seemed to work.

"Navigator, copilot," Adrian called. "Dick, are we good on this turn?"

"Affirm," Conrad called from the navigator's station. "Give me twenty more seconds on this heading."

"You got it."

The flak bursts stopped altogether. Pure satin blue lay ahead, unsoiled by explosives.

"Damn, copilot," Conrad called. "You're so good they just gave up."

"Don't count on it," Karl said. He wanted to believe it, but it didn't make sense. The Germans would never let scores of Forts waltz into airspace over an industrial center like Bremen this easily.

Fifteen seconds passed as peacefully as if *Hellstorm* were flying a training mission over Texas. Then a dirty rag unfurled in the sky directly in front of the second combat box. Then another, and another. Instead of appearing at random, the bursts now kept pace with the formation.

The flak gunners had fine-tuned their lead, Karl realized. Two of the aircraft ahead of *Hellstorm* already appeared damaged. One had a smoking engine, and another was missing part of its rudder.

"Huns got us dialed in," Adrian said. "Those guys in the front are getting chewed up pretty bad."

"Just keep those turns coming," Karl said. "Wait for the flight leader to call a climb."

During that blissful break in the flak bursts, the Germans had recalculated. They could pick you up on an optical sight and use a stereoscopic range finder to get your altitude. That information got fed down an electrical cable to a director that automatically computed lead. It worked much the way an expert shotgunner could shoulder his weapon, place his cheek to the stock, and swing the barrels ahead of a speeding grouse. When the lead looked just right, he'd touch the trigger and watch the bird crumple and fall.

Something struck a glancing blow to Karl's windscreen, like a single grain of sleet. Left a gouge in the glass. An instant later, another black stain smeared the sky in front of *Hellstorm*.

"This is gonna get ugly on the bomb run," Conrad called over the interphone.

"I know it," Karl said.

Ahead, the lead squadron's ships began a turn. The Fortresses banked steeply, revealing the white stars on their left wings. Karl consulted his plotting chart. This turn wasn't evasive action; the lead bombers had reached the initial point and were turning toward the target.

"Here we go," Adrian said.

"Welcome to the main event," Karl said.

Karl tried to convey more enthusiasm than he felt. He wanted, *needed,* to serve his country, his dad's adopted country. Except right now, he wanted to be anywhere but here.

A loud bang sounded just to his left. Startled by the noise, he ducked instinctively. He turned to see his side window shattered by shrapnel. Cracks spiderwebbed across the pane.

Settle your nerves, boy, he told himself. *Settle your nerves.*

"Copilot, navigator," Conrad called. "Coming up on the IP. I'll call the turn."

A pencil mark on Karl's plotting chart showed the initial point: a railroad crossing, barely visible from this altitude. Radio compass bearings backed up the visual reference. Karl held up the chart for Adrian and indicated the pencil mark with his thumb. Adrian nodded.

"Ready, ready, turn," Conrad called.

The horizon tilted as Adrian banked the aircraft thirty degrees to the left. In the turn, the combat box dissolved and the planes reassembled into one deadly line for the bomb run. The flak bursts disappeared behind and to the right. Adrian rolled out on his new heading just as a command came from their squadron's lead ship:

"Fireball, climb, climb now."

Adrian shoved the throttles and put *Hellstorm* into a thousand-foot climb. *We just threw the flak gunners a change in both heading and altitude,* Karl thought. *Maybe that will screw them up for a few minutes. Pretty hard to hit a grouse that's climbing and turning at the same time.*

Karl checked his watch and monitored the minutes, then the seconds. By now, he knew, bombs would be falling from the Forts up ahead. Moments later, a call from the group commander—in the lead ship from the first combat box—sent Karl scrambling for his target charts.

"Fireball squadrons, be advised we have good hits on the primary target," the commander announced. "But there's not any wind at ground level, and you've got smoke obscuration over the primary right now. Proceed to the secondary. Acknowledge with your call signs."

Several bombers checked in while Karl waited. When his turn came, he radioed: "Fireball Able Five."

The secondary target charts showed the location of submarine pens at the edge of the River Weser. Paper-clipped to the charts were photos taken days ago by high-altitude P-38 reconnaissance planes. In the photos, the sub pens appeared as rectangular masses of gray concrete.

"Navigator, pilot," Karl called on interphone. "You copy our new target?"

"Working on it, sir. I'll have you a new heading in a second."

"How about you, bombardier?" Karl asked.

"Got the photo out now," Pell said. "Get me there, and I'll blast it."

That would require some luck, Karl realized. Pell would probably display his usual accuracy—but *Hellstorm* carried ten five-hundred-pound general-purpose bombs. Adequate for an aircraft plant built before the war, but not the tool of choice for hardened submarine pens. Still, the GP bombs would at least give the Kraut shipyard workers a rough day—and maybe even do a little bit of actual damage. Karl and his crew would fight with what they had.

"Pilot, navigator," Conrad called on interphone. "Come left heading three-four-zero."

"Three-four-zero," Karl said. "Let's go bomb some U-boats."

"Three-four-zero," Adrian said as he began the turn.

The sky ahead remained clear of flak bursts for several minutes.

But then the black puffs reappeared, walking along ahead of the aircraft. The flak gunners' tracking capability reminded Karl of a hateful Doberman that lived on his paper route when he was a kid. Young Karl could pedal hard on his Schwinn, turn off his route, and cut down a side street, and that damned dog would still catch up, nipping at the cuffs of his jeans.

The first four puffs blossomed silently, unaccompanied by the sound of shrapnel striking the airplane. Then something hit the fuselage so hard, Karl felt the shock through his seat.

"What's happening, guys?" he asked. "Everybody all right?"

Long seconds without an answer. Karl thought he heard shouts from behind him, off interphone.

"Baker's hit," Ryan called. "Big chunk of steel came right through the radio room."

"How bad?" Karl asked.

Karl wanted to get up and go see for himself, but this close to the target and under fire, he dared not leave the command seat. The momentary silence on the interphone was maddening.

"How bad?" Karl repeated.

"It's his arm, sir," Ryan said.

That told Karl little. Was the arm scratched or severed? Despite his impatience, he understood the reason for the slow answers. The guys probably couldn't see the wound at all through the radio operator's heavy flight clothing. At the very least, they needed to get his jacket sleeve off.

"You want me to go back and have a look?" Fairburn asked from the top turret.

"Negative," Karl said. "Stay on your guns. I don't think fighters will come up through this flak, but you never know."

As an experienced aircraft commander, Karl had become used to making those kinds of decisions. As much as he wanted to give Baker extra help, he had to think of the entire ship and crew. There wasn't a lot of room back there, anyway, and the waist gunners could handle it by themselves.

Adrian followed new headings provided by the navigator, and the flak bursts scattered to the right of the airplane. After a few minutes, Baker himself spoke up on the interphone. His voice sounded weak, but his words remained clear:

"Pilot, radio. I'm still with you, sir. Arm's tore up, though. They put a tourniquet on it."

"Good to hear your voice, Baker. Let 'em give you some morphine."

"Don't need it right now. Arm's just numb. I'll save the morphine in case I need it later. We got a long way to go."

"Good man."

"Oh, and, sir, the liaison radio's dead. Shrapnel busted it."

That meant *Hellstorm* had lost her long-range communication. Not good, but at the moment, the least of Karl's problems. Now he concentrated on getting the aircraft over the target, dropping the ordnance, and flying the egress route. At this point, turning for home to get the radio operator to a doctor sooner was not an option. A lone B-17, especially one with an engine acting up, would make easy prey for the *Luftwaffe*.

With Baker's arm in a tourniquet, Karl thought, *he'll probably lose it. He might face a lifetime of disability because we wanted to get this mission done.*

Somewhere in the back of his mind, guilt tugged at Karl. He'd always felt ashamed of his cousin's membership in the German American Bund. After the attack on Pearl Harbor, Gerhard lit out for Mexico and hadn't been heard from since. The FBI was waiting for him if he ever came back. The Eighth Air Force knew about it, too, and Karl had faced a grilling before he could enter flight training. Eventually the military had satisfied itself about Karl's loyalties, but he'd always felt he had something to prove.

Am I so afraid of getting tarred by Gerhard's nonsense, Karl wondered, *that it skews my judgment? Is that why Baker's back there bleeding right now?*

Forget about it, Karl ordered himself. *Don't be a Hamlet. Concentrate. You've got a job to do.*

A smudge appeared on the horizon at the two o'clock position. The primary target, Karl realized, with a pall of smoke hanging over it.

"Looks like the other squadrons pounded the Focke-Wulf plant pretty good," Adrian said.

"You got that right," Pell said from the bombardier's station. "Glad I don't have to bomb through that smoke."

The aircraft droned nearer to Bremen, and the river hove into view. Karl searched for anything that looked like a submarine bunker. A heavy concentration of flak bursts polluted the sky across the entire city; the Germans were not going to make this easy. From the navigator's station, Conrad called up two more heading changes, and the crew began to set up for the bomb run. At the side of the river, Karl spotted what looked from this distance like a big rectangular rock.

"Target in sight," Pell called. "Follow the PDI."

The Pilot Direction Indicator displayed a needle that swung left or right to tell the pilots which way to steer toward the target. Easy enough on a training mission, but a lot harder with flak in the air, and with cold, tired aviators at the controls. The autopilot offered more precision than hand flying, and Karl needed maximum accuracy. Uncle Rainer lived somewhere in the urban landscape below.

"I got faith in my copilot," Karl said, "but I want to do this on autopilot." He glanced at Adrian, who nodded. No further explanation required. By now, Karl believed, he and Adrian could almost read each other's thoughts.

Karl had already turned on and warmed up the AFCE, *Hellstorm*'s Automatic Flight Control Equipment. He flipped a bar switch to engage the AFCE. The control yoke rocked slightly as the autopilot's servos kicked in. To fine-tune the autopilot's inputs, Karl twisted the sensitivity knob until the ailerons chattered, then backed the knob down just a hair. When the plane drew closer to the target, Karl placed his thumb on the control transfer switch and clicked the switch to the Second STA position. Second station meant the bombardier. Through the autopilot, synchronized with the gyros of the Norden bombsight, Pell now steered the aircraft for maximum accuracy.

"All right, bombardier," Karl called. "Your airplane."

"'Captain Norden' has the plane," Pell said.

Four B-17s floated in line ahead of *Hellstorm,* boring toward the target. The nearest ship was *Crescent City Maiden,* call sign Fireball Able Four. *Maiden*'s bomb bay doors yawned open, and a moment later, Karl heard Pell open *Hellstorm*'s doors, too. As an electric motor cranked the doors into the slipstream, the wind's one-note symphony grew louder.

In concert with the wind, flak bursts multiplied across the sky, a *danse macabre* to the slipstream's crescendo. Pockmarks fouled the air above Bremen from the northern edge of the city to the south: This was Curtain Fire. No need for the antiaircraft gunners to calculate lead when they know exactly where you're going. Just put up a wall of hot steel and let you fly into it.

Invisible claws raked at *Hellstorm*. Karl heard shards puncture the plane's aluminum skin from nose to tail, but at least for the moment, they hit nothing vital. The bomber continued flying normally, and the crew reported no new injuries. The plane directly in front of *Hellstorm*, *Crescent City Maiden*, appeared undamaged as well—but then she took a hit in the number-three engine. Black oil splashed over the cowling, and flames licked past the leading edge of the wing. Two heartbeats later, heavy smoke trailed from the engine. *Maiden*'s pilots feathered the prop; Karl watched the propeller spin down to a stop, blades turned into the wind for minimum drag.

"That ain't good," Adrian said.

Crescent City Maiden began to lose airspeed, and *Hellstorm* started catching up to her.

"Careful not to overrun them," Karl said. Adrian eased the throttles back.

Maiden's wings rocked. The number-four engine began to burn, and flames wrapped around the entire cowling.

"Fireball Able Four's on fire," a voice called on the radio. Sounded like Rawlings, *Maiden*'s aircraft commander.

"Don't push your luck, Four," Karl radioed. "Get out while you can."

Maiden began a wide, smoking turn to get off the bomb run. She began to descend: Rawlings was trying to build speed and blow out the flames. The fires only spread farther.

"If they keep screwing around," Adrian said, "a tank's gonna blow."

Before Karl could respond, tiny figures began dropping from underneath the stricken aircraft. One by one, their parachutes opened.

The radio voice spoke again: "Fireball Able Four going down."

"Ball turret," Karl called, "*Maiden*'s bailing out. Count the chutes for me, will you?"

"I got four," Russo said. "Five, six, seven, eight."

Maiden's right wing now trailed a sheet of flame. Two men remained aboard. Maybe the pilot and copilot were trying to set the autopilot or the trim tabs to steer the stricken plane away from the rest of the formation. But that became pointless as the control surfaces burned up.

The flaming aircraft began to roll over: She had slowed below the minimum control speed for two engines out, and now she began a smoking death spiral.

"Get out, Rawlings," Karl said into his oxygen mask.

A black speck fell away from the burning B-17, then another. The ninth and tenth parachutes opened just as *Crescent City Maiden* exploded. An orange smear in the sky threatened to envelop the last two parachutes, but the flames stopped just short of igniting the silk canopies. Debris rained from the cloud of fire. The only piece recognizable as part of an airplane was the left wing. The wing tumbled like an autumn leaf until it struck the ground with a splash of flame.

"Shake it off, guys," Karl said on interphone. "Can't do anything for them now but hit the target."

"One minute," Conrad called.

The flak bursts intensified until black spots nearly blotted out the atmosphere's natural blue, as if the sky had contracted a medieval disease. *Hellstorm*'s wings dipped and rolled, and Karl looked out the window to see a chunk of metal bitten out of the left aileron. But the aircraft held true on course, guided by inputs from Pell, hunched over the Norden down in the nose.

"Thirty seconds," Conrad announced.

The concrete rectangle on the ground loomed close now. The first B-17 in the formation flew over the structure, and a line of steel eggs fell from the bomb bay. When the first one detonated, a blast wave radiated out from the target like a fast-moving ripple. More ripples came in quick succession. Most of the bombs exploded on top of the submarine bunker, and a couple fell beside it. Karl could not assess the damage; he was focused on his instruments and target chart, ready to take over in case of autopilot failure.

"Ten seconds," Conrad called.

Karl wanted to remind Pell of the urgency for an accurate drop. But that would have been pointless—and the regs demanded silence on the interphone during the bomb run except for critical calls. The autopilot corrected course two degrees to the right.

A smoking concrete mass began sliding under the aircraft's nose. The Norden's mechanical computer counted down to bring two tungsten contacts together. The contacts sent an electrical signal through the bombardier's control panel.

Behind him, Karl heard the bomb shackles release.

8

Dire Thunders

The heavens' wrath—booming, whistling, howling wrath—rained down as Wilhelm and his crewmates huddled inside Bunker Valentin. He held his hands over his ears, but the explosions overhead assaulted his eardrums until he could hear little but a tone and a dull roar. The men turned their oil-smeared, bearded faces toward the ceiling—as they had when depth charges detonated over the *U-351*. The building shuddered. Dust and grit filled the air. The lights swayed and flickered with every blast, and ripples danced across the black water in the U-boat slips.

As Wilhelm kneeled with his comrades, he remembered stray lines from his literature classes back when he was in gymnasium, before the naval college. Something from Virgil's *Georgics*:

> *Germany heard a clashing of arms all over the sky;*
> *the Alps trembled with uncommon earthquakes . . .*
> *Never did lightnings fall in greater quantity from a*
> *serene sky, or dire thunders blaze so often.*

Long before the First Reich, did this Roman poet foresee the fall of the Third? Foretold or not, the Reich's destruction seemed pretty certain now if this many B-17s could fly into Germany.

So far, at least, the seven meters of concrete held firm—but Wilhelm found it hard to believe any man-made substance could withstand this onslaught. The bombs just kept coming—how many damned Flying Fortresses did the Yanks have, anyway?

What god did I anger, Wilhelm wondered, *that my whole existence always comes back to this? Huddling in the dark, waiting for explosions to stop.*

Some of the U-boat men cursed, but no one panicked; like Wilhelm, they had experienced this before, just not on land. To Wilhelm, once logic surfaced in his mind through the ocean of god-awful noise, this situation actually seemed easier: He might get crushed by falling concrete—but even in the worst case, at least he would not drown.

The bunker's two-story-high steel sliding door remained partially open; the men had not managed to close it all the way before the first bombs struck. Through the meter-wide column of daylight, Wilhelm saw the *U-351* moored at her pier, helpless and exposed.

A bomb struck the far end of the pier. Wilhelm saw an eruption of fire. He felt the shock wave force itself through the door opening. His sleeves flapped, and heat singed his face. Smoke poured in through the slot. Men coughed and cowered.

And the lights went out.

The bunker fell pitch black except for the wedge of daylight by the doorway, now dimmed by smoke and dust. The *U-351* still bobbed beside the pier. The pier itself had suffered a deep gouge in the concrete, but the sub remained intact. Her previous battle damage would still be repaired, and she would still go out on a pointless suicide mission and become her crew's coffin. For him to order the men back aboard her would amount to murder.

Despite exhaustion and sleep deprivation, Wilhelm's thoughts came clear and fast. He realized the darkness and confusion of the air raid gave him his best opportunity to escape. He rose to his feet, bumped and elbowed through his men to reach the far end of the submarine pen—away from the light, toward the door that led to the offices and machine shop.

Like many U-boat men, Wilhelm kept a flashlight in a pocket of his fatigues. But he chose not to use it yet. In the deep shadows, he felt his way to the door. It opened into a hallway as black as a submarine with total power loss.

Another salvo of bombs rocked the bunker. Men cried out from somewhere down the hall. Grit shook loose from the ceiling and sprinkled onto Wilhelm's head and shoulders. Amid explosions, screams, and solid gloom, Wilhelm found his surroundings . . . fitting. To abandon all for which he'd lived and fought felt like a kind of death, a portal through blackness to another phase of existence. If a U-boat bunker under attack by heavy bombers wasn't purgatory, it would do until the real thing came along. He stepped into the dark hallway and closed the door behind him.

Behind the intermittent roar of bombs, another set of explosions sounded a steady percussion line. Antiaircraft cannon, Wilhelm realized, pounding away at the Flying Fortresses. It seemed little more than token resistance. The flak batteries might take out an airplane here and there, but the bomber stream came on, relentless as Valkyries.

Confident he had slipped away from his crewmates unnoticed, Wilhelm dug into his pocket and withdrew his flashlight. When he turned it on, the beam lit shafts of dust suspended in the air by the shocks of bombardment. He had often used this same light to help bring a dying U-boat back to life: fumbling for emergency power, working to regain control before the vessel sank to crush depth. Now the light led him farther from his crew.

Wilhelm entered the machine shop he'd visited earlier. Among the lathes, drill presses, and tool cabinets, he saw men crowded onto the floor, sitting with their arms around their knees. Some rocked back and forth on their hips. These were the same poor wretches he'd seen ordered out of the truck by the SS guards. The guards now stood over them, wielding flashlights and machine pistols.

One of the SS men met Wilhelm's gaze. The man's hatchet face put Wilhelm in mind of a rat. *Every gymnasium has a bully who looks like that,* Wilhelm thought, *and this is their idea of serving the Fatherland. How much courage would this man show in the middle of the Atlantic against a foe that shoots back? We'll never know,* Wilhelm considered, *because he's probably too damned stupid for U-boat service.*

The SS man shouted to make himself heard over the air raid Klaxons and flak guns.

"Sir," the guard yelled, "we'll get these pigs to work on cleanup as soon as the all-clear sounds."

Wilhelm made no reply. None of the slave laborers looked at him, but a few stared up at the ceiling. *Are they praying for deliverance? And in what form?*

Perhaps they wished for one of those Grand Slam concrete-busters to blow off the roof and take them out of their misery. In their position, Wilhelm would have wanted exactly that. But whatever the Yanks were dropping now seemed insufficient to the task.

No bombs fell for several seconds, and Wilhelm wondered if the attack had finally ended. He moved out of the machine shop and continued down the corridor, pondering his next move. *Get out of the base and as far away as possible,* he decided. *And I'll do it quickly while everyone is still dazed.*

He followed his flashlight beam to a steel door at the end of the hallway. From the ensign's tour earlier, Wilhelm thought he recalled that the door opened to the outside.

Without warning, the door ripped from its hinges and flew past his head. The air turned to a soup of fire and debris. A vacuum sucked the breath from his lungs. He found himself on his back, struggling to breathe, to understand. Tasted blood in his mouth. Something hurt his eyes. Glare. He realized the glare came from the sun. A bomb had struck just outside the building at a place not reinforced as strongly as the main bunker. The blast had ripped open the door and part of the wall, and Wilhelm lay amid the rubble. Dazed, he found himself unable to move for several minutes.

Gradually his sense of balance returned. He tried to sit up. Placed the heel of his right hand on the ground. A jolt of pain shot through his arm, as if he'd been electrocuted. Wilhelm fell onto his side and rubbed his left thumb across the back of the injured hand. He found his right thumb dislocated, wrenched from its socket at a grotesque angle. Each breath hurt; some of his ribs were probably broken. Blood dripped from a gash on his left arm. When he coughed, he barely heard the sound. The blast had partially deafened him.

Wilhelm wanted to check on his crewmates, to let a doctor treat his hand, to bathe, to shave, to sleep. But the Yanks and their endless bombs had, in a way, presented him with a gift: a chance to get away, one that would not last. At such an opportune moment, Wilhelm had learned, a good officer seizes the initiative. In his mind, he set his new course.

Using his left hand this time, Wilhelm pushed himself to a sitting position. His first priority was to get that thumb back into place if possible. He placed three fingers against the dislocated joint and pushed. That hurt so much, he ground his molars, sucked in air between his teeth.

And he hadn't pushed hard enough. The thumb remained out of position.

Wilhelm had seen a sailor deal with a similar injury while at sea. With no doctor on board, and weeks of patrolling ahead, the man had little choice but to fix it himself. The sailor hooked his thumb around a rung of the U-boat's tower ladder and yanked hard. He screamed as the pain put him on his knees, but the joint popped back into place. Wilhelm realized he'd need to find a similarly brutal field remedy.

He placed the heel of his boot on the first joint of his thumb, pinning his right hand to the ground. Placed his left hand around his right wrist. Closed his eyes, drew in a deep breath, and pulled hard.

He'd thought he wouldn't scream like that sailor. And he didn't. He screamed more like a girl. The agony brought tears to his eyes; he felt he'd torn the thumb off altogether. He rolled onto his back. But when he looked at his hand, the thumb was back in its socket. Still hurting, but back in place.

Wilhelm took three painful breaths. Forced himself to stand. He braced himself on a chunk of fallen concrete and took an unsteady step. That brought no additional pain; at least his legs weren't broken. His eyes watered from dust and grit. Wilhelm took out a handkerchief and dabbed at them, blinking. Brushed dirt from his beard. Wiped the cut on his left arm and placed the bloody handkerchief back in his pocket.

A dead silence took hold. At first, Wilhelm wondered if he'd gone completely deaf, but he heard, faintly, the grinding of rubble under his boots. He listened carefully and realized the flak guns had qui-

eted. So had the air raid Klaxons. Thank God, the bombers had finished their work for today.

On unsteady feet, Wilhelm entered what had been the area of
new construction. Where a new concrete wall had stood, he saw only
a crater of mud. Scaffolding and I beams lay in a heap of twisted
metal. A toppled crane rested across the burning remains of the
truck that had brought in the slave laborers. Black smoke boiled
from the wreckage, and it smelled like a torpedoed oil tanker. No
sign of life anywhere.

A chain-link fence, still intact, surrounded the construction zone.
Wilhelm picked his way to the fence, hoping to find an opening. Mud
sucked at his navy boots. He took two more steps and sank in muck
to his knees.

"Scheisse," Wilhelm said.

He began to lift his left foot, heavy with mud, when something
about five meters away caught his eye: a filthy puddle, the black-and-
white stripes of a prison uniform, a burgundy swirl. A black hand,
scorched fingers curled into a claw. Nothing else resembled any part
of a human body. Some poor devil caught in the open, or perhaps
the remains of the prisoner shot dead by the SS goon before the
bombing. In any case, this man's troubles were over, and he was
probably better off than his comrades huddled inside the machine
shop.

Wilhelm had believed he fought a chivalrous war. U-boat crews
operated by a code of honor. For example, one never fired on a ship
rendering aid. Wilhelm remembered a night when the *U-351* made a
surface attack on a British freighter. One shot hit her amidships, and
one shot sufficed. The freighter's back broken, flames towered into
the darkness while her crew lowered lifeboats from their davits. The
stricken ship had sailed with a large convoy, and Captain Brauer
wanted to score more victories that night. The torpedo tubes stood
loaded and ready, and the convoy's destroyer escorts crisscrossed
the sea in all the wrong places. The *U-351* remained unseen, deadly,
and poised to strike again.

Another freighter hove alongside the flaming wreck. An easy shot
on a fat target. Brauer seemed about to add another five thousand
tons to his kill record. But the men in the lifeboats began rowing

across to the freighter. Sailors lowered scramble nets from her railings. Wilhelm heard, quite distinctly, one of those sailors call out in that odd, flat-sounding American English: "Climb aboard, fellas. We'll get you some dry clothes and hot chow."

Captain Brauer doffed his cap and crumpled it in his fist. He wore an expression like he'd just lost a chess game.

"Close the tubes," Brauer ordered. "We'll get her on another night."

The mission was to stop Allied supplies, not kill fellow mariners. Of course, some of the mariners on torpedoed ships would die, but those deaths came as a regrettable secondary result. Mercy had its place across the windswept leagues of the Atlantic. That was especially true in the stories Wilhelm had heard about U-boat ace Otto Kretschmer. The legendary Kretschmer had been known to surface among the lifeboats of men he'd just torpedoed, call out in fluent English, and make sure the castaways had food, water, and a course to land.

But even if the *Kriegsmarine* fought with honor on the seas, Wilhelm realized, horrors ensued on shore. Horrors in the name of the nation he loved. Almost at first sight, he had despised that hatchet-faced bully in the SS uniform. Now Wilhelm wondered, *Are he and I cogs in the same machine?*

Wilhelm slogged through the muck to reach the chain-link fence, where he found drier ground. The effort winded him, and hard breathing made his cracked ribs stab him all the worse. He paused for a moment, hooked his fingers through the fence, and scraped his boots against the links to rid them of mud.

While he kicked and scraped, he looked out across the river and into the city. The water flowed dark, the color of engine oil, and it looked about as drinkable. Debris bobbed in the current: splintered lumber, bottles and cans, a wad of clothing. No, that wasn't a wad of clothing; it was a body floating facedown.

Nothing flew overhead now except a single crow, black as the depths, gliding above the Weser. Pillars of smoke rose in a half-dozen places as if Thor had emerged from the pages of Germanic mythology and thrown down thunderbolts.

Wilhelm came to a break in the fence. Not a gate, but merely a rip in the chain links, perhaps the result of a chunk of concrete or metal sent flying in the bombardment. The opening wasn't wide enough for him to step through, so he grasped the torn edge of the fence and pulled. He worked at both sides of the rip, yanking with his good hand while he braced himself with one boot against the fence. Each pull sent blinding pain through his ribs, and twice he had to stop and let the silver dots clear from his eyes. When Wilhelm opened a hole barely big enough to admit his shoulders, he ducked through. A broken link snagged his inner thigh. The sharp wire tore a hole in his fatigues and left a bloody scratch.

Now, where to go?

Wilhelm's maternal grandparents lived in an old section of Bremen. He had last seen his *opa* and *oma* just before his first patrol. He had no idea if they remained here or if they'd moved to safer environs in the country. As a deserter, would his presence put them in danger? Perhaps. But given Wilhelm's spotless record up until now, the *Kriegsmarine* would probably consider him merely missing— and not conclude he'd deserted—for at least a day or two. They might even think he'd been blown away in the bombing.

I'll stay just one night, Wilhelm thought. *I haven't seen them in so long. I'll tell them only that Valentin was bombed and I survived; that much is true. I'll get cleaned up, catch up on my sleep, and then I'll move into the countryside and wait out the war.*

He climbed an embankment studded with patches of dead weeds. At the crest, Wilhelm came to a paved access road that led from the naval base. No cars moved along the road; the city remained silent. He walked along the road's edge. With each step, his ribs burned. His hand throbbed where the thumb had been knocked out of joint. The thumb remained in place, but a bruise the color of deep seawater was spreading across his palm.

A devastated city lay before Wilhelm. The bombers had come many times before, and it was hard to tell which damage had taken place two years ago and which had happened half an hour ago. He stumbled past the remains of a shipyard's office buildings. Two intact walls loomed over a mound of bricks. A steel desk, twisted and charred, rested atop the rubble. Except for a relatively new Mercedes with tires burned off the rims, the scene resembled photos Wilhelm had seen from the First World War.

The bombed-out shipyard so riveted Wilhelm's attention that he failed to look where he put his feet, and he did not see the object that tripped him. Something snagged his boot, and he staggered and nearly fell. Suffered more stabs of pain from his ribs. He looked down and saw a metal bar, painted black except for a yellow tip.

Wilhelm picked up the object and examined it more closely. From its taper—and the English lettering—he realized he was holding a propeller blade. Evidently, a flak shell had found its mark in the skies above him. At least one Flying Fortress crew was having a bad day. *Serves them right,* Wilhelm thought, *raining explosives on this once-beautiful city.* But then he realized the men on the civilian freighters he'd sent to the bottom would say he deserved getting depth charged.

Professionals, Wilhelm thought. *We were all professionals doing a job. Well,* some *of us were professionals,* he considered. *Not that motherless goon in the SS uniform. What skill, what study and aptitude, did his job require?*

Wilhelm tossed away the propeller blade. It clanged onto the skeleton of a fallen shipyard crane. The noise startled a stray cat. The calico hissed and disappeared into a tangle of rusting cable. Wilhelm saw the cat hiss, but did not hear the sound; his ears remained dulled. He put one boot in front of the other, continued his journey toward the unknown.

9

The Butcher Birds

Karl switched off the autopilot and racked *Hellstorm* into a steep left turn. Freed of her bomb load, she weighed five thousand pounds less, and she handled more nimbly. Electric motors closed the bomb bay doors.

Below, blazes flickered across Bremen. From this altitude, the fires and smoke gave the city the appearance of an inflamed ulcer, septic and bleeding. Pell had reported his bombs on target, and Karl believed him, but the damage wreaked by the formation looked general and indiscriminate. Karl forced himself not to think about Uncle Rainer and Aunt Federica; he still had a hell of a long way to go, and he needed to concentrate. As he rolled the wings level on his egress heading toward the North Sea, he heard Russo calling from the ball turret.

"Bandits nine o'clock low and climbing fast," Russo said. "Here they come!"

Karl peered out the left window. Dark specks moved over the ground, maybe ten of them. Hornets kicked from their nest, armed and enraged. The *Luftwaffe* intended to exact a price for the raid on Bremen, and Karl felt he'd gotten into a street fight with one arm in a sling. With Baker wounded, there was no one to fire the gun in the radio room. The B-17 carried other guns, of course, but Karl wanted every weapon ready to start blazing. To make matters worse, his aircraft would now have to defend itself alone. The Fortresses had strung out all across the target area, and they no longer provided mutual support from interlocking fields of fire.

"They're trying to get ahead of us," Pell reported.

Sure enough, the specks were flying parallel to the bombers' course and pulling ahead. Faster than heavy bombers, German fighters could use their speed advantage to set up for attack. They'd get a few miles in front of the formation and a little above it, then turn and slice through the Forts.

"Yeah," Karl said. "They're going to get on our twelve o'clock and come in. Stay ready, gunners."

Karl felt tempted to tell them to use short bursts and keep interphone chatter concise. But he'd already reminded them at least once, and the gunners knew their jobs. In their training, they'd fired BB machine guns at moving targets on an indoor range, and they'd learned to lead targets at various angles by firing shotguns at clay pigeons. Then they'd gone up on training flights to shoot at towed targets. The factors of lead, bullet trajectory, target speed, and angle all came together in a deadly science known as flexible aerial gunnery.

In the distance, the fighters began to turn. As they banked, Karl recognized them as Focke-Wulf 190s. That angle revealed the *Balkenkreuz* markings—the black crosses on the fuselages and wings. The 190s also bore swastikas on their vertical stabilizers. Each fighter carried a pair of machine guns synchronized to fire through the propeller arc, along with twenty-millimeter cannons mounted in the wings. According to Eighth Air Force intel reports, German pilots nicknamed the Fw 190 the "Butcher Bird."

"Anybody see any friendlies?" Adrian asked.

"Negative," Fairburn called from the top turret.

"Wait," Anders responded from the tail gun. "I got four Mustangs coming down from five o'clock high."

"How far out are they?" Karl asked.

"I don't know," Anders said. "Maybe four miles."

The 190s were closer, and they continued to turn. In a few seconds, the attack would begin. Karl could almost sense his gunners watching the Butcher Birds through their sights. He prayed the Mustangs would intercept the enemy planes in time.

Karl's oxygen regulator blinked black and white faster and faster as he breathed more rapidly. Flying Fortresses had a reputation for being hard to shoot down, so the Germans tended to concentrate their fire toward the flight deck. Though Karl had always considered himself a strong man, at the moment he felt frail and squishy. In the cockpits of those 190s, drawing closer by the second, sat highly skilled and motivated young men determined to put sharp, hot metal through Karl's body.

The Butcher Birds banked more steeply, maneuvering in front of the B-17s.

"They're at twelve o'clock and closing," Karl said. Tried to keep his voice as even as possible.

From above *Hellstorm*, the Mustangs appeared in Karl's field of view. They dived and turned to meet the 190s. Tracers began spitting from their wings. Some of the Butcher Birds turned to engage the Mustangs. But others held course and pressed their attack.

The oncoming Butcher Birds grew larger in the windscreen. Some aircraft veered to hit other bombers in the scattered formation, but one bored directly at *Hellstorm*. Flashes began to blink on the leading edges of its wings: cannon fire.

Karl banked to begin an evasive turn, but it was a token effort. The Fort could never outmaneuver a fighter. With a mere flick of its ailerons, the German aircraft stayed on *Hellstorm* and closed fast.

Hellstorm's gunners opened up. Rips of fire erupted from the ball turret, the top turret, and one of the cheek guns in the nose. Tracers cut parabolas toward the German aircraft, but the Focke-Wulf seemed to absorb them without effect. Perhaps the rounds impacted without inflicting fatal damage. Empty casings from Fairburn's twin fifties clanged and clattered behind Karl and Adrian.

The German aircraft began firing. Bangs sounded from *Hellstorm*'s left wing. The aircraft shuddered as if stomped by a giant boot.

The fighter headed right for the windscreen; Karl pushed down on the yoke and began to dive. At the last instant, the 190 pulled up. It screamed over the top of the Fortress, just feet away. Anders opened fire with the tail gun; Karl felt its thumping, quieter and more distant than the turret guns just above his head.

The yoke began to vibrate, and when Karl looked out his window, he saw why. Half the left aileron had been shot away. What was left hung ragged and torn, fluttering on its hinges. Worse, the number-two engine was smoking and burning. Spasms of panic twisted his gut, but Karl forced himself to focus.

"Feather number two," Karl ordered. He wanted to shut down the stricken engine and stop its propeller. A motionless, feathered prop presented less drag than a windmilling prop.

Adrian put a gloved finger on the center console.

"Confirm two," Adrian said, asking Karl to double-check he was shutting down the correct engine. Bad time for a stupid mistake to leave them with two dead engines.

"Confirm," Karl said.

Adrian flipped switches to close the fuel valve and shut off the boost pump for the stricken engine. Placed his middle finger on the feathering button for number two.

"Confirm two," Adrian repeated. His voice sounded strained from inside his oxygen mask.

"Confirm."

Adrian shoved the button, and the number-two propeller slowed to a stop. He opened the cowl flaps on the bad engine and switched off its magnetos. The smoke trailing from number two thinned, but did not stop. Karl advanced the throttles for the three remaining engines to max continuous power. Now he'd have a tough time maintaining speed and altitude, and he prayed the Butcher Birds would content themselves with one pass.

No such luck.

The 190 that had just put cannon rounds into *Hellstorm*'s wing and engine cut a wide, smoking arc around the formation and headed for home. Karl's gunners had done some damage, after all. But another fighter circled and climbed, searching for prey. Wounded and burning, *Hellstorm* made an obvious target. The German pilot would want to finish her off, record her death with his gun camera, and claim a confirmed kill.

"Here comes another one," Karl said. "Ten o'clock high."

The Butcher Bird steepened its bank while it gained altitude, as if performing a chandelle in an air show. An elegant move in a lethal ballet. At the zenith of the maneuver, the German pilot let his nose drop until his guns lined up with *Hellstorm*'s forward fuselage. The

190's cannons began to wink. Fairburn and Russo started blasting from their turrets.

Karl banked hard to the left and began a descending turn. He hoped it might throw off the fighter's aim—but the German pilot needed only to nudge a rudder pedal to adjust fire. The Fort's tracers cut spears of light toward the enemy, while the 190's muzzles strobed with cannon rounds.

The Butcher Bird dived so near that Karl saw the pilot's eyes inside his goggles. Three impacts jackhammered somewhere out on the right wing. The yoke lurched in Karl's hands.

The windscreen exploded.

Cold air blasted Karl with such force that it slammed the breath from his lungs. Glass shards peppered his cheeks. *Hellstorm* spasmed and trembled. Steepened her dive. The needles inside the gauges shook so hard that the instruments became unreadable.

Karl pulled back on the yoke. The aircraft did not respond. The nose fell through the horizon, and *Hellstorm* pointed toward the ground.

"Pull with me," Karl said to Adrian.

No response.

Karl glanced to his right and saw why.

The cannon round that had punched through the windscreen had struck Adrian square in the chest. His flak vest was meant to stop shrapnel, not high-velocity projectiles. Frothy blood from the copilot's lungs bubbled through a wound the size of a softball. He hung in his harness, head lolled to one side. Streamers of blood, driven by windblast, tracked across the sleeves of his leather jacket. The blinker on his oxygen regulator stood motionless.

With no time to process the horror beside him, Karl pulled hard on the yoke. The aircraft continued its plunge. The howl of the slipstream rose to a scream, and acceleration pressed Karl against his seat. He couldn't read the airspeed indicator, but he knew *Hellstorm* had to be nearing VNE—its never-exceed velocity. Beyond that speed, the aircraft might start coming apart.

With so little pitch control, Karl guessed cannon rounds must have ripped away part of the tail surfaces. He braced with his left boot and hauled back with all his strength. Felt something release. Maybe a control cable had come unsnagged. The nose began to rise.

"Right wing's on fire," a voice called on the interphone. Sounded like Fairburn, but Karl wasn't sure. Frigid air blasting through the broken windscreen nearly drowned out conversation.

"How bad?" Karl shouted.

When he spoke, he heard no sidetone in his headphones.

"Crew, pilot," he called. "Anybody hear me."

No answer. The interphone had just gone out.

Karl pulled hard on the controls. Brought the aircraft back to level flight—more or less. The instruments still bounced in their cases, but now he could see the altimeter needles well enough to read fifteen thousand feet. *Hellstorm* had just lost six thousand feet.

And she flew alone. Karl saw no other aircraft, friendly or enemy. Both sides had probably given *Hellstorm* up for dead.

They had guessed correctly, too. The nose kept pitching up and down despite Karl's best efforts to hold altitude. An attempt to turn to the north, back onto the egress route, produced no results. Aileron control gone. Karl leaned forward to examine the right wing. Flames enveloped the number-four engine and threatened to spread. He punched the feathering button to stop the propeller. This mortally wounded aircraft would not fly much longer.

One of the most common causes of death for aircrew members was a delayed decision to bail out. Karl had seen it, too: Flying Fortresses wreathed in flame, dropping out of formation like meteors burning through the atmosphere, no parachutes unfurling. The aircraft commander undoubtedly thinking, *We want to go home, not to a POW camp.* Karl had always told himself he'd never do that to his men; if an emergency demanded it, he'd act decisively and quickly. But the choice came hard. His crew had *completed* their final bomb run. They'd earned the freedom of civilian life, the status of honored veterans. The doorway to home lay just a few hundred air miles away in England.

Hellstorm could no longer take them there. Karl just hoped to keep her stable long enough for the crew to get out. Instead of a joyous homecoming, his closest friends now faced interrogation and internment—if they were lucky. And with the interphone out, he had only one way to communicate his order. Karl flipped the switch for the bailout bells.

Thank God, at least the three electrically powered bells still worked. They clanged a long, one-note dirge. Bailout procedures called for the navigator and bombardier to exit through the forward hatch. The pilots, engineer, and radio operator would drop through the bomb bay, and the ball turret gunner, waist gunners, and tail gunner would leap through an exit on the side of the fuselage. The bomb bay doors yawned open again. That meant Pell, at the bombardier's station, had heard the bailout signal and reopened the doors.

The rush of the wind changed pitch as someone opened the forward hatch. Good—that meant Pell and Conrad were wasting no time getting out of the airplane. Karl intended to stay at the controls until everyone else exited; then he'd put the B-17 on autopilot—if the autopilot would engage. Maybe that would keep the wings level long enough for him to reach the bomb bay.

Fairburn dropped from the top turret and stood behind Karl's seat. The engineer buckled his leather flying helmet and zipped his fleece-lined jacket. Placed his hand on Adrian's shoulder. Looked at the dead copilot, then at Karl.

"He's gone," Karl shouted over the windblast. "Get out."

Without a word, Fairburn turned and vanished. Karl thought he heard shouts from the aft section of the plane, though the wind noise made it hard to tell. He hoped that meant the gunners were helping Baker get to the bomb bay. Maybe even pulling the wounded man's rip cord for him just as they pushed him out.

The shouts and thumps lasted for a few seconds. Then Fairburn reappeared on the flight deck. Karl turned to him and yelled, "I told you to get out!" Fate had given *Hellstorm*'s crew precious time to escape—a luxury not always granted to stricken Fortresses. Karl didn't want to waste a moment of it.

"Going now, sir," Fairburn shouted. "Just wanted to tell you everyone's gone but us."

Damn, that's a good man, Karl thought. *With the interphone shot out, I needed another way to make sure the entire crew bailed, and Fairburn read my mind.*

Karl nodded to his engineer. Fairburn slapped Karl's shoulder, then disappeared into the bomb bay.

For several seconds, long enough to make sure Fairburn got out, Karl did something few men had ever done: He flew alone in a B-17. Then he released the buckle on his harness. Reached down and flipped on the autopilot. The yoke rocked as the servos engaged—or tried to. Karl let go of the controls. *Hellstorm* started a descending turn to the right. Her ailerons and elevator were too damaged for the autopilot to hold her steady.

Get moving, Karl told himself. He popped the quick-disconnect on his oxygen hose, pulled a drawstring to shed his flak vest. Yanked out his interphone cord. Placed the heel of his hand on the center console and pushed himself up from his seat. Glanced one last time at Adrian. The blood on the copilot's clothing and gear was beginning to freeze. It seemed so very wrong to leave him here.

Your aircraft, buddy, Karl thought. *May it fly you to a better place.*

Karl made his way aft, stumbling as the airplane banked. He balanced on the bomb bay catwalk. An icy blast whipped at his pants legs. Thousands of feet beneath him, the German landscape scrolled by. The River Weser came into view, along with the smoking city on its banks. Karl realized *Hellstorm* had made a full turn and crossed back over Bremen. The autopilot lost what little control it ever had, and the airplane banked more steeply.

Karl realized that any second now, the flak guns would open up again or the airplane would overbank and stall. Or both. He placed his hand on his rip cord and stepped off the catwalk and into the void.

A tumbling rush overwhelmed Karl's senses. Earth and sky blurred and swapped places. Vertigo brought such delirium that Karl felt propelled *upward* toward a ceiling of land. For several seconds, he gave no thought to pulling his rip cord. Finally enough reason gathered in Karl's mind: He jerked the D-ring.

His limbs flailed with the parachute's opening shock. The horizon righted itself, and the sight rocked Karl's inner ear so hard that bile rose in his throat. He swallowed hard, managed not to vomit.

He looked up and saw he had a good chute. Sunlight filtered through the round white canopy. Around him, Karl saw nothing else in the air. No airplane, no other parachutes. He prayed everyone had gotten out safely and their chutes had opened. God only knew where they'd landed.

But where was the aircraft? Karl saw no telltale fire on the ground to mark its crash site.

Distant booms began to echo. Karl scanned the skies around him and saw black puffs, maybe three miles away and several hundred feet above him. The flak gunners were firing at his airplane, still aloft. Amid the flak explosions, the B-17 rolled into a ninety-degree bank and began to plunge. *Hellstorm* in its death spiral, manned only by Adrian's ghost.

Karl felt a fullness in his throat. *If I'd turned back when I had the chance,* he thought, *Adrian would still be alive. We'd have flown another mission in a day or two, and then we'd have gone home.*

Hellstorm tightened her spiral, traced a black corkscrew of smoke toward the ground. Karl kept his eyes locked on his airplane through her final moments. The left wing separated and tumbled away in flames. The rest of the B-17 impacted at the river's edge. The explosion showered debris into the Weser, and the fire cast a wavering reflection across the water.

10

The Clothes of a Dead Man

The flak guns across the river began pounding again. Wilhelm looked up in surprise to see a strange sight: A single Flying Fortress twisted a flaming path to the ground. Wilhelm lost sight of the aircraft behind a screen of trees, so he did not see the bomber hit the earth—but he heard the impact. A flat *crump* from a kilometer away, a bit like the sound of a depth charge exploding.

Wilhelm knew little of air tactics, but he thought it odd for a lone bomber to venture over an enemy city. Why would its crew do something so clearly suicidal? Then a possible answer occurred to him: The crewmen had either died or bailed out, and with no one at the controls, the bomber had circled back over its target. The guns fell silent, and Wilhelm decided this incident did not concern him.

What did concern him was the devastation he found as he neared his grandparents' neighborhood. Cratered streets led to flattened apartment buildings and scorched chimneys standing sentinel over bare foundations. Even in blocks that remained undamaged, houses appeared empty. Boards were nailed over windows, and weeds grew through cracks in the sidewalks. Dead leaves littered stoops. A scene of abandonment and loss entirely out of accord with Wilhelm's childhood memories.

As a little boy, he had walked these streets with his grandparents and their dog, a big Alsatian named Bruno. Whenever *Oma* and *Opa* stopped to chat with neighbors, Wilhelm would pet Bruno between the ears and ignore the adult conversation. After a few seconds of this, the dog would lie down and roll onto his back, wanting his belly scratched.

And—perhaps unusual for an Alsatian—Bruno loved the water as much as Wilhelm. During trips to the lake at Bürgerpark, the dog liked nothing better than to swim after a stick that Wilhelm would throw as far as he could. Bruno used to paddle back to shore, drop the stick, and shake water from his fur in a spray that covered a laughing ten-year-old Wilhelm. When Wilhelm got older, Bruno would ride in the sailboat with him, a loyal mate on the first vessel Wilhelm commanded.

These happy memories brought tears to Wilhelm's eyes. It was an entirely different life back then, when boats were tools of pleasure and not instruments of destruction. Homes were solid and permanent, and loved ones lived long lives.

Bremen's streets had changed so much that Wilhelm did not recognize some of them. Stumps marked where mature trees had once stood. Wilhelm wondered if bombing had destroyed the trees or if desperate residents had used them for firewood. He lost his bearings and wandered aimlessly along an alley with no identifying sign. But when the alley dead-ended onto Wachmannstrasse, he knew exactly where he was.

His grandparents' street.

Stumps lined the crumbling pavement. Wilhelm could close his eyes and bring the lindens back to life, see them before him as if they grew there still. He wandered down the sidewalk, avoiding trash barrels, bricks, and other debris. Half the homes on Wachmannstrasse were destroyed or damaged. The rest appeared empty. At his grandparents' address, instead of a four-story town house, he found a pile of rubble. Bombs had leveled the entire block.

He had experienced such happy times here. Christmas mornings. Family reunions. Birthdays. Evenings when his grandfather read him sea stories and his grandmother made apple strudel.

The last time he'd been ashore he'd found his parents' home abandoned—and now his grandparents' house was gone.

Wilhelm sobbed, sank to his knees. The motion spiked pain through his ribs. His entire world seemed upended, everything he stood for either betrayed, perverted, or blown away. *I did my job,* he thought. *Why wasn't that enough to prevent this?* For a moment, he felt tempted by the easy way out: to place the barrel of his Luger against the roof of his mouth and end the nightmare.

Instead, he wiped his eyes and cheeks on the sleeves of his fatigues and reminded himself to act like a German officer.

From the remains of his grandparents' home, he selected a chunk of brick. A piece shaped in a rough pyramid, about the size of the horizon mirror on a sextant. He put the fragment in his pocket. Wilhelm did not know why he did this. A piece of the past to carry him into the future, perhaps.

On the next block, Wilhelm found an intact row of townhomes. Smoke rose from one of the chimneys. Wilhelm knocked on the door.

An old man in a tattered naval sweater answered the knock. He wore a great gray moustache with waxed points in the style of the previous century, and his ocean-blue eyes flashed with more than a hint of annoyance. But when he saw Wilhelm's fatigues and cap, his expression softened.

"What can I do for you, *Oberleutnant*?" the man asked.

"Very sorry to disturb you, sir," Wilhelm said. "I just came back from patrol. My grandparents lived on this street. Can you tell me what became of them? The Göttingers?"

The man stroked his moustache, regarded Wilhelm.

"Would you like to come in?"

The words sounded muffled. *Is this an invitation?*

"What's that, sir?" Wilhelm asked. "My hearing, it's a little off."

"Would you like to come inside?"

"No, thank you. I have to be on my way. But I saw what happened to my grandparents' house."

"I am sorry you had to come home to that, son." The man spoke more loudly now. "I know your grandfather. Good man, Kurt Göttinger. He moved away."

"And my grandmother? Was she hurt in the air raids?"

The old man stood silently for long seconds. Wilhelm knew that could mean nothing good.

"No," the man said finally. "I see that you do not know, and I am sorry to be the one to tell you this. Your grandmother Ingrid was very sick. When she passed, Kurt could not stand to stay in the house. I do not know where he went. Bombs hit the street about a month after he left."

Wilhelm stared down at the masonry that made up the old man's stoop. Forced himself to keep his composure. Oma *is gone? Could the navy not have managed one radiogram to inform me?*

"Come inside, my boy," the old man said. "I can see you have fought hard. Submariner's patrol beard and all. I have a shot of schnapps for you."

The schnapps sounded tempting. Wilhelm was tired and hungry; maybe the old man would offer food, too. Against Wilhelm's better judgment, he accepted.

"You're very kind," Wilhelm said. "I won't impose on you for long. I'll be on my way in a few minutes."

Inside the old man's sitting room, Wilhelm needed a moment for his eyes to adjust to the darkness. The man bade him to sit on an overstuffed sofa. Books lined the walls, and a wood fire burned in a hearth made for coal. Above the hearth hung a painting depicting the 1916 Battle of Jutland: roaring guns of British and German battleships and destroyers locked in one of the greatest naval engagements of all time.

There was no mention and no sign of a wife; Wilhelm guessed his host was a widower. The man disappeared into another room for several minutes. He returned with two small glasses and a bottle of pear schnapps. Poured three fingers of schnapps into each glass and handed one to Wilhelm.

"I started heating the kitchen stove," the man said. "I can offer you some schnitzel in a little while."

"Thank you very much," Wilhelm said. "I take it you're a navy man."

"I was. Forgive me, I should have introduced myself. My name is Rudolf Brandt. I was a captain in the *Kaiserliche Marine.*"

The old Imperial Germany Navy. The glory days of Tirpitz and Spee.

Wilhelm took a tiny sip of the schnapps. He was being careful. He hadn't had alcohol in weeks and food in hours, and he feared the drink would go straight to his head. The schnapps tasted like a freshly picked pear, with a burning sweetness behind it. Wilhelm's throat and stomach warmed instantly.

Brandt pointed to the cut on Wilhelm's left arm. "What happened to you?" the old man asked. "Got a little too close to the Tommies and Yanks?"

"Uh, no, sir. I slipped and fell on the deck the other day. It is nothing."

Wilhelm knew it was a lame story, but it seemed to satisfy Brandt.

"I heard the bombers," Brandt said. "Did they hit the submarine base?"

"I fear they did, but I was not there at the time," Wilhelm lied.

Wilhelm placed his glass atop a coaster on an end table. Despite his best efforts at courtesy, he closed his eyes and drifted off to sleep. The sound of rattling dishes woke him twenty minutes later. Brandt brought him a plate of *jägerschnitzel,* along with a knife and fork.

"Thank you, sir," Wilhelm said. He sat with the plate on his knees and sawed at the schnitzel. Working with the knife made his sore thumb hurt again, but Wilhelm didn't care. The meat's aroma filled his mouth with saliva. He tried to eat slowly and to mind his manners, but the effort took self-control. It was the first hot food he'd had in days.

"You eat like you just got off the boat," Brandt said.

"I have, sir," Wilhelm said, chewing. "I wasn't sure how long I'd have on leave, and I didn't want to miss seeing my grandparents, but . . ."

"An awful thing to learn as soon as one sets foot on shore."

"Yes, sir." Wilhelm decided to change the subject—and maybe get some information that could help him. "What is the latest news of the land war? I've been a bit disconnected from that lately."

"I've been disconnected from it, too," Brandt said, "so I am afraid I cannot help you. I no longer listen to the broadcasts. You see, my son died on the *Bismarck* back in '41. Since then, I don't care a cup of bilgewater for anything about this war."

Wilhelm had been onshore at Kiel when the *Bismarck* went down. Of course, everyone in the navy had followed the reports closely. The *Bismarck*, the greatest capital ship of the *Kriegsmarine,* destroyed the British battlecruiser HMS *Hood* in the Battle of Denmark Strait, between Greenland and Iceland. The Tommies wanted vengeance, and the Royal Navy launched a five-day sea-and-air hunt for the German warship. They caught her six hundred kilometers off the coast of France.

A torpedo dropped by an aircraft from the carrier *Ark Royal* damaged one of *Bismarck*'s rudders, and that proved a fatal wound. Unable to maneuver with a jammed rudder, she steamed in a circle as the British battleships *King George V* and *Rodney* moved in for the kill. A raging duel ensued, with the Tommies firing hundreds, maybe thousands, of shells. The shells set *Bismarck* afire stem to stern, and torpedoes finished her off. From a crew of more than two thousand men, only about a hundred survived.

"I'm very sorry for your loss, Captain Brandt," Wilhelm said.

Brandt waved his hand almost dismissively. Wilhelm thought it a strange gesture. Then the old captain looked into the fire, stared at the flames for a long time as if trying to control his emotions. Keeping all parts of his mind at battle stations, Wilhelm thought. Maybe Brandt was done with pity, long past wanting anyone's sympathy.

When Brandt looked up again, he changed the subject.

"Son," the captain asked, "do you need a place to stay during your leave?"

The offer tempted Wilhelm, but he could not accept it. Soon the navy would suspect he'd deserted. Then other parts of the government would get involved—agencies without the navy's codes of honor and professionalism. Anyone sheltering him would be endangered. Wilhelm decided to ask for a couple of small favors, then move on as soon as possible.

"I appreciate that, sir," Wilhelm said, "but I have to be on my way. If you don't mind, though, I'd like to wash up and shave off this beard. And, as much as I hate to ask, borrow some civilian clothing. All my clothes were in my grandparents' house."

"By all means," Brandt said. He pointed to a staircase. "The bathroom is at the top of the steps. My son's old room is the door to the right. You're a little taller than he was, but you may have any clothes you find. Pardon the dust. I don't go in that room anymore."

"What was his name, sir?"

"Meinhard. *Leutnant* Meinhard Brandt."

Wilhelm finished his schnitzel, repeated his thanks, and climbed the stairs. On the second floor, he found a cramped bathroom with a pedestal sink and a claw-foot bathtub. Next to the wall, a radiator pinged and hissed.

With a flick of his wrist, Wilhelm turned the hot-water knob for the bathtub faucet. Tested the water with his hand and found it ice cold. While he let the water run, he entered Meinhard's room. The door groaned open on hinges clearly not used to moving. As Wilhelm's host had said, dust coated the bedstead, mirror, and dresser, thick enough to lend a gray haze to every surface. Only one object sat on the dresser: a framed photograph of a smiling boy in a midshipman's uniform. Beside the midshipman stood a younger version of the old man downstairs, resplendent in the dress coat of a *kapitän zur see.*

Wilhelm felt he had intruded on a shrine, invaded some sacred place where he had no business. *What would the old captain say if he knew I was a deserter? Probably throw me out in a rage and call the Gestapo,* Wilhelm thought. *Or would he?* Young Meinhard's death now seemed so pointless, so unnecessary.

God willing, Wilhelm thought, *my absence will let my crew escape the pointless death that awaited them. They can't patrol without an executive officer; the* Kriegsmarine *would never send out a boat without a second in command. Perhaps the navy will split up the crew to fill absences on other boats—ones without insane suicide orders.*

The petty officers and seamen with their whole lives ahead of them might get to live those lives and not become ghosts that haunt rooms such as Meinhard's.

But am I fooling myself? Wilhelm wondered. *Will they not just name another exec and send my comrades on a one-way patrol? No way to know. At least I won't be complicit in the crime,* Wilhelm considered. *As a navy man, I have sacrificed my honor to save it.*

Wilhelm looked into the dusty mirror. Gave a bitter, bewhiskered smile, and thought: *Ah, yes, try explaining* that *at your court-martial.*

He opened the top dresser drawer. The odor of mothballs rolled into the air. The drawer contained two stacks of shirts, each one quite properly folded into a square as if ready for inspection. Just what a good midshipman would have done. Wilhelm selected the first shirt on the right stack, a long-sleeved flannel garment. Held it up against his chest. A little small for him; the sleeves were too short. No matter, he'd roll up the sleeves.

In the second drawer, Wilhelm found trousers. He unfolded a set of canvas britches and held them against his waist. Like the shirt, they were a little small, but they'd do. With the clothes draped over his arm, he considered whether to look for anything else. He didn't want to: Taking anything at all seemed a desecration. But he needed to blend in with civilians, and the old captain had said he could take what he wanted.

Wilhelm opened a closet. Four sets of uniforms hung from coat hangers, cleaned, pressed, and waiting for duty. Waiting eternally. Wilhelm also found two civilian suits and a leather civilian jacket. He took the jacket and retreated into the bathroom. Placed the clothes over a towel rack and once more tested the water flowing from the bathtub faucet.

The water flowed hot now; steam fogged the window. Wilhelm stoppered the tub and let it fill. Unbuckled his belt and placed the belt and holstered Luger on the floor. Untied his boots and pulled them off, stripped out of his filthy fatigues. He kept on his navy-issued watch, the dial marked *KM*. The watch had endured years of salt spray and storm; a few droplets of bathwater wouldn't hurt it.

Wilhelm closed his eyes as he lowered himself into the water. Just like at the end of any other patrol, a hot bath felt like a wild extravagance. The water stung the cut on his left arm and a dozen other scratches, but the pain passed. As he sat down in the tub, his sore ribs ached, and he shifted his weight until he found a comfortable position. He opened his eyes and examined his hand where the thumb had been dislocated; the thumb remained in place, and the bruise radiating from the joint had grown larger and uglier. Wilhelm leaned against the back of the tub, closed his eyes again, and fell asleep.

When he woke up, the water felt cool. A film of grime floated on the surface. Wilhelm glanced at his watch and saw that he'd slept for fifteen minutes, just enough to take the edge off his exhaustion. In the U-boat, he had gone days with little more rest than that. Wasting no more time, he took a cake of soap from the soap tray, scrubbed himself thoroughly, stood up and dried himself, and pulled the tub's drain stopper. The water drained away to leave a ring of the filth he'd washed off. Wilhelm turned on the cold tap, cupped his good hand to catch the water, rinsed away the ring, and turned the water off again.

The bathroom cabinet contained a straight razor, but no shaving cream. Wilhelm wiped a towel across the fogged mirror. The face that stared back at him looked at least a decade older than his twenty-five years. He filled the sink with hot water and substituted soapsuds for shaving cream. He razored his beard away carefully; the effort took several minutes, and despite his caution, he cut himself in a couple places. But the cuts stopped bleeding after he dried his face.

Wilhelm dressed, put on his boots, and donned the jacket. Took the Luger from its holster and placed it in his waistband. Hardly the most comfortable way to carry the weapon, but he figured it was safer to keep it concealed instead of wearing it openly with a holster in civilian clothing. He found his flashlight in his fatigues and placed it in a jacket pocket. Also from his fatigues, he pulled the brick fragment from his grandparents' house, and he placed it in a trouser pocket. Rolled his old, dirty clothes around the empty holster and tucked the bundle under his arm. Clomped down the stairs to say his good-byes.

"Captain," Wilhelm said as he offered his right hand, "I cannot thank you enough for your hospitality."

Brandt took Wilhelm's hand in both of his own. The shake hurt the bruised hand, and Wilhelm tried not to let his pain show.

"It is nothing," the old officer said. "Be careful."

The perfect way to end the conversation, Wilhelm thought. He liked "Be careful." Not "Give 'em hell," not *Heil* Hitler." Just "Be careful."

Wilhelm let himself out Brandt's front door and stepped into the street, wearing the clothes of a dead man.

11

Shell Shock

Karl hit the ground with his knees slightly bent, just like he'd been taught. That kept him from breaking his legs, but it didn't keep him from getting dumped on his ass like a sack of potatoes. He tumbled onto his side and bruised his hip. Scraped his elbow, too, hard enough to hurt through his flight jacket. His pistol holster dug into his armpit. The white silk canopy settled beside him. The wind had calmed, and Karl felt grateful for that. A gust might have reinflated the canopy and dragged him across the ground.

He rose up on one knee and looked around. A weed-strewn dirt parking lot surrounded him, but no cars were in the lot. A large building, perhaps some kind of factory or shipyard facility, lay in ruins just yards from Karl's landing site. Most of the walls had collapsed, but the back section of the building, near the river, remained intact. He saw nobody, but he knew that kind of luck wouldn't last. He'd parachuted into an urban area he'd just bombed. That meant lots of people who might find him, and they'd probably not like him very much when they did. He took in several heavy breaths, and his heart pounded so loudly he could hear it.

If I'd bailed out into the Black Forest, Karl thought, *I might have stood a chance. As it is, I'll probably wind up in a stalag before nightfall.*

Still, he had to try. First priority was to hide his chute and find cover. He clicked the releases on his parachute harness and shrugged out of the straps. Wrapped the risers and canopy over his arms until the parachute became a white mass of cloth that he held against his chest. Karl jogged toward what remained of the building by the river.

He knew time worked against him. Now that the raid had ended, people would start coming out at any moment. Karl had heard of downed fliers beaten to death by enraged mobs. Since he spoke German, he figured he stood a chance of blending in if he could evade capture long enough to get out of his uniform.

A door at the rear of the bombed-out factory stood ajar. Karl crouched by the door, the bundle of parachute still in his arms. Looked inside and listened. He heard nothing and saw no one. Just an abandoned desk, a floor strewn with bird droppings, and a bulletin board with a yellowing poster. The poster's foreground depicted a bare-chested factory worker wielding a hammer and a set of tongs. The background showed the shadowy image of a soldier in a German Army helmet, and the lettering read: DU BIST FRONT!

"You are the front," Karl thought. *Pretty standard propaganda for factory workers.* He stood up and began to slip through the door, but he stepped on a shroud line drooping from the bundle in his arms. He tripped and fell into the room. The impact startled a pair of pigeons on the sill of a broken window. The birds flushed from their roost.

Stupid, stupid, stupid, Karl thought as he scrambled to his feet. He dropped the parachute and kicked it behind the desk. Unfastened his throat microphone and threw it to the floor. Unzipped his flight jacket and withdrew his .45. Pulled back the hammer to cock the weapon and checked that the thumb safety was engaged. Stood as still as he could, held his breath, and listened.

Distant voices called out in excited tones; Karl could not make out the words. Neighbors coming out to check on one another, or perhaps some sort of official survey team.

Near the bulletin board with the propaganda poster, an open door led to a hallway. Karl moved toward the door, holding his pistol with both hands. Clicked off the safety. Pressed himself against the wall by the doorjamb and peeked down the hall.

Nothing illuminated the hallway except the gray daylight that spilled through windows and the few open doors. Industrial-type pendant lamps hung from the ceiling, wire guards protecting dead lightbulbs. The place looked like it had been bombed years ago and the Germans had judged it not worth repairing.

Karl crept into the hall, holding his Colt out in front of him. He didn't quite know what he sought except a better place to hide, and maybe some clothing. Dressed in a USAAF flight jacket and a gabardine A-4 flight suit, he might get shot on sight.

He came to the first room on his right. The door was closed. Karl listened intently, heard nothing behind the door. Only the shouts outside. They sounded closer now. He twisted the doorknob and pushed.

The room lay empty. A cracked translucent window admitted milky, filtered light into a chamber about half the size of a typical classroom. Maybe, in better times, this was the office of a low-level supervisor. Karl did not go inside the room; it contained nothing of use to him and offered no good place to hide.

He eased farther down the darkened hallway. The door to the next room, on his left, stood open. Metal lockers and tool cabinets lined the walls. Clipboards of yellowed paper cluttered a table. At the far end of the room, a glassless window opened into what had been a much larger room—probably an assembly line. Bombs had blown off the ceiling, and rubble covered the concrete floor.

This must have been the tool crib, Karl thought.

Workers would come to the window and check out tools. Somebody wrote down who had each tool and when the employee brought it back.

Very German.

Inside the tool crib, Karl looked around for anything he could use. A set of welder's coveralls hung on a coat hook behind the door. Not exactly the kind of civilian clothing he wanted, but he gave the coveralls a closer look. Stiff and dusty, they smelled of mildew. Spiderweb across the collar. Even filthier than his flight suit, which was damp with sweat.

Just as Karl figured he'd pass up the coveralls and look for something better, someone spoke from across the bombed-out factory floor.

"Was it here?" the voice asked in German.

"I don't know," another voice answered. "They said they saw a bomber go down."

Karl lifted the coveralls off the hook and hid under the table. Gripped the .45, readied himself to shoot.

Then he realized the weapon was useless. He might get the first guy. He might get the second. He might get all of them. But the sound of gunfire would bring more soldiers, police, SS, whatever. He'd never win. Karl placed the pistol on the floor. Surviving the next few days—or the next few minutes—would depend on his wits, not his weapons.

Now what? Put on the coveralls, fool, he told himself. *And make up a story pretty damn fast.*

Karl rolled over into a sitting position. Bumped his head on the underside of the table. Unlaced his boots. Stopped and listened.

Footsteps and murmurs came from outside. Men were poking around the building, but not in any ordered fashion that Karl could discern. Deep inside him, an animal instinct screamed to forget this quick-change nonsense and just run like hell. But he knew that would only lead to capture or worse.

His heart thumped as he peeled off his flight jacket. With trembling fingers, he unbuckled his shoulder holster and pulled it off. Stopped and listened again.

Silence.

Where have the men gone?

All right, Karl thought, *it's now or never.*

He unzipped his flight suit from neck to crotch. Freed his arms from the sleeves. His dog tags clanked, so he took their chain from around his neck and placed it on the floor by his Colt. Then he leaned back, raised his hips off the floor, grabbed the waist section of the flight suit, and slid it off of his legs. Now he wore only his boxer shorts, a T-shirt, and his green G.I. socks.

Footsteps echoed in the hallway behind him.

Oh, perfect, Karl thought. *What will people think if I get killed or captured like this?*

He unzipped the welder's coveralls. A startled spider crawled out of one sleeve. Karl shoved one leg into the garment, hoped another spider didn't bite him.

Do they have black widows in Germany?

"No one is in here," a voice said from just yards away.

"We better check, anyway," someone replied.

Karl yanked on the other pants leg and pushed his arms into the dirty, cold-soaked sleeves. Tried to pull up the zipper, but it wouldn't budge.

You gotta be kidding me, Karl thought. *I'm gonna die because of a rusty zipper.*

The footsteps sounded closer.

"My cousin used to work here," a voice said.

"What happened to him?"

"Drafted. Killed on the Russian front."

"Spooky in here now."

Karl jerked at the zipper once more, and the tab zipped only about halfway up his chest before it stuck again. Good enough. The pants pockets of the coveralls were deep enough to accommodate his pistol, so he jammed the .45 into the right pocket. Grabbed his dog tags and stuffed them into the left pocket.

Oh, hell, Karl thought. *Nearly forgot my ID.* Karl did not bring his wallet on combat missions, but he did carry his military identification card in a pocket folio. Fumbled into his flight suit and retrieved the ID. Stuck it in the pocket with the dog tags. Pulled on his left boot and tied it. Pulled on the right boot, and its heel scraped on the concrete floor.

"Hey," a voice called from somewhere close. Now just feet away. "I heard something."

Karl wrapped his flight suit around his jacket and holster. Rolled from under the table. Stood up and opened a steel tool cabinet, no longer caring what noise he made. Stuffed the bundle of clothing into the cabinet. Looked down and realized he'd never tied his right boot. Too late. Maybe even a good thing.

"Stop," someone shouted. "Identify yourself."

Karl turned to see a man in the doorway. An older guy, probably in his fifties. Gray temples, bulging stomach. He wore a military uniform, but not one Karl recognized from intel briefings.

Not SS, thank God. Not regular army, either.

Two men about the same age stood in the hall behind him. They wore the same type uniform. Their helmets bore a set of wings with lettering that read *Luftschutz.*

Oh, yeah, Karl thought. *Civil defense force.*

Mouth open, Karl looked at them as if he didn't understand.

"I said, identify yourself," Gray Temples said.

"Uh, Karl. My name is Karl," he said in German. The fewer lies he told, the less he'd need to remember. "What's your name?"

"I'm asking the questions here, you imbecile. What is your full name?"

"Karl Hagan. *Oberschütze* Karl Hagan." A private. Senior rifleman.

"What's a private doing here by himself?"

"Uh, well, I heard them bombs and got scared, so I ran in here." Karl thought hard, tried to remember the ungrammatical, lower-class German his father used when he got angry.

The men looked at one another. Gray Temples said, "No, idiot. I mean, why aren't you at the front?"

"Oh, I was. They gave me leave. Me and my friends got hit—I mean, there was this mortar shell. My mama lives over there." Karl pointed. "I worked here before I got drafted. Me and some guys had some comic books in here back then, but I can't find them no more. Did you see any comic books around here?"

"The Führer has banned such smut, you moron."

The *Luftschutz* men murmured among themselves. Karl heard Gray Temples say, "I think the boy's touched in the head."

"Shell-shocked," the second man whispered. "He doesn't even talk normal."

"Saw it many a time, back in the Great War," the third said.

Gray Temples turned to Karl and asked, "Did you see an airplane crash nearby? Any airmen coming down in parachutes?"

"Um, no, sir. I been hiding in here the whole time."

Gray Temples nodded and pursed his lips, as if he'd known all along he'd get no useful information from such a dunce. "The air raid is over," Gray Temples said. "Go on home."

"I will, sir," Karl said.

The men began moving down the hall, and Karl felt flush with relief. Sweat dampened his whole body.

Then he realized he'd left his escape kit in his flight suit.

Now that someone had seen him, he needed to get away from here as quickly as possible. The Three Stooges from the *Luftschutz* might find his parachute in that other room at any moment. But he might need the escape kit later.

He decided to risk it. He went back to the tool cabinet, opened it, and dug through his discarded clothing for the escape kit. Took the olive-colored pouch from his flight suit and closed the tool cabinet.

Looked up to see Gray Temples watching him.

Standing by the tool cabinet with the escape kit in his hand, Karl's mouth turned dry. His palms slickened.

"What are you doing?" Gray Temples asked. "I told you to go home."

Karl hesitated for just a moment, thinking. Then he held up the escape kit and smiled like an eight-year-old on Christmas morning.

"Found it," he said. "My old lunch bag. I knew I left some stuff in here. I'm going home now. My mama will wonder where I am."

Karl brushed past the *Luftschutz* man. Made sure his fingers covered the lettering on the pouch: KIT, SURVIVAL. E-17. USAAF. Strode down the hall as casually as he could fake it, fighting the urge to sprint. Behind him, he heard one of the men say, "God help us if we have many like him at the front."

That's right, Karl thought. *Just keep thinking that. I'm the biggest dumbass you ever saw. Not too bright to begin with, and then I got shell-shocked.*

He stepped past the room where he'd hidden his parachute. Took care to keep his eyes straight ahead. Emerged from the building and walked across the parking lot where he'd landed. Stuffed the escape kit into one of his pockets.

With no idea where he was going, except away from his landing site, Karl headed down a road that led through the industrial area, along the river. Bremen began to come back to life. Sirens screamed in the distance. Not air raid Klaxons, but fire trucks, Karl assumed.

A military truck with an open bed approached; the vehicle carried figures in uniform. When the truck rumbled past him, he saw it carried more *Luftschutz* men. Karl waved.

Keep doing that, Karl told himself. *You're hiding in plain sight. And remember—no more English. Don't even think in English. Don't even* breathe *in English. Thank God my father insisted on German at home,* Karl mused. *"It iss de language of* mein *heart,"* Dad used to say.

And the language that could keep my ass alive and free, Karl thought. *Maybe. If I'm very, very lucky.*

Karl began to shiver, despite the sweat all over his body. He guessed the temperature was about forty degrees. His flight jacket would have felt good now. He wondered where his crewmates had landed; the aircraft commander in him wanted to look for them. But that was impossible—*Hellstorm*'s dying turn on autopilot had put Karl out of the airplane miles from everyone else.

He hoped at least some of them had linked up and could travel together, and he prayed that if they got caught, they got caught by the military and not a mob. Rotting in a stalag would beat some of the alternatives. *Godspeed, boys,* Karl thought.

A plan began to form in Karl's mind, each word in German: *Find Uncle Rainer and Aunt Federica? Forget it. You don't have their addresses, and you'd get them into trouble. Big trouble. Try to head south and west. The Allied armies will come from those directions. Keep playing the dumbass on leave. Stop second-guessing about how you could have turned back; that's all done now. This situation's awful but it's what you got. Most important, don't hurry and do something foolish. Weeks or months could pass before you see another American. Take. Your. Time.*

At least you still get to live, Karl added. *You just saw a bunch of guys get blown up. And you owe it to Adrian to get home and tell his parents what a first-rate pilot and officer he was. Keep your eyes open, and—as far as possible—keep your mouth shut. Keep putting one foot in front of the other. You're a ground trooper now.*

12

Sailing Alone Around the World

With little plan except to avoid human contact as much as possible, Wilhelm set out on a journey of unknown destination. The absence of a goal felt strange; a sailor always had a course to steer, a port to reach. Lines on a chart indicating route and purpose. Not today.

He turned down an alley that led to a main artery through town. Paused to dump his old uniform and holster in a garbage bin. Wilhelm lacked a map, but if memory served, the adjoining road would take him out of this neighborhood, through another industrial area, and eventually out into the country south of town. People were beginning to come out of their houses. They opened their doors partway, peered up into the clouds, and stepped onto their stoops and walkways as if they expected the sky to fall at any moment. No one paid Wilhelm any attention.

The alley led Wilhelm toward an ash tree that had somehow survived repeated bombings. Just as he passed under the tree, a cool breeze swept through Bremen's streets and gave voice to the leaves overhead. They rustled and whispered and reminded Wilhelm that autumn was deepening. The air did not carry the crispness of fall, however. The breeze brought odors of smoke and fire, cordite and oil.

A vague unease gnawed at him. Wilhelm had plenty of reason for unease: the wrenching decision to end his career and leave his crew-mates, the mortal danger of life on the run as a deserter. But he was used to mortal danger, to the risk of a death as awful as anything the SS might do to him. No, something else rankled him. As he wandered down the sidewalk with his hands in his pockets like a vagabond, fingers around the brick fragment from his grandparents' house, his mind settled on the reason for his unease: solitude.

Wilhelm could not remember the last time he'd spent waking hours alone. On patrol, of course, he lived in close quarters with forty-nine other men. Even in port, they remained close by, playing cards, drinking, singing. He already missed the camaraderie. When not with navy men, Wilhelm usually had female companionship. Women seemed drawn to the derring-do of U-boat men, and Wilhelm considered fleeting wartime trysts one of the few side benefits of his profession.

The unaccustomed loneliness reminded him of a favorite book he'd read during his academy days: *Sailing Alone Around the World,* written by the American mariner Joshua Slocum. During the time Wilhelm read that book, he was learning the navy's way of doing things. The *Kriegsmarine* drilled teamwork into cadets until it seeped into their bone marrow. Without a highly trained crew working together with the precision of a Swiss watch, a submarine amounted to nothing but expensive plumbing. Alone we are nothing, the cadets learned. But in concert with our mates, we become a deadly weapon in service to the Fatherland. Slocum's true-life story stood in sharp contrast to this navy ethic.

The tale captivated Wilhelm. In 1895, Slocum sailed from the state of Massachusetts in an eleven-meter oyster sloop he'd rebuilt himself, the *Spray.* Captain Slocum braved gales, doldrums, pirates, and monster waves—and glided back into home port three years later. No one before had ever circumnavigated the globe alone. Slocum accomplished the feat as an old man in his fifties.

Wilhelm knew a lot of brave men, and he counted himself among them. And he'd worked among brave men long enough to know courage came in many varieties, much the way boats and ships came in many classes and types. He found Slocum's brand of courage particularly inspiring, given its blend of skill, self-reliance, and self-confidence. Setting out across the ocean in a U-boat took guts enough. But what if you had no radio to communicate with shore, no modern instrumentation, no specialists to fix what broke down? In the journey before him, Wilhelm knew he'd need to follow in Slocum's wake, to find the courage to keep faith in his own judgments.

Traffic began moving on Bremen's streets again, mainly trucks and Army vehicles. A Mercedes-Benz L3000 stopped several meters in front of Wilhelm. When troops began piling out of the back, Wilhelm recognized their uniforms. They were *Luftschutz* men, surveying the damage. Their *truppmeister*, a paunchy man in his forties, strutted about as if he thought he was an admiral instead of an air-raid warden. A leather belt stretched around the man's stomach and strained at the last notch.

The *truppmeister* barked to Wilhelm, "You there. Who are you? Do you live around here?"

Careful, Wilhelm told himself. *Resist the temptation to put this pompous tub of lard in his place. Try not to give your name. Or any name.*

"I am an *oberleutnant* of the *Kriegsmarine*, and I have just returned from patrol," Wilhelm said.

The *truppmeister* blanched. "Uh, very sorry, sir." The man saluted, and Wilhelm returned the salute. "May I trouble the *oberleutnant* to show his identification?"

"You may."

Taking his time, Wilhelm held the bundle of his old fatigues under one arm, withdrew his pigskin wallet, and found his navy card. He tried not to wince; he used his injured hand, and it still hurt. Let his middle finger cover most of his name as he held it before the *Luftschutz* man.

"Yes, sir, very good, sir," the *truppmeister* said. "I take it that you are on leave, since you are out of uniform."

"You take it correctly."

"Sir, we have reports that an American bomber went down not far from here. Did you happen to see the crash or any parachutes?"

"As a matter of fact, I did," Wilhelm said. No reason not to tell the truth. "I saw a Flying Fortress go down in flames. I did not see where it impacted, and I didn't see any parachutes."

Wilhelm returned the card to his wallet, placed the wallet back into a hip pocket. He tried not to show his relief—and he knew the next encounter with military authority might not go so well. Fooling these simpletons was one thing; they were trained to make reports and sweep up broken glass. Fooling the Gestapo was quite another. And the SS had units specifically assigned to hunt down deserters.

Wilhelm left the *Luftschutz* to its duties and continued his walk. He passed a shuttered butcher shop and an apothecary with shelves so bare it might as well have stayed shuttered, too. Inside, a pharmacist in a white coat dusted his bottles. The pharmacist glanced through the window at Wilhelm, returned his attention to his dusting, then looked up again.

Wilhelm understood the reason for the man's double take: One did not often see young, able-bodied men by themselves, either in civilian clothes or uniforms. Military men usually traveled in groups while on duty. Even on shore, officers were usually found in twos and threes. A captain and his exec on the way to refresher training, for example. And soldiers home on leave nearly always had parents, buddies, or sweethearts by their sides.

This would be a problem, Wilhelm realized, whether he kept on the civvies or changed back into his dirty, torn fatigues. Wearing his fatigues would not have remained an option for much longer, anyway. The farther he got from water, the more out of place he'd look in a navy utility uniform; that's why he'd wanted the civvies in the first place.

A matter of tactics, just like stalking a freighter. *Always consider tactics,* Wilhelm told himself. *Don't let your guard down for a minute.*

To Wilhelm, sometimes it seemed that war and everything about war—the politics behind it, even the running away from it—amounted to a deadly game. Your machine against mine, my wits against yours. Lethal chess. Conflict did have its addictive appeal; Wilhelm never felt so alive as during a surface attack at night, spume flying over the bridge, the Target Bearing Transmitter trained on a victim. He supposed men of much higher rank felt a similar thrill as they marked maps spread across tables in the Reich Chancellery. Wilhelm doubted those leaders would tackle peacetime responsibilities with the same relish. What if they had been marking sewer lines instead of battle lines? Damn their souls, did they even *want* peacetime duties?

As Wilhelm passed through several more blocks, the well-appointed town homes of Captain Brandt's neighborhood gave way to run-down apartments. The apartments looked like typical residences for factory and shipyard workers. By now, it was five in the afternoon, and women and older men shuffled in and out of the buildings. Shift change, perhaps.

About a hundred meters ahead of him, Wilhelm noticed a knot of people gathering under a tree. At first, he supposed they were waiting for a coach or some other transport to take them to work. But as he came closer, he saw that the twenty or so people did not peer down the street in anticipation of a ride. Instead, they looked up into the tree. Some pointed. They spoke in hushed tones. A blond-haired young woman placed her hands over her eyes for a moment, then ran down the street. She did not look at Wilhelm as she brushed past him. Her face appeared as ashen as that of a submariner long submerged.

Wilhelm came close enough to hear the people talking. "Serves him right," one man said.

"I bet he was a Communist," another muttered.

"Will they cut him down before—" The woman did not finish her sentence.

Under the field maple, its few remaining leaves still afire with autumn color, Wilhelm joined the spectators. A man, quite obviously dead, hung from an upper branch. A hemp noose encircled his neck, and his hands were tied behind his back. The corpse's head lolled to the side at an impossible angle. A thickened black tongue protruded from twisted lips, and the face was a shade of purple Wilhelm had never seen. The dead man wore the uniform of an *obergefreiter,* a regular army lance corporal.

Someone had tied a cardboard sign to the body: *I have been hanged here because I was too cowardly to defend the Reich. I did not believe in the Führer. I am a deserter.*

The blood in Wilhelm's veins ran as cold as the Baltic. He stared into the bulging dead eyes, and he wondered if he was looking into a mirror, gazing at his not-too-distant future.

"I saw the SS string him up," a woman said. "Watched the whole thing from my apartment window. He kicked and flailed for about five minutes."

Wilhelm looked at the woman. Middle thirties, dressed for a factory job. Her voice betrayed no revulsion. She spoke in a matter-of-fact tone, as if these things happened all the time. Maybe they did.

"Good," a man said. "He didn't deserve a bullet."

The man gave Wilhelm a hard look, as if he knew a deserter on sight. *No, he doesn't know,* Wilhelm told himself. *You're just getting paranoid. You must keep your head no matter what. If you can focus while depth charges explode around you, you can focus now. Enough real threats lurk—from every point on the compass. You don't need to imagine false ones.*

To blend in, Wilhelm decided he needed to say something. So he said, "This is the Reich's justice." A statement that was true enough.

"You're darn right it is," a bystander said. Same fellow who'd speculated that the hanged man was a Communist. Looked old enough to have served in the Great War. An emblem on his lapel consisted of a swastika encircled by a ring gear: the membership pin of the DAF, the German Labor Front. "Are you new in town, young man?" he asked. "I don't believe I've seen you before."

Steady as she goes, Wilhelm told himself. *Make just enough small talk to get out of here gracefully.*

"I am sort of new, sir," Wilhelm said. "I'm a U-boat officer. Just returned from patrol, and I hope to visit my parents." All true. Except he had no idea when, if ever, he would see his parents again.

A broad smile creased the older man's face. The grin revealed tobacco-stained teeth and gold fillings.

"Ah, one of our brave sea wolves," the man said. "I might have known. I see steel in your eyes. Tell me, son, have you sent many of Roosevelt's ships to the bottom?"

"A few, but my crewmates must get the credit."

"Yes, yes, of course, young man. You sea wolves work together as we all should. *Ein Volk, ein Reich, ein Führer.*"

Drunk on ideology, Wilhelm thought. *They're untroubled by the harsh realities in the seas, in the skies, and on the fronts. What sort of bloodlust could turn a hanging into an impromptu social event?*

While Wilhelm wasn't looking, while he'd thrown himself into his job, what had happened to his people?

Wilhelm decided he'd said enough right things to these jackals to avoid incriminating himself. Now he could move on and put this scene astern.

He took a final glance at the body of the deserter, then shouldered his way out of the crowd. As he continued down the street and out of the residential area, he wondered about that boy hanging from the field maple. Perhaps he had never been a good soldier. Or perhaps, like Wilhelm, he had fought long and hard until deciding there was no more point. What might he have done with his life after the war? A damnable waste.

Wilhelm recalled a passage from Captain Slocum's book. As the *Spray* negotiated the Strait of Magellan, at the southern tip of the Americas, Slocum searched for wildlife. He needed to gather food, and he did find mussels near the shore. But he saw few birds in that bleak stretch of water where gales threw sheets of mist against granite mountains. On one desolate hill, the captain noticed a beacon, and he supposed the man who put it there probably died of loneliness. *A bleak land,* Slocum wrote, *is not the place to enjoy solitude.*

13

A Sailor Home from the Sea

Despite the family connections, Karl had never visited Bremen. A steelworker's family could hardly afford trips to Europe. And Karl sure as hell never expected to see the city this way: a downed aviator in civilian camouflage, playing the role of an idiot.

At least he fit in, thanks to the welder's coveralls. Now that it was late in the day and apparently time for shift change, workers crowded the sidewalks. No one gave him a sideways glance, though a few called out, *"Guten abend."* Karl returned each greeting, but kept walking to avoid getting involved in conversation.

In a way, he felt kin to everyone he saw—and not just by German ancestry. Until they opened their mouths to speak, these folks could have passed for the people he'd grown up with, his dad's friends and coworkers. Same kind of clothing, same kind of jobs, same place in society.

Except for the bomb damage and the signs in German, even the streets looked like home. Karl had spent all of his life in Bethlehem, Pennsylvania. The factories and shipyards of Bremen looked a lot like the steel mills of Bethlehem, Allentown, or Pittsburgh.

As Karl continued his walk, he nodded to a gray-haired guy carrying a lunch box and a set of canvas gloves. If he knew, Karl thought, he'd probably smash in my head with that lunch box. Yet he looks like one of Dad's buddies back at the mill.

During Karl's childhood, he'd always enjoyed meeting his father's friends. Sometimes during the summer when school was out, his dad would take him to the steel mill. Of course, as a child he was never allowed near the blast furnace, but he could visit the machine shop, the break room, and the tool crib. One time, a supervisor even let him watch new ingots, glowing orange, get transferred into the rolling mill. The supervisor explained the big picture to young Karl: You melt iron, remove impurities, and alloy it with carbon to create a metal as hard as iron, but not nearly as brittle. It goes through the fire and comes out stronger.

Don't get careless, Karl ordered himself. *These German workers look like friends. In better times, they* would *be friends. But you just tried to blow up their workplaces. Some folks don't take kindly to that.*

"*Guten abend,*" Karl said to Guy With Lunch Box. Then he looked away to make sure he had to say no more.

Dusk began to envelop the town. Though the weather remained clear, Karl never noticed streaks of sunset. On clear days back in Pennsylvania, the dying sun painted the sky the color of a hot steel ingot. But here, smoke from air raids and factory stacks obscured all color.

As darkness approached, lights inside buildings winked on. At most windows, a hand immediately lowered a blackout curtain. *Whatever else the Eighth hit today,* Karl mused, *we didn't get the power stations. Not all of them, anyway.*

Very German, he figured, *to stay organized enough to keep electricity humming even under repeated air attack. No doubt their production minister—What was his name? Speer?—placed highest priority on the electrical grids in industrial towns. The farming villages are probably out of luck.*

Apart from a general intent to head southwest, Karl had no idea where he was going. His silk escape map covered all of central and western Europe; it offered no detail on Bremen or any other city. He had bailed out with his aeronautical charts still in his pockets, and he wished he'd thought to bring the AAF Target Chart with him. That one offered the greatest detail for his current location, but he'd left it in his discarded flight suit.

Lacking anything to guide him, Karl decided to find a place to hole up for the night. In the darkness, he came to an abandoned warehouse. No lights shone through the windows, and when he moved closer, he saw that some of its walls had collapsed. By now, he had left the crowds behind. He looked around to make sure no one was watching him, then made his way to the bomb-damaged building.

A wooden door hung open on one hinge. Karl ducked through the doorway. Once over the threshold, he groped blindly; this room had no windows, and its intact walls blocked what little light came from outside. He nearly tripped over debris on the floor, invisible in the blackness. He stood still and let his eyes adjust.

As his pupils opened, he perceived a hint of illumination—just a cottony vagueness—a few yards in front of him. The moment hinted of fever dreams, the mind's wild imaginings during deep sleep. Karl almost wondered if he *was* dreaming; this predicament surely rivaled his worst nightmares. But distant traffic noise, the honk of a tug on the river, and the odor of grease and oil vouched for reality. He lifted a foot and took one long, careful step toward the light. Nothing impeded him, so he took another step.

Eventually he found himself at another doorway, with his eyes fully accustomed to the night. The doorway led to an open warehouse floor almost as big as a football field. The far wall lay open, and the pale glow of a nearly full moon provided just enough light to see.

Chunks of machinery sat in rows, most of them covered by tarps. Karl speculated they must have been engines needing a rebuild. If they were new, they certainly wouldn't be sitting here abandoned. He pulled the tarp off one of them. The engine was a huge thing, long rows of cylinders. These were probably engines for ships or submarines.

Karl decided to spend the night in the warehouse. Seemed as safe as any place, though that wasn't saying much. He dragged the tarp to a corner, underneath a broken window, intending to use it as a blanket later. Pulled his escape kit and pistol from his pockets and sat down cross-legged. He hadn't eaten since breakfast at 0300, and he was hungry. Hated to use up the food in his escape kit on the first day, but he saw no other options.

Karl opened the escape kit and inventoried it as best he could in the dim light. The pouch contained two cellulose flasks that could double as canteens. Each flask had a clip-on lid. Karl opened the first flask and shook out its contents onto the tarp. He found packs of spearmint gum and Charms candies—which he'd never liked. The items also included bouillon powder, matches, a fishing kit, a button compass, razor blades, a hacksaw blade, and three condoms.

He chuckled at the sight of the condoms. *Guess they think I'll get on well with the natives,* he mused. But he knew the condoms were really for keeping matches and other items dry.

With no water to make broth, Karl couldn't use the bouillon powder now, so he settled for the Charms. Opened one of the hard candies and popped it into his mouth. The damned thing contained just enough food value to make him even hungrier. While he crunched on the Charms, he opened the other flask. It contained a small first-aid kit, tweezers, aspirin, some five-mark German bills, and a toothbrush. *If it were up to me,* Karl thought, *I'd have traded the candy for a little tube of toothpaste.* The second flask also included an item Karl had added on his own: a Camillus folding knife. Not as fierce-looking as the Bowie knives and Arkansas toothpicks favored by macho types. More like the knife a gentleman farmer might carry in his work pants. In Karl's estimation, far more practical.

He reassembled the escape kit, placed everything back into the flasks except the Charms. Resolved to get away from the city tomorrow and out into the country. There he might find a stream, and he could use the water to shave, clean up, and make the bouillon. The less he looked like an unshaven derelict, the better he'd blend in when he couldn't avoid people. He also hoped to find some kind of coat; he was already cold and the nights would only grow colder. But he had no idea how he might go about scavenging a coat or a jacket without getting caught. One crisis at a time, he told himself.

For now, he made do with wrapping the tarp around him. It smelled like an engine and was filthy, but it kept him warm. Karl placed his .45 on the floor near his right hand and leaned back against the wall. After just a few minutes, he fell into a deep sleep.

A great trembling of the earth shook him awake. Karl opened his eyes in a state of utter confusion; for a moment, he could not remember where he was. Realization hit him like a gut punch—yes, he'd actually gotten shot down. And the nightmare had just become worse. The ground shuddered; the building rattled. A tremendous roar sounded from a couple miles away. Not distinct explosions, more like a continuous, pulsing eruption. Air raid sirens shrieked.

The Lancasters, Karl thought. That's the RAF up there, heavy aircraft filled with bombs like insects full of eggs, impregnated with destruction.

Allied doctrine called for round-the-clock bombing of Germany, and the Brits took the night shift. Karl huddled in his corner, his senses overwhelmed by nonstop thunder. So this was what it was like to be on the receiving end of heavy bombardment. *No,* he reconsidered, *this is only a hint. The bombs aren't hitting on this side of the river.*

Even at a distance, the detonations sounded like the end of the Earth. The rolling booms grew louder. Flashes lit up the broken window above him, and the glass clattered with each shock wave. Were the bombs walking their way toward him?

Karl sweated under his tarp. Wondered if the next bomb would take him out of this world. Night bombing was imprecise; it amounted to area bombing. After all, this new kind of industrial war was a war on cities. Stop the enemy's factories, de-house his workers. In darkness, all of Bremen became a target.

An animal impulse in Karl's mind cried out for him to flee. But flee where? He could only curl up in a fetal position and wait for the Armageddon outside to stop. Until it did, each second could bring death. Karl had once heard a Londoner say he didn't worry about bombs, because they'd either hit you or not. If not, no problem. If one does hit me, the man said, I won't even know it. So why worry?

But this wasn't an either/or proposition. Karl could think of a thousand possibilities between escaping without a scratch and dying a quick death. Flying debris could maim you. Fire could trap you. Crumbling walls could bury you. Maybe that Londoner had downed a couple pints when he scoffed at aerial bombardment.

The noise pierced Karl's eardrums and flowed straight into his brain. *Is this what I wrought every time I flew?* Karl asked. From *Hell-*

storm's flight deck, the bombs were silent; they struck the ground with soundless blooms of smoke and fire. Now he realized just how appropriate a name had been given to that aircraft.

He did not regret his choices. This war was a fight between good and evil, simple as that. *Cousin Gerhard couldn't understand it,* Karl thought, *and that's why he chose the wrong side.*

But such bad things had to happen before the good could win. Hamlet was right: cruel to be kind.

Through the ringing in Karl's ears, he heard the boom of flak guns. He hadn't heard them before, and that's when he realized the bombing had ended. The gunners continued their barrage, perhaps hoping to pick off stragglers from the formations. After a time, the pounding of flak batteries stopped—replaced by sirens, shouts, and the rumble of trucks and ambulances.

He kept still and tried to get back to sleep, though he doubted he could sleep again tonight. Closed his eyes and listened to the sounds of Bremen attempting to recover from another attack. Seconds later— or was it an hour?—the sound of footsteps told him two things: Yes, through sheer exhaustion, he had fallen asleep again. And someone else was in the warehouse.

In the next room, boot heels ground against dirt and glass on the floor. The steps came slowly and deliberately. Karl wondered if someone had seen him come in here and reported him to authorities. He picked up his .45, clicked off the thumb safety, and held it with both hands.

The smoke and haze had cleared somewhat, and now the moon poured enough bourbon-colored light to throw shadows. A silhouette emerged at the warehouse entrance. Karl couldn't tell if the man was armed; the figure kept his hands at his sides. With his Colt aimed at the stranger, Karl waited and hoped the man wouldn't see him.

The figure turned slowly, scanning the warehouse.

Maybe Karl breathed too hard. Maybe moonlight glinted off his watch. Whatever the reason, the stranger ducked behind an engine block. Now Karl could see little but a pair of hands. Holding a pistol.

"*Wer bist du?*" Karl called.

"And who are you?" the stranger said.

"I asked you first."

"I am a naval officer. Off duty. My home was destroyed."

Karl said nothing. Wondered about the right thing to do.

"You're just looking for shelter?" Karl asked finally.

"Yes, yes. You too?"

"I used to work here in a factory," Karl said. "I'm a soldier on leave. My mama's house got bombed." Tried to keep his sentences simple and childlike.

"Then we have no reason to point weapons at one another."

"Okay, put yours down."

The figure rose from behind the engine block. Lowered the pistol, but did not put it down. Karl tilted his muzzle toward the floor, but kept his finger inside the Colt's trigger guard.

"Come on out," Karl said. Realized he'd used his command voice, and he chided himself. *Remember,* he thought, *you're a simpleton.*

The stranger stepped toward Karl, into a shaft of moonlight. Karl recognized the man's handgun by its distinctive shape. A Luger. The man eyed Karl's weaponry as well.

"This could end well or badly," the man said. "I mean you no harm."

Of course, you don't, Karl thought. *I'm a fellow German, for all you know. Why would the guy say that? Does he suspect?*

Neither man moved to put away his handgun.

"Are you from here?" the stranger asked.

"My mama lives here, like I said."

"That's not a Bremen accent."

Damn it, damn it, damn it, Karl thought. *I'm gonna have to shoot this guy.*

"That's not a German pistol, either," the stranger said. "As a matter of fact, that's a Colt Model 1911. Standard issue, I believe, in the United States Armed Forces."

"Yeah, my papa got it in the war. I mean the *other* war."

"And you just happen to be wandering around tonight with family heirlooms."

"Well, I—"

The stranger raised his Luger higher, but he did not point it at

Karl. "Let us drop this charade, Sergeant. Or Lieutenant, or whatever your rank is. You are an American airman. And a lucky one, to have made it this far. Your German is good, too, wherever you learned it."

"I learned it at home, just like you," Karl said.

The stranger regarded him over the Luger, holding the weapon out with straightened arms, a look on his face like a man working through some difficult puzzle.

"Do you know what you have done to my people, to our cities?" the man asked.

Now I'm under interrogation, Karl thought. He dropped the simpleton act, kept his finger on the trigger. "I got a pretty good idea. Especially after tonight."

"I should shoot you right now."

Karl remained still, his weapon held ready, but not aimed directly at the naval officer. He tightened his fists around the Colt, clamped the grip safety down hard. Set his finger against the trigger. Every part of the weapon—spring and sear, hammer and firing pin—gathered within a breath's pressure of unleashing a bullet.

Just a matter of who's half a second faster, Karl thought.

He examined his would-be executioner. Young guy, probably only a little older than Karl. But with the eyes of a man who'd witnessed too much. That was clear even in this dim light. Karl knew the look; he'd seen it before. On his friends and in the mirror.

"You seem to have lost your taste for killing," Karl said.

"I never had a taste for killing," the man said. Answered quickly, too. But a long moment passed before he added: "I just had a job to do."

"I know what you mean."

"Do you, now?" The stranger sounded like he wanted to argue. But he let his question hang in the air without any elaboration.

After several seconds passed, Karl said, "You said you *had* a job to do. Past tense. They discharged a naval officer at a time like this? And that's why you're in civilian clothes, hiking through an air raid by yourself?"

The man let his eyes wander as if considering how much to reveal. With the stranger off guard, Karl noted this would be a good time to fire. But he saw little profit in that right now.

"I am a sailor home from the sea," the man said. "For good."

Karl tilted his head back, raised his eyebrows.

"You mean you've just quit?" Karl asked. "Walked away from your base?"

Long silence. "Yes," the stranger said finally.

"Then you're in more trouble than I am," Karl said.

PART II

PART II.

14

Truce

Wilhelm had often brought the enemy into his sights, through the periscope, through the TBT. But never this closely, to look into the enemy's eyes, to hear his words, to see his face. Wilhelm wanted to pull the trigger; these bomber crews had rained destruction on his boat, his men, his home. Now came a chance to exact highly personal retribution. Vengeance would take nothing more than a slight tensing of his hand muscles. That would send a nine-millimeter slug exploding through this American's brain. A sense of power rushed through Wilhelm even more energizing than when he stalked an Allied convoy.

Yet he did not fire.

Over the Luger's sights, he observed the airman. In the low light, the American appeared oddly familiar: Young. Frightened. Resolute despite the fear. Wilhelm had seen that same look many times—the same widened eyes and set to the jaw—on the faces of his crewmates. Already he missed them so badly.

The American could have fired his Colt several times by now. Why hadn't he? Wilhelm's hesitation could have proved suicidal if the Yank hadn't hesitated, too. Perhaps a part of Wilhelm *wanted* to die. What had he done? What had his world come to, when he could talk to no one tonight but an enemy flier, a conversation over the muz-

zles of cocked pistols? He could trust no one. But he felt an instinc-
tive need to trust *someone,* if only for a few seconds. He decided to
take a chance.

"Safe your weapon, Yank," Wilhelm said in English, "and I will safe
mine."

Wilhelm lowered his Luger and engaged the safety. The American
lowered his Colt, and Wilhelm heard a soft click. The airman let out a
heavy sigh, like a submariner whose damaged boat has finally
stopped taking on water. Now he just looked tired. And alone.

"What is your name?" Wilhelm asked.

"Karl Hagan. First Lieutenant, United States Army Air Forces. You?"

"Wilhelm Albrecht. *Oberleutnant, Kriegsmarine.* U-boat service."

"Pleased to meet you, *Oberleutnant* Wilhelm Albrecht."

"Is that so?"

"Well, you didn't shoot me. That's a start."

"Where is the rest of your crew?"

The American hesitated before answering. The question put an
end to his flip manner.

"I . . . I don't know," he said. "They bailed out. Except my copilot.
He's dead."

"I am sorry."

"I just bet you are."

"No, I am," Wilhelm said. He placed the Luger back in his waistband and held up his hands to show they were empty. The American
nodded and put down his Colt. "We all know how this war will end,"
Wilhelm continued. "Any further deaths are an ungodly waste, but an
ungodly waste we will have."

Wilhelm took a step to get a better look at Lieutenant Hagan. The
American made no threatening move.

"What the hell," the Yank said. "Have a seat."

Wilhelm joined the flier in the corner of the warehouse. He sat
with his back to the wall, knees pulled close to his chest.

"You want some Charms?" the American said. "I hate these
things."

What in God's name is a charmz? *A strange lot, these Americans.*

When the Yank spoke again, he switched back to German, with
the diction of the working class. "So," he said, "you got tired of
shooting torpedoes at merchant ships and drowning civilians?"

A flash of anger burned in Wilhelm's chest. Who was a bomber pilot to judge him? He jabbed his finger in the air as he spoke.

"They were legitimate military targets—"

"Shh," the Yank said. "Keep your voice down. If you're a deserter, you don't want to get caught any more than I do."

Wilhelm wanted to punch this impudent flyboy. But the man was right about the need to keep quiet. No point arguing grand strategy with a peasant American, especially late at night with SS on the prowl. How did he speak such good German, anyway? Lower class, to be sure, but fluent.

"You said you learned German at home," Wilhelm whispered. "Now that we have stopped pretending, where did you learn it? Did you study here before the war?"

"I learned it at home, like I said. My father came from outside Koblenz. He moved to the States before I was born."

Interesting. This American was all but German himself. Wilhelm had first wanted to kill the Yank. Now another idea flowed through his mind like a tide race: Should the two of them stay together? The Reich's lines were collapsing by the day; Wilhelm knew that sooner or later, he might encounter Allied forces. U-boats had terrorized Allied shipping for years. What might Allied troops do to a U-boat officer?

But if I help this downed pilot, Wilhelm thought, *perhaps he'll help me. Maybe stop his compatriots from blowing my head off.*

"We seem to have reached an unlikely truce," Wilhelm said. "That hardly means we're comrades—let me make that clear. But if we traveled together, I could help you evade detection. And if we encountered your countrymen, perhaps you could help me get inside American lines."

"How do I know you won't try to save your ass by turning me in?" the American asked in English.

"If you had seen what I saw today," Wilhelm said, also in English, "you would know there is no turning back for me. I could not save myself by betraying you." Wilhelm described the hanged soldier and the sign left on the body.

"Damn, that's ruthless," the Yank said.

"So you see," Wilhelm said, "my own country considers me an enemy now."

"All right. I get your point."

Several minutes passed in silence. On the road outside, a vehicle rumbled by, but did not stop. Eventually the Yank said in German, "I guess you know your way around here?"

"Somewhat," Wilhelm answered. "My grandparents used to live in Bremen."

"I have relatives here, too, but I don't know exactly where they live."

Wilhelm stared at the American pilot.

"Wait," Wilhelm said. "You mean to tell me you dropped bombs on a city where you have family?"

For the first time, the American looked angry.

"I mean to tell you I dropped bombs on a submarine pen," he said. "And I mean to tell you it's none of your damned business."

Clearly, a sensitive subject for the Yank. The pilot folded his arms and stared straight ahead. He looked spent, wrung out. Understandable for a man who had just parachuted from a doomed airplane; Wilhelm had seen exhaustion among his crew many times. But the American's fatigue seemed of a higher order—a breaking point as much spiritual as physical.

One part of the Yank's misery required no speculation from Wilhelm, and that was loneliness. *We were both leaders of finely honed teams,* Wilhelm considered. *Social by nature, proud of our technical expertise and that of our men. And here we are, by choice and chance, bereft of our power, our machines, and our friends.*

After a few minutes, the American continued his thought. "I did what I had to do," he said. He sounded like a man trying to convince himself of something. "Look where it got me. Look where it got my crew."

This man is as alone and hopeless as me, Wilhelm thought. "We had our missions," Wilhelm offered. "We did the best we could. That part of our war is over now."

The Yank appeared to mull over this for a moment. Finally he said, "All right. If you want to travel together, we can do that."

"Very good. Perhaps we can keep one another alive. I know the region better than you, and your presence could help me if we meet American troops."

"You're going to need me a lot more if we run into your own troops, especially the SS."

Wilhelm frowned. "Why do you say that?"

"If an SS squad puts their rifles in our faces and starts asking questions, who would you rather be: a German deserter or a downed American flier? I'll tell them you're my navigator. It's probably safer for me that way, too."

Wilhelm raised his eyebrows. "Well, Lieutenant Hagan," he said, "you're not stupid. I will give you that. Yes, I'd rather spend a few months in a stalag *luft* than get strung up from a tree."

"Can you speak English well enough to pull it off?"

"Of course," Wilhelm said in English. "My English is fluent."

The American did not seem impressed.

"Your English is also British," the Yank said. "We'll have to work on your American accent."

"That is impossible."

The pilot chuckled. He took a tarp that he'd taken off one of the engines and pulled it over his shoulders. "Let me sleep half an hour," he said. "Wake me up whenever you're ready to move."

Why is he *giving the orders?* Wilhelm thought. *Ah, well. No matter. We have not killed each other. That is progress enough for one night.*

Wilhelm tried to rest, too. He drifted off to sleep, and he woke much later than he wanted. When he opened his eyes, he saw the first gray flush of dawn. He shook the Yank by the shoulder.

"Wake up, Lieutenant," Wilhelm said. "We slept too late. We need to get moving."

The American stirred, blinked, and looked at Wilhelm with wildness in his eyes. Clearly, in the moment of awakening, he did not remember their meeting. Overwhelmed by instinct, the man started to reach for his pistol. Then his expression changed, and his eyes showed recognition. He kept his hand off his weapon.

"That would have been a bad way to start the morning," Wilhelm said in English.

"Pronounce it *bin*," the Yank said. "Not *beeeen*."

"Ach. As if I don't have enough problems already."

The American slid the tarp off his body and rose to a kneeling position. In the morning light, Wilhelm could see him better now. Instead of a flying suit, he wore an old set of work coveralls; heaven only knew how he'd found those. Stubble darkened his chin, and his cheeks bore streaks of dirt or grease. He could have passed for a submariner back from a long patrol except for the tanned face and lack of a full beard. However, the skin around his eyes remained white—presumably the result of wearing aviator's glasses as the sun streamed through his windscreen. The effect made him look a bit like a *waschbär*, or raccoon, as English speakers called it.

"Excuse me," the Yank said. He walked to a far corner of the warehouse, unzipped his coveralls, and urinated. Wilhelm didn't like the idea of relieving himself in such an improper way, but circumstances did not allow for normal niceties. He found his own corner and emptied his bladder as well. The two men gathered their things and met in the front room of the warehouse.

Peering through a shattered window, Wilhelm observed the street outside. A transport truck rolled past, followed by two vehicles filled with *Luftschutz* men. Though the eastern sky had begun to lighten, enough darkness remained that the trucks burned their headlights, thin beams shaded through blackout lenses.

"How do you feel?" Wilhelm asked. "Are you ready to move?"

The American pilot hugged himself, ran his hands along his upper arms for warmth.

"A little cold and hungry," the pilot answered in English, "but ready as I'll ever be. That's an Americanism. Say it."

Wilhelm rolled his eyes and said, "Ready as I'll ever be."

The American shook his head and said, "Rome wasn't built in a day."

They stepped out of the building and began walking. A wire fence built with hook-shaped concrete posts lined the road. Ceramic insulators studded the posts; Wilhelm realized the fence was electrified. Or had been. Beyond it lay the remains of another bombed-out industrial building. Grass grew tall among the shattered masonry: The bombers had knocked out this place some time ago. Death might have come as a welcome relief, Wilhelm supposed, to the slave laborers confined behind that electric fence.

The position of the rising sun told Wilhelm the road led southwest. He wanted to get off the road and away from any major lines of travel, but he did not want to climb that fence. The wires were probably no longer hot, but he didn't intend to test that theory.

The sound of approaching traffic diverted Wilhelm's attention from the fence. He could not yet see the traffic; a curve in the road about half a kilometer ahead concealed it. It was too late to run for cover; to be seen running would amount to a confession. The American must have sensed Wilhelm's apprehension.

"Remember," the American said. "You're my navigator. We were in a B-17 Flying Fortress."

A flatbed truck appeared from around the curve. Slits of light shone through its blackout lenses. The vehicle swayed on worn springs as it struck a pothole.

Wilhelm and the Yank moved into the ditch to let the vehicle by. A cloud of dust rolled over them when the truck juddered past. The driver and passenger wore *Luftschutz* helmets, and they barely gave the two pedestrians a glance. A row of black bags lined the truck bed.

Bodies.

The submariner and the pilot exchanged a grim look, then stepped out of the ditch and back onto the roadway. Wilhelm appreciated the way the American had reminded him of his cover story. *So he's cool under pressure,* Wilhelm thought, *like a good U-boat man.*

"We need to get off this road," the Yank said in English.

"Right away." Wilhelm tried to place an ease into the vowels, less crispness into the consonants.

"Better," the Yank said.

The electric fence gave way to coils of concertina wire along the roadside. Tendrils of climbing nightshade intertwined with the concertina, and the poisonous red berries looked like drops of blood on the wire's razor edges. Behind the concertina lay an open field littered with barrels, concrete blocks, and a rusted-out car. At the far edge of the field, abandoned apartment buildings overlooked the River Weser. Between the broken buildings, Wilhelm caught glimpses of the river. Steam fog rose from the black water in wisps, and it made Wilhelm think of the spirits of dead submariners rising from ocean depths.

Without any suggestion from Wilhelm, the American stepped across the ditch and began picking his way through the razor wire. A blade snagged the leg of his coveralls, and he muttered a curse. With his thumb and forefinger, the pilot freed the fabric from the wire, then winced and shook his hand. A runnel of blood appeared on his thumb. He wiped the blood on his sleeve and placed the side of his thumb in his mouth. Spat another English curse, and stepped through the last coil and into the field.

Wilhelm followed close behind, receiving his own small wounds and rips in his pants. Somehow he got a long scratch on the back of his hand. Concertina wire really was the devil's own invention: It would slow down any escaping laborer long enough for guards to aim an easy shot. Assuming, of course, the would-be escapee didn't get fried by the electric fence first.

The two men waded through dry weeds toward the apartment block. They stumbled over chunks of brickwork and bent rebar, and Wilhelm guessed this open area had not really been a field. Another row of buildings had probably stood here. They'd been bombed out, apparently, and bulldozers had scraped away most of the rubble. To Wilhelm's left, broomstraw nearly concealed a set of concrete steps that led to nothing.

The weeds gave way to a crumbling strip of pavement and the remains of the apartments. At the first structure, spars of wooden shoring propped up a leaning brick wall. The other three walls had collapsed; Wilhelm wondered why anyone had bothered to keep one standing. The wall's two windows stood hollow, all the glass broken out. A row of four starlings perched on a sill. The birds scattered at the men's approach.

This vantage point afforded a better view of the river. No one stirred on its banks, but a tugboat wallowed upstream along the main channel. Black smoke rolled from its stack, and the tug's engine emitted a throaty grumble that sounded to Wilhelm like worn pistons.

Perhaps the tugboat's noise prevented Wilhelm from hearing another engine. Maybe his ears remained dulled from the explosion back at the submarine base. Or maybe he simply let his guard down. For whatever reason, the American took Wilhelm by surprise when he grabbed him by the shirt collar and yanked him behind the shored-up wall. For an instant, Wilhelm believed the Yank had suddenly thought better of traveling with a German, deserter or not, and decided to kill him.

The bomber pilot pushed Wilhelm to the ground, onto his stomach. Still not comprehending the Yank's purpose, Wilhelm rolled and started to reach for his Luger. But the Yank made no more threatening moves. Instead, he dropped and lay flat. Wilhelm now found himself confused and in pain; the jarring of sore ribs sent waves of fire through his chest.

"Shh," the Yank said. "Car coming."

The whine of an engine rose as a vehicle neared. Sounded like something smaller than the truck they'd just seen. Rather than speeding past, the vehicle slowed. The engine idled.

"They might have spotted us," the Yank said.

Slowly Wilhelm rose up on his knees until he could peek over a window opening. The movement caused another stitch in his chest.

On the road by the fence line sat an old Kfz.13 Adler armored car, with an MG34 machine gun mounted on a pintle. Three soldiers sat in the car. Two got out, while one manned the machine gun. One of the dismounted soldiers carried a Mauser, and the other carried a *Sturmgewehr* 44. The runes on their collar tabs indicated their branch of service.

The SS.

15

Hunted

Behind the blasted brick wall, Karl gripped his .45 and held his breath. He and the German deserter dared not take another look around the wall. To avoid being seen, they could only hide, listen, and wait—assuming the SS troops hadn't pinpointed them already.

Karl felt his pulse thumping. The slightest sound became amplified; the master control knobs for all of Karl's senses got turned up to the stops. The crunch of approaching boots grew louder with each step.

The footsteps stopped.

"*Wo?*" one of the soldiers asked. Where?

"I don't know. I thought I saw movement in the field."

Karl mouthed a silent curse. They must have seen something just as they rounded the curve. He tapped the U-boat man's shoulder. When the German looked at him, Karl pointed two fingers toward his own eyes, then pointed to the right side of the wall. He pointed to the German, then at the left side. Raised his pistol. *You cover the left; I'll cover the right.*

The German got the message. He set himself on one knee, Luger aimed to the left. Karl covered the right side and the windowsill above him.

The odds of surviving this engagement, if it came, tallied up even at best. With luck and straight shooting, Karl figured, he and the German might take down the two SS men who'd dismounted from the armored car. No, the odds came up far worse than even: It looked like at least one of the men had an automatic weapon. And what about the guy on the truck with the big machine gun? He could open up from the road.

Doesn't matter if he can't shoot through the wall. He can still keep us pinned down here, Karl realized. *Until more Krauts come. Which won't take long.*

A pair of boots clomped closer. The soldier took two steps, then stopped. Two more steps. Stopped.

The man was stalking. Hunting.

"Here?" a voice asked.

"Somewhere," came the answer.

"Probably a stray dog, Johann. You see an escaping Jew around every corner."

If Adrian had to die, Karl thought, *thank God he died in the air. What would he have gone through if these people had caught him? Yeah, come on around this corner, you goose-stepping son of a bitch.*

The SS troops outgunned him, but Karl knew his .45 fired a heavy slug. Just one in the torso would put a big man down. Karl hoped he could at least take one enemy with him.

We'll report to Saint Peter at the same time, he thought. *And part ways after that.*

The steps advanced even nearer. Stopped. The enemy soldier stood so near that Karl could hear his breathing. The man coughed. Spat. Took another step.

Karl raised his weapon higher. Tried to picture where the SS man's torso would first appear. Wondered if his parents would ever learn what happened to him.

"Come on, Johann," a voice called. "You will make us late."

"Verdammt," came the response, just feet from Karl's head. "Very well."

A scuffing sound followed, perhaps a boot heel scraped in frustration. When the footsteps began again, they moved away from the wall.

Yeah, Karl thought, *you don't want to be late, wherever the hell you're going. We Germans are ever punctual.* Relief flowed through his muscles like a narcotic.

Karl lowered his .45 and turned to look at the U-boat man. The sailor rested his Luger against his knee as if the weapon had suddenly grown too heavy to lift. He furrowed his brow and pressed his lips together in a puzzled look.

I know what you're thinking, Karl mused. *You almost got your first taste of land combat, and who had your back but an enemy officer? I was just thinking the same thing.*

A door slammed on the armored car, and the vehicle's engine revved. With one hand, Karl braced himself against the wall and prepared to look over the windowsill. His new German acquaintance held up a finger to wait.

Did the U-boat man suspect a trick? Maybe. These SS guys weren't Boy Scouts. They wore the *totenkopf,* the death's-head insignia, for a reason. Probably knew all kinds of ruses to play on scared people trying to hide.

Sure enough, the armored car's motor raced for several seconds—without going anywhere. Karl imagined all three occupants scanning the field and the apartment block, waiting for someone to break cover. After a minute or so, Karl heard someone put the armored car into gear and drive away. He eased himself upward, unbending his knees, and peered over the bottom right corner of the window opening.

The field lay empty; the SS men had gone.

"Cagey customers, aren't they?" Karl said in English.

The U-boat man looked puzzled for a moment. He seemed to ponder Karl's figure of speech just for a second, then toss it out of his mind.

"We have not seen the last of them," the sailor said in German. "Their job requires little expertise, but they have mastered what few skills they need."

The sailor's contempt for the SS dripped from every word. That surprised Karl a little, but he thought he understood. This *Kriegsmarine* officer carried the pride of a mariner, a professional. Much like an aviator. If he had deserted because of cowardice, he would have forgotten all about military professionalism. *So maybe this guy isn't a coward. So much the better.* Karl did not care to spend time with a man who took counsel of his fears.

"We better keep moving," Karl said.

"Ja."

The two men rose from behind the wall and walked through the shattered apartment buildings. Karl pocketed his Colt, and the German put away his Luger. Gaps among the buildings offered views of the river. Karl gleaned two bits of information from the water: He and the sailor were moving upstream, which meant roughly southeast. And the river carried little traffic. Karl had seen no vessels since that tugboat a while ago. So, for now at least, it was probably safer to walk along the river than anywhere near a road.

Though the German never said so, he seemed to think the same thing. He led the way down an embankment that sloped to the water's edge. Riprap placed for erosion control made walking difficult. Chunks of limestone and broken concrete rolled underneath Karl's boots. A black film, almost like charcoal dust, covered everything. Perhaps the result of industrial pollution, Karl supposed, or possibly ash from fires touched off by incendiary bombs. In places, rubble from a destroyed building had tumbled down the riverbank, and in those sections, it became hard to distinguish the riprap from bomb damage.

Karl could not tell whether the destruction along the water's edge had happened last night or months or even years ago. From the lack of activity, he began to judge the damage old.

Then he found a body among the weeds and concrete and stones.

A man lay facedown, ten yards from the water. The corpse showed no sign of decay; it had not even begun to smell. The clothing was dry, so the man had not floated down the Weser. Apparently, he had died where he fell, a victim of shrapnel or flying debris, perhaps. The man was gray-haired and heavyset.

The sailor gave Karl a sharp-edged glance. *Yeah, I know,* Karl thought. *A victim of the air raid, more than likely. A civilian casualty. Just like the civilian crews of freighters.* Karl decided not to have that argument again. Instead, he said only, "I hate to see that."

"As do I."

The dead man wore a brown woolen jacket. A gust rippled the river's surface and flowed cool on Karl's neck and face. The breeze reminded him how cool the night had been, and how the weather would only grow colder.

"And I hate to do this," Karl said.

He kneeled beside the body. With thumbs and forefingers, he pinched the fabric of the dead man's sleeve and trousers. Steeled himself for any vision of horror that might result from what he was about to do. Lifted, pulled, and turned the body over.

Karl expected to see ghastly wounds, mangled features, or worse—teeming maggots. He saw none of that. Just an old man's stubbled face with shallow, bloodless scratches. A senior shipyard worker, perhaps, or maybe an old pensioner. Probably alive and well only hours ago. Unseeing eyes stared up at the sun, pupils milky with death. Karl saw no injury to suggest a cause of death; it was as if the man had strolled along the river and dropped dead of a heart attack. Remotely possible, Karl supposed. But more likely some sort of blunt trauma had ended his life. Maybe a brick blasted into the air had struck his head. During wartime, death had so many ways of coming out of nowhere. Karl knew of a fighter pilot who got killed sitting on the ground at home base. Poor guy flipped a switch for a fuel boost pump and an electrical short ignited a full tank of gas.

Whatever the old man's cause of death, this riverbank littered with rubble seemed a forlorn place to end one's earthly existence.

A zipper, zipped halfway, secured the jacket across the man's belly. As soon as Karl touched the zipper tab, the jacket's tightness pulled the zipper all the way down. The corpse's stomach bulged as the jacket opened, and the sight put Karl in mind of gutting a big fish. He looked up at the U-boat man, expecting words of reproach, but the sailor said nothing.

Karl lifted the man's arm and took hold of the jacket sleeve. Tried to pull the dead arm out of the sleeve, but the arm slid only a couple inches. With much tugging and yanking, Karl learned it was a lot harder to take clothing off a dead man than you'd think. While he worked, a dead shad floated by near the river's edge, a shard of silver bobbing belly up in the dark water. By the time Karl freed the jacket, he'd jerked the corpse around enough that a box of matches and a green cigarette pack fell from the dead man's shirt pocket. The label read *Eckstein No. 5 Cigaretten;* Karl took the matches, but left the smokes. Not that he didn't want them; he could have used a cigarette right now. But he decided he should take only things he needed to survive, even from the dead. Especially from the dead.

He shook out the jacket to remove some of the dirt and bits of dried vegetation. Put it on and zipped it up. Too big, but it would do.

"I thought you might yell at me for robbing the dead," Karl said.

The U-boat man shook his head. "You need a coat," he said, "and yesterday I did something very like what you just did."

Karl wondered what that meant, but didn't ask. He pulled his Colt from a pocket of his coveralls and rechecked it: hammer cocked, thumb safety engaged. Ready for quick use. He tried to put the weapon in a jacket pocket, but the large-frame pistol was too big for that. Karl returned the .45 to his coverall pocket. Looked down at the corpse one last time.

"Thank you for the coat," Karl whispered in German. "I'm real sorry."

He thought of his German relatives nearby. Any of them could have wound up like the man at his feet. He recalled getting to know Uncle Rainer and his wife, Aunt Federica, when they visited the States while he was still in high school. Federica was known for her apple strudel—which Karl could still taste. Apples, cinnamon, vanilla ice cream. And Rainer had been so delighted when he learned Karl liked to hunt and fish. Rainer promised to send him a drilling, the combination rifle and shotgun favored by German outdoorsmen. The perfect solution, Rainer said, for the grouse hunter who happens across a stag. Just flip the selector and shoot the stag with the rifle barrel. To Karl's American sensibilities, joining a fowling piece with a high-powered rifle seemed a strange hybrid. In the end, it didn't matter. Because of money problems, the drilling became too dear a gift for his uncle to afford. Eventually Rainer lost his job—and Karl's dad had heard nothing from him since. Karl recalled Adrian's speculation: Had Rainer spoken out against slave labor or some other Nazi abuses? Entirely possible.

Uncle Rainer, so eager to share his love of the outdoors, was about the age of the dead man whose jacket Karl now wore.

"Let's move on," the U-boat man said. "We should get out of the city as soon as we can."

The aviator and the submariner climbed to the top of the river-bank. Amid the riprap and other debris, each step forced them to feel for balance and foothold. Karl realized he couldn't afford to get hurt. If he fell and broke his arm, seeking a doctor to set the bone would amount to surrender and imprisonment. For a flier downed in enemy territory, high stakes accompanied even the smallest choices: Do I put my heel on that broken brick over here or that stub of rebar over there? And for the German, Karl realized, the stakes ran even higher. For a deserter, capture meant death. To remain alive, the U-boat man would need to remain free until Germany's inevitable defeat played itself out.

They continued southeast, staying close to the water. A diesel engine snarled somewhere up ahead, deep-throated and loud. Something on the surface, not in the air. Karl placed the sound when a tugboat rounded a bend in the river.

The tugboat dragged a barge loaded with scrap metal. Swells from its bow rippled the Weser's flat calm. Karl guessed the scrap would wind up in some furnace downstream, melted down and turned into new tanks or rifle barrels. In wartime, no steel went to waste.

The submariner motioned for Karl to follow, and he pointed to a street that paralleled this section of the river. Karl took his meaning: *Let's get farther from the water so that tug crew doesn't spot us.* The boat probably had a radio, and the captain could report suspicious characters skulking along the waterfront. Karl and the U-boat man could not remain invisible; it was impossible to travel through a city without being seen. But better to be seen by random civilians than by someone with quick and easy communication to the police or shore patrol.

The two fugitives stepped over a low concrete wall that lined the street. They walked as casually as they could, and they came to an avenue that ran directly away from the Weser, through another residential area. A left turn placed the men among brick town houses, some intact, some destroyed by fire or bombs. An oak had grown from a hole in the sidewalk, but now the tree stood charred and dead. The bark had turned to charcoal, mostly black, but in some places burned to gray ash. The block of townhomes beside the tree had burned away as well, leaving blackened brickwork.

Off the riverbank and less conspicuous, Karl and the German turned and watched the tug and barge float by. As the barge passed, Karl got a better look at the cargo of scrap metal.

The barge carried the carcasses of crashed airplanes. Maybe the casualties of last night and yesterday, given German efficiency. The wreckage offered mute testimony to the aerial combat over this spot: hammering flak, spitting guns, tumbling bombs, and machines and men raining to earth.

The scrap included a Messerschmitt's wing, a Lancaster's empennage, and a Focke-Wulf's fuselage and canopy. Flames and explosions had scorched away most of the paint, but one wingtip bore the German *Balkenkreuz*. Another displayed the red-white-and-blue roundel of the RAF. Karl saw no American markings, but he did recognize the cowling of a Wright engine, possibly one of *Hellstorm*'s. Or perhaps not. From his parachute, Karl had seen his plane hit the ground and blow up. There were probably no pieces of it left as big as an intact engine.

Karl considered the journey of the American metal on that barge: from a mill at Bethlehem or Sparrow's Point to the Boeing plant to an air base in East Anglia. Then to a battlefield in the sky. Now down to this floating mass grave where the remains of Axis and Allied machines comingled. Back to the furnace for reincarnation as another weapon. Karl turned his back on the scrap barge and followed the German down the avenue, looking ahead for the next sign of trouble.

Karl realized he was scanning around him, much the way he'd done in the cockpit—looking as far ahead as possible, hoping to see the fighters early enough to alert the gunners and take evasive action. Old habits died hard, and maybe that was a good thing.

He saw no people, but he noticed an odd sight. Piles of dirt, or maybe coal dust or slag, littered the pavement. Three or four feet across, maybe a foot high. They came in no regular pattern, and one appeared every few hundred yards. When Karl came to the next one, he gave it an experimental shove with his boot. The substance turned out to be blackened sand.

"Leave that alone," the U-boat man said.

"What is it?"

"They use sand to smother incendiary bombs."

Remnants of last night's visit by the Lancasters, Karl realized. He could still feel the heat through the sole of his boot.

16

Amber Waves

By now, Wilhelm believed, the navy had probably reported him as a deserter. Under other circumstances, they might have waited longer to reach that conclusion: An officer with a stellar record suddenly goes missing after an air raid? Perhaps he'd taken a blow to the head and now wandered dazed and lost. Perhaps an explosion had thrown his body into the river.

But an officer goes missing shortly after receiving an order for a suicide mission? A different story entirely. Traversing the firebombed neighborhood, Wilhelm stepped around a still-smoking pile of sand, and he warned the Yank that the danger had likely just increased.

"Remember how those SS men in the armored car worried about being late?" Wilhelm asked.

"Yeah."

"They were heading in the direction of the naval base. Maybe for a briefing about a missing *oberleutnant*."

"You think so?"

"Very likely."

The American looked into the distance as if in deep thought. *Perhaps reconsidering whether it's a good idea to travel with me*, Wilhelm thought.

But if the aviator entertained misgivings, he did not voice them. He said only, "Then we better make tracks."

Another Americanism, Wilhelm supposed. *Why couldn't these Yanks make do with standard English?*

Traffic began to move through the streets. A bus trundled past Wilhelm and the American. It steered around the sand piles, weaving along cracked pavement until it stopped at a corner two blocks ahead. The bus's door opened and five civilian workers boarded. The door closed, the brakes hissed, and the vehicle swayed around another sand pile as it continued on its way.

Hunger gnawed at Wilhelm's gut. He imagined the Yank pilot was hungry, too, though the American had not said so. Wilhelm had a few marks in his wallet, so paying for food was not the problem. The problem stemmed from the very act of visiting a butcher or baker. Interaction with anyone posed a risk. Would civilian shopkeepers be alerted to watch for deserters? Even without an official alert, would some ardent National Socialist automatically suspect any young man not in uniform? The sailor-on-leave story probably had a short shelf life.

Perhaps I did not think this through, Wilhelm considered. *Maybe I've traded one suicide mission for another.*

Still, they had to eat.

"I'd like to find a butcher or a grocer to get some food," Wilhelm said, "but not so near the waterfront and the naval base."

"That's probably a good idea. You got money?"

"Some."

"I have a few marks, too. I can spot you some cash if need be."

"Spot" me some cash? That made no sense in English *or* German. "What are you doing with German money?" Wilhelm asked.

"They give it to us in case we wind up going on a hike with a U-boat officer who's called it quits."

"Called it quits"? Verdammt, *this American slang is annoying.*

"I have enough money for one meal for both of us, at least," Wilhelm said.

"Thanks. Then I'll pay for cocktails at dinner tonight."

Wilhelm sighed. "Is that supposed to be funny?"

"I'm a regular Bob Hope."

"Who in God's name is Bob Hope?"

"You don't know Bob Hope? How about Jimmy Stewart? They're actors. You know, Jimmy Stewart's a bomber pilot, too."

Actors? Bomber pilot actors? What is this nonsense?

"We do not watch many motion pictures in the submarine service."

"How about Marlene Dietrich? Bet you've heard of her."

"A very brave woman."

"Yeah, the two of you ought to get together after the war. I bet you'd have a lot in common."

Yes, I'll just call her the next time I'm in Hollywood, Wilhelm thought. *The famous German actress who denounced the Nazis will cancel her dates with celebrities and rush right out to see me. How are these Yanks winning the war if they are so foolish?*

Wilhelm's hunger was making him irritable. Even the basic necessities would present challenges from now on. Though Wilhelm had faced mortal danger on a daily basis aboard his submarine, he'd nearly always had enough to eat. Sometimes the food was awful, especially near the end of a patrol. But only rarely did sailors face short rations.

Captain Slocum had written of subsisting on potatoes, salt cod, and biscuits during his sail around the world. Even that rough fare sounded good to Wilhelm right now. He decided he would get away from this section of Bremen, then maybe take a chance on entering a shop farther along.

A staff car appeared ahead, coming straight on. Wilhelm and the Yank stood in plain sight for the car's occupants; it was too late to hide. Wilhelm felt his palms grow damp—and the car whooshed past. An admiral sat on the backseat; Wilhelm caught a glimpse of the thick gold braid on the man's sleeves. The admiral never looked up from his papers, and the car never slowed.

A close call averted by luck or providence, Wilhelm speculated—or perhaps something else? Maybe two men walking together looked less suspicious than one, especially if an alert had gone out for a single deserter.

At the next intersection, the pair came to a cobblestoned side street. Wilhelm pointed silently, suggesting they go down the cobblestone—only because he saw no traffic on the street. No bombs had fallen here; no craters or firestains marred the stones smoothed by hundreds of years of hooves and feet. Wilhelm took a vague comfort from the street's permanence, but the uneven surface made for uncomfortable walking. Cobblestones apparently worked better with horseshoes than navy boots. Still, Wilhelm appreciated the quiet of this street. The American had stopped yammering, so for a few moments, the quiet became complete. No sound but the faint buzz in Wilhelm's ears left by the blast at the U-boat bunker.

A large redbrick building appeared on the right. It, too, appeared undamaged, but sat vacant. No vehicles drove up to it; no pedestrians entered its doors. At first, Wilhelm guessed it to be a big office building, but as he got closer, he realized it was a school. A set of concrete steps led to a pair of double doors, and above the double doors, a marble stone inlaid in the edifice read GYMNASIUM WESER. Boards covered classroom windows, behind which students had gone about their lessons in mathematics, history, Latin, and Greek. And in more recent years, racial studies. The building reminded Wilhelm of his own schooling: happier days, when the world seemed full of promise.

"An empty school?" the Yank asked.

"Yes. I suppose the children have been moved out from under your bombers, since you consider this city such a target."

The American pilot folded his arms and nodded. "Probably," he said after a few seconds. "The Brits have moved their kids out into the countryside, too. For the same reason."

Ten years ago, Wilhelm had sat in classrooms very much like the ones inside this abandoned school. He recalled how his classmates and teachers buzzed about the death of President Hindenburg, and how they wondered what it meant for the country now that Hitler had declared himself both chancellor and head of state. A new day was coming for a new Germany, Wilhelm and his friends had believed. Those excited conversations seemed so recent; Wilhelm could remember some of them word for word. And at the same time, that part of his life seemed so long ago. So distant, in fact, that it might have happened to someone else.

Intense discussion had taken place at his family's dinner table in those days. Though Wilhelm never gave much thought to religion, his parents did—especially his mother. Some members of their congregation had joined the *Deutsche Christen,* which sought to bring the pulpit into line with National Socialism. His parents thought it made no sense to meld a centuries-old faith with a brand-new political order, and they were thrilled when a delegate from their church signed the Barmen Declaration. The declaration rejected what it called false doctrines—such as the notion that National Socialism had anything to do with Jesus Christ.

Later, that delegate, Herr Kraus, was forced to leave Germany. Wilhelm's parents escaped notice because they'd kept their opinions confined to the dinner table. But now Wilhelm wondered what might have happened if more Germans had spoken out like Herr Kraus. Would bombs not be falling on Germany around the clock?

No way to know. When swept up in an ideology, people's passions ran high and overrode common sense. Perhaps no amount of dissent could have stopped the Reich from racing toward calamity.

The reassurance Wilhelm had drawn from the cobblestones left him now.

"Let's go," Wilhelm said. "The empty school makes me sad."

"Me too."

The pilot appeared genuinely concerned about the impact of his bombs. But Wilhelm felt he'd gained no ground in whatever moral skirmish was happening between them. Nagging questions kept coming up in his mind: Did we bring those bombs on ourselves? And what about the impact of my torpedoes? Sometimes fuel would spill from a stricken freighter's bunkers, spreading a sheen of diesel across the swells. Lighter than water, the sheen would remain intact and afloat. When it ignited, the waves themselves would burn.

On one of those occasions, Wilhelm watched from the *U-351*'s bridge as an American merchant seaman—a civilian—abandoned a sinking ship. With no choice but to leap into a flaming ocean, the man stood by the rail. Wilhelm could imagine what the sailor was thinking: Take a deep breath, swim underwater for as long as possible, come up for air beyond the fuel's spread.

The sailor gulped air, held his breath, and jumped. He dived like an Olympian, arms over his head, hands together, his form so proper he hardly made a splash. Had he been an athlete? A competitive swimmer or high diver?

He vanished beneath the fire. Wilhelm wished him success and imagined him underwater, taking long strokes, propelling himself to safety. But when the sailor's lungs burned for air, the water above him burned, too. He had not swum far enough. He surfaced amid the fire and inhaled flame instead of air. Thrashed on top of the water for a few moments and sank forever.

That image numbered among many that haunted Wilhelm. It came to his mind unbidden, whenever it wanted, as if the seaman's ghost had gotten into his head.

Another two hours of walking brought Wilhelm and the American flier out of Bremen's southern suburbs and into the country. They followed the route of one of the new autobahns, but the fugitives kept several hundred meters from the road. At a distance, Wilhelm reasoned, motorists could not tell young men from old and might take the two for farmers, ever loyal to the Reich, working the fields to feed the soldiers.

The ploy seemed to work. Staff cars, armored cars, and military trucks rattled along the highway, and no one slowed down to look. Wilhelm and the aviator waded into a barley field. Nearly ready for harvest, the stalks had turned golden brown, with just a few green streaks remaining in the seed heads. Though Wilhelm was no farmer, it seemed exceptionally late in the year for barley to remain in the fields. Perhaps exigencies of war had delayed spring planting. The stalks bent with a light breeze and moved in unison, creating terrestrial swells.

"Amber waves," the Yank said. He uttered the phrase in English—and as if it was supposed to mean something. Wilhelm had no idea what he was talking about and did not ask. Waves that color reminded him of waves on fire.

The barley field stretched for about two hectares and ended at a wooded area. The forested space wasn't deep—only about fifty meters—and it consisted mainly of mature poplars. They grew in neat rows, maybe planted by the current landowner's grandfather or great-grandfather. Their boughs threw dappled shade onto the forest floor. Wilhelm stepped among the trees, leaned on a trunk, and closed his eyes.

In this place of quiet and concealment, he felt the nearest thing to peace and safety he'd experienced in years. A bird called from somewhere in the limbs overhead. Tranquility flooded into him like fresh air filling a surfaced U-boat through a newly opened hatch.

Here, Wilhelm sensed, no harm would come to him. If he could freeze this moment and stay within these magical woods, he could live out the rest of his days untroubled. Yet he knew he had to move beyond the trees, back into the world and all its dangers. The same illusion of safety had torn at his heart in the days when the *U-351* docked in Lorient. Back then, he often sat at a table in a fine restaurant with a French beauty across from him. Clinking glasses, glinting silverware. The life of a king. All the while knowing he would soon cast off lines to begin a new patrol—and an Allied depth charge might get him before he ever left the Bay of Biscay.

The downed American must have guessed the train of Wilhelm's thoughts. The pilot, despite all his silly talk earlier, had the grace to allow a few minutes of silence.

In the field on the other side of the trees, a tractor labored across the soil. It dragged a plow, turning under whatever crop had grown there. The crop wasn't barley; these plants grew in furrowed rows. Wilhelm, reared in the city, at first did not recognize the plants. The tractor drew nearer, dust rising from the plowshares, a broad-brimmed hat on the farmer's head. Wilhelm and the Yank stayed hidden within the trees. When the tractor reached the end of the row near the forest, Wilhelm saw that the farmer was using the plow to dig up late-harvest potatoes.

At the end of the row the farmer pulled a lever to raise his plow. He turned into the next row, pushed the lever, and the plow bit into the dirt once more. Potatoes began cascading off the plowshare.

"We can use some of those," the Yank said.

"I was just thinking the same thing," Wilhelm replied. "Let him get a little farther out. Then we'll grab a few potatoes and be on our way."

When the tractor got halfway across the field, with the farmer's back to the fugitives, both men slipped out of the trees. Wilhelm picked up only two potatoes. He would have liked more, but he did not want suspicious bulges in his pockets if he encountered anyone. He dusted off the potatoes and placed one in each of his front trouser pockets. The Yank gathered three and managed to make them disappear in his workman's coveralls.

The men eased back into the poplars and traveled to the edge of the autobahn. A line of *Wehrmacht* trucks rumbled by, canvas tarps draped over their cargo. No other traffic followed, so Wilhelm and the Yank stole across the pavement and climbed over a wooden fence into a pasture. Black-and-white Holstein cattle grazed on a hillside that pitched down and away from the road. Wilhelm led the way downhill, drawing stares from the livestock and taking advantage of the slope to avoid being seen from the road.

From this vantage point, Wilhelm spotted a village in the valley at the far end of the paddock and fields. Smoke rose from chimneys set among slate roofs. A forested hillside rose on the other side of the town. Though his hunger had grown from a vague ache to an acute pang, he did not relish the prospect of raw potatoes. He judged it reasonable to take a chance on finding a shop to buy something more appetizing. The burghers in the little town probably would have no knowledge of a navy deserter on the loose from Bremen—at least not yet.

"Shall we see if someone will sell us some wurst?" Wilhelm asked.

"Lead the way, if you think it's safe."

"Nothing is safe."

As if to underscore Wilhelm's point, a low hum began sounding in his ears. Not the buzz of deadened hearing, but something more distinct. At first, he supposed it to be farm equipment—another tractor somewhere, or perhaps a well pump. But the buzz deepened to a grind that came from no discernible direction. The noise seemed to emanate from the ground itself. The grind rose in volume and spread from horizon to horizon. Wilhelm looked across the hills and fields, tried to determine the source of this unearthly sound.

The American aviator pointed into the sky. For a moment, Wilhelm could make no sense of the white grooves cutting through the deep blue. He had seen condensation trails of high-flying airplanes before, usually one at a time. But now there were dozens of them. Maybe hundreds. He could make out black dots, barely visible, at the advancing heads of the vapor lines.

Liberators and Flying Fortresses. Innumerable, inexorable, and en route to a target.

17

Heil Hitler

The cows began to run. They fled in all directions. Some ran into one another.

Karl understood why. Their primitive minds could not comprehend the sound of hundreds of engines, the scores of spreading contrails. The creatures knew only to run from danger, and the danger seemed everywhere.

Though Karl had flown in such formations many times, he felt a touch of animal fear himself. He knew the bombers wouldn't unload here; perhaps they were headed all the way to Berlin. Still, he couldn't help but stand in awe. Not until this part of the twentieth century could anyone have witnessed a sight like this. It appeared some force from another planet had invaded to rip the earth and sky apart.

At the same time, the scene tantalized him. So close and yet so far. Right up there, right *there,* was his world, his element. A seat and a set of controls more familiar than his car. Well-rehearsed procedures and a Stanley flask filled with coffee. Friends and colleagues all around him. Surely, he knew some of the men who now flew miles above. He wished he could reach up into the blue and let them pull him aboard.

The airplanes passed directly overhead. The cattle ran around until they exhausted themselves and stood lowing, steam rising from their tongues. As the formation droned eastward and out of sight, the noise faded and, one by one, the Holsteins resumed grazing. The bombers' passage left lines chalked across the sky. The contrails began to widen and dissipate. Isolation closed in on Karl like a vise.

He followed the U-boat man down the hill toward the village. Every few yards, they had to step around cow manure, but they managed to keep their boots unsoiled. To keep his sudden loneliness at bay, Karl thought of food. Something to go with the potatoes in his pocket.

"Do you think they'll have a grocery down there?" Karl asked.

"I'm hoping for a baker or a butcher shop. They certainly have plenty of cows here for beef."

"These are milk cows."

"So you are a farmer, too?"

"No, my dad is a steel worker. But we have lots of farms in Pennsylvania."

In fact, the terrain looked a lot like rural Pennsylvania. But the farmers here had a slightly different lifestyle. Back home, a farm family lived in the midst of its fields and pastures. Driving through dairy country, you'd see a house surrounded by a cluster of barns, stables, and silos. Then a couple miles down the road, you'd see another house and barn lot. Here, at least in this area, the farmers lived in the village and went out to their fields each day.

Karl supposed they lived together because back in olden times, it was too dangerous to reside out in the country all alone. He'd heard plenty of German fairy tales from his parents, and many of those tales described a dark world filled with monsters, murderers, and robbers. There were witches and goblins; awful things happened to children. The tales probably reflected the lives and fears of real-world medieval Germany.

The monsters on the loose in Germany now wore armbands, and they did far worse things than anything imagined in the Middle Ages. *I tried to help slay the monsters,* Karl thought, *and I got swatted from the sky. So here I am—thousands of miles from home, stuck on the ground, hungry and stepping over cow patties, waiting to get shot. That's progress for you. Fighting a wicked witch or a troll under a bridge would seem easy by comparison.*

"When we get into the village," the German said, "let me do the talking."

"Sure."

The pasture adjoined the back lots of the houses and shops of the one-street village. Karl and the German sailor climbed the fence again, this time to exit the pasture. Along the way, Karl looked for a discarded tin can or anything else he could use for makeshift cookware. But the Krauts were too damned tidy; he saw no trash of any kind.

The two men proceeded down a cobblestone alleyway between a traditional timber-framed Middle German house and a blacksmith shop. The sliding wooden door to the blacksmith shop stood open. Inside, the smith reached into his forge with a pair of tongs. The man glanced up as Karl and the U-boat man passed, then returned to his work. He looked up again, this time with a questioning expression. Karl tried to avoid his eyes.

On the street in front of the shop, a horse clopped by pulling a cart. An old man sat at the front of the cart and held the reins, and a boy of about eight rode behind him. The old man ignored them, but the boy waved. Karl waved back.

The street smelled of wood smoke and horse manure. From a closer view of the buildings, he saw that not all the roofs were made of slate. A few were built from wooden shingles or even thatch. Most featured window boxes overflowing with geraniums and other flowers. This late in the year, the plants had turned stalky and yellow, but had not yet died from a hard freeze.

The villagers appeared to go about a typical workday. A man holding a rope bridle led a tremendous Holstein bull out of a stable. The bull's solid mass of muscle and hide reminded Karl of a Sherman tank. A woman carried a bucket of milk. Another woman pushed a baby carriage. A black cat ran across the street and leaped onto a doorstep, waiting to be let back into its home. Two boys talked excitedly and pointed up at the contrails, which were beginning to disappear altogether. Everything looked normal for a German farming village except there were no young men, just like back in Bremen.

Curious glances greeted Karl and the U-boat man as they walked down the street. In a town this small, Karl realized, everyone knew everyone—so two strangers might have attracted stares under any circumstances. But with a war on, the villagers had to be wondering: *Why are you here?*

The woman with the milk bucket smiled as she neared the two men. In her twenties, she wore her blond hair in a long braid, and her peasant dress didn't hide her pleasing figure. Karl flattered himself that she found him attractive. But then he remembered he sported a day's growth of beard and was wearing rumpled work clothes. She probably hadn't seen a man anywhere near her age in a long time, and she'd have taken a second look at any guy. Maybe she assumed he and the sailor were heroes of the Reich, home on well-earned leave.

"*Guten tag,*" the woman said as she passed.

"*Guten tag,*" the U-boat man replied.

As his new traveling companion had asked, Karl kept his mouth shut. He realized he shouldn't be happy about an encounter with a German civilian, even one as easy on the eyes as this woman. He should be terrified, because the slightest misstep could spell disaster. If these people knew he was an American bomber pilot, this pretty girl might well join a mob and skewer him with a pitchfork.

The town looked prosperous for a farming community. Power lines sagged from wooden poles, so the homes had electricity. The farmer back in the potato field must have been doing well, since he plowed with a tractor instead of a mule or a horse. Maybe Germany had modernized more than Karl expected, or maybe the villagers had the right connections. The latter possibility worried him. If the town was full of especially loyal Nazis, then this was a very bad place for a German deserter and a downed U.S. airman.

Don't get paranoid, Karl told himself. *Just stay calm, cool, and collected. As if you're flying an instrument approach through fog. Little room for error, but manageable if you focus.*

Though Karl began to see lots of dangers, what he didn't see was a place to buy food. Had he and the sailor taken a big chance for nothing? Maybe these farmers lived so independently they didn't need a butcher or a grocer. Some of the old-timers back in Pennsylvania never bought anything for the kitchen except coffee and sugar.

The U-boat officer was probably thinking the same thing. He scanned the doorways and gable ends, perhaps looking for a shopkeeper's sign.

Just when Karl had begun to lose hope of eating anything other than the potatoes in his pockets, the German pointed and said, "There."

On the right side of the street, a sign over a doorway: METZGEREI. Butcher.

Apart from the wording above the door, the building looked much like the surrounding homes. Karl and the German sailor crossed the street, stopping to wait for another horse and cart. At the butcher shop, a pair of tiny brass bells hung from yarn tied at the top of the door. The bells tinkled when the sailor pushed the door open.

Inside the shop, wurst, sausages, and hams dangled from hooks in the ceiling. The aroma made Karl's mouth water instantly. A balding man, with a black apron tied across a wide belly, was placing cuts of meat in an iced case. He stared for a moment and said, "How may I help you?"

"Good day," the U-boat officer said. "I'd like to pick up some bratwurst and *blutwurst,* please." He stood with his hands on his hips, trying to look like a casual shopper.

"Ja, natürlich," the butcher said.

As they began the transaction, Karl looked around the shop. A framed photo of old Adolf himself hung from the rear wall. A scale rested atop one of the meat cases, and another of the cases contained a whole hog, skinned and dressed. Behind the cases, a radio and a telephone sat on a wooden table. The radio was turned off.

This guy must be doing all right for himself, Karl thought. *The radio makes sense, but in a village this small, who needs a phone? A status symbol,* he figured. *Like folks back home moving up from a Chevy to a Buick.*

"I do not know you gentlemen," the butcher said. "Are you visiting someone in town?"

"Ah, no," the sailor said. "We are on leave from our regiment. We thought we'd enjoy a hike in the countryside for a change."

The butcher grunted, pulled a long blade from a drawer, and cut down a length of wurst. Karl looked more closely at the knife. The butcher had hooked his thumb through a steel ring attached to the grip. A muzzle ring. This wasn't a butcher knife; it was a damned bayonet.

"In my soldiering days," the butcher said, "the last thing I'd have done on holiday was go for a long walk."

With his hands in his pockets, Karl put his fingers around the Colt. *Where is this little exchange going?*

"It's just such a pleasure to hike across the ground instead of crawling on my belly," the U-boat man said.

The butcher made no reply. Instead, he cut down one more wurst and waved the blade as if to ask whether they wanted more.

"Three, please," the sailor said, indicating *three* in the German style, with his thumb, index finger, and middle finger.

"Ja," the butcher said. Very matter-of-fact and businesslike, Karl observed. No chitchat, no questions about how the war's going. Karl eased his grip on the pistol. *Maybe we won't wind up stabbing and shooting,* he thought, *but this guy's a rude son of a bitch.*

The butcher placed the wurst inside a muslin bag, weighed the meat, and tallied the charge. The sailor took bills from his wallet and paid. The butcher handed over the bag, snapped his heels together, raised his arm, and barked, *"Heil* Hitler."

The U-boat man returned the salute and greeting. Karl, caught with his hands in his pockets, did not. The butcher gave him a dirty look, but said nothing. And now it was too late. That salute was to be given quickly and automatically.

Damn, Karl thought, *did I just blow it?* He hadn't thought about this stupid greeting; hell, he'd had so much else to consider.

"Danke," the sailor said. Hefted the bag under his arm and headed out the door. Karl followed him outside, and the door with its brass bells tinkled shut. The U-boat officer's heels clacked on the stone sidewalk, and he seemed to walk a little faster than before.

"Should I have *heiled,* too?" Karl whispered.

"It doesn't matter."

The sailor didn't look at Karl as he answered. He just kept walking, package tucked under his arm, staring straight ahead into the wooded hills beyond the town. His mood had obviously changed. Maybe a conversation with such an ardent Nazi had rattled him. But that couldn't have come as a surprise. Surely, any German, let alone a *Kriegsmarine* officer, had seen plenty of ardent Nazis.

When they passed the last building on the street, Karl noticed a sign over the door: BÄCKEREI.

"Shall we run in there and get some bread to go with that wurst?" Karl suggested.

"No."

What's wrong? Karl wondered if the German had suddenly become angry with him. *If he's steamed about the Nazi salute thing,* Karl thought, *then he should have briefed me on what to expect.*

"You want to tell me what's going on?" Karl whispered. "You think I screwed up back there?"

"No, that's not it. But did you see what the butcher did just as we left?"

"No."

"He went straight to the telephone."

18

Hares and Hounds

The village street turned into a country road, and Wilhelm chose the first dirt path he saw that led off the road and into the forest. He wanted to get out of sight and as far away from the village as possible. Perhaps he had grown paranoid, but he could easily imagine the SS or Gestapo at the other end of the butcher's phone line.

As they entered the forest, the path became a tunnel underneath a canopy of juniper and spruce. The trees gave off an evergreen scent that Wilhelm associated with Christmas. In another era, the tall spruce trees might have served for mainmasts, but today they provided a screen between the village and two fugitives trying to disappear.

Wilhelm heard no truck engines or anything else to suggest pursuers. He began to think the butcher's suspicion was more a product of his imagination than of reality. Unrelenting exposure to danger could have that effect. Wilhelm had seen submariners whose nerves became shot after a series of harrowing patrols. Every splash became a depth charge; every creak meant a collapsing hull. Fear could send your mind into a spiral of psychological warfare with yourself.

The forest floor sloped upward like the deck of a U-boat on a gentle ascent, just enough to make for labored walking. The American pilot kept pace; apparently, he was in good physical condition, and he had enough sense to keep quiet.

"We'll eat when we get well away from the town," Wilhelm said in a low voice.

"Yeah, that place gave me the willies, too," the Yank said in English.

That was an expression Wilhelm knew. In German folklore, willies were virgins jilted on their wedding day. They died of a broken heart, and their spirits haunted the woods. They killed any man they encountered by forcing him to dance until he dropped dead of exhaustion.

At the crest of the hill, the two men came to another barley field. Wilhelm saw no one in the field, but he decided to remain in the trees, anyway. As they skirted the field border, the American stopped and dug into one of his pockets.

"Wait a minute," the Yank said. "How well do you know this area?"

"I have never been here before."

"Then let's get our bearings. Keep your eyes peeled while I take a compass reading." The pilot took out some sort of flask or box and pulled off the lid.

"Eyes peeled?" Good heavens. Wilhelm scanned the forest and barley field, while the American set himself to the task. The flier lowered himself onto one knee and took from the flask a tiny compass and a silk map. At a glance, Wilhelm could see the map's scale made it almost useless; it covered much of the continent. But the little compass intrigued him. The Yank held the compass on the ends of two fingers and let the needle settle on magnetic north.

"All right," the pilot said, "we're still headed south, more or less. Just wanted to make sure my sense of direction wasn't failing me."

Good procedure, Wilhelm noted. From here, the River Weser was no longer visible, so they couldn't navigate by that landmark anymore. He supposed aviators developed the same keen inner compass possessed by mariners—perhaps even keener. Since their craft moved so much faster, they had much less time to discover and correct a navigational error.

The Yank folded the map, put away the compass, and closed the flask. Pointed into the forest.

"If we keep going south," he said, "it will take us off this path but still in the woods, and I think we need to stay off paths, anyway."

"Agreed," Wilhelm said. They needed no chance encounters.

The southerly bearing brought them over an unbroken carpet of fallen spruce needles, with more underbrush than had existed along the path. A hare bolted from a thicket, and Wilhelm flinched at the noise. The hare's long ears bobbed as it zigged and zagged, gray quicksilver darting through the trees. Wilhelm heard the rustle of its hind paws striking the ground for a couple seconds after the hare became invisible.

Run, little rabbit, Wilhelm mused. *Someday you may find yourself hunted like the two of us. Will you escape the men and their dogs, the* Drahthaars *baying behind you?*

The stray thought reminded Wilhelm of something he'd read about Hermann Göring, head of the *Luftwaffe* and president of the *Reichstag.* Göring's numerous other titles included *Reichsjägermeister*, or master of the hunt. This close confidant of Hitler so loved the Fatherland's woods and waters that he'd developed regulations governing hunting, fishing, and forestry. Göring had even built an enormous country home and hunting lodge outside Berlin—named Carinhall, for his late wife.

For Wilhelm, that knowledge lent a vaguely sinister aspect to the forest. Turned its shadows darker. Suggested a regime whose reach extended to nature itself. Did such a forest offer refuge, or entrapment?

The two men stole along the wooded hillcrest. The decaying spruce needles quieted their footfalls, and Wilhelm and the American made almost no noise as they ghosted through the trees. They walked long enough for Wilhelm's legs to tire, about an hour's hike from the village.

The trek became a little easier when the grade of the land angled downward. A stream murmured in the distance, barely audible. Cold water would go well with a meal. Wilhelm judged that he and the Yank had journeyed deep enough into the forest to call a halt.

"I think I hear water," Wilhelm said. "When we get there, we can rest and eat."

"Sounds like a good idea," the pilot said.

The slope grew steeper until both men had to shuffle their way downhill, balancing occasionally against a branch or a trunk. The water's gurgling grew louder, and the stream appeared in a crease of the hillside. A shaft of sunlight pierced the leaf canopy to where the stream eddied around a group of stones, and there the water sparkled like champagne. At the water's edge, Wilhelm took a seat on a boulder patched by lichens while the American sat cross-legged beside him. Wilhelm waved his hand toward the brook.

"After crossing oceans and seas," he said, "I come back to water ankle-deep."

"And after flying over Germany a bunch of times," the Yank said, "here I am on the ground. Ought to be some kind of moral in that story."

"What do you mean by that?"

The American thought for a moment and said, "Nothing. Because I don't know what the moral would be."

Though Wilhelm did not say so, he did find a moral in the Yank's story of dropping bombs on his ancestral home. The American pilot had been forced to choose between nation and family, and he had chosen his nation.

Until now, Wilhelm had thought he knew something about patriotism. He had seen throngs in long straight lines, offering stiff-armed salutes and singing "The Horst Wessel Song." Reflexive expressions of fealty to the Führer, emotions stirred by propaganda bombardment through radio and film. Vows to overcome our enemies: the Jews, the Slavs, the *untermenschen* of the world.

But this man—this bomber pilot, damn him—loved his country on a more personal level. His loyalty stemmed not from hating anyone, certainly not from hating Germans. Lieutenant Hagan loved his country much the way Wilhelm loved his crewmates. Wilhelm had made his own terrible choice because of that love. Opposite sides of the same coin.

Wilhelm opened the muslin bag and withdrew a link of *blutwurst*. He patted his pockets and realized he had no knife.

"I'll cut it for you," the pilot said.

The American opened his escape kit and found a folding knife. Wilhelm handed over the wurst. The flier flicked open the knife, sloshed its blade in the water, and selected a flat, wet stone from the streambed.

"This'll have to do for a cutting board," he said in English.

He placed the wurst against the rock and sliced a portion about two centimeters thick. Handed the slice to Wilhelm.

"*Danke,*" Wilhelm said.

The *blutwurst* tasted heavenly. He chewed for a moment and swallowed. The first taste of food made him even hungrier. The Yank passed him two more slices, then emptied the escape kit onto the ground and dipped the container into the water.

"Have a drink," the pilot said, again speaking in English.

"Thank you," Wilhelm said. He tipped the container to his mouth and drank half the water. Felt its coldness sliding down the inside of his chest. Handed the water back to the American. Wiped his mouth on his sleeve and said, "So, how do our chances look to you now?"

"Zero-point-nothing," the flier said, cutting a chunk of wurst for himself. Wilhelm wondered if that was some kind of aviator talk, but he could not mistake the meaning.

While they ate, Wilhelm noticed vegetation growing along the brook. The stems branched into sets of leaflets with sawtooth edges, and the weeds had produced brownish seedpods with the approach of late autumn. He could not identify the plants, but they looked like some sort of herb. They prospered in this wet ground, lining both of the brook's banks.

"If we cannot have sauerkraut with the wurst," Wilhelm said, "watercress would do."

The Yank looked at the plants. "That ain't watercress. It's water hemlock. You don't want to eat that. Don't even touch it."

"It's poisonous?"

"Kill you dead as a hammer."

Mein Gott, *another stupid Americanism.* "You are a naturalist as well?"

"Nope. Just a flyboy. But they teach us a little about ground survival."

"Very good."

Wilhelm's survival training consisted of the things a sailor should know: how to improvise a raft, catch fish, read stars. Land meant port, a destination, a haven. But now land had become as hostile as a swath of ocean pinged by Allied sonar.

And here we are in Göring's forest, Wilhelm thought. *So fitting that poisons line its streams.* He watched the water tumble over sunlit rocks and wondered where each drop of it might go. This stream probably widened and became a tributary of the Weser. The Weser flowed into the North Sea, and the North Sea led to the open Atlantic. The very water at Wilhelm's feet might someday grow salty and splash across the bridge of a U-boat or the bow of a destroyer. Mingle with the oil of a torpedoed vessel or the blood of a dead mariner.

The bomber pilot cut another chunk of wurst with his folding knife and popped it into his mouth. While he chewed, he said, "If you don't mind my asking, what made you go over the hill?"

" 'Over the hill'?"

"Well, you didn't really *go* over the hill. That means deserting and going to the other side. But what made you quit?"

"No," Wilhelm said, "I did not go to the other side. Make no mistake about that."

The American waved his folding knife. But not in a threatening manner. He held it by his thumb and forefinger, with his other fingers outstretched. Almost a gesture of apology.

"No offense, bud," the Yank said.

The downed American had no business asking such questions, and Wilhelm felt no desire to discuss his motives. Not with anyone. Certainly not with an Allied pilot. But as Wilhelm thought about it, he realized the Yank wasn't necessarily impugning his motives.

The bomber pilot, Wilhelm thought, *is probably deciding how far he can trust me. Fair enough.*

"My crew was given a suicide mission," Wilhelm said finally. He told Lieutenant Hagan about the order to ram Allied vessels when torpedoes ran out.

"And you didn't want to die for nothing?"

"I didn't want to kill my crew for nothing."

The Yank stopped chewing. He looked straight at Wilhelm and said, "I understand. I took my guys into harm's way, and I got at least one of them killed. But I wouldn't have done it for nothing."

The pilot cut another piece of wurst and offered it to Wilhelm. Wilhelm did not take it.

"Do you really think you understand what I've been through and what I've done?" Wilhelm asked.

"Well," the American said with his hand still extended, "let's just say I get it."

Wilhelm accepted the slice of wurst and continued eating. They sat in silence for several minutes, resting and drinking water. No sounds intruded except the brook's burble and the jingle and chirp of birdsong.

Until dogs began barking in the distance.

"We need to move," Wilhelm said.

"Nazi butcher dropped a dime on us, all right."

Wilhelm ignored the nonsensical expression. He stuffed the remaining food back into the muslin bag, while the Yank dumped the water from his container and put his survival gear back into it. They followed the stream downhill for a few hundred meters, then waded through a hemlock patch and stepped across the brook.

Heading south became only a secondary concern; right now, Wilhelm wanted only to move away from the dogs. The barks sounded like at least three animals, and the sound grew louder, accompanied by indistinct shouts.

From the streambed, the forest sloped upward, and Wilhelm and the American clambered through spruces that grew ever more sparse. Open fields appeared to the right and left. The men had entered a finger of forest that stretched into agricultural land. They were about to lose their wooded haven, and the dogs sounded closer with each yap and snarl.

The hares and the hounds, Wilhelm thought. *And we two are the hares.*

They reached the top of a rise. Both men leaned over with their hands on their thighs, winded from the rapid climb. Wilhelm pulled his Luger from his waistband, used his sleeve to wipe sweat from his brow, and turned to the American.

"You do what you want," Wilhelm said, "but I won't let them take me. I have seen what they'll do if they capture me." He double-checked that the weapon had a round chambered, then placed it back under his belt.

"Don't give up the ship just yet," the Yank said. "We might find a way out of here."

The American had a point. If the two of them could stay out of sight and well away from the animals, they might escape.

They had come to the borders of two fields where the trees tapered off. Barley grew in the field to the right, and the thigh-high grain offered poor concealment. But to the left grew corn. Perhaps it remained in the field at this season because of a shortage of fuel or labor. The dry stalks stood at least a foot taller than either of them. The corn rows sprawled for at least two hundred meters through loamy black soil. Another forest beckoned from the far side of the field. Wilhelm pointed into the corn. The bomber pilot nodded.

They plunged into the stalks. The rust-colored leaves scratched at Wilhelm's cheeks. To protect his eyes and face, he kept his hands up like a man in a fistfight, still holding the food bag in his left. A couple of rows to his side, he heard the rustle of the American's passage through the field. The noisy stalks made it difficult to hear the barking.

Wilhelm couldn't tell if the dogs were getting closer or not. In the dense stalks, he might never see a dog about to run him down from behind. He still hadn't caught a glimpse of the animals, and for all he knew, the barking might have come from some old frau's pack of poodles. But they sounded like big dogs, and he had to assume they were shepherds in service to the SS.

In the middle of the field, Wilhelm paused to listen. He heard the American rustle on ahead of him. The barking continued, but fainter now.

Wilhelm pressed on through the field. At the end of the rows, he found the pilot breathing hard, scanning into the distance.

"I don't hear the dogs anymore," the American said. "Do you?"

Wilhelm cocked his head and held his breath. At first, he heard only the crinkle of stalks set into motion by the breeze. The noise masked another sound that became apparent very gradually: a distant buzz, like a bilge pump far astern.

For a moment, Wilhelm thought the noise came from within his own damaged ears, but then the American pointed to a dot above the horizon. The dot moved closer and materialized into the shape of a small airplane.

Wilhelm recognized it as a Fieseler Fi 156 *Storch*. The ungainly single-engine aircraft actually looked like a stork with its long, straight landing-gear struts. In Wilhelm's old aircraft recognition charts, it would have been listed as a friendly model, used for liaison and reconnaissance.

Or searching for fugitives.

19

Knights-errant

Karl no longer wondered whether German authorities were look-ing for him and the sailor. The appearance of the *Storch* elimi-nated all doubt. The aircraft made its first pass about two miles to the west, cruising low, at less than a thousand feet. As it turned, Karl rec-ognized that it was flying a grid search pattern. The wide wings, painted in a green-and-gray mottled camouflage, banked steeply until the *Storch* rolled out on a reciprocal heading from its original pass.

"Get in the trees," Karl said. "Get up against a tree trunk and just hold still."

"Maybe we should run deeper into the forest," the U-boat man said.

"No. Trust me. That's the last thing to do right now."

As a pilot, Karl knew how hard it was to spot something on the ground. You couldn't just gaze out the windscreen; you had to scan your instruments, mind your power, watch your fuel consumption. Even if you had a backseat observer with nothing to do but look, the observer had a lot of real estate to cover. The thing that tended to catch your eye was movement.

During Karl's cadet days, back when he flew lighter airplanes, he got schooled on the difficulties of searching from the air. The schooling came not from the training syllabus, but from awful necessity. It happened during his primary flight training in Oxnard, California.

Under the tutelage of civilian contract instructors, the cadets flew the Stearman PT-13B, a big yellow biplane with a 220-horsepower engine. Karl hit it off pretty well with his roommate, a lanky Houston boy named Benny Ardmore. Son of an oil well roughneck, Ardmore kept Karl laughing with stories from the oil patch. Complained about nothing except that he had to wear his uniform all the time and couldn't show off his Stetson and snakeskin boots. Good pilot, too—or so it seemed.

Maybe Cadet Ardmore made a mistake or maybe he suffered mechanical failure. But one day he failed to return to base from a solo cross-country training flight. The commander sent up six Stearmans to search for Ardmore, one of them piloted by Karl with an instructor.

The Stearman didn't have an electric interphone like the B-17 and other combat aircraft. The instructor had to yell at the student through a Gosport system. The Gosport amounted to little more than a speaking tube that divided into two hoses extending to the ear pads in the student's leather helmet.

As best he could, Karl scanned the ground for any sign of a crash or a downed pilot. Even out in the open, a lone individual was just a tiny dot. If the tiny dot wasn't moving, it became even harder to spot. He saw hitchhikers, farmers, and campers—but no one who looked like a stranded aviator.

When none of the Stearmans found Ardmore or his crash site along the planned route of flight, the search became even more difficult. If he'd gotten lost, where had he gone?

"I have the aircraft," Karl's instructor shouted through the Gosport. "I'll show you how to fly a search grid."

Like boats dragging a lake for a drowning victim, the biplanes crisscrossed the search areas. Karl monitored compass headings, checked wind drift, and tried not to waste gas by droning over the same place twice. They found nothing on the first day of the search. Or the second. Or the third.

Finally, on day four, Karl caught a glimpse of yellow amid the trees in the Los Padres National Forest, miles from Cadet Ardmore's planned route. The army trucked in some enlisted men who reached the crash site on foot. They said it looked like Ardmore had died on impact. No one ever found a cause for the crash.

Later, Karl lost more friends to training accidents—more than he cared to remember. The folks back home heard about combat deaths, but they had no idea how many airmen died in training. From this first painful loss, he took several lessons. One came back to him now: *If we don't panic and run, that pilot will probably miss us.*

As the *Storch* came around again, Karl and the German flattened themselves against two spruces.

"That's it," Karl said. "You're a tree. Think like a tree."

The look on the Kraut's face made it clear he thought Karl had lost his mind. *But he's still listening to me,* Karl thought. *He hasn't gone sprinting through the forest. An important quality for an officer: Know when to listen. Since this guy has sense enough to listen,* Karl figured, *maybe he's pretty smart.*

The *Storch* passed almost directly overhead, so low that Karl could hear not just the banging of its cylinders, but the whoosh of air over its airframe. Built for just this sort of slow flight, the thickly cambered wings let the *Storch* practically crawl through the sky. Just an oversized Piper Cub, to Karl's thinking. Multiple glass panels made the cockpit look like a greenhouse, so the pilot had a terrific view. But he must not have seen the men on the ground, because he flew across the forest on the same heading until he turned for another fruitless pass. Looking up through the canopy of leaves, Karl watched the plane flicker in and out of sight.

"Like running deep and silent with a destroyer above us," the U-boat man said.

"Just hold still and let him finish his grid."

The *Storch* crossed the forest border and flew over the cornfield again. For a few seconds, Karl had an unobstructed view of the aircraft. Then it disappeared again, obscured this time by corn tassels. After two more passes, the *Storch* vanished altogether, and the gurgle of its engine died away.

"Not much of a search," the sailor said as he stepped from under the tree. "Typical *Luftwaffe.*"

"Why do you say that?"

"Those eagles of the Fatherland are not nearly as good as they say they are. They couldn't keep your antisubmarine planes off me, and they can't keep your bombers out of our skies."

The comment surprised Karl. The *Luftwaffe* was damned good, as far as he was concerned. Good enough to shoot down far too many Fortresses. And to kill Adrian. *Maybe this U-boat guy has his expectations set too high for what air power can do. Might make for a fascinating conversation,* Karl thought, *if we could sit down and compare notes for several hours.*

But you couldn't really hold a military science seminar while running for your life.

For the rest of the day, the two men continued their trek through the countryside. They crossed two more creeks, and at the second creek, Karl emptied the contents of one of his survival flasks into his pocket and filled the flask with water. The fishing gear and other equipment chafed against his thigh, but the need for water overrode any concern for comfort.

From time to time, Karl checked his button compass to keep on a south-by-southwest course. Several times, he thought how it would have been great simply to press a talk switch and say, "Hey, nav. Gimme a heading." And each time he wondered what navigator Conrad and the other crew members were doing right now.

Who was dead? Who was captured? Were any of them still evading capture? No way to know, and they might remain missing for years. Then maybe way out in 1975, some German farmer would dig up a set of dog tags that traced back to an American flier from a bomber called *Hellstorm*.

At dusk, Karl and the sailor stopped in a glade set among a stand of birch trees. No sound of road traffic intruded. Karl hoped the nearest highway or village lay miles away, but he couldn't be sure.

"We might as well rest here," Karl said in English. "We gotta sleep sometime, and at night, I guess, we're less likely to have a farmer stumble onto us while we're asleep."

"Agreed," the German said.

Karl sat with his back against a birch trunk, the bark peeling like parchment. He pulled off a section, and it looked like a ripped page torn from the book of Fate. But the page contained no words, no advice, no guidance. Karl rolled it up into a little scroll and started to flick it away with thumb and forefinger, but then decided to keep it for kindling. Took out his Colt and set it on the ground beside him.

Somehow the trees and the pistol and the danger and desperation made him think of a Hemingway novel he'd read back at base. Right now, he took no great meaning from *For Whom the Bell Tolls*. Rather, he took a practical tip. Robert Jordan, the American teacher turned guerrilla in the Spanish Civil War, kept his pistol tied to his wrist so he wouldn't lose it. That seemed like a smart idea, especially since Karl, in his haste to change clothes after he first bailed out, had left his holster behind.

He removed the survival tools from his pocket in one great handful and spread them out in front of him. He found a length of parachute cord bound up with a rubber band. Slipped off the rubber band and uncoiled four feet of line.

"What are you doing?" the sailor asked.

"Making a lanyard."

With his thumbnail, Karl snapped open the folding knife and cut the line. Threaded one end through the lanyard loop at the base of the pistol's mainspring housing and tied a simple overhand knot. Pulled on the cord, and the knot began to slip.

"Good heavens," the sailor said in English. "Can you not tie a lanyard knot?"

Karl shrugged. The German held out his hand. Karl handed over the Colt and the parachute cord. The Kraut shook his head and muttered, "You aviators."

Immediately Karl wondered if he'd made a mistake in passing his weapon to the sailor. *What if the Kraut got spooked by that* Storch, Karl asked himself, *and decided he's better off without me? Will he shoot me as soon as I'm no longer convenient?*

The submariner made no threatening move; he just untied the parachute cord and began his own knot. Still, Karl reminded himself not to let his guard down.

The German's fingers moved so quickly, Karl could not follow the work. But when the Kraut handed back the weapon, a neat loop attached the cord to the mainspring housing, fastened with a knot so tight it felt like a pebble between Karl's fingers.

Karl tied the other end of the lanyard to his wrist. This time he used a square knot, one of the few other knots he knew. Gave the German a questioning look.

"It would not pass muster in the Sea Cadets," the U-boat officer said, "but it will hold."

Karl chuckled. He cut another four feet of line and tossed it to the Kraut.

"I guess you'll need one, too," Karl said.

"Thank you," the German said. In less than a minute, he secured his Luger the same way Karl had lanyarded the Colt.

The gray in the eastern sky deepened toward black. The breeze fell to a dead calm, the kind that would have made for nice, smooth flying: one of those evenings when you could control an airplane with the tips of two fingers. The thought turned Karl's mind to the unfairness of it all. He and his crew should be done and packing for home. *Why, why, why?* Karl closed his eyes and bumped the back of his head against the birch three times, once for each *why.*

Now that he had a chance to stop and catch his breath, a rage built within him. Karl wanted to lash out at something, tear a limb from a tree and beat the ground with it. Scream curses and threats at Hitler, the *Luftwaffe,* Gerhard, and anybody who'd ever pissed him off.

But that would only wear him out and make the sailor think he was crazy. And after ten minutes of losing his mind, he'd still be right here, stuck on the ground in enemy territory. *You better stay focused and in control,* Karl told himself, *or you'll wind up extremely dead.*

The air began to chill, and Karl felt the sweat on his back growing cold and sapping his body heat. He doubted the temperature would drop below freezing tonight, but it sure would get cool enough to make him miserable unless he did something. In the last of the fading light, he pushed himself away from the birch tree and up onto one knee. Studied the ground for a moment, and selected a flat spot far enough from any trees. He wanted a place without too many roots.

He brushed away the leaves and spruce needles to make a circle about three feet in diameter. Then he began to dig with his bare hands.

Karl made little progress against the dry top crust. The soil rubbed his fingertips raw and hurt as it clotted under his nails. He reluctantly opened his folding knife and chopped at the ground. Hated to do it because it would dull the blade.

"What on earth are you doing?" the sailor asked.

"Digging a fire hole."

"A hole?"

"Yeah. It'll keep us a little warmer, but the flame won't show."

"Can I help?"

"Try to gather some kindling. The lighter the better, like the bark off these birches." Karl pointed at the trees with his knife blade. "Then some bigger stuff, like twigs."

"Very good."

While Wilhelm began peeling bark from trees, Karl continued digging. He wished he'd started sooner; night fell around him and he dug purely by feel. He felt like an idiot for not having a flashlight— but his escape kit was designed for rapid bailout, not an extended camping trip.

From the corner of his eye, Karl saw a sliver of light shine from the German's fist. So the U-boat guy had a flashlight. Of course, he did. Probably got pretty damned dark in a submarine when the power went out.

"Can you hold that light over here for a minute?" Karl asked.

"*Ja.*"

The Kraut tromped over to the half-finished fire pit. Dropped a handful of bark and twigs beside the hole, shaded the flashlight with the palm of his hand, and shone it where Karl was working.

The light revealed a root in the way, about the size of Karl's little finger. He jabbed at the root with his blade, pulled it out of the pit, and flung it away. Kept dumping handfuls of soil beside him until he had dug down to his elbows. Then he opened another, smaller hole, and he tunneled with his fingers to connect the two pits. When he finished, he rested on both knees and wiped his forehead. Brushed his hands against his thighs to shake off some of the dirt. Noticed the German's questioning look.

"The little hole's for ventilation," Karl said.

"Excellent. Did they teach you that in your air force?"

"Boy Scouts."

Working by the shaft of illumination from the flashlight, Karl selected some of the bark and twigs the sailor had gathered, and he added the little birch bark scroll he'd made. Placed it all at the bottom of the fire pit and found his matches. Not the ones from his escape kit, but the matches he'd taken from the dead man by the river. Slid open the matchbox, took one wooden match, and pressed its head against the striking surface on the side of the box.

Don't waste these, Karl told himself. *You don't know how long you'll be out here.*

He struck the match, and it ignited on the first attempt. The match burned with a sulfurous flare that assaulted his nostrils. He touched the flame to a tatter of birch bark and waited for the fire to catch. When the bark started curling and reddening, Karl dropped the match and held another shred of bark over the flame. Gray smoke stung his eyes, but gave him a little surge of victory now that he'd started the fire.

After a couple minutes, the flames licked at the top of the pit. The Kraut added larger sticks to the fire and gathered more deadfall to burn during the night. Once the concealed campfire became well established, both men sat beside it and warmed their hands. The U-boat man opened the bag from the butcher shop and brought out more of the wurst. Karl wiped his knife blade on the sleeve of his coveralls and started cutting slices of wurst. The knife had dulled a bit, but it still made clean slices. When he finished, he wiped the blade again, closed the knife, and returned it to his pocket. The wurst seemed enough for a meal, so Karl decided to save the potatoes for later.

The air smelled of wood smoke and evergreens, and the landscape fell silent except for the occasional call of a night bird. Stars wheeled overhead, silver dust embedded in obsidian. Karl took a handful of wurst and began to eat. In the forest's peacefulness, he could almost imagine himself and Wilhelm as a pair of friends on a hunting trip. Or perhaps two knights-errant of old, traveling medieval Germany to right wrongs and rescue fair maidens.

After the meal, Karl lay on his back and stared up at the sky. *We're not friends on a hunting trip,* he told himself. *That Kraut is the enemy. Will he stab me while I'm sleeping?* Karl rested his hand on his Colt and wondered whether he'd sleep at all.

20

Silent Running

In a fitful sleep, Wilhelm dreamed of Captain Slocum's solo voyage, imagined himself as master of the *Spray*. The sloop's deck and lines felt entirely real as Wilhelm tied up to a dock in Samoa. There, he accepted an invitation to visit the widow of Robert Louis Stevenson, just as Slocum had done. Wilhelm felt so honored to accept her gift of a set of Mediterranean sailing directories once owned by the late author.

How glorious it must have been to sail the world alone and in peace, obligated to no man, dependent on nothing except one's own commanding expertise as a mariner. To use an old Martini rifle for nothing more lethal than firing warning shots when "savages" came too close. To view the world and its inhabitants with an affirming nod, and to accept every individual as a likely friend.

Wilhelm awoke in war, on land, surrounded not by waves, but timber.

He looked up at treetops smothered by low clouds. A fine mist hung in the air, barely able to wet the hairs on his arm. Despite the moisture, Wilhelm felt less chilled than yesterday; evidently, a warm front had moved in during the night. He sat up and saw the American trimming bark from a meter-long branch. The Yank pilot had broken off its twigs to form a fairly straight staff, and now he scraped with his folding knife as intently as if forming fine sculpture.

"Are you making a walking stick?" Wilhelm asked.

"Yep," the Yank said in English, "until I use it for a fishing pole."

"*Sehr gut,*" Wilhelm replied. He did not feel like starting lessons in American English this early in the morning.

The Yank took the hint. "Do you want to get moving?" he asked in German.

"I want to make some progress, but I don't think we should tempt fate as we did yesterday."

The two men discussed how best to continue their travels, weighed one risk against another. They decided to move mainly through wooded areas during the day. When crossing open country, they'd try to move at night, at least when the moon and stars provided enough light to see.

The American, apparently satisfied with his work, stopped scraping at the stick and gestured toward the forest with his knife.

"I wonder how deep these woods go," he said.

"No idea," Wilhelm said. "We will find out today."

"You know, we're going to have to get back to the River Weser and cross it at some point."

The Yank was right. They needed to move south and west, toward the American and British forces. With the Red Army invading from the east, Wilhelm did not want to risk getting captured by Soviet troops. In their hands, he'd probably fare no better than if the SS arrested him. The Reds would probably kill the Yank, too. If they caught him evading with a German *Kriegsmarine* officer, they'd never believe he was really an American airman.

The Yank began kicking dirt into the fire hole. The soil showered onto the red embers and white ash and choked off the final wisps of smoke. He kept shoving the dirt with his boot until he had filled the pit. Then he scattered twigs and fallen evergreen needles until the place where the fire had burned looked almost undisturbed.

"All right," the Yank said. "Let's move."

The American checked his miniature compass, pocketed the instrument, and pointed into the forest with his new staff. Wilhelm nodded and followed him into the spruces, carrying the muslin bag from the butcher shop. The bag felt much lighter now; they had eaten most of the wurst, and Wilhelm hoped the Yank really knew how to catch fish with whatever gear he carried in his escape kit.

As Wilhelm had hoped, the woods stretched for a good distance. The men walked for an hour with no sign of a break in the trees. Gentle wooded hills gave way to a flat forest floor. The change in terrain suggested a river valley, Wilhelm thought. Perhaps they had not strayed too far east.

The cloud cover remained low, so at least search planes posed no threat for the moment. The only sound came from rhythmic thumps as the American's walking stick struck the ground with each stride. A short distance ahead of Wilhelm, the pilot looked like an Alpine trekker on a weekend jaunt.

As the morning wore on, Wilhelm considered the obstacles between him and escape. The river presented the first challenge. Could they take a chance on stealing a boat? Could they risk crossing a bridge? Where were the bridges, anyway? Would he and the Yank have to swim? Did this flyboy even know how to swim? If the days turned colder, would wet clothes mean death by hypothermia?

Even if they crossed the river safely, plenty of other dangers remained. Not just from the SS hunting deserters, but from retreating German troops. Then came the problem of approaching a British or American unit. Some of the soldiers would have fought all the way from the beaches of Normandy and might be quick to line up their sights on strangers.

Twice during the day, the Yank found narrow brooks where he refilled his water flasks. At both stops, the men drank until they'd quenched their thirst, then filled the flasks again.

At midafternoon, the horizon became visible through breaks in the timber; Wilhelm and the American had reached the edge of the forest. The Yank pilot pointed ahead, then placed his index finger across his lips to gesture for silence. Wilhelm nodded and the two slowed their pace. Before each step, Wilhelm checked the ground for twigs and other debris lest a snap give them away. The effort seemed natural. Silent running came instinctively to a submariner.

Near the forest border, but still within the cover of trees, the flier dropped to one knee and leaned with one hand on his walking stick.

Except for his coveralls, he could have been a wanderer from almost any century of human history. Wilhelm kneeled beside him and surveyed the terrain beyond the woods.

The landscape sloped downward from where the spruces ended. Hectares of fields extended across a valley several kilometers wide. Stone walls, less than a meter high, divided the fields. Just as Wilhelm had suspected, a river wound through the valley. To the south, barely visible in the distance, Wilhelm discerned the edge of a town nestled on the riverbank. He tried to get his bearings, though any sailor would find that difficult without proper charts. Mentally he traced the route he and the American had taken for the past two days.

"What's that town?" the Yank asked.

"I was just wondering that," Wilhelm said.

"Whatever it is, we'll just cross the Weser down there and keep heading southwest."

"*Ja,* but the problem is I don't think that's the Weser," Wilhelm said.

"What is it, then?"

"I think that town is Verden, and if it is, you are looking at the River Aller."

"Is that a bad thing?"

"It means we have come farther south than we realized, and we now have two rivers to cross if we mean to join up with your compatriots. The Aller flows into the Weser near here."

"So once we cross that river," the Yank said, pointing with his staff, "we'll come to the Weser again pretty soon."

"Yes. Too bad you cannot part waters with that stick like Moses."

"Yeah, I'm all out of miracles."

The fugitives watched the valley for an hour. Not a single person appeared. The Yank sat down, took out his folding knife, and whittled at his staff, apparently trying to make it smoother to the hand. Curls of wooden shavings accumulated in his lap. Wilhelm stared across the fields and into the town.

"If I recall my history," Wilhelm said, "Verden is where Charlemagne ordered a massacre of thousands of Saxons."

The American looked up from his carving. "This part of the world has a bloody history, doesn't it?"

"Yes, and becoming more so by the day."

"Guess we won't be traipsing into Verden and reading the historical markers, will we?"

Yes, of course, Wilhelm thought. *Here you go with your silly remarks again. The silence was too good to last.*

But to Wilhelm's surprise, the Yank did not yammer on. He put away the knife, laid the staff across his lap, and sat quietly. Dug his thumbnail into the soft wood he had exposed by whittling. When he finally spoke again, he did not make a foolish joke.

"Speaking of historical markers," the American said, "there won't be any for our battles."

"What do you mean?"

"Think about it. You can go visit the spot where Charlemagne did this or Napoleon did that. You can go see Waterloo, or back home, I can go to Yorktown or Gettysburg. But nobody will ever visit the sites where we fought. No markers up at twenty thousand feet."

True enough, Wilhelm considered. "Or down at two hundred meters," he added.

"Just a bunch of contrails that are gone in fifteen minutes."

"Or oil slicks that vanish in a day."

Only wind and water, Wilhelm thought, currents of air and sea, and a thousand memories.

As the sun began to set, the American pointed to a small stone structure built at the end of one of the rock walls down in the valley, a few hundred meters away. The little building stood about one meter high and not more than two meters wide.

"I'm guessing the farmers here use those things to store tools next to their fields," the flier said.

Wilhelm shrugged. "Perhaps. I am not a farmer."

"Back home, we have big toolsheds in our barn lots, but you do things different here. Maybe you leave tools in the field for the night if you don't want to carry a hoe all the way back to your village."

"So?"

"So, big shed or little shed, I wonder if there's something we can use in there."

What nonsense is this? Wilhelm wondered. "What are you going to do with a hoe or a shovel?" he asked.

"Nothing. But maybe I'll find something else."

"Do you want me to come with you?"

"No," the Yank said in English. "Stay up here in the woods. If I get caught, just skedaddle." He left his walking stick in the woods beside Wilhelm and waded into a fallow field overgrown with weeds.

Wilhelm watched the pilot's progress. No other person appeared, and no cars or tractors rolled onto the farm paths between the fields. When the Yank came to a cornfield, he disappeared into the stalks. Alongside the cornfield, a rock wall extended to the stone shed.

After several minutes, Wilhelm saw movement at the shed; the Yank had reached his goal. The American pilot examined several items he found inside. Some he kept; others he rejected. He bound up the things that he kept in what looked like a bundle of cloth.

To Wilhelm, this all seemed a waste of time and an unnecessary risk. He began to wonder if traveling with the Yank was a good idea, after all. He wished he could have commanded this crazy aviator to forget the silly idea of scrounging for something useful. To Wilhelm's military mind, every situation demanded a chain of command, a clear idea of who was in charge. But the two men were of roughly equal rank and experience, and neither would accept a subordinate role.

Dusk deepened as the Yank made his way back to the woods. Wilhelm waited in the trees, feeling the weight of the Luger under his belt. From his trouser pocket, he extracted the brick fragment from his grandparents' home. Held it in his fist, felt its sharp corners. Pressed his fist to his lips and wondered if he'd ever see any of his family again.

The first stars became visible, and Wilhelm took a vague comfort from the sight. This was nautical twilight, when the brightest stars appeared and mariners used them to take bearings. At this time of year, the constellation Aquarius would soon make itself visible in a section of the sky known for its association with water. Near Aquarius, one would find Pisces the fish and Cetus the whale.

The heavens themselves were arranged to help sailors find their way, Wilhelm thought. *Yet here I am adrift without ship and crew.*

More stars took form in the night sky, and the evening became so quiet Wilhelm heard only the tick of his watch. He began to worry: Had the pilot lost his way? Had he decided he was safer alone? But then, the shuffling of footsteps sounded from the fields below, and a figure took form in the darkness, carrying a bundle in his arms.

Wilhelm put the brick fragment back into his pocket and said, "I was beginning to think you weren't coming back."

"Just being careful," the Yank said. "I took my time and low-crawled so nobody would see me."

"It worked. I did not see you until just now. What did you find?"

The bomber pilot dumped his bundle onto the ground. "Can you shed some light on the subject?" he said.

After puzzling for a moment, Wilhelm realized this was the American's idiotic way of asking him to turn on his flashlight. He shielded the lens with his fingers, clicked on the light, and let a tiny beam illuminate the things the Yank had stolen from the shed.

Coils of hemp rope secured a folded canvas tarpaulin. The pilot unwrapped the rope and opened the tarp. The tarp contained nothing but a metal bucket.

"What on earth will you do with that?" Wilhelm asked.

"Cook. But first I want to make a knapsack."

"A what?"

"Just hold the light for me, will you?"

With his folding knife, the Yank cut a four-foot square from the tarp. At each corner of the square, he made a small incision that looked much like a buttonhole. Then he cut a length of hemp and threaded it through the holes. Held up the ends of the rope for Wilhelm.

"You're the knot expert," the Yank said.

Wilhelm handed the flashlight to Hagan and secured the makeshift backpack with a reef knot. With the excess, he improvised a carrying strap by tying a bowline on a bight.

"All right," the Yank said, "I'm impressed."

Then you're easily impressed, Wilhelm thought. *A five-year-old fisherman's son could have tied these knots. It is a wonder landlubbers can even tie their shoes.*

The Yank passed the flashlight back to Wilhelm and picked up what was left of the tarp. He spread the canvas on the ground; the tarp looked large enough to cover the back of a small truck. The aviator kneeled on the tarp, and with his folding knife, he cut the canvas into two equal portions.

"Now we got blankets," the Yank said. "Or maybe a couple pup tents."

The pilot closed his knife, placed it in his pocket. Folded his half of the tarp, then got back down on his knees and began to dig with his hands.

"Another fire hole?" Wilhelm asked.

"Yep."

The American constructed a fire pit just as he'd done the night before. As he dug, he compared the diameter of the hole with that of the bucket's base. Evidently, he wanted to make sure the hole was smaller than the bucket, so the bucket could sit on the ground over the flames. Wilhelm gathered fuel, and the pilot fumbled for his matches and lit the fire. When the blaze began to crackle and spread, the Yank emptied a flask of water into the bucket and placed the bucket on the fire pit.

"Gimme your potatoes," the Yank said in English.

Wilhelm handed over his two potatoes. Using the folding knife, the flier cut each potato into halves, quarters, eighths. Left the skin on. Dropped the diced potatoes into the water, which was beginning to steam. The Yank also cut up the potatoes he'd carried in his own pockets.

From his handfuls of survival gear, the American selected a small screw-top tin. In the orange flicker of firelight, he opened the tin to reveal several bouillon cubes wrapped in foil. The pilot unwrapped two cubes and dropped them into the bucket, which now served as a soup kettle. He found a fallen branch, broke off a stick, stripped the stick of twigs and evergreen needles, and used it to stir the soup.

"Since we don't have bowls," the Yank said, "once the potatoes cook, we'll just have to let the bucket cool enough to pick it up and drink straight out of it."

Wilhelm nodded. This meal would be no more difficult to eat than many he'd had aboard the *U-351:* In a pitching, rolling boat, it was easier to drink cold soup from a can than to handle a bowl and spoon.

After a few minutes, the bouillon dissolved and Wilhelm detected the aroma of chicken. The pilot stirred the soup from time to time, leaning over and sniffing the vapor that rose from his makeshift kettle. The Yank seemed inordinately pleased with himself that he'd found a way to cook, but then Wilhelm decided he was judging the man too harshly. Better to accomplish something and derive a morale boost from it than to give in to despair. Wilhelm had seen proof enough of that on patrol. On a submarine in the middle of the Atlantic, one could improvise solutions for almost anything except a bad disposition.

Wilhelm sat with his back against a tree and tried to purge his mind of all thoughts, to sense nothing but the smell of food and the quiet of the night. His eyelids fluttered, and he might have dozed off if the Yank hadn't announced, "Soup's ready. Now we just have to let it cool a little."

Using a handkerchief to protect his fingers from hot metal, the Yank slid the bucket off the fire. A few seconds later, he tapped the bucket's rim to test its temperature. Shook his hand, placed his finger in his mouth. *Of course, it's still hot, you dummkopf,* Wilhelm thought.

The Yank continued to stir, and every few minutes, he tapped the rim again. Eventually he placed his palm against the side of the bucket for a few seconds. When he could keep his hand on the bucket without getting burned, he said, "Dinner's served. You go first."

The bucket had no handle, so the Yank used both hands to lift it by the rim. Passed it carefully to Wilhelm, who placed one hand on the bottom and one hand on the side. The metal remained hot, but not painfully so. Wilhelm felt the soup's vapor rising into his face.

"Danke," Wilhelm said. He raised the rim to his lips, tipped the bucket. Some of the soup splashed into his lap, but he managed to take in a mouthful. It tasted surprisingly good, just a little salty. Wilhelm swallowed, chewed the potato chunks that remained in his mouth, swallowed again. Took another sip and passed the bucket back to the Yank.

While he waited for his turn to drink more soup, Wilhelm reminded himself to take what solace he could from the quiet, the stars, the hot food. And from the comradeship, even if his comrade was a blathering American. *Value each moment,* he told himself.

Because tomorrow I may feel a rope around my neck.

21

The Geometry of Dying

Karl woke up in the early dawn, cold and groggy. Rays of sunlight slanted through the timber and highlighted wisps of fog. The air smelled of charcoal—hints of the campfire from last night. Frost coated his tarp, which he'd used as a blanket. The white crust reminded him that sleeping outside would soon become very uncomfortable. He raised himself on his elbows and looked around.

The German was gone.

From somewhere deeper in the forest, Karl heard rustling. Footsteps. More rustling.

Son of a bitch lit out on me, Karl thought, and that could be the SS on the way. He sat up, tossed away the blanket. Reached into his coveralls for the .45, still tied to a lanyard on his wrist. Flicked off the thumb safety. The rustling grew louder.

No use running now, Karl realized. *They're too close. Shoot it out or let 'em take me?*

That depended on who they were and how many. Karl held the Colt with both hands, ready to make quick decisions.

He lowered the weapon when he saw the source of the noise: the Kraut sailor, alone, dragging a log.

The sailor pulled the log next to the fire pit and dropped it. Eyed Karl's pistol.

"What the hell are you doing?" Karl asked. "I don't plan to be here long enough to build a log cabin."

"Neither do I."

"I don't think building a great big bonfire is a good idea, either, if that's what you have in mind." Karl placed his weapon on safe and put it back in his pocket.

"Neither do I."

"Well, are you just going to keep me in suspense?"

"You were very resourceful yesterday with your improvised cooking. Today I will try to follow your example. I will get us across that river."

Without another word, the Kraut marched back into the woods. He returned a few minutes later with another log. This one was smaller, only a little bigger around than the end of a baseball bat. He dropped it next to the first log.

"I get it," Karl said. "A raft. But how do we get it to the river?"

"We carry it."

Karl frowned.

"Do not worry," the U-boat man continued. "I will make it small. We wait for darkness, and then we move. Our little raft does not need to carry us across the Atlantic. It only needs to get us over the Aller."

Karl folded his blanket and packed it in the knapsack he'd made. After his night's sleep, he had a cottony taste in his mouth and a pang in his stomach. He wanted nothing more than breakfast; the powdered eggs and weak coffee back at the 94th would be a banquet to him now.

It was all a matter of circumstance. So many days he'd sat in that chow hall longing for home. Now he longed for the chow hall, which seemed like home. With his crew around him, each man healthy and young, their whole lives ahead of them.

He forced his mind off that track, as if punching off an autopilot that steered the wrong heading. On that course lay nothing but despair and guilt, neither of which he could afford right now. Karl turned his attention back to the U-boat man, who was dragging yet another tree limb.

That little construction project, Karl thought, *will at least give us something to think about other than where we'd rather be.*

The German rubbed his hand; apparently, his injuries still pained him. But he made no complaint as he looked down at the logs and limbs he'd gathered so far.

"This will be a rough version of a raft because we don't have an ax," the U-boat man said. "Otherwise, I would cut everything to an even length and make notches to fit the logs together."

"You couldn't use an ax if we had one," Karl said. "Too much noise. The sound of an ax blade chopping into hardwood carries a long way."

"Very true." The Kraut placed a hand to his ribs and looked at Karl. "We must not make unnecessary sound. You would have made a good submariner."

The sailor marched into the forest once more, rustled around, came back with two more fairly straight limbs.

"What can I do to help?" Karl asked.

"Give me the rope you found in the shed," the German said. Then he raised his hand to show the parachute cord lanyard attached to his Luger. "And do you have any more of this?" he asked.

"Yeah, I got more parachute cord. Not enough to make a raft, though."

"We will do the best we can. How sharp is your knife?"

"Not very. But I can fix that."

"Very good."

With that, the Kraut turned on his heel almost as crisply as a Prussian soldier executing an about-face. Tromped into the woods again.

Why is he in such a good mood? Karl wondered. Then he thought, *No, that guy has probably never been in a good mood in his life. But the sailor is . . . intent. Yeah, that's the word:* intent.

Karl understood why. Building a raft, heading for water, put the man back in his element. Made him feel a little more in control.

I'd feel better, too, Karl thought, *if I could make an airplane out of tree limbs and fly the hell out of here.*

He went to the knapsack he'd made, pulled open its drawstring, and withdrew what was left of the hemp rope. Gripped one end of the rope and wrapped coils around his elbow and across his hand, looping over and over until he'd coiled all twenty feet. Karl had no idea how sailors normally stored rope, but he wanted to leave it for the Kraut in some semblance of neatness. *Otherwise,* he figured, *I'll get some remark about how this wouldn't pass muster in the Sea Cadets.*

Karl placed the hemp next to the German's pile of logs and branches, and he dug through his pockets for his parachute cord. The cord came out in a tangled mass that put him in mind of a bird's nest. He set to work untangling it, and when he finished, he spooled it around a stick and left it beside the hemp.

A few minutes later, the U-boat man returned, dragging two branches as big around as a man's lower leg. Eyed the hemp and the parachute cord and said, *"Gut. Danke."* Marched back into the forest.

With the toe of his boot, Karl began to kick at rocks hidden underneath fallen leaves. At the edge of the forest, near the open field, he found what he was looking for: a fairly flat stone, big enough to cover his palm. For his purpose, the stone wasn't as good as real Carborundum, but it would do. He took the rock back to the German's growing log pile, sat on one of the logs, and took out his knife. Opened the blade and began scraping it across the stone.

The sun had risen higher by now and Karl could see that the day was dawning clear. Scattered cumulus dotted the sky, and they scudded along fast enough that he could see them moving. He felt only a light breeze through the forest, but the winds aloft must have been clipping along at forty knots or so.

The U-boat officer came back with an armload of sticks no bigger around than his wrist. He put them down beside his other logs and branches, then stood for a moment surveying his raw materials.

"So," Karl said in English, "are we gonna make like Huckleberry Finn?"

The German looked annoyed for a second, but then his expression changed.

"Ah," he said, "now there is an Americanism I recognize. Yes, we will ride the raft like Mark Twain's character. I read Twain in gymnasium."

"No kidding? You must have pretty good schools."

Wilhelm shrugged, and his expression changed again. "Well, we did at one time."

The sailor started moving his logs and sticks around as if he couldn't decide how best to begin construction. Finally he laid the four biggest logs, side by side, then paused to untie his pistol lanyard and gain freer use of his hand. He selected a branch that forked into three smaller branches. Leaning over, he placed his heel on the branch and pulled on it with both hands. The branch cracked and broke. The German rubbed at his injured thumb, then broke off more of the branch until nothing remained except a fairly straight pole.

"I can do that for you," Karl said.

"*Nein.* I can do it myself faster than I can explain what I want. But I would like to borrow your knife in a few minutes."

"Sure thing." Karl turned over the pocketknife and ran his thumb along the blade. "I think it's getting a little sharper."

The earthy smell of the woods, the freshness of the breeze, brought Karl back to his childhood. He might have been playing in the woods with neighborhood boys, gathering limbs and branches to build a fort. Firing over the barricades with toy pistols, imagining themselves on an adventure with Tom Mix and Hoot Gibson in the Wild West.

Karl had felt the same boyish sense of adventure on his first training flights. But that brand of thrill had gone from his flying long ago. Flying the mail might have been an adventure. Barnstorming in a biplane might have been an adventure. But fighting your way through flak and Messerschmitts to drop bombs on a target was nothing but hell.

And so is evading capture on the ground, Karl reminded himself. *Don't forget that with the possible exception of this one Kraut, everybody for a hundred miles would like to kill you.*

The sailor continued breaking branches until he'd made eight poles, which he laid crosswise over the logs. They weren't all straight, and the uneven lengths of the logs and poles gave the emerging raft a snaggletooth appearance. The Kraut took the rope and threaded some of it around the end of a log. Lashed a pole to the log with some complicated sailor's knot that Karl couldn't have begun to replicate. The German looked over at Karl and held out his hand. With thumb and forefinger, Karl took his knife by the blade and placed the handle in the sailor's palm. The U-boat man placed the cutting edge against the rope. Hesitated, moved the blade closer to the knot. Apparently, he wanted to conserve as much rope as possible.

"Measure twice, cut once," Karl said.

"What?"

"Nothing. Old saying."

Before Karl could explain further, he heard aircraft. Not the steady burr of an approaching bomber formation, but a snarl that rose and fell, rose and fell. From the sound, he guessed he heard two or more lighter aircraft, probably single-engine. Constant power changes; somebody was jockeying a throttle.

"The *Storch* again?" the German asked, looking up from his task.

Karl did not look at the sailor, but gazed upward, scanning through the trees. He dropped his sharpening stone and shaded his eyes. Through the leaves and branches, he saw the flash of a wing as a fighter aircraft banked hard. Another plane followed. Staccato pops accompanied the engine noise.

Is somebody firing?

With a glance downward across the fields to make sure no one was watching, Karl moved to the edge of the trees for a better view. For a moment, he saw nothing. Then a Bf-109 shot out of a cloud at damn near three hundred knots. Fairly low, maybe two thousand feet. A few hundred feet above it followed a P-51 Mustang, gaining on the Messerschmitt. The American fighter's V-12 engine screamed, and its polished aluminum glinted in the sunlight.

A dogfight.

A faint smile crossed Karl's face. "Get him," he whispered. "Get him."

Karl looked around for other planes; fighters worked in pairs at least. He heard more engines, but at the moment he saw only the 109 and the Mustang. The 109 snapped into a hard right turn just as the Mustang fired. The stream of tracers flashed by the German aircraft with no effect.

The German plane clawed for altitude, turning and climbing in a chandelle. Clearly, the Kraut pilot wanted to shake the Mustang from his six o'clock, get off the defensive, and maneuver for offense.

The Mustang pilot would have none of it. Following from above, he lowered his nose and turned his altitude advantage into a speed advantage. In the dive, he banked nearly ninety degrees, rolled out of the turn, and pulled up hard. The U-boat man joined Karl at the forest's edge just as the Mustang lined up behind the 109 and fired again.

Tracers painted a yellow line straight into the German aircraft. The Mustang seemed to fire lightning rather than .50-caliber ammo.

Smoke trailed from the 109. The German fighter continued climbing at an ever-steeper angle, slowing as it gained altitude. The Mustang leveled off and turned like a shark circling its kill. When the 109 went nearly vertical, on the edge of a stall, Karl knew its pilot was either dead or incapacitated.

At the apex of its climb, the German aircraft slowed nearly to a stop and became enveloped in its own smoke. It fell over into a hammerhead stall and began to spin. The 109 traced a spiral of black smoke for a thousand feet. Then it hit the ground and exploded.

Fire and debris showered the fields. The 109 had impacted less than half a mile away, and Karl could almost smell the smoke.

Karl looked over at the sailor, who watched grim-faced. By now, the smile had faded from Karl's lips, too; death, even that of an enemy, gave him no urge to gloat.

The Mustang had disappeared, though Karl still heard the rasp of engines. And the noise still sounded like more than one aircraft. Maybe the Mustang had vanished behind a cloud and was joining up with his wingman. Karl searched the sky, still shading his eyes with his hand. He wondered what must be going through the Mustang pilot's mind. Karl's war seemed technical and industrial, but a dogfight was personal. Almost like a duel: Who could fly and shoot better? Who had a better machine? Who had better eyes? Karl had heard fighter pilots say the first flier to see the other usually won, the living and dead determined before the first shot.

A throaty grumble rose from somewhere behind and above Karl. He turned and spotted movement between the leaves and branches—two fighters in close formation. Maybe these were the Mustang pilot's compatriots.

But when the airplanes crossed over the forest border and scissored away from each other, Karl saw they were 109s.

One of them pulled up abruptly and banked hard to the right. Why such a sudden climbing turn?

An instant later, Karl saw why. The Mustang had emerged from behind a lobe of cumulus; the German aviator must have spotted it. The American aircraft flew straight and level, almost at a right angle to the flight path of the approaching 109.

Turn, Karl thought. *Dive, for God's sake. Get low and fast.*

Where was his wingman? Probably already shot down.

The Mustang took no evasive action. Maybe the pilot had his eyes inside the cockpit, checking engine instruments for signs of damage to his plane. Maybe, flush with victory, he picked the wrong instant to get complacent. Or maybe he was just tired. But he didn't seem to see the approaching German aircraft.

The lead 109 fired as the Mustang crossed in front of him. The Kraut aviator employed the deadly geometry of a deflection shot; the tracers arced ahead of the American plane until they began punching into the engine cowling. The rounds stitched backward along the fuselage. Karl couldn't tell whether they pierced the canopy and hit the American pilot. He felt sick to his stomach.

The Mustang shuddered. It rolled to the left and wrote a downward curve in black smoke.

The burning, smoking aircraft dropped behind a low hill. The earth seemed to absorb the Mustang, as if the plane had penetrated the terrain the same way it would penetrate a cloud. A second later, a billow of flame rose above the hill.

22

Fishing Instructions

Wilhelm felt no justice, no sense of vengeance, when the American fighter aircraft crashed. He saw only another unnecessary loss of life. Without any discussion, he turned back to building the raft, glad for a task to occupy his mind. He took his time with the rope, cord, logs, and branches, knowing he had all day to complete the task. Only at nightfall would he and the American try to carry the raft down to the river.

While he worked, guns stuttered in the distance, sometimes so far away he thought he just imagined the sound. The smoke and flame of the dogfight remained in his mind. Wilhelm did not indulge in thoughts of peacetime. He did not picture himself going about some boyhood adventure. He would employ the raft in a desperate escape attempt, not a pleasure cruise with the dog Bruno in the Bürgerpark.

The raft came together as a crude affair, no more worthy of the Sea Cadets than a knot tied by the American pilot. Barely wide enough for two men, it seemed a poor comparison to the raft sailed by Huckleberry Finn. Forks of branches too thick to break by hand jutted at odd angles. Without any sort of planing tool, Wilhelm had to leave in place all the knots and imperfections. He fancied that the earliest mariners, working only with stone tools, might have built such a craft.

It has come to this, Wilhelm thought. *I have gone from a Type VII U-boat to the vessel of a caveman. Somewhere in the depths,* he mused, *amid the wreckage of ships I torpedoed, Neptune must be snickering at me.*

Wilhelm stood back from the raft and eyed it. He rubbed at his sore thumb joint, which hurt worse now from all the handwork he'd just done. He took out his Luger and retied its lanyard to his wrist.

"Not bad," the Yank said, gesturing toward the raft. "Looks like it'll get us across high and dry."

"Hardly a work of great naval architecture," Wilhelm said, "but it will serve."

When midday came, lunch consisted of a few bites of wurst for each man, and that finished the meat from the butcher shop. The small snack only whetted Wilhelm's appetite. To take his mind off hunger, he stretched out on his back beneath the trees and let himself catch up on badly needed sleep. He dozed for two hours, and he woke to the sound of faint rustling in his left ear.

He raised himself onto his elbow. Amid the dry leaves, Wilhelm saw the source of the sound: two large black ants locked in combat. The insects tumbled across a curled, dry leaf, their front legs wrapped around one another, antennae twitching furiously. Using their pincers as weapons, the ants bit and struggled, with neither gaining advantage.

What could they possibly be fighting about? Wilhelm wondered. *A crumb we dropped? Territory? Some matter of ant pride, an insult followed by a duel? To them, this forest must seem as vast as the Atlantic, yet they don't believe there's room enough for both of them.*

The ant battle reminded Wilhelm of a spider fight on board the *Spray.* During a stop in Tierra del Fuego, Captain Slocum brought a log onto his sloop. In this log nested a spider, which left its hiding place only to encounter a spider of similar size that had ridden all the way from Boston. The two spiders went at one another immediately, and the Bostonian won. After killing the Fuegian spider, the New England spider pulled its opponent's legs off, one by one.

Perhaps God sees our wars as trifling as battles between bugs, Wilhelm thought.

The ants rolled off the leaf, struggled across the ground, and disappeared under another leaf. Wilhelm did not bother to move the leaf and see the fight's outcome.

Near dusk, the aviator took a pouch from among his handfuls of gear. The American opened the pouch and shook out its contents, which included a spool of braided fishing line and a set of small hooks. The Yank reached for his walking stick and sat cross-legged on the ground.

"What are you doing?" Wilhelm asked.

"I want to rig up a fishing pole while I still have light to see."

"When do you plan on fishing?"

"When we get to the river, if it looks safe enough."

Wilhelm folded his arms and regarded the Yank pilot. "Are you mad?" Wilhelm asked.

The American looked up with an injured expression. "What's that supposed to mean?"

"You plan on a fishing excursion out in the open, along the river-bank?"

"Well, yeah. But only if it looks safe."

Wilhelm frowned. *We are on the run as a deserter and a downed enemy airman,* he thought. *How would anything ever look safe?*

"Aren't you hungry?" the Yank added.

"Of course, I am hungry."

"Well, then, you're welcome."

Still skeptical, Wilhelm watched the pilot tie the fishing line to his walking stick. The Yank unspooled about three meters of line, then cut the line with his folding knife. He examined his fishhooks with what appeared to be a practiced eye. Finally he chose one. They all looked the same to Wilhelm, but the differences seemed to matter to the Yank.

Though Wilhelm considered himself a good sailor, his love of the water had never extended to fishing. Eventually his skepticism gave way to curiosity.

"May I see that?" he asked, pointing to the pouch that had contained the line and hooks.

"Sure." The Yank tossed the pouch to Wilhelm.

Inside the pouch, Wilhelm saw lead sinkers, two corks, and three artificial flies. He also found a folded set of instructions. When Wilhelm opened the instructions and read the English wording, it told him little about how to catch fish. The instructions served more as a pep talk:

> FISHING INSTRUCTIONS
> *Of all the instructions which can be given to a man,*
> *or to a group of men, the most important is this: KEEP*
> *YOUR HEAD. You have in this kit, sufficient equipment to*
> *keep you alive for an indefinite period. You can use*
> *your own good sense and these instructions to keep*
> *yourself reasonably comfortable and safe.*
> *The materials here can be used for fishing in fresh or*
> *salt water. Many types of fish will take the lures included*
> *here.*

The "fishing instructions" went on to add that eels were edible, but sea snakes were not. The instructions ended with this final note:

> *Keep cool—and you'll come out of your experience a*
> *better man. BEST OF LUCK AND REMEMBER THAT*
> *COURAGE ALONE HAS WON MANY A BATTLE.*

Is this how Americans usually think? Wilhelm asked himself. *To hold such unbridled optimism, to believe every problem has a solution? How very strange to find insight into a national character by reading a scrap of paper inside an airman's emergency fishing kit.* Wilhelm looked up at the Yank. *Yes, that's an American for you,* Wilhelm thought. *Downed in enemy territory, and he's merrily rigging up a fishing pole. If the American national character includes the dauntless fighter,* Wilhelm decided, *it also includes a hint of the affable dunce.*

The Yank pilot threaded the braided line through the eye of the fishhook, and he tied what looked like a passable clinch knot. When he pulled on the line to test the knot's soundness, the knot held. He trimmed off the excess line with his folding knife and wrapped the line around his walking stick, now transformed into a fishing pole.

"With all your time on the water," the American said, "I bet you got to do some good fishing."

"Fishing was never a priority in the *Kriegsmarine*."

The pilot shrugged. He placed the fishing pole across his lap and rested his arms over his knees. Looked around at the forest floor for a moment. Then he got up and began kicking at leaves and fallen branches.

"Now what are you doing?" Wilhelm asked.

"Looking for bait."

"What?"

"A bug. An earthworm. Anything."

Good heavens. Now the American was scrounging for insect life. *Maybe the man is a genius, finding ways to keep his mind off the horrors of war and the slim chances of ever seeing home again. Maybe he is just very, very hungry. Or perhaps he's simply lost his mind.*

The flier eventually reached down and, with thumb and forefinger, grasped something on the ground. He picked up a large black beetle, its six legs waving in the air. The Yank carried the beetle to his fishing pole, found the hook at the end of the line, and pierced the insect's thorax. He pushed the hook all the way through until the beetle, legs still wriggling, was impaled on the hook's shaft. The American secured the line and bait by pressing the hook into the bark at the base of the fishing pole.

Nightfall brought stillness and chill. Wilhelm zipped up the leather jacket he'd taken from the room of young *Leutnant* Brandt. He rubbed his hands along his upper arms and thought how this jacket alone would not answer for the coming winter. *But it may not matter,* he told himself. *This crazy American and I will not likely live that long.*

Night insects began to trill. After a few minutes, a deeper buzz joined the crickets: the drone of aircraft engines. The engines sounded a mere undertone in the darkness, too faint to reveal direction. Wilhelm scanned the stars, but saw no planes.

"I hate to leave the tarps behind," the American said, "but with the raft, we got enough to carry already."

"True," Wilhelm said.

"We might as well get moving. I don't see any headlights or anything."

"To be sure."

By the light of the moon and stars, the pilot lashed his fishing pole to his improvised backpack, then hoisted the backpack over his shoulder. Wilhelm kneeled beside his raft and took hold of the largest of its logs.

"I will take the heavy end, since you have the knapsack," Wilhelm said.

"Either way is fine."

The aviator crouched opposite from Wilhelm and grasped a log on his end. Together, they lifted the raft as they stood. Wilhelm found his rough-hewn craft lighter than he'd expected.

"This ain't too bad," the Yank said in English.

The two men shuffled with the raft, moving it out of the woods and to the fallow field. Their burden wasn't heavy, but there was no way to move it quickly. At the edge of the field, they paused and lowered the raft so that it rested on its side. Wilhelm scanned the fields and river valley much the way he'd scanned for shadows on the night sea. He saw nothing but stars, heard nothing but the same distant engines.

"Let's get this done," Wilhelm said.

"Aye-aye, Skipper."

They lifted the raft again, and Wilhelm raised his end high enough so that the logs and branches did not drag through the weeds. He didn't want to leave an obvious trail from the forest to the river. As they shuffled down the gentle slope, Wilhelm supposed they were trampling some of the vegetation, though darkness made it difficult to tell how badly. What if someone noticed their tracks in the morning?

Wilhelm resolved to float downstream for at least a few hundred meters instead of crossing the river directly. That way, if pursuers followed the tracks to the river, there would be no continuing trail on the other side.

The faint thrum of aircraft engines grew a little louder. Then came the *thud-thud-thud* of explosions, many kilometers away. Wilhelm could not tell if the blasts came from aerial bombs, antiaircraft fire, or ground artillery. The Yank looked up at the sky in the direction of the thuds, but made no comment.

The abandoned field of weeds ended where the land became perfectly flat. A low stone wall separated the weeds from a cornfield. Wilhelm and the American leaned the raft against the stones and paused for a moment.

"We're gonna tear up some corn when we take this thing through that field," the Yank whispered.

"I know." Wilhelm explained his plan to float downstream a ways.

"Good idea."

Both men listened carefully for the sounds of any threat. Wilhelm placed his hand under his jacket and put his thumb around the grip of his Luger. Would he use it now if some farmer caught him sneaking through the fields? Could he gun down a fellow German?

Not an innocent farmer, Wilhelm decided. *I'll shoot an SS goon if I have to,* he thought. *But a man simply checking his fields has as much right to live as I do.*

Wilhelm decided that if a farmer came out waving a shotgun, he would either surrender or try to make up some sort of lie. He just hoped the farmers had all gone back to their village homes.

"Ready to move on?" the Yank asked.

"*Ja.*"

The pilot and the sailor hoisted the raft and stepped across the stone wall. The Yank parted the dried corn leaves with one arm and led the way into the field. The raft tangled in the stalks immediately. Wilhelm and the flier jerked it free, to the sound of tearing vegetation. For a moment, Wilhelm worried about the noise, but he supposed anyone listening would hear little but the booms in the distance. The two men shuffled a few more meters into the field until the raft tangled again. The corn made for much slower progress than when they'd crossed the open field of weeds, and the effort of constantly ripping the raft through the stalks winded both of them. They stopped to catch their breath in the middle of the field.

The American wiped his brow with his sleeve and said, "One time, a B-17 came back to our base with corn stalks stuck in the bomb bay."

"Why had it flown so low?"

"To get away from your fighters."

Wilhelm and the flier struggled through the cornfield for another twenty minutes. They emerged, breathing hard, at a dirt path. Beyond the path lay the River Aller, a ribbon of reflected moonlight. A light breeze stirred ripples across the water's surface and rustled the corn stalks behind Wilhelm. The distant booms stopped; the bombing raid—if that's what it was—had ended.

Drawn to his natural element, Wilhelm kept his eyes on the river, judging its current and depth. He did not take time to survey the dirt path, and he did not notice that it curved sharply to his left. The cornfield obscured the path beyond the curve. Perhaps the corn also muffled the sound of the approaching truck. Wilhelm did not become aware of the vehicle until it rounded the curve and appeared with shaded headlights throwing a narrow beam right into his eyes.

23

Mercy, Unaffordable

Karl and the German dropped the raft at the field's edge and retreated into the corn rows. The truck sputtered past them, and for a moment Karl thought its driver had seen nothing. But then the vehicle slowed and stopped. With a grinding of gears, it reversed. The truck backed up until it came to where the two fugitives had ducked back into the field.

Karl crouched, reached into his pocket, and withdrew his Colt. The Kraut went down on one knee and shook his head. Karl shrugged. He had no desire to kill civilians, but had even less desire to get interrogated by the SS. He kept his fingers around the grip of the .45.

The driver wrenched a parking brake into position and opened the door. A passenger opened the opposite door.

Oh, great, Karl thought. *Two of them.*

"What did you see, Papa?" a child's voice asked. The kid walked to the front of the truck. The play of light and shadow made it hard to tell, but Karl guessed the boy at about ten.

Perfect, Karl thought. *A kid.*

Karl kept his thumb on the Colt's safety. Could he shoot a man in front of his son or grandson? He sure as hell didn't want to. And he realized that even if he did, the act would not bring escape. He could never shoot the boy. And the boy would run straight to the nearest house and alert the whole world. Karl lowered the gun. Tried to breathe as quietly as possible.

"I don't know what it was," the driver said. The man got out of the truck and peered into the field. "Something ran into the corn."

Go away, Karl thought. *Please just go away. You didn't see a damned thing.*

The driver turned and got back in the truck, and Karl sighed with relief. But then, the man got out again and clicked on a flashlight.

It's over, Karl thought. *A miracle that we got even this far.*

The man waved the flashlight beam across the stalks, and Karl expected him to find the raft, which they had left at the edge of the field. Part of the raft lay within the stalks, but one crooked branch stuck out from the corn.

"Was it a stag?" the boy asked. "I saw a stag yesterday."

The flashlight beam stayed high. The man never pointed it toward the ground, and he did not seem to notice the raft.

"Maybe that's what it was," the man said. "The deer have nearly destroyed my garden."

Yeah, Karl thought. *I'm a deer. Go the hell away.*

"Let's go home, Friedrich," the man said. He turned and sat in the truck, closed his door. The boy hopped into the passenger side and slammed his own door. The parking brake groaned, and the truck rolled away.

For several minutes, neither fugitive moved. Karl listened intently, berating himself for not hearing the truck earlier. No more sounds came from the path. Between the stalks, he saw a distant flash brighten the horizon, a quick inflammation in the sky, and then it faded.

"We gotta get out of here," Karl said.

"*Ja,*" the U-boat officer said.

The two rose from their hiding place within the corn and lifted the raft. With haste now instead of stealth, they carried it across the path and shuffled down a grassy embankment to the river. The sailor pushed the raft into the water and held it in place with one hand. He jostled his creation, appeared to try to judge its seaworthiness. Then he whispered, "Give me your fishing rod."

"What for?" Karl asked.

"I want to use it to pole us away from shore. Then I will give it back."

"Sure thing." Karl slid the pole from his pack and handed it to the German. The Kraut took it with one hand while still holding on to the raft.

"Climb aboard," the Kraut said.

Karl swung the pack off his shoulder and heaved it onto the raft. He waded into the river, and the cold water made him suck in his breath between his teeth. He took hold of the raft with one hand, slid his hips on board. The makeshift craft wobbled, and for a moment water swamped the logs and branches—and his butt and legs. Karl thought the raft was about to sink, but then it bobbed higher and floated true. The German sloshed into the river and pulled himself aboard.

Both men sat on the raft to keep the center of gravity as low as possible. With the fishing pole, the submariner pushed away from the bank and let the current take the raft. He lifted the dripping pole from the water and passed it back to Karl.

The raft's ride left much to be desired. Whenever Karl or the German shifted his weight, water flowed over the logs and soaked their trousers. The cold water made Karl shiver, but he still judged the raft better than wading or swimming and getting drenched head to toe.

In the middle of the Aller, the current flowed more rapidly. The forest that had hidden them receded into the darkness, and the raft floated past more fields. Few lights shone in the distant town of Verden, and the lights soon vanished with the raft's progress.

After several minutes, Karl felt he'd gotten the hang of keeping his balance on the raft, and he decided to give his fishing pole a try. He found the hook still embedded in the pole's base, and the beetle still impaled on the shank. Karl plucked the hook free and unwound the fishing line from around the pole.

This primitive tackle felt nothing like the bamboo fly rod he'd used the last time he'd fished—two years ago in the Wiconisco Creek, north of Harrisburg. He had visited the Wiconisco alone, to enjoy a few hours of solitude and natural beauty before heading into the maelstrom of a world war. Karl recalled standing in the creek in his hip waders, casting a Quill Gordon that he'd tied himself. The Gordon imitated a mayfly, and he let it float across a rocky riffle and swirl in the eddy of a deep pool.

In the clear water, he saw a big rainbow trout rise toward the fly like a submarine coming up from the depths. The trout lunged at the fly and took it in a splash of diamond droplets. Karl caught a glimpse of scales the color of cognac, and his line pulled tight.

He played the fish for several minutes, feeling its strength transmitted through the line and into the bend of his fly rod. When the rainbow tired, Karl brought it to the net. He kept the net submerged, however, and he watched the fish rest in the water, gills pumping, tail and fins waving like feathers in a soft wind.

With a set of needle-nose pliers he kept in his fishing vest, he extracted the hook and turned the fish out of the net. The rainbow hesitated for a moment, then sensed its freedom. Vanished into the Wiconisco with a flick of its tail.

Karl felt satisfied to see the fish swim away unharmed. There would be plenty of killing in the months to come, and he felt no desire to do any more of it than necessary.

Tonight, however, he and the German needed to eat. Karl flung the baited hook over the edge of the raft and let it drop into the Aller. In the darkness, he could not see where it struck the water. He wasn't even sure if it was floating or not; he had used no sinkers on his line. After letting the hook drag in the water for a few seconds, he lifted his line again and swung it out ahead of the raft. That way, the beetle could drift more naturally.

"Can fish see that in the dark?" the U-boat man whispered.

"I don't know if they see it or smell it or feel it, but I've caught fish at night before."

As if on cue, Karl felt a tug on the line. He jerked the pole to set the hook.

At a spot two feet from the raft, the water practically exploded. Whatever had taken the beetle pulled hard enough to nearly yank the pole from Karl's hands. It ran for the bank. Karl lowered the pole's tip to give the fish a little more room to run, but he still feared the line would break. If he'd been fishing with a reel, he could have set the drag and let the fish take all the line it wanted. As it was, he could only hold on and hope for the best.

This was no rainbow trout, either. If he hadn't known better, Karl would have thought he'd hooked an alligator. The fish pulled hard enough to tow the raft at an angle to the current. Karl realized that if he'd been fishing from the bank, the line would have already snapped. It held only because the raft could move.

"I cannot believe you're actually catching a fish," the Kraut said.

"Haven't caught it yet," Karl said in English.

The fish leaped from the river. Karl saw only a shadow, but the thing looked as long as his arm. It fell back to the surface with a splash as if a limb had fallen from a streamside tree. When it hit the water, it took off again, and through the line, Karl felt the surge. With no net, he wondered how he'd ever bring such a large fish to hand.

"How much farther downstream do you want to go?" Karl asked.

"I don't know. I'll just look for a place that seems secluded," the Kraut said.

"All right. You handle the navigation, and I'll handle this fish."

"I think the fish is deciding where we go."

"He is, but he'll get tired after a while if he doesn't break the line."

The fish turned and ran under the raft. The line bent around an outer log, so tight it fairly hummed in the water. Karl felt sure he was about to lose the fish, but the creature reversed direction and headed for the bank once more. His quarry still had plenty of fight, but Karl sensed a slight weakening. The fish ran for shorter distances, and it changed direction more often.

The raft drifted across a sandbar and ground to a halt. The fish struggled on, but Karl no longer worried about the line breaking.

"I could push us off this sandbar, but we might as well stop here," the sailor said.

Karl looked behind him, surveyed the sandbar as best he could in the moonlight. The sandbar ran all the way to the bank; he judged that he could wade to shore without getting any wetter than he already was.

"All right," Karl said. "I'll get off the raft and try to drag the fish to shore."

"*Ja.*"

Karl stepped onto the sandbar, felt his boots sink into the sand. Cold water flowed into his boot. He held the pole high and backed up through riverbank weeds.

The fish slid, flopping, across the sandbar and into the wet vegetation. Karl moved forward and placed his right foot on the fish to hold it still.

From the fish's bullet shape, he saw that he'd caught neither trout nor bass, but a northern pike—or whatever they called a pike in Germany. He knew the pike would have a mouthful of needlelike teeth, so he dropped the pole, reached down, and picked up the fish by the gills. The pike flopped and struggled and sprayed him with water, but Karl held on. He backed up onto dry land, put down the fish, and felt for his knife. Cut the line and left the hook in place: He had no intention of putting his fingers between those teeth.

Karl reached for his pole. Whacked the fish on the head to kill it and end its flopping. He fished for survival now and could not afford the mercy he'd shown the rainbow in the Wiconisco Creek.

The sailor took hold of the raft and dragged it into the rushes along the shore. He concealed it as best he could among the weeds, but as he stood looking down at the raft with his hands on his hips, he appeared worried.

"May I use your knife?" the German asked.

"What for?"

"To dismantle the raft, at least partly."

"Why not just let it float on downstream?" Karl asked.

"Because we do not know where it will drift ashore and who will see it."

Karl passed the knife to the U-boat man. The sailor cut some of the lashings that held the raft together and kicked the logs apart. He shoved a few of the logs back into the water. The German collected as much of the rope and parachute cord as he could salvage, grabbed Karl's knapsack from among the raft's wreckage, and took the water flasks from the knapsack. He filled the containers with river water and joined Karl on the bank.

"A good day's work," Karl whispered. "We got across the river and we got something to eat."

The Kraut made no reply. Karl lifted the pike into the knapsack.

Swung the knapsack onto his shoulder and raised his fishing pole, ready to use it in its former role as a walking stick.

"I hear another vehicle," the German said.

A second later, Karl heard it, too: the clattering and wheezing of an old engine. A good reason to get away from the river as quickly as possible.

"Let's move," Karl said.

A field of waist-high weeds lay next to the water. Karl led the way into the field, and when the hooded lights of a truck bounced into view, he motioned for the U-boat man to get low. Both men crouched among the weeds. Karl could smell the pike in his knapsack; he imagined its slime getting all over his gear.

The truck rolled along the river road, fifty yards from the water. Though Karl could not see it well in the night, the vehicle appeared to be another farm truck. The truck never slowed; its driver appeared to notice nothing out of the ordinary. After it passed, Karl and the sailor rose and made their way into the trees on the far side of the field.

"That was pretty close," Karl whispered.

"If the truck had come while I was beaching the raft, we would have been seen."

The Kraut reached for his flashlight, clicked it on, and shaded it with his hand. He began leading the way deeper into the woods. The men did not need to discuss the urgency of putting distance between themselves and the river road. After the sun came up, someone would likely notice their tracks on the riverbank or the path they'd torn through the cornfield. Worse, villagers might notice both and make a connection.

The fugitives hiked for two hours. In thicker sections of the woods, the moon and stars offered little illumination. After a low-hanging branch caught Karl full in the face, he began using his walking stick as a guard, holding it in front of him to locate obstacles the way a blind man might use a cane. Once again, his thoughts turned to his crew. Where were they tonight? In a POW camp? Dead? Or on the run in some other forest?

If I had turned back, Karl thought, *we'd be in our beds at Rougham. Maybe anticipating a short milk run to complete our tour. Then home.*

Stop it, he told himself. *Stop it, stop it, stop it.*

Karl found his mind like an airplane that wouldn't stay trimmed; it kept wanting to veer off in the wrong direction. To fight that tendency, he resolved not to think back on anything, and to think ahead no further than necessary. To anticipate what might happen tomorrow brought little except dread. So he would look ahead only to the next couple of hours.

We'll stop and dig another fire hole, Karl decided. *I'll fillet the pike as best I can with my folding knife, and we'll sharpen sticks to hold chunks of fish over the fire. After we eat, we'll use the fire to dry these wet clothes.*

One task at a time.

Don't think of trigger-happy villagers, he ordered himself. *Don't think of the innocent farmer who might catch you, and don't think about the calculus of who deserves to live. Don't think of SS interrogators and firing squads. Or of Adrian with a hole blown through his chest. Or of Conrad, Pell, or Russo and whether their parachutes opened at all. Don't think of the impossible distance to cover before reaching friendly forces—or of the danger of approaching those forces in the unlikely event you get that far.*

Think of rainbow trout rising to take dry flies, Karl mused. *Or think of something useful, like how you need to sharpen your knife again before you fillet the fish. Or how you'll need to slice off the skin because that will go faster than trying to scale a fish with a pocketknife.*

One task at a time, Karl thought. *One task at a time.*

24

Executioners

In the glow of the fire pit, Wilhelm held his second piece of fish over the flames. The American sat across from him, uncharacteristically silent, eating slowly and staring into the fire. On the ground nearby rested the bones of the filleted pike, with the head and tail still attached. The exposed skeleton put Wilhelm in mind of the bleaching timbers of a long-grounded schooner.

Another bomber formation droned overhead. Wilhelm braced himself for the thuds and flashes, but none came. Presumably, the aircraft headed for a target so deep in the Reich that its destruction would take place out of earshot. They appeared to fly unopposed, at least for this portion of their route; Wilhelm heard no antiaircraft fire.

Yes, he realized, *this war is well and truly lost.*

"There go your friends," Wilhelm said, glancing up at the heavens.

The American finished a bite of fish, licked his fingers, wiped his hands on his trousers.

"Yeah," the Yank said, looking aloft. "But my closest friends were shot down with me. I sure hope they're safe on the ground somewhere. I know my copilot's dead, but I want to think the others made it."

"Many of my classmates are at the bottom of the Atlantic," Wilhelm said. "You and I, all our comrades, have been so busy fighting, we have had no time to grieve."

"I guess not."

Wilhelm kept his next thought to himself: *And you and I will likely never get time to grieve.*

The next hour passed in silence, and the two dried their clothing by the fire. With no sounds of dogs or other pursuers, the two men judged it safe to try to sleep—but they got little rest. A breeze came in on a cold front that dropped the temperature nearly to freezing. For warmth, they lay close together with their backs to each other. Wilhelm slept only in snatches, and he suspected the Yank fared no better. Wilhelm did not voice his next thought: *If we do not reach the Allies before winter sets in, we will either freeze to death or surrender. We do not have the gear to survive out of doors in deep cold.*

The first light of dawn revealed high overcast the color of steel. The fugitives had camped in a grove of pin oaks, with a carpet of ferns across the forest floor. Autumn had turned the ferns from green to yellow. Wilhelm and the American kicked dirt into their fire pit, and discussed a plan for the day. They decided once again to travel for as far as the woods would conceal them, then assess the terrain where the trees ended.

They hiked slowly and kept their footfalls as quiet as possible. Every few hundred meters, they stopped to look and listen. At one point, Wilhelm thought he saw a rifle barrel aiming from behind a tree, but it turned out to be only a dead branch, fallen from canopy above and resting at an odd angle.

You're seeing things, he told himself. *Either through paranoia, lack of sleep, or morning mist.*

Wilhelm thought of the optical illusions that haunted superstitious sailors. He'd learned in the naval college about the fata morgana, a kind of mirage that can appear just above the horizon, especially during a temperature inversion. Named for Morgan le Fay, the sorceress of Arthurian legend, a fata morgana resulted from light rays bent so crazily they could make a ship appear to float *above* the ocean. Such mirages probably explained the wild tales of the ghost ship *Flying Dutchman,* doomed to sail the seas forever.

Good thing ghost ships do not really exist, Wilhelm thought. *If they did, spectral submarines and their targets would eternally crowd the Atlantic.*

At midmorning, the men came to the edge of the forest. The view beyond revealed not picturesque farmland, but a rail-marshaling yard. Watching from a distance of more than a kilometer, Wilhelm's heart sank. He and the Yank would have to circle through the woods for a long distance to get around the bustling rail yard. Dozens of workers busied themselves coupling and decoupling locomotives. Guards stalked the property, Mausers held crosswise across their chests. Smoke rose from an office chimney.

"That ain't good," the Yank muttered in English.

"My thoughts exactly."

"Guess we'll just have to wait till dark and go around."

Wilhelm and the aviator remained hidden in the trees, watching the rail yard. A locomotive chugged out of the yard, pulling a dozen empty boxcars, and Wilhelm wondered what their purpose might be. Another engine, without cars, screeched and groaned into position, and rail workers connected a flatbed car that carried an antiaircraft gun. Soldiers swarmed across the flatbed, loading it with shells for the flak cannon.

"Hell of a way to ride shotgun," the Yank said, again in English.

"How's that?"

"The gun isn't there to be transported; it's there to protect the train."

"I see."

Hunger pangs began to torment Wilhelm again. He'd eaten his fill of fish last night, but neither man had eaten since. Sitting at the base of a tree, he plucked dry blades of grass, twisted them into little balls, and popped them into his mouth. He found the taste and texture not so bad when he thought of the grass as salad without dressing.

The Yank toyed with a small stone. Flicked it in the direction of the rail yard.

"I knew a guy who rode the rails all over the country back during the Depression," the flier said. "Said it was a heck of an adventure, but he wouldn't want to do it again."

"Why would he do such a thing?"

"Looking for work, mainly. Lots of guys did it. They called them 'hobos.'"

"They were looking for work, but they could afford a ticket?"

The Yank laughed. "No, they weren't buying tickets. They were hopping freight cars. Illegal and dangerous as hell. You could fall off a train and lose an arm or a leg, or get cut in half."

"The times got difficult here, too," Wilhelm said, "but I never heard of anyone doing anything like that."

"Yeah, it was crazy. Railroad bulls would catch them and beat them up, but they'd come right back. You couldn't find a job anywhere. But everybody's got a job these days."

"When I was little, I thought all Americans were rich gangsters like Al Capone. Where is your railroad-riding friend now?"

"Working at a shipyard in Mobile, Alabama."

"I might have known. You Americans keep sending so many ships."

For the next hour, the rail workers connected cars behind the flatbed that carried the flak gun. Two cars contained loose coal. Four held rolling stock: various military trucks and utility vehicles. Behind the rolling stock came two tanker cars, presumably carrying gasoline or diesel fuel.

"Where do you suppose that stuff is going?" the Yank asked.

"No idea," Wilhelm said. "I never concerned myself with army matters."

"I'm sure the navy had you busy enough." The American spoke those words with a bit of an edge, but Wilhelm let it pass.

The overcast began to break up, revealing patches of blue overhead.

As if cued by the sky's opening, the buzz of radial engines sounded from above. Wilhelm counted four, then six aircraft. No, eight of them. Single-engine fighters arranged into two elements of four, they plummeted through a break in the clouds. Dived toward the earth at a steep angle. The fuselages looked thick and bulbous—not sleek like Messerschmitts.

"*Scheisse*," Wilhelm said.

"Ain't gonna be pretty," the Yank remarked in English.

A siren began to wail in the marshaling yard. Men ran for bunkers. Three soldiers leaped aboard the flatbed and manned the flak cannon—a twenty-millimeter *Flakvierling* 38. They spun wheels, yanked levers, raised the four barrels of their weapon.

"I do not know those planes," Wilhelm said.

"P-47 Thunderbolts."

The flak gun began pounding so loudly, Wilhelm felt reverberations in his rib cage. Smoke spat from the muzzles, and the flatbed rocked with the weapon's recoil.

The antiaircraft fire passed harmlessly over the attacking Thunderbolts. In their haste, the gunners had elevated the barrels too far.

The lead Thunderbolt leveled at treetop height. Scythed across the ground toward the rail yard. Three others followed close behind, while the other fighters circled higher.

When the P-47s opened fire, bright motes of light spat from their guns. Rounds streaked from the wings and danced into the rail cars. The strafing sent up showers of dust and debris. Some of the rounds struck the flak gun and the car that carried it. The tracers rended metal, wood, and flesh. Wilhelm saw two gunners dismembered in a reddish mist. One of the trucks chained down on a rail car began to burn.

Another antiaircraft gun started booming. Wilhelm had not noticed the second flak cannon. It fired from a position on the ground at the far side of the rail yard. Its shots, too, missed their mark.

The first four aircraft pulled up and banked left just in time to clear the target for their mates. The second element of attackers swooped toward the men and machines on the ground.

All of Wilhelm's instincts screamed, *Alaaarm! Dive, dive, dive into the soil! Sink below the surface and maneuver before this hellfire immolates you.*

But, of course, that was impossible. This stationary target lay at the mercy of the aircraft, and the P-47s had no mercy to give. Wilhelm could scarcely imagine the terror of the men in the rail yard. He had faced similar attacks in the *U-351,* but he'd always had a means of escape: A good U-boat crew could crash dive in as little as thirty seconds. At the first cry of "Alarm," everyone ran for their diving stations. Sailors slammed shut the hatches and vents. The crew flooded the forward ballast tanks, and to speed the process, anyone not otherwise engaged scrambled forward to help lower the bow. An attacking aircraft might find nothing to strafe but a foamy swirl.

But to Wilhelm, the aircraft hitting the rail yard seemed more like executioners than attackers. With at least one of the antiaircraft guns

out of action, the planes could work their will. No defensive fire
came up at the next four Thunderbolts.

Two of the P-47s opened up with their guns, but for a moment,
the other two did not fire. Wilhelm wondered if their weapons had
jammed. Then they loosed a salvo of rockets.

Wilhelm had never seen this particular brand of destruction. In
the U-boat, he had faced aerial bombs and strafing by bullets and
cannon fire, but never rockets. These flaming darts cut bright vectors
of light. Several speared the tanker cars.

In quick succession, the two tanker cars exploded. A flaming mass
engulfed half the rail yard. A hot shock wave slammed Wilhelm's face
as if he'd jerked open an oven door. Smoke swelled and towered,
and from behind the smoke, the four winged executioners pulled up
and climbed skyward.

Fire seethed throughout the rail yard. Screams melded with the
crackle of flames. Wilhelm had seen tanker ships loaded with fuel oil
burning on the seas—but not with this kind of fury. The tanker cars
must have carried gasoline. Maybe high-octane aviation fuel for the
Luftwaffe.

Wilhelm looked over at the American, who watched without expression. No doubt this aviator had orchestrated similar hell from his
Flying Fortress, but he would not have witnessed the results up
close. In the Yank's unblinking eyes, Wilhelm saw flames reflected.

Yes, Wilhelm thought, *now you see what your bombs have done.*

Somewhere amid the conflagration, a secondary explosion cooked
off. Twisted chunks of metal arced upward, spinning and smoking,
and fell back to a burning earth.

The first four P-47s banked in the distance, leveled their wings,
and came on fast for another strafing run. They disappeared behind
the pall of smoke just as they began firing; Wilhelm could not determine their targets. Perhaps they fired at previously untouched rail
cars on the other side of the flames. Wilhelm had no way of knowing,
and it did not matter. The rail yard was already thoroughly destroyed.

The P-47s pulled up, and all eight joined into formation and
climbed. The aircraft vanished into cloud cover now dirtied by rising
smoke.

Wilhelm wanted to sprint into the burning rail yard, help fight the
fire, pull men from wreckage. But he knew that was impossible. He

was out of the war and on the run, and he could do nothing but run until the war was over.

A series of loud pops sounded within the fire, followed by another secondary explosion and a shower of flame. Perhaps some of the rail cars contained ammunition. Whatever the reason, the fire raged larger and hotter.

"We should move," the Yank said. "Everybody will be fighting the fire, watching the fire, or looking up at the smoke."

"And not concerned with two vagabonds."

"That's what I'm hoping. And maybe we can scrounge some more food."

How can the American think of food at a moment like this? But then Wilhelm realized he was hungry, too. Survival instincts would not be denied.

He stood up, stiff in all his joints. He and the Yank backed farther into the shadows of the forest. From somewhere out of sight, the sirens of fire engines blared.

After one final look at the devastated rail yard, Wilhelm turned and entered the forest. He wondered about the men who had just been burned or shot to death. How many? Some may have been diehards like that Nazi butcher back in the village, but others were just rail workers doing a job.

And I can do nothing, Wilhelm thought, *except use their misfortune as cover for movement.*

He was like a rat stowed away on a ship, always running and hiding. Constantly looking for advantage: a scrap of food, a sip of water. Just trying to hang on and survive until the ship sails into port.

25

Cold Mercy

Wilhelm and the American skirted the forest, stopping every half mile or so to estimate their distance from the rail yard. At several points, they crept through the trees to view the set of railroad tracks. The two men hid in underbrush, just meters from the railroad ties, until they felt sure that nothing and no one was coming down the tracks. They stole across the tracks, up a dirt embankment, and into the trees on the other side. Wilhelm hoped they could continue their progress toward friendly forces once clear of the rail network that led away from the marshaling yard.

As the day wore on, the air grew colder, adding to their misery. Clouds gathered and joined into a solid overcast. Wilhelm's stomach hurt for want of food. With the approach of winter, he knew their luck or their tactics would have to change. Cold and hunger would force them to take bigger and bigger chances just to stay alive. The two men trudged silently; they barely had the energy to place one foot in front of the other, let alone to talk.

Mist drifted from the overcast, and they slogged through a drizzle that turned to a light rain. A gentle wooded slope led down to a narrow stream. There, the Yank stopped to drink. He kneeled by the water, opened his pack, and took out a water flask. Dipped it into the stream, drank, passed it to Wilhelm. Wilhelm drank and refilled the container.

They continued their forest trek through the rain, which grew steady. Wilhelm had hoped walking might warm him some, but he only grew colder. The pine needles and juniper boughs took on a crystalline sheen; the rain was beginning to freeze.

This will end soon, Wilhelm thought. It might not end well, but it must surely end soon. In his cold, glazed purgatory, Wilhelm began to consider a new plan. Perhaps he could turn himself in and say he'd been wandering after taking a blow on the head: Debris had struck him during the bombing of the U-boat bunker and he'd traveled in a daze.

Surely, the navy, the government, would understand. Then he could rest, sleep in a warm bed. Yes, when they came to another road or village, he would take leave of this Yank and turn himself in.

The rational part of his mind brought him up short. Every good sailor knew the signs of hypothermia, and one of them was altered judgment. Men freezing to death had been known to remove their coats and gloves as their core temperature dropped and fouled their thinking.

Your brain, Wilhelm told himself, *has run aground. If you turn yourself in, the SS or Gestapo will execute you. Publicly, shamefully, and painfully. You have no choice but to press on,* Wilhelm realized. *And you are a submariner; you have faced discomfort before.*

A few meters ahead, the pilot stopped. He turned to Wilhelm and, with his fingers outspread, motioned for a halt. Then the Yank pressed a finger to his lips for silence.

Deeper in the forest, perhaps thirty meters away, Wilhelm saw the reason for his partner's behavior. Some sort of structure lay among the trees, its lines clearly man-made.

A bunker? No, a bunker would be better hidden, and it would not have lengths of sheet metal built at right angles. One flat surface looked at least six meters long with . . . guns.

There were two guns pointing out into the woods. The long, heavy barrels of an air-cooled automatic weapon.

The American took a tentative step forward. Then another, and another. Wilhelm followed close behind. As the object came into better view, Wilhelm recognized it as a B-24 Liberator.

Or part of a Liberator: Wilhelm could make out a section of the fuselage, along with the distinctive H-shaped tail with its twin rudders at either side. Just the back half of the airplane. Jagged metal and frayed cables hung where the airplane had ripped apart. No sign of wings, engines, or a nose section anywhere.

"This is a B—" the Yank began.

"Twenty-four. This airplane I know," Wilhelm interrupted. "You have a version of it modified for hunting U-boats."

Rain droplets pattered on the aluminum skin. A faded white star against a blue background marked the Liberator as a U.S. aircraft. Bullet holes across the fuselage served as mute evidence of the aerial battle that had downed the plane. Decaying fallen leaves covered part of the horizontal section of the tail; this wreckage had lain here for a while. Perhaps the bomber had targeted the rail yard many months ago.

The two fugitives approached the Liberator's remains. The aviator reached the wreckage first. Taking care not to get cut, the Yank placed a hand on the sharp, ripped aluminum where the airplane had torn open, and he looked inside. Shook his head sadly.

"*Was ist das?*" Wilhelm asked.

"Somebody didn't get out," the flier answered in English.

Wilhelm caught up with the Yank pilot at the opening to the fuselage. He expected to see a putrefying corpse, but instead he saw bones. A skull lay beside a yellow oxygen bottle. A collarbone rested a meter away from the skull. A rib cage was visible inside a torn flying suit, and next to the suit lay a shearling jacket. Dry leaves littered the floor; apparently, wind had blown them inside during the long months since this aircraft came to grief.

"Animals must have scattered the bones," Wilhelm said.

The aviator said nothing. He stood very still and stared at the disassembled skeleton. After a minute, he ducked inside the fuselage and began searching. He unzipped the flying suit and examined the ribs. Scanned the floor. Moved aft to the gunner's station in the tail.

"What are you looking for?" Wilhelm asked.

"His dog tags. I'm sure he's still listed as missing. His family needs to know."

"Dog tags"? Oh, yes, Wilhelm thought. *Identification tags.*

The American kneeled at the gunner's station. Reached down and picked up a leather glove. Tiny bones tumbled out of it and rattled onto the floor.

"Damn it," the Yank muttered. He dropped the glove.

"I'll help you look," Wilhelm said. He tried not to think about what destruction this Liberator might have wrought on his country. The airman whose bones lay at his feet had been another fighting man just doing his job.

Wilhelm squatted and ran his eyes across the wires and tubing, the expended brass cartridges, and the mangled sheet metal. After a few minutes of searching, he noticed a corroded chain underneath the leaves. He picked up the chain with thumb and forefinger, and as he lifted it, two metal tags clanked together.

"I found them," Wilhelm said. "They look different than ours."

He took hold of one of the tags. Exposure to the elements had discolored it, but he could still read the lettering:

> *CARLTON S. MEADE*
> *17497345 T43*
> *JANET R. MEADE*
> *834 MAPLE HILL DR*
> *KNOXVILLE, TENN*

"Give me that," the American said. "Now." Held out his hand.

"Sorry, I—"

Wilhelm handed over the identification tags. The flier read them and placed them in his pocket. Gazed up at the ceiling of the aircraft as if he could look through it—at something much farther away. Wilhelm wondered if the Yank was imagining the aerial combat that took down the Liberator.

"Are you all right?" Wilhelm asked.

The American cut his eyes at Wilhelm. In that instant, they seemed made of flint. No warmth. The eyes of an enemy instead of a friend. The Yank let a long moment pass without comment.

"This kind of thing is a little close to me right now," the pilot said finally.

"Quite understandable. I'm sorry you had to see this."

The American placed his hands on his hips, looked around at the bones, the wiring, the flying suit.

"No, I'm glad. Janet Meade won't have to wonder for fifty years what happened to her tail gunner husband."

A mercy, Wilhelm thought, *albeit a cold one. To have proof positive of a loved one's fate.*

The wives, sweethearts, and parents of lost submariners never got back such an item. No one could reach into a steel tomb at a thousand fathoms and retrieve personal effects. Undoubtedly, some wives of lost U-boat men held out irrational hope that their husbands had escaped the sinking. Had drifted to the Azores or the Bahamas. Had ridden flotsam to salvation and would someday recover and return.

The Yank started looking through the wreckage again. He leaned into the tail gunner's compartment, reached down, and said, "Here it is." Hoisted an unopened parachute.

"Why didn't he use that?" Wilhelm asked.

The aviator sighed hard. "Any number of reasons," he said. "He might have been dead before the airplane came apart. Or the g-forces might have pinned him in place after the tail broke away." The American twirled his finger to illustrate a tail section spinning to the ground. "If they got hit up at twenty thousand feet or so, the other half of this plane could have hit the ground miles from here."

"You sound as if you have seen this."

The bomber pilot rolled his eyes. "More than I care to remember," he said.

The Yank pulled the rip cord, and a mass of white silk tumbled out. He sat on a crossbrace, reached into a pocket, and opened his folding knife. Began cutting the lines that attached the silk to the parachute harness.

"I hate to take this," the Yank said, "but it will help keep us warm."

He worked at the silk for a few minutes and eventually separated the fabric from the cords and straps. Then he split the cloth down the middle and rolled the two halves into tight bundles of cloth. Cut several lengths of parachute cord and secured the bundles with the cord. Placed them in his makeshift pack.

The pilot turned his attention back to the dead flier's remains. He knelt beside the shearling jacket and flying suit, and he lifted— very gingerly—the jacket away from the suit. For a moment, he seemed to consider taking the jacket, but then he set it aside. Without asking, Wilhelm understood why: Both he and the American already had coats—and this United States–issued jacket would make it hard to blend in with the populace.

A holster and web belt had lain hidden under the jacket. The Yank opened the holster and found a Colt inside. He ejected the magazine and checked it. Racked the slide, and a cartridge flipped out of the chamber. Retrieved the round, slid it into the magazine, and pushed the magazine back into the pistol. Racked the slide to rechamber the cartridge.

"I think this thing still works," the American said. "You want a .45? I already got one."

"*Danke.*"

The aviator placed the weapon back in the holster and handed the holster and web belt to Wilhelm. Wilhelm buckled the belt around his waist.

"Magazine's full," the pilot said. Wilhelm nodded. Though he still had his Luger, he felt grateful to have the Colt as well. In the event of capture, the U.S. handgun would make his claim to be a downed American a little more plausible.

Wilhelm tried to imagine that scene: Could he really make an SS officer believe he was a Yank flier? Could he mimic this pilot's accent, use some of his American turns of phrase? *I'm a sailor,* Wilhelm thought, *not an actor.* But an idea came to him that could make the ruse less likely to fail.

"I do not like to suggest this," Wilhelm said, "but I think I should wear those dog tags, as you call them."

The American, still kneeling beside the flying suit with the rib cage inside, stared up at Wilhelm. His expression darkened.

"Hell no," the Yank said.

"You say I should try to pass as a U.S. aviator if we become captured. Those identification tags will make the story easier to believe. You know how we Germans love official papers and tags."

"Forget it. These dog tags need to get back to his wife."

"But if the SS kills me, they will probably kill you in the next instant. And Janet Meade will never know what happened to her husband."

The Yank glared at Wilhelm. Clenched his jaw and kept silent for a long moment.

The wreckage around us probably heightens his grief and anger,
Wilhelm thought. *If I suddenly came across a U-boat right now, how
would I feel? I'd imagine it manned by all my lost comrades.*

"It's bad enough to take his parachute and gun," the aviator said
finally. "I'm not letting you steal his name, too."

"I understand your reverence for fallen comrades," Wilhelm said.
"Believe me, I do. But I think Sergeant Meade would want *you* to survive."

The Yank appeared unmoved. If anything, he looked angrier.
"What if you get killed with his dog tags on you, and they ship you to
the States?" he said. "Then his family gets the tags on the wrong
body. What are they going to think? How will they feel then?"

"Let us hope neither of us dies or gets captured. But if we do face
the SS, we will need to use every resource at our disposal."

The Yank sighed hard, and he looked down at what little remained of Sergeant Carlton Meade. Reached into his pocket for the
dog tags and chain. Still grim-faced, he passed them to Wilhelm.
Once more, Wilhelm read the lettering on the tags.

"Thank you for your help, Sergeant Meade," Wilhelm said. He
slipped the chain over his head and dropped the dog tags inside his
shirt.

The two fugitives remained inside the B-24 hull and waited for the
rain to pass. The Yank remained sullen. Normally, Wilhelm would
have welcomed a pause in the man's quips and Americanisms, but
the silence felt hostile. *Perhaps he blames me, symbolically, for the
death of that airman,* Wilhelm thought. *And for the fate of his
friends.*

The two men wrapped themselves in sections of parachute cloth
and settled in to rest. This time, the Yank kept his distance despite
the cold. Wilhelm nodded off immediately. When he woke up, the
rain had stopped. A familiar buzz filled his ears. He emerged from his
bedding like a caterpillar sloughing off a cocoon and stumbled to the
open end of the fuselage. Looked up through the trees.

He saw no aircraft, but he could tell the clouds had lifted enough
for planes to fly. And he could not mistake that noise: the *Storch,*
once again crisscrossing in a search pattern.

Behind him, the American stirred.

"So they haven't forgotten about us," he said.

26

Breakdown

The noise from the Kraut puddle jumper put Karl in an even worse mood. He thought he'd shaken that damned thing. Karl and the German waited inside the B-24 until dusk, when the *Storch* gave up the search and growled away into the distance.

Now Karl just wanted to get away from the wreckage—for a lot of reasons: Inside the crashed bomber, he could not get Adrian and his other crewmates out of his head. Also, his mind, stressed and fatigued, wandered to strange places. Karl kept imagining the Liberator intact. He wanted to climb into the cockpit and magically take off and fly home. But, of course, there was nothing forward of the bomb bay except German forest.

Out loud, Karl gave a more practical reason for moving.

"I don't know if the *Storch* pilot saw this tail section from the air," Karl said. "Maybe not, since it isn't what he's looking for. But if I spotted half an airplane lying in the woods, I'd sure get on the radio and tell somebody."

The U-boat man agreed, so they rolled up their bedding and stuffed it into the knapsack. Checked their weapons. Headed farther into the forest without a backward glance at the resting place of Sergeant Carlton S. Meade.

The night made for rough walking. Though the cloud ceiling had lifted, it had not dissipated. And clouds at ten thousand feet blocked the moonlight as effectively as clouds just above the ground. Both men muttered curses as invisible branches slapped their faces and unseen roots tripped them. From time to time, they paused to check their course. The German, shading his flashlight with his hand, aimed a slice of illumination at Karl's button compass. At each stop, they confirmed a southwesterly course toward the Weser. The light reddened the Kraut's fingers as if the blood inside them glowed. During one compass check, the sailor's shivering jiggled the light everywhere except onto the compass, and Karl lost patience.

"Keep that damned thing still, will you?" Karl hissed. Stress, strain, and grief shortened his fuse, and he didn't care if this enemy naval officer knew it.

The Kraut said nothing and looked at Karl with a wounded expression. Gripped the flashlight with both hands and managed to focus the beam onto the compass.

What the hell is he doing, Karl wondered, *shining that light all over the place? Trying to get us caught?*

All along, the sailor had said for him there was no turning back. The German authorities would execute him for desertion, immediately and without trial. No mitigating circumstances would help. He had crossed the Rubicon, blah, blah, blah.

But maybe he's having second thoughts, Karl imagined. *Getting cold feet about running away from the navy. Looking for an exit, an open escape hatch. Thinking about turning me in.*

Thoughts as dark as the night forest tormented Karl as he groped through the trees. He could not see the Kraut; he could only hear him: footsteps a few feet away in the blackness. *This whole thing is crazy,* Karl thought, *wandering through the Reich, trusting a German deserter. As soon as we get cornered, he'll put a bullet in my back. I'll live just long enough to think how it shouldn't have come as a surprise.*

Karl tried to bear all his burdens with stoic silence. But when a low-hanging branch brushed by the German smacked him in the mouth, he lost control. The blow stung like a leather strap. Karl stumbled backward, dropped his knapsack. Let loose a string of curses.

"Stupid son of a bitch," Karl said. "Watch what the hell you're doing."

"Shh," the sailor said, his voice disembodied by darkness. "Calm yourself."

"Screw yourself."

The German let the insult pass. After a minute or so, he said, "We are cold and tired. It's no wonder you're at the end of your tether. Let's stay here for the night and not walk into any more trees. We'll just wrap up in that parachute cloth you saved."

Karl was too tired to argue. He felt for the pack he'd dropped. Tried to open it, but could not find the knot for the drawstring.

"Gimme some light, will you?" Karl asked.

The U-boat man clicked on his flashlight. The beam grew dimmer now; the batteries couldn't last much longer.

One crisis at a time, Karl told himself. With numbed, shivering fingers, he untied the pack and pulled out two rolls of parachute silk. Tossed one to the Kraut. Unrolled the other for himself. Sat on the cold ground, wrapped the silk around him, and lay with his back on the forest floor. Kept his distance from his traveling partner.

The parachute blanket warmed Karl some, but not enough to make him comfortable. He gazed into an overcast sky, so black he might as well have lain in a grave. Exhaustion overtook him, and he fell asleep despite the cold. His last conscious thought of the night: Getting blown up in *Hellstorm* would have been so much easier.

Karl awoke beneath clouds the color of dirty cotton. Light breeze in the evergreens. Dusting of frost on everything, including the parachute cloth. Distant crumps and thuds—bombs falling somewhere miles away, with flak guns pounding at the bombers. Touched a finger to his upper lip, which was still sore from getting smacked by the branch last night. He raised himself onto his elbows and saw the U-boat man already up, rolling his blanket of parachute silk.

"Are you feeling better?" the German whispered.

"Not really."

All Karl's doubts came flooding back. It could only be a matter of time before they ran into German soldiers or police. What would the sailor do then?

"The river cannot be much farther," the Kraut said.

Karl dug into a pocket and found his button compass. Threw it at the U-boat man.

"You lead the way, if you think you know where we are."

The German caught the compass as it bounced off his chest. He gave Karl a puzzled look, but did not ask for explanation. The explanation would have been: *I want you in front of me where I can see you. Yeah, you didn't give me away when we saw those SS men on the first day. But I gotta size you up every day.*

With no breakfast except a handful of leaves, the two men resumed their trek. They kept to the woods for the better part of the day; their hunger, thirst, and cold worsened as the hours wore on. At a narrow forest stream, they stopped to refill their water containers. Karl drank deeply, and he felt some of the cold water run from the corners of his mouth and into his whiskers. He supposed he must look like one of the hobos he'd mentioned to the German. He needed a shower, a shave, and a hot meal. Especially a hot meal. The longings did nothing to help his frame of mind.

In the late afternoon, as the German led the way among a tall stand of firs, he stopped to examine something on the ground. A path, barely discernible, ran among the leaves and underbrush. It looked a lot like the cow paths Karl had seen in Pennsylvania pastures, though not nearly as well beaten. *Is a farm nearby? Or is this some kid's path to Grandma's house?*

"We should probably stay away from wherever that path goes," Karl said.

The U-boat officer kneeled, looked up and down the path.

"I'm not so sure," the German said. "I have never been much of a hunter or fisherman, but I know people who are. Germans like to build cabins up in the wilderness. I think you Americans would call them 'fishing camps.'"

"So?"

"So maybe we can find a place to get out of the weather. Maybe even get provisions."

Stupid idea, Karl thought. When evading capture, he'd been taught, an individual should avoid any line of communication where locals travel. A road, a canal, a path. You want to be where people *aren't.*

"If this path leads to a fishing or hunting cabin," Karl said, "it sounds like a good way to run into a pissed-off guy with a gun."

"But look at the path," the sailor said. "It is not well traveled. Who-ever uses it is probably riding a panzer these days. If he's still alive."

"I don't care. We need to stay hidden."

"We need to rest and eat."

A flush of anger burned in Karl's chest. He was too exhausted and had too much on his mind for some Kraut sailor's bright ideas.

"Forget it. I don't need the SS hooking my balls up to a car bat-tery."

"Lieutenant Hagan," the German said as he stood up again, "win-ter is coming. Even well-equipped soldiers have a tough time surviv-ing winter in these latitudes. We have nothing. Do you know how many German troops have frozen to death on the Eastern Front?"

Not enough, Karl thought. He started to say so out loud, just to get under the Kraut's skin. But then another thought intruded through the fog of fatigue—one much more serious.

"You want to lead me into a trap," Karl said. "Now that you've got-ten a little tired and hungry, you've had enough playing Davy Crock-ett. You think they'll go easy on you if you hand them my ass on a platter."

"Who is . . . ," the Kraut said. "Never mind. Just listen to me. I know my people and their habits. A cabin can stay closed up for months, even in peacetime. You are the one who is overly tired."

The sailor advanced toward Karl as if he was about to place his hand on Karl's shoulder to give him a good shake. That was too much. Karl slapped away the German's hand, grabbed him by his jacket lapels.

"Get your damned hands off me, you goose-stepping bastard," Karl said through gritted teeth. Shoved the Kraut against a tree hard enough that his head knocked against the trunk.

The German responded with a left hook he must have learned at the naval college. Son of a bitch had never said a word about a box-ing team, but the blow landed hard enough to knock Karl off his feet. Karl staggered backward and fell, but he stayed on the ground only for a second. Fueled by pure rage, he ran at the Kraut, grabbed him around the waist with both arms, and tackled him.

On the forest floor, the U-boat man rolled hard and came up on top of Karl. Gripped Karl's throat with his left hand. Drew his Luger with his right. Karl froze.

The German breathed hard, with dirt and leaves in his whiskers. Despite the cold, a drop of sweat fell from his nose.

"I could have killed you a hundred times by now if I'd wanted," the sailor said. "I do not wish to take another life, or cause the SS to take yours." He drew in a long, ragged breath before he continued his thought. "But unless you come to your senses, I will put a bullet in your forehead and leave you in these woods."

The Kraut took his hand off Karl's throat, but kept the Luger's muzzle to his skull. Karl coughed, turned his head, spat onto the ground. He let his heart slow down, let his anger cool.

Maybe he'd been wrong. He looked up at the German—who looked angry, but very much in control of himself. A prickly burn of embarrassment replaced Karl's white-hot rage.

Of the two of us, he thought, *I cracked first. Okay, so I screwed up. Can't ever get that moment back. Nothing for it but to press on.*

"All right, Jack Dempsey," Karl said. "Lead the way."

The sailor pushed himself off Karl's torso, brushed dirt from his jacket. Held the pistol angled toward the ground. He still looked pissed off. He looked pained, too. The Kraut put a hand to his side and winced. Ribs still sore, evidently. He put away the weapon and pointed his finger at Karl's nose as if lecturing an errant recruit.

"I am sorry about the loss of your friends," the German said. "Truly, I am. But find another way to mourn."

Karl shrugged. He couldn't quite bring himself to apologize to a guy who'd devoted his career to serving the Third Reich. But Karl had to admit the guy's point: He *had* been getting worn out from fatigue and stress and thinking about the rest of *Hellstorm*'s crew.

"All right, then," Karl said. "This cabin better have a freezer full of steaks." He hoped his tone conveyed new confidence—which he really didn't feel.

A mother-of-pearl cloud layer drifted overhead as Karl and the German made their way along the path. Occasional fissures in the overcast admitted rays from a setting sun and limned the cloud breaks with copper. Though the sky looked beautiful from this angle,

Karl knew how much more spectacular this scene would appear from above the overcast, and he wanted very much to be there. What paradise to drone toward home base, planning the let-down through the cloud layer, anticipating coffee, sandwiches, and a shot of debrief whisky.

Well, you could wish for anything.

What was that song from the Pinocchio *movie? "When You Wish Upon a Star." Yeah,* Karl thought, *just keep wishing.*

As his fatigued mind wandered, it stumbled on an unpleasant thought. He voiced it immediately.

"Hey," Karl said, "how do you know we're going *toward* your supposed cabin and not away from it?" His knapsack slid from his shoulders and he stopped to tug at the straps made from parachute cord.

"I don't."

Huh? We don't know? Just like that? Flip of the coin, heads or tails. Fifty-fifty. Karl felt so tired, he didn't care.

He jogged a few steps to catch up with the German and found that the path ahead pitched downhill. The trail widened under a canopy of pines, and pine needles carpeted the path. Karl nearly slipped as a sheaf of pine needles shifted under his feet. When he regained his balance, he looked downhill and caught glimpses of pewter between the trees.

Water.

The German stopped, turned halfway back toward Karl, and motioned for him to stop, too. Eased himself down to a kneeling position. Gazed at something out in front, something in or near the water. After a couple minutes, he gestured for Karl to come forward.

Karl padded ahead on spongy, decaying pine needles. Kneeled by the sailor's side. The U-boat man hadn't reached for one of his pistols, and Karl took that as a good sign.

Wordlessly, the German pointed. From this vantage point, Karl could tell the water was a lake, not a river. The surface lay still and mirrored the illuminated overcast; the sight put Karl in mind of dross floating on molten steel. But the sailor wasn't pointing to the lake. Peering through the trees, Karl needed a moment to find what the German had seen.

There. An angled roof appeared among the trees. Observing from the wooded hillside above, Karl could see little else of the structure. But it appeared to be a two- or three-room shack situated on the lakeshore. It probably had been there awhile; moss covered most of the wooden shingles. A stone chimney stood cold; no smoke rose from the flue.

"Shall we go see Hansel and Gretel?" Karl asked.

27

A Warning Branch

Wilhelm and the Yank watched the cabin for an hour and saw no activity. For at least one night, Wilhelm decided, they had found safe anchorage. At dusk, they used the last of the day's light to commit a breaking and entering.

As they picked their way downhill through the pines, the cabin came into better view. Three rooms at most. A cracked four-pane window. No plumbing, apparently; a wooden outdoor privy stood several meters from the main cabin. Someone had stacked cords of firewood next to the cabin. The split wood had weathered to the color of well-done steak.

Two large stones served as a doorstep. On the door, a dried, curved tree branch hung from a nail.

Upon closer inspection, Wilhelm saw that someone had stripped most of the bark from the small branch, bent it into a loop, and tied the ends together with twine to hold that shape. Wilhelm had no idea what it meant—but strangely enough, the Yank did.

"A *warnbruch*," the American said.

"Warning branch?"

"Yes. My uncle Rainer told me about German hunting traditions. You guys use branches for signals, like 'I shot the deer here.' This one means 'danger in the area,' like poachers or a tree about to fall."

Wilhelm sighed. *"Danger in the area"? Indeed.*

"In this case," the Yank continued, "I'm guessing it means keep out."

"They're serious about it, too," Wilhelm said. He pointed to chains that held the door shut. The door had no knob, just a hole bored into the wood. From inside the cabin, a chain passed through the hole. Another length of chain hung from an angle iron nailed to the outside wall, and a padlock secured the two chains together.

"I don't got a key," the bomber pilot said, "but I got a boot."

"You will never break that chain."

"Yeah, but I'll break the wood."

The Yank put down his knapsack, untied the pistol lanyard from his wrist, and took off his jacket. Motioned for Wilhelm to step aside. Set himself in front of the door, raised his knee, and let fly with a hard kick.

The door shuddered when the Yank's boot made contact. The chains rattled, but everything held firm. The Yank flexed his knee and rubbed his shin as if it hurt, then poised with his other knee. Slammed his boot into the door again. Cracking noises came this time.

Wilhelm inspected the hardware. The nails holding the angle iron in place had begun to tear loose.

"Take a rest," Wilhelm said. "Let me hit it once or twice."

Wilhelm gave the door an experimental shove with the toe of his boot, then stepped back two paces. With a running start, he rammed his heel into the door.

His boot struck with a sound like a woodsman's ax whacking into an oak. The angle iron tore loose in a shower of splinters. The door swung partly open and stopped when the padlock—still attached to the chain—lodged against the hole bored in the wood. The end of the chain affixed to the inside wall still held. Wilhelm's effort reignited the pain in his ribs.

"Probably another angle iron holding the chain on the inside," the flier said.

"Not for long."

Despite the pain, Wilhelm kicked once more. The door slapped open, chains swinging and creaking.

A musty odor rolled from inside the cabin. Not an unpleasant smell: some combination of cooked onions, wood smoke, and mothballed bed linen. Pure darkness within. Wilhelm held his side for a moment, then dug for his flashlight, clicked on its weakening beam, and stepped inside.

A wood-burning stove sat in the middle of the main room, with a kettle and empty pot on top of the cooking surface. An L-shaped stovepipe extended into the rock chimney. The furniture consisted of a rough-hewn pine table and four ladder-back wooden chairs. Two oil-burning lamps, both dark, sat on the table. Cobwebs sagged from the corners of the ceiling.

"Are your matches still dry?" Wilhelm asked.

"Yeah," the Yank answered. The single syllable carried an edge, suggesting he was insulted at the suggestion he'd let his matches get wet. Wilhelm didn't care. Letting your matches get wet was no more stupid than starting a fistfight.

The aviator found his matches among his survival trinkets. Guided by the beam from Wilhelm's flashlight, the American lifted the glass chimney from one of the oil lamps and turned the knob to raise the wick. Struck a match, touched fire to the wick, and replaced the glass. The room filled with a soft, golden glow.

"You wanna just save the oil in the other lamp?" the Yank asked.

"*Ja.* One is enough."

Lamplight revealed the room's primitive décor. A set of antlers hung on one wall. The antlers had not been mounted on any sort of plaque; they'd simply been nailed to the log wall, complete with a section of deer skull. Another wall featured something of an icon: a framed painting of Saint Hubertus. In the moldering picture, Hubertus appeared next to a stag. Between the stag's antlers gleamed a crucifix. At the bottom of the painting, these lines appeared in German Gothic script:

> *This is the hunter's badge of glory,*
> *That he protect and tend his quarry,*
> *Hunt with honor, as is due,*
> *And through the beast to God is true.*

Wilhelm told the American the story of Saint Hubertus. Sometime during the seventh century, the future saint's wife died in childbirth, and in his grief he abandoned all responsibilities. He began spending his time afield, hunting with his dogs. One day, in the midst of a chase, a great stag stopped and faced him. An astonished Hubert saw the Holy Cross shining amid the stag's magnificent rack. A voice said to him: "Hubert, thou must turn to the Lord, lest ye go down unto hell." In the pious life that followed, Hubert became the patron saint of hunters, mathematicians, and metalworkers.

"A good sign, no?" Wilhelm said. "Especially for you of the American steel industry."

"I don't know," the Yank said, "but I'll take whatever luck I can get."

The aviator began looking in corners and opening doors. Two of the doors led to small bedrooms, each furnished with little but a cot. In one of the bedrooms, a wooden gun rack hung empty on the wall. Someone had taken care in its construction; the U-shaped brackets had been lined with felt to prevent scratching the guns. Quite different from the metal locker that contained firearms on the *U-351*.

Wilhelm opened a narrow door to find a pantry filled with fishing tackle and nonperishable foodstuffs. Spinning rods and a fishnet leaned in a corner. A wicker basket set onto the pantry floor contained potatoes sprinkled with lime. Shelves held glass jars full of canned onions, tomatoes, and some sort of fruit—perhaps pears. A muslin sack contained dried beans. A cupboard stored stoneware plates and bowls, utensils, and a few canisters of seasonings.

"Oh, my God," the Yank said. "This looks as good to me right now as the dining room in the Waldorf Astoria. Score one for you, Popeye the Sailor Man."

"We should stay here only long enough to regain our strength," Wilhelm said. "We get dried out and warmed up, and we eat our fill. Then we move on."

The temptation to get too comfortable presented additional danger. The men who had hunted and fished here might well be dead on the Eastern Front, Wilhelm believed, and that's why he'd taken this calculated risk. But, on the other hand, some old pensioner could come along any day.

"I'm sure you're right," the American said. "I'll light the stove if you'll wash some of those potatoes."

Perhaps the bomber pilot had returned to his senses. While the Yank brought in wood and kindling, Wilhelm took the pot from the stovetop and placed five potatoes in it. He carried the pot outside and shuffled through the darkness down to the water. Just enough lamplight shone through the window for him to see to go about his task. He dipped the pot into the lake and stood sloshing the potatoes with the fingers of his right hand. Poured out the water, careful not to spill the potatoes, dipped the pot again. He could not see how well he had removed the lime, so he swirled the potatoes a second time. Poured out the water once more, dipped the pot, and carried the water and potatoes back toward the cabin.

Just as he reached the door, silken flashes lit the horizon. The bombers had returned, striking somewhere in the direction of Bremen. *Even this lakeshore heaven*, Wilhelm mused, *must have its reminder of hell.*

Inside, the smell of fresh smoke greeted Wilhelm. The American had started a fire in the stove. Wilhelm placed the pot on top of the stove, removed the potatoes from the water, and placed them on a plate. He found a kitchen knife in the cupboard and began quartering the potatoes. When steam began to rise from the pot, he tilted the plate over the water and used his blade to sweep the potato chunks into the pot. Droplets splashed onto the stovetop and sizzled.

The Yank went to the pantry and came back with a sealed jar of onions. Unscrewed the zinc cap and emptied the onions onto a plate for Wilhelm to cut.

"My ex-hobo buddy would have called this 'mulligan stew,'" the flier said.

"How's that?"

"Stew made from whatever you got."

"Indeed."

Wilhelm sliced the onions and added them to the pot. Shook in a few dashes of pepper. They considered adding more from the pantry, but decided to conserve the rest of the food. The pot began to simmer and filled the cabin with the mouthwatering aroma of onion and potato soup. When the Yank took a turn at stirring, Wilhelm sat, folded his arms across the table, and put his head down. He could have fallen asleep right there, but for his hunger.

The Yank went outside and returned with his water flasks filled. Set them on the table, stirred the pot once more, and declared, "Soup's ready." Ladled the soup into stoneware bowls and placed a bowl and spoon before Wilhelm.

Wilhelm could have wept. Food, sleep, and warmth. The mere fact of having his basic physical needs met seemed an unpardonable indulgence. The war had taken much from him—and had taken so much more from so many others. He wished he could wall off this cabin in the woods from all the violence and insanity—except he'd have preferred to get walled off with one of his French girlfriends instead of this talkative, wayward American.

He sat up straight. The Yank took a seat opposite him. Wilhelm took a spoonful of soup and placed it in his mouth. Burned his tongue, so he immediately grabbed a water flask and took a drink. *But oh, the taste of warm food.* He dipped the spoon again, blew on the soup, and watched the tiny ripples. Took another bite, this time without pain.

For fifteen minutes, the men ate without speaking. Each refilled his bowl. The American spilled soup on his whiskers and wiped it with his sleeve. He seemed more in command of his emotions now. Perhaps his breakdown had brought some sort of catharsis—or perhaps the food and shelter had simply brought him needed relief. He looked up from his bowl and said, "You said your last name was Albrecht, right?"

"That's correct."

"May I call you that?"

"Certainly."

"Mine is Hagan. Karl Hagan."

"Yes, I remember."

The men continued eating in silence. After Wilhelm finished his third bowl, he tilted the cook pot to see how much soup—or mulligan stew, as Hagan had called it—remained. Two pieces of potato and a chunk of onion swam in shallow broth, perhaps half a bowl's worth.

"You can finish it," the Yank said.

"Are you sure?"

"All yours, Popeye. Too bad we don't have spinach for you."

"Very kind of you," Wilhelm said. He ate until nothing remained but a mouthful of broth, then put down the spoon, lifted the bowl, and drank off its final contents. Hagan took the bowls and stacked the cookware and utensils on the end of the table.

"I'll wash all these in the lake tomorrow," the Yank said. "I'm going to bed."

Hagan lifted his knapsack, dug out the blankets of parachute silk, and selected one for himself. Shuffled toward one of the bedrooms like a very old and tired man. At the bedroom door, he turned back toward Wilhelm.

"Put out the lamp before you go to bed, will you?" Hagan said.

"Of course," Wilhelm answered.

The American disappeared into the bedroom. The door squeaked on little-used hinges as he closed it.

Wilhelm sat at the table and stared into the oil lamp's yellow flame. The flame imprinted itself on his retinas, and he could still see the oblong tongue of fire when he closed his eyes. The ghost flame floated in darkness like the funeral pyre of a distant tanker torpedoed in the North Atlantic. Wilhelm rested his head in his hands. He began to nod off, and he startled awake when his elbows slipped on the table.

What makes the difference, he asked himself, *between an enemy and a friend?* On the run from his own compatriots and having befriended an American, Wilhelm felt he should find some lesson, some concluding moral. But in his exhausted state, he could not work his mind toward that harbor.

Maybe it will come to me, Wilhelm mused, *as a final thought when the SS stands me in front of a wall.*

He got up from the table and lifted the makeshift silk blanket that Hagan had left out for him. Carried the blanket to the other bedroom and placed it on the cot. Spread out the blanket, sat on the cot, and took off his boots. His toes cracked as he flexed them. He untied the pistol lanyard from his wrist and stripped off his jacket. Took the Luger from his waistband and placed it on the floor. Unbuckled the American gun belt from his waist and put the holstered Colt on the floor as well.

Wilhelm returned to the main room and gently lifted the oil lamp. He carried the lamp into his bedroom and placed it in a corner. Looked around the room enough to get his bearings. When he felt sure he could find his way to his cot in the dark, he scrolled the lamp's wick down until the flame went out, as if the burning tanker had finally slipped beneath the waves.

28

The Future Doesn't Belong to You

Karl woke to a dawn so heavily frosted that at first he thought snow had fallen. When he stepped outside to relieve himself, his boots crunched on dried grass and fallen leaves fuzzed with rime. The frost looked much like the kind of ice that would form on the B-17's leading edges when flying through mist above the freezing level. The Fort didn't take well to that; she could carry a heavy load of bombs, but not a load of ice. Fuzzy wings meant you needed to get out of icy weather.

The outdoor privy smelled foul, and that concerned Karl. The odor implied recent use. He wondered if he and Albrecht should move immediately. But the thought of another night in the open made him shudder. *Just one more day,* Karl thought, *to get our strength back.* He pissed through the hole in the bench and closed the door behind him. Outside the privy, he took a deep and grateful breath of clean air as he surveyed the forest and lake.

The water's surface lay still and bright silver like a pool of mercury. All around the shore, whitened evergreens rose from the lake on gentle slopes. A cloudless sky stretched overhead, still dark enough in the west for Karl to make out a couple of stars.

From the woodpile, he selected three pieces, all quartered sections of oak. He carried the firewood into the cabin and set it down next to the stove. Opened the stove, took hold of the poker, and stirred the ash. The effort revealed glowing coals.

Piece by piece, Karl placed the firewood into the stove. He stacked the wood crosswise to let air circulate, and he closed and latched the stove door without adding kindling. The coals from the night before still looked hearty enough to ignite fresh firewood by themselves.

At the table, he gathered up an armful of dirty bowls and cookware. Carried them outside and down to the water's edge. The lake's surface no longer stood motionless; a pair of mallards had landed a hundred yards away, and they cut ripples in the shape of twin vees as they swam.

Karl kneeled, put down the cookware, and dipped one of the bowls into the water. Grasped wet sand with his thumb and three fingers and smeared the sand into the bowl. Scrubbed with his fingertips until the bowl looked fairly clean; then he rinsed it and set it aside.

As he continued washing the dishes, he heard aircraft engines and looked up. For several seconds, he scanned the sky, but saw nothing. Then the planes appeared from behind the screen of trees to the east. Six Focke-Wulfs prowled low, no more than three thousand feet above ground level. They held a tight formation, their cruciform shapes black against the morning light. Each aircraft sported a yellow band around the fuselage near the tail. Their engines skirled loudly enough to send a vibration through Karl's rib cage, and the ducks lifted off the water in an explosion of spray and flapping wings.

The fighters flashed across the lake and receded to the west. Karl speculated about their target. Their altitude suggested they intended to strafe troops on the ground instead of engaging bombers in the cold, thin heights. And that implied Allied lines were moving closer.

Good news, if true. Yet Karl knew he'd need a lot of luck to live long enough to reach Allied lines. He also found it strange to interpret a *Luftwaffe* formation as any kind of good omen. For so many months, he'd seen squadron mates fall to *Luftwaffe* guns, and he'd expected to meet his own death the same way. His death now seemed even more certain—except it would happen on the ground instead of in the air.

When he finished washing the dishes and spoons, Karl carried everything back inside. He found the cabin's interior pleasantly warm; the firewood he'd placed in the stove must have caught quickly. Albrecht was up, rummaging through the pantry and cupboard.

"Good morning," Karl said. "What are you looking for?"

Albrecht answered without looking at Karl. He picked up something from a pantry shelf.

"Found it," the German said. "I was hoping someone had left a razor here. There is a fragment of mirror hanging on the wall in my room. I see no shaving powder, but I did find soap." Albrecht waved an ivory-handled straight razor.

"Excellent," Karl said. He scratched his beard. "I'd love to get rid of this bird's nest. Look a little bit less like a hobo."

"First we eat breakfast." The U-boat man lifted a jar from the cupboard. "Pears, perhaps?"

"Anything."

Karl placed the cleaned dishes back in the pantry. He found two forks, and he and the sailor ate the pears right out of the jar. The fruit had a syrupy taste, sweeter than raw pears. It had been cooked so thoroughly that it melted in Karl's mouth like cotton candy at a county fair. When one pear half remained, Albrecht offered it to Karl.

"You gave me the last of the soup," Albrecht said, "so now it's your turn."

"Thanks," Karl said as he speared the pear half. Then he held the jar toward Albrecht. "Don't waste the juice. You drink it."

"Danke."

The German lifted the jar with both hands and drank the syrup. He paused once, to wipe his mouth on his sleeve, then drained the jar completely.

"I'd say I wish we had coffee," Karl said, "but that would be getting greedy."

The U-boat man nodded, swallowed, wiped his mouth again. "I'll warm up some water to shave and wash," he said.

"All right," Karl said. "While you're cleaning up, I'll see if I can catch us some dinner."

Albrecht picked up the cook pot Karl had just scrubbed and took it outside. He returned a minute later with the pot filled with water, and he placed it on the stove. Karl began looking through the fishing tackle the cabin's owner had left. He found a rod fitted with a casting reel, and the reel held a spool of line that looked like braided cotton or linen. Some German fisherman had left an artificial lure tied to the end of the line—just a simple silver spoon with a treble hook. Though Karl had his own rudimentary fishing kit, he decided to use the lure already tied on: After all, the Kraut who owned this rod probably knew the fishing here better than anyone else.

On the pantry floor, Karl also found a landing net. He took the rod and net outside and down to the water's edge. As he looked across the lake, he saw no fish breaking the surface; if they were feeding at all, they were feeding at lower depths.

The lure hung by its hook on one of the rod's line guides. Karl plucked the lure off the guide and let it swing at the end of the line. Clicked the spool release and held the spool with his thumb. Raised the rod over his head and flicked it forward. At the same time, he lightened the pressure he held with his thumb, which allowed the spool to spin and the line to pay out.

The lure sailed out over the water in a long parabola. The sight reminded Karl of lines of tracers arcing from *Luftwaffe* guns. The spoon hit the lake with a muted *sploosh,* and ripples spread from the impact point. The ripples put him in mind of the shock waves of bomb strikes viewed from high altitude, and he wondered if the war had doomed him to see everything through a prism of destruction.

Karl waited a heartbeat to let the lure sink. Then he began turning the reel, retrieving the spoon just fast enough to keep it off the bottom.

No fish struck on his first cast, and he reeled in the lure. Pulled it dripping from the lake. Pressed the spool release, thumbed the spool, cocked his arm for another cast.

And stopped cold.

What in heaven's name am I doing? Karl asked himself. *This could be Keystone Lake back home in Pennsylvania,* he thought, *with me on a day off without a care in the world.*

Except he had all kinds of cares, more than he liked to consider, and they all added up to a very slim chance of survival. What the hell kind of war was this? He'd gotten shot down where the air was so thin he couldn't breathe it, then returned to the earth unharmed under a canopy of silk—and now found himself on a nature hike with an enemy officer.

Madness.

Hell, maybe I already got killed, Karl thought, *and this is the fever dream of a dying brain. Or else I'm in purgatory, doomed to wander a war zone with another soul as lost as me.*

But the weight of the Colt in his pocket reminded him this was all too real. He remained an officer of the United States Army Air Forces, with all the attendant responsibilities—and not a kid playing hooky from school to go fishing, or a troubled shade at large in Hades. *Keep proper vigilance,* he reminded himself. He eyed the opposite shore, turned his neck to watch behind him. No sign of anyone.

Karl let fly with another cast. This time, he didn't hold enough tension with his thumb, and the reel backlashed. The line bunched up around the spool and balled up into a large tangle. Karl cursed under his breath, examined the fouled line. Turned the reel forward and backward and spent the next fifteen minutes untangling the mess he'd made.

If eating depended on my casting skills, he thought, *we'd starve to death at this rate.*

After he'd cleared the backlash, he tried another cast. Better this time. The spoon flew about twenty yards before splashing down, creating no bird's nest inside the reel. Karl waited a thousand one, a thousand two, then began retrieving the lure.

Adrian should be here, Karl thought, *telling me I can't cast worth a damn. Dear God, wouldn't he find this rich? On the lam through Germany with a disillusioned Kraut. If there's a heaven,* Karl mused, *and if Adrian's looking down on me, he's probably laughing his ass off.*

Unless he's mad at me for not turning back when I had the chance.

Karl realized he'd stopped turning the reel's crank, and he'd let the lure settle on the bottom. He tried to start retrieving again, but the spoon's hooks hung up on something.

Great, Karl thought, *now you've done it.* He tugged this way and that, but the lure remained stuck fast. Nothing for it but to pull straight back. *If the line breaks, the line breaks.*

He lowered the rod tip and started walking backward. The line tightened until it sang and vibrated—then fell slack as something gave. Either the line had parted or the lure had pulled free.

Karl started retrieving again and felt the small weight of the lure. So he still had it. *And no, Adrian was all about the mission,* Karl decided.

He wouldn't be angry with me for trying to hit a valuable target inside the Reich. And he wouldn't be laughing at me; he was too serious a guy. He'd say, Now your mission is to survive: Catch some rest, catch some fish, eat, get back your strength, and keep moving.

A fish's strike interrupted Karl's thoughts of his dead friend. The rod jolted as if electrified, and Karl felt the fish surging at the end of the line. He raised the rod tip high to keep tension on the line, and he began cranking the reel. The fish ran in short bursts, quick zigs and zags, but it never pulled hard enough to strip line even though Karl had set the drag lightly. Not a big guy, then.

When Karl reeled his quarry within five yards of the shore, the fish broke the surface. Just a butterscotch flash, then it submerged again. But that glimpse was enough to tell Karl he'd hooked a trout.

That knowledge tilted his thoughts toward mercy. To Karl, a trout was a noble fish, of a higher order than catfish or carp. An ichthyologist might disagree, but it seemed a creature leaping after minnows and stoneflies had evolved further than one scavenging the bottom for dead things. *If it's a little trout,* Karl decided, *I'll let it go.*

The fish made one more show of fighting; it swam hard to Karl's left and made the rod tip dance. It surfaced again, feathery tail wavering, and Karl reeled until it lay in the shallow water at his feet, gills pumping. The lure hung from the fish's lower jaw. A small trout, as Karl had suspected. Maybe seven inches. Not big enough to bother with the landing net.

Karl kneeled, leaned the rod across his thigh, and ran his fingers down the line until he could take hold of the treble hook's shank. As soon as he did so, the trout began to flop and splash. One of the hook points jabbed into Karl's thumb, though not deeply enough to sink the barb. Karl swore, shook his hand, and held up his thumb to examine the puncture.

A small globe of blood oozed from the wound. Karl rinsed it in the water, then took hold of the hook shank again.

"Now hold still," he whispered in English. "I'm trying to do you a favor."

With his other hand, Karl grasped the fish's jaw. It flopped again, more feebly than before. But this time, Karl held its mouth steady and managed to avoid getting jabbed again. All the while, he held the trout under the surface except for its head; he knew the fish would have a better chance of surviving if he kept it in the water and didn't break the mucus membrane that enveloped its body.

With a twist of his thumb, he wrenched the hook free. If he'd been trout fishing back home in Pennsylvania, he'd have used the pliers he carried just for this purpose, but today he made do with his own pierced thumb. When he let go of the fish, it flashed away like a miniature torpedo, leaving a swirl of mud and bubbles.

Karl held the lure in front of his face and examined the hooks. Two of them had bent from when he'd gotten snagged earlier. He looked on the ground until he found a pebble about the size of a golf ball, and he used that to bend the hooks back to their original shape.

He set to cast again, but an unpleasant thought made him pause. Today he fished to survive; would he ever again fish for pleasure, just to enjoy nature? Doubtful.

No, he told himself, *you gotta stop thinking like that.* But another part of his mind argued: *It's the truth.*

Then don't think about it, he decided. *Think about what you'll do during the next couple of hours. Maybe the next couple of days. But not beyond that. Stop thinking about a future that doesn't belong to you any more than this rod and reel or this cabin.*

Karl flung the lure again, made a nice long cast with no tangle or backlash. That made him feel a bit better. One of those little achievements, like an especially smooth landing or a good joke that made your buddies laugh.

He retrieved without getting a nibble, and he continued casting, sometimes to his left, sometimes straight out in front, sometimes toward his right. He lost count of his casts, never got a bite, and began to wonder if the first fish was the only one he'd get today.

Just when he began thinking about either trying a different lure or a different spot, the rod came alive. The line went tight and pulled hard. Karl hauled back on the rod to set the hook.

The hook's sting must have angered the fish—and this one felt strong. It strained against the line, even took out a few more feet of line as the drag whined. The rod bent into a U, and Karl reminded himself not to try to horse this fish to the net. Good way to break the line. Just let him run and get tired.

He held just enough pressure to keep the line taut, and tried to reel in only when the fish turned and ran toward him. Then it zagged right, and the water seemed to boil where the fish surfaced.

Karl saw that he'd hooked a big German brown trout. Maybe it would go fifteen pounds. The fish thrashed on top of the water like a bass, threw spray with its tail, then dived again. Karl pulled a little harder to give the trout more resistance. Sometimes a big fish like that could be smart enough to swim around an underwater snag and pop the line.

The fish found no snag, but it put up a hard fight. Its strength and will to live transmitted up the line, down the rod, and into Karl's hands. He played the fish for twenty minutes before he began bringing it closer to shore. Karl would reel in five or six feet, then lose three or four.

But eventually, through patience, he brought the fish within reach. It lay in the shallows, gossamer fins wavering. Flush from the fight, its underbelly glowed yellow, and dark speckles covered its back.

A shame to take its life, Karl thought, *but we have to eat.*

With one hand, he reached behind him and found the net handle. Pulled on the rod with his left hand, scooped the net with his right, and lifted the trout, dripping, from the lake.

29

Machines, Wounded and Bleeding

Wilhelm had known this idyll at a lakeside cabin must end soon and could end badly. In the late afternoon, after he and the Yank had finished the fried trout, the end came. Stray snowflakes began spiraling across the windowpanes, and Wilhelm felt sleepy amid the cabin's warmth and wood smoke. Hagan took a bucket of warm water into his room to shave and wash.

Wilhelm sat alone at the table and sipped coffee—yes, coffee, though he could hardly believe it. They had found a half-empty bag of grounds in the pantry, and Hagan made what he called "coffee the cowboy way." He'd boiled water, stirred in the coffee, then dropped in a cold stone to settle the grounds. Wilhelm found the coffee quite passable, and he was holding the warm cup in his hands when he heard footsteps approaching the cabin.

"Hagan," Wilhelm called out by way of warning.

He put down the coffee and reached for his Luger. Felt spiders crawling through his gut. Stood with his back to the wall, facing the door. He wished he'd grabbed the Colt he'd taken from the dead American gunner, the better to claim to be a Yank. But that weapon remained in its holster on the floor beside his cot.

Hagan did not answer Wilhelm's call; perhaps he hadn't heard it. The footsteps approached the cabin door. The door burst open with a hard kick.

In the doorway stood a white-headed old man pointing a rifle. Gray stubble softened the lines of his jaw. He leveled the muzzle in Wilhelm's direction just as Wilhelm raised his Luger.

Neither man fired.

"What are you doing here?" the man shouted. "Why are you in my lodge?"

The man wore hunting clothes: a woolen field jacket and an Alpine hat. He carried an old bolt-action *Gewehr* 1888, and now he held it with his cheek on the stock, one eye closed, and the other peering down the barrel at the center of Wilhelm's chest.

"Uh, we . . . I am a s-soldier," Wilhelm stammered. "I got separated from my unit. I am sorry to trespass, but—"

"You don't look like a soldier," the old man snapped. "Where is your uniform? What is your rank? You are a deserter or a thief."

Before Wilhelm could answer, Hagan threw open the door to his room. Crouched low in the doorway, his cheeks pinked by a fresh shave. Gripped his .45 with both hands.

The old man swung the rifle toward Hagan and fired. Wood chips flew from the doorjamb. When the old man started to work the bolt on his antique weapon, Wilhelm struck. He sprang from the table and drove a left hook into the man's jaw. Stunned, the old man staggered backward into the wall and dropped the rifle.

"Don't make us hurt you," Hagan said in German.

Wilhelm stood over the man and held the Luger loosely, finger outside the trigger guard. The man looked up, wide-eyed. Then he closed his eyes, hard. Waiting for the shot, apparently. But he said nothing.

"I understand," Wilhelm said. "You fear for your life. Sir, we have no intention of harming you."

The old man opened his eyes and said, "Go to hell." Rubbed his jaw. Glared up at Wilhelm.

"We are not robbers," Wilhelm continued, "and we beg your pardon. Just let us go on our way." He kicked the rifle out of the man's reach.

"Are you deserters?" the man asked. "Do you not have the guts to defend your Fatherland?"

The question stung, and Wilhelm didn't answer. At this point, he wasn't sure whether to play a downed American, but it really no longer mattered: Whether the old man thought they were deserters or Allied aviators, he would surely alert authorities as soon as he could hike to a telephone. But he was an innocent civilian, merely protecting his property. Shooting him was out of the question.

Hagan rose from his crouch, Colt now held with one hand. "All right," he said in German, "I guess we need to get moving."

Wilhelm reached down and picked up the man's rifle. He and Hagan couldn't leave a long-range weapon in the hands of someone who might take shots at them.

"Who are you people?" the man demanded.

"I told you," Wilhelm said. "We are trying to make our way back to our unit. As a matter of security to the Fatherland, you should forget you ever saw us."

Very little chance of that, Wilhelm thought. *The old man will surely tell someone. If the SS brings dogs, the animals will identify our scent here and follow it. We will leave tracks in the snow, too, unless it snows a lot harder and covers them.*

Wilhelm felt events closing in on him, much the way ocean swells could converge and form a rogue wave. Those mountains of water had tossed his U-boat like a toy. Crewmen could only hold on and pray; they would either survive or not, and there was little they could do about it.

"Hagan," Wilhelm said. "I hate to do this, but we should tie him up."

"Yeah," the Yank said, "I guess you're right."

Hagan hurried around the cabin, gathering up gear. He grabbed a jar of tomatoes from the cupboard and stuffed it into his knapsack. Then he pulled a length of parachute cord from the knapsack and handed the cord to Wilhelm.

Wilhelm pulled a chair from the table and placed it in the middle of the room. "Sir," he said, "please have a seat."

The old man didn't move.

"Get in the chair!" Hagan shouted. He pointed his handgun. The old man glared as he took his seat.

Wilhelm jammed his Luger into his waistband. Tied the man's hands behind the back of the chair, then tied his feet to the chair's front legs. He took care not to pull the bonds so tightly that they'd cut off circulation. He knew that kindness would cost them: The man would eventually free himself. But perhaps this would delay him long enough to give them a chance to escape.

When he finished the last knot, Wilhelm went to his room, found his American pistol belt, and buckled it on. Wrapped up the parachute silk that had served as a blanket. Tucked the rifle into the crook of his arm. Then he and Hagan left the cabin. Wilhelm did not look back at the old man, shouting curses at them as they departed.

Snow fell harder now. Flakes collected in the curls of fallen leaves, and ice pellets mixed with the snow. The ice made ticking sounds as it struck Wilhelm's jacket, and the pellets stirred the lake surface with endless tiny ripples.

"Let's just keep to the woods," Wilhelm said. "It doesn't matter which way we go, except away from here."

"Yeah," Hagan answered, "I'm sure he'll head for the nearest phone as soon as he works himself loose."

The two men followed the shoreline until the lake narrowed at a cove. A wooded hillside rose from the opposite shore, and a narrow stream spilled into the lake at the cove's tip. As they splashed across the stream, Wilhelm noticed ice forming in the still pools. A dusting of snow covered each crust of ice.

Cold began to seep through Wilhelm's jacket. He did not relish the thought of another night out in the wilderness, but he saw no other option. Navigating the straits between German and Allied lines presented plenty of danger even in ideal conditions. With the added threat of freezing to death, the task seemed impossible. The fugitives could only take one day at a time—one hour at a time, really.

The Yank led the way up the forested rise. As they trekked deeper into the timber, Wilhelm forced his mind onto any train of thought except the cold. He tried to recall more of Captain Slocum's adventures on his sail around the world. The wily old sea dog spread carpet tacks across his deck when he slept in hostile harbors. That way, the yelps of barefoot pirates would wake him in time to fight back.

Slocum recorded no encounter that forced him to kill—a record

Wilhelm now envied. The American sailor glided into his home port unblooded, though not without a reminder of man's propensity for killing. While Slocum sailed on his voyage of peace and self-discovery, the Spanish-American war broke out. Just north of the equator, he spotted the mast and flags of the battleship *Oregon*. Her signals queried, "Are there any men-of-war about?" Slocum signaled no, and the *Oregon* steamed on its way.

And in those waters near the equator, Wilhelm thought, *Slocum would have been warm. Deliciously warm.*

Wilhelm willed his mind onto other bearings. After all, he'd begun thinking of Slocum's journey on the *Spray* expressly to avoid dwelling on the cold. And he reminded himself not to get too envious of Captain Joshua Slocum, given the old mariner's eventual fate. In 1909, he set sail on the *Spray* for another voyage, and he was never seen again.

Dusk descended before the men made three kilometers, and the snow never let up. The evening brought a heavy quiet; Wilhelm heard neither bark nor engine—and no shouts or shots or anything else to suggest pursuers on their trail. But he knew not to take comfort in that. Eventually, the old man would alert authorities. The only question was how long the cord would hold him.

The light among the trees turned violet as night came on. When the ticking sounds stopped, Wilhelm knew the ice pellets had given way to pure snow. Maybe the snow would erase their tracks. He felt flakes caressing his face like frozen feathers, and he began to shiver. The men finally stopped when it became too dark to find their way through the forest.

"Still got your flashlight?" Hagan asked in English.

"Yes," Wilhelm said, "but its batteries are weak."

"All right. I'll make this as quick as I can. Gimme some light, and I'll rig up a little tent to keep the snow off us."

Wilhelm wished the Yank had thought of that before the daylight ran out—but then changed his mind. They'd probably made best use of visibility by getting as much distance from the cabin as possible. He took the flashlight from his jacket pocket and thumbed the switch. The light cast a pale yellow beam hardly bright enough to penetrate two meters of the darkness.

"Probably the last use we'll get out of that thing," the Yank said. He kicked through snow-covered leaves, apparently looking for something. Found a crooked branch, tossed it aside.

"What do you need?" Wilhelm asked.

"A fairly straight stick."

Wilhelm joined Hagan in shuffling through the decaying leaves and other detritus on the forest floor. Just as he found a branch that might answer for the task, the flashlight's beam faded completely.

"Oh, great," Hagan said.

With overcast hiding the moon, the woods turned black as bilge-water. Wilhelm heard Hagan pulling at his clothing, perhaps opening pockets. The Yank muttered curses, fumbled in the dark. Then Wilhelm heard the rattle of matchsticks and the rasp of a match strike.

Hagan's face appeared in the smoky flare of the match.

"Take these," he said. Handed the matchbox to Wilhelm—the same matches they'd taken days ago from the dead man by the river. "Let's try not to use too many."

The Yank shook out the match held between his thumb and fore-finger. By feel, Wilhelm took another from the box and lit it. Working by the light of the second match, Hagan opened his pack and found parachute cord. Just as the American reached for the straight branch Wilhelm had found, the match burned down close to Wilhelm's fingers. He felt the heat, shook out the match, and dropped it. By the time he lit another, Hagan had begun lashing the branch to a tree trunk. When that match burned down, he shook it out and lit yet another. Now Hagan was spreading out parachute silk.

The effect was like watching a motion picture with frames missing. Each match gave Hagan enough illumination to start a small task such as tying a knot. The Yank would complete the task in darkness, then begin the next step by the light of a fresh match. Effective enough, Wilhelm noted, but they burned through their limited matches at a spendthrift's pace. When Hagan finished staking out the corners of the makeshift pup tent, only two sticks remained in the matchbox.

"Might as well save those two," Hagan said. "We can eat in the dark."

The Yank took more parachute cloth from his knapsack, and Wilhelm ducked into the pup tent and put down the rifle he'd taken from the old man. With parachute cloth, Hagan and Wilhelm wrapped themselves against the cold as best they could. Wilhelm heard clinks of glass as Hagan opened the jar of cooked tomatoes he'd taken from the cabin. A few seconds later, Hagan handed over the jar. Working by feel, Wilhelm fished a tomato from the jar and ate using his fingers. The tomato had little taste, but it was better than nothing, and Wilhelm liked the way the seeds popped between his molars.

"How far do you think we will get?" Wilhelm asked, wiping his fingers on his trousers. He still worried about dogs and scent trails.

"Your guess is good as mine," Hagan said in his own language. "We made it this far."

"I do not take much comfort in that," Wilhelm said, also in English. "I do not believe we have an endless supply of luck."

"Me neither. And like I said, you gotta learn to talk like an American if I'm gonna pass you off as my navigator. Use your contractions. You *don't* take much comfort in that."

Affecting an American accent seemed a hopeless task to Wilhelm, but he supposed it might help pass the time.

"I *don't* know," Wilhelm said. Tried to flatten his vowels.

"Better. All right, let's try some Americanisms."

"Like what?"

"Lemme think." The Yank paused for a moment. "Well, there's one," he said. "Say 'lemme think.'"

"Let me think."

"No. Drop the *T* and run the words together like you've just had two beers."

Wilhelm groaned. "Lemme think," he said.

"A little better." Hagan paused again. "All right, how about this. Say 'Get your hands off me, you goose-stepping Kraut bastard.'"

"That is not funny."

"It's not meant to be. It might save your life. Try it."

Wilhelm repeated the sentence. Attempting the accent made him feel like a bad actor in an amateur play.

"Not real convincing," Hagan said. "Try it again."

Wilhelm repeated the line once more. It didn't sound right, so he said, "Let me hear you say it again."

The Yank uttered the sentence, and Wilhelm tried to mimic him.

"Maybe a little better," Hagan said. "If we do get caught, say one or two things in English, but keep it to a minimum. Tell 'em you studied German in college."

"I hope to tell them nothing at all."

"Yeah, but it helps to have a plan. If you playact as my navigator, you'll need to know a few things about my unit, too."

"Such as?"

"If we get interrogated, we don't have to give anything but name, rank, and serial number. You're a first lieutenant. But if you need more back story, you're from the 94th Bomb Group, 331st Squadron. Repeat that back to me."

"Ninety-fourth Bomb Group, 331st Squadron," Wilhelm said in English.

"Exactly. They know our unit designations, so you'll need to get that right. Our ship's name was *Hellstorm*. She had a square *A* on the tail."

"*Hellstorm*. Appropriate."

Hagan paused. He stared past Wilhelm as if suddenly troubled.

"Those dog tags I gave you might keep you alive," the Yank said, "but there's a problem. I should have thought of it before now."

"What is that?"

"If we wind up in a stalag and they process you under Meade's name and serial number, they'll send that information to the Red Cross. His wife will get word that her husband is safe in a prison camp."

Wilhelm had not considered that, either. He chided himself for his thoughtlessness. "That won't do," he said.

"You're damned right it won't do."

Wilhelm pulled the chain from under his shirt. He started to lift it from around his neck.

"No," the Yank said. "Keep them. Just—lemme think for a minute."

Hagan sat quietly for a few moments. Wilhelm let the dog tags dangle between his fingers. He tried to imagine the grief of a wife getting a telegram saying her husband is missing. But how much worse to receive false hope that's later dashed?

"Throw these things away if you must," Wilhelm said.

"No. Keep them, like I said. If we get captured, let the SS or who-ever see them to make it look like you're one of us. But when they start doing paperwork," Hagan added, "you don't give them Meade's real name and number. Make up a name, lose the dog tags, do whatever you gotta do."

Wilhelm placed the tags back into place under his shirt and said, "I give you my word."

"Good."

Smart thinking by the Yank, Wilhelm believed, *to plan for a bad turn of events.* Wilhelm certainly had seen the value of preparing for emergencies. His crew had practiced crash dives, firefighting, and other procedures until they became second nature. He had pored over technical manuals constantly, because one never knew when a little tidbit of knowledge might save the day. Hagan had probably trained similarly as a bomber pilot. And like Wilhelm, he had likely begun his career by thinking of it as a grand adventure. Wilhelm wondered about that, so he decided to ask.

"When I joined the navy," Wilhelm said, "I thought it would be all glory, but I found out differently very quickly after the war started."

"Yeah, I know what you mean."

"When did that happen for you?" Wilhelm asked. "If you do not mind my asking."

"If you *don't* mind my asking," Hagan said. "And I don't."

"Don't," Wilhelm repeated. The contractions still sounded unnatural.

The Yank let a few moments pass before answering. "It wasn't one of the big missions," he said finally. "It was one that probably didn't even make the newspapers."

Hagan told of a mission he'd flown back in June, days after the Allied invasion at Normandy. The Eighth sent a relatively small force— thirty planes—to hit an airfield near Leipzig. His crew suffered no injuries and his plane sustained no damage.

"But when we got back to Rougham," the Yank said, "one of the ships that arrived after us shot up a red flare in the landing pattern. That meant wounded aboard. They had taken some flak on the run-in, and then they got bounced by fighters. The ship was *Cajun Cassie.* Jackie Bilodeau was the aircraft commander. Louisiana boy."

Hagan explained how he watched *Cajun Cassie* taxi into the hardstand next to his own aircraft, *Hellstorm.* Bilodeau's bomber had suffered heavy damage; the rudder and vertical stabilizer looked torn as if clawed by some giant predator. Shrapnel had peppered the fuselage and slashed holes in the wings. Near the right waist gunner, a cannon round had opened a puncture the size of a basketball. The Fortress leaked fluid as it groaned to a stop.

"At first, I thought she was losing oil or brake fluid," Hagan said. "But it was leaking from the seams of the waist door. And it was red. The airplane itself was dripping blood."

A shell had torn off a gunner's leg, Hagan recalled, and the radio operator's arm had to be amputated later. The bombardier and the right waist gunner were dead.

"When the ground crew opened the waist door," Hagan said, "blood poured out. Fifty-caliber casings were floating in it. Just dripped into a pool underneath, like the airplane was a big whale somebody had harpooned."

Wilhelm did not know how to respond to such a story. He had seen people lose their lives in awful ways, but he had never witnessed anything quite like the blood-spattered horror described by Hagan. Saying the wrong thing now seemed worse than saying nothing, so Wilhelm kept silent. After a few minutes, the Yank spoke up again.

"I can still see that," he said. "Like it was yesterday. I can see it right now."

"I suppose we have all seen things we wish we could erase."

They talked no more that night, and Wilhelm slept fitfully. The cold kept him awake for much of the time. When he managed to fall asleep, he dreamed of a U-boat cruising submerged, trailing swirls of blood.

30

Improvising on the Verge of Disaster

At first light, a buzzing assaulted Karl's ears. The sound came to him in that middle world between sleep and wakefulness, and the conscious part of his mind worked to distinguish between dream and reality. The noise persisted and grew more distinct as he drifted closer to full awareness, like runway lights growing brighter as he descended from a cloud deck.

Karl jolted to complete alertness when he recognized the noise's source: Once more, it was that damned *Storch*.

He shook Albrecht. "Get up," Karl hissed. "They're looking for us again."

The U-boat man sat bolt upright. Tossed aside his parachute cloth blanket as if he needed about half a second to wake up. Probably got conditioned to do that during his sea duty.

"The old man reported us," Albrecht said.

"Was just a matter of time." Evidently, the cord had not held the old man for long.

"Strike the tent?"

"No, let's leave it," Karl said. "Just get ready to move."

The *Storch*'s engine grew fainter. Karl crawled from under the makeshift tent and scanned upward through the snow-lined trees. He caught no glimpse of the aircraft. Two inches of fresh snow lay on the ground, but as long as Karl and the German stayed inside the woods, a pilot would have a hard time spotting their tracks.

Karl stuffed a blanket into his pack. Grabbed his matches and fold-ing knife, tossed them into one of the flasks of his survival kit. Dropped the kit into his pack. Drew his Colt from his pocket and checked its status: round chambered, hammer cocked, thumb safety engaged. Tied the pistol's lanyard around his wrist and pulled the knot tight with his teeth. Albrecht emerged from the tent with his Luger in hand.

"You probably should ditch that Luger," Karl said in English.

"'Ditch' it?"

"Drop it when we get away from the tent. Leave that old man's rifle, too. If you gotta use a weapon, use that .45 I gave you. Makes you look more like an American."

"Very good."

The *Storch*'s engine grew louder. Coming back for another pass on the grid. But they had outwitted the search plane before; maybe they could do it again, Karl thought.

"Remember," Karl said. "When that thing gets close, just get up against a tree and hold still."

"*Ja.*"

In the early-morning light, Karl led through the woods. Lacking a detailed map, he had no idea where he was going except generally farther from the old man's cabin. A few hundred yards from the tent, Albrecht tossed away his Luger. The German pistol skittered on the forest floor. The U-boat man pulled out his wallet, removed a card, and threw that away, too.

The *Storch*'s engine grew louder, and Karl looked up to find the aircraft banking just a couple hundred feet above the treetops. The thing flew so close, he could make out the cord attached to the pilot's leather flying helmet. Karl backed up against a tree and stood still. Looked over at Albrecht, who had done the same. Karl listened to the aircraft pass overhead, and he watched it level its wings and take up a new heading. At first, he heard only its engine and prop. But as the aircraft droned farther away, he heard barking. Then indistinct shouts.

"Do you hear that?" Karl asked.

Albrecht looked up at the sky, shook his head. But then his eyes widened as the barking grew louder.

"Damn it," Karl said. "They're coming."

The sailor glanced at the snow-covered forest floor, and Karl knew what he was thinking: If they find our tracks, they have us.

Karl fought a surge of panic; for an instant, he felt like a field mouse trying hopelessly to hide from a circling hawk. "We gotta move," he said.

The two fugitives began running through the forest at a quick jog. Twice, when the *Storch* flew near, they leaned close to tree trunks, panting. The land pitched downward, and Karl hoped that meant there was a shallow stream at the bottom of a cut, which they could cross and break up their tracks in the snow.

The slope did not lead to a stream. At the base of the hill lay the curve of a paved road. Through the trees, Karl saw trucks moving along the road. Military trucks. Black *Balkenkreuz* crosses painted on the sides, just like on the Focke-Wulfs.

"Son of a bitch," Karl muttered under his breath.

"Let's stay up on the hill and keep to the trees," Albrecht said. "That way." He pointed roughly north; Karl didn't take the time to dig out his pocket compass. Navigating no longer mattered, anyway; hiding was the only goal. With dogs and men behind them, and troops on the road in front, Karl felt the options narrowing by the second.

They followed the hill's contour, climbing to stay well above the road. Karl stumbled and went down on both knees. When he got up, patches of snow stuck to his lower trousers. The curve continued into a tight switchback, and the two men found themselves in a tongue of forest looped by pavement. The barking grew louder.

"We're gonna have to take a chance and cross that road," Karl said. "Maybe the woods get deeper on the other side."

Albrecht nodded. Both men let themselves slide and stumble downhill. About fifty yards from the road, Karl grabbed a sapling to stop himself, and he raised a hand to motion for Albrecht to stop, too.

"I hear more traffic," Karl said. "Let's wait for it to pass, then double-time it across the pavement."

The rumble of heavy tires increased, and two more trucks passed.

Karl listened closely to make sure the vehicles kept moving. When the noise died away, he whispered, "Let's move."

He jogged down to the base of the hill, his knapsack bouncing across his shoulder blades. Heard Albrecht's footsteps right behind him. Crouched at the forest's edge and looked both ways. He couldn't see far in either direction because of the curve's sharpness. But he saw no trucks or soldiers in his limited field of view, so he stood up and charged across the road. Albrecht followed close behind. Just as they entered the woods on the far side, another truck whooshed around the curve.

Karl did not look back. For a moment, he held out hope that they hadn't been spotted. But then, he heard the truck screech and groan to a stop. Doors slammed. Shouts rose. Karl could make out the German:

"Halt!"

"Which way?"

"There! I think I saw two!"

The two men sprinted through the forest. Albrecht pulled slightly ahead of Karl. His boots threw little showers of snow.

A rifle shot cracked behind them. Neither man fell. A warning shot, perhaps? Karl didn't care. He simply ran. Madly. Hopelessly. Low-hanging evergreen boughs slapped his face. His lungs burned.

The fugitives scrambled up a wooded rise, then slid down the hill's far side. The knapsack caught on a branch and tore from Karl's shoulders. He left it.

Somewhere through the trees, he heard engines gunning, more doors slamming. Yaps of more dogs. Another rifle shot split the morning. Bark flew from a tree just to Karl's right.

"Stop!" a voice commanded.

"Zeus," another voice called. "Attack!"

Did I hear "Zeus"?

Karl did not have to wonder long. He heard the thumps of fast paws behind him.

And then the dog was on him, all teeth and snarls. The animal grabbed him by his trousers. Karl felt teeth sink into the back of his left thigh. He tumbled to the ground. Fell hard on his shoulder. Rolled to find a German shepherd leaping for his throat. Lips curled back to reveal flashing teeth. Karl blocked with his elbows to keep the animal off his head and neck.

The dog grabbed Karl's forearm. Karl felt teeth break the skin—teeth like spikes. With his free hand, he grabbed at the dog's collar. The animal fought and writhed; Karl had no idea a damned dog could be so strong and fast.

From somewhere out of Karl's field of vision, Albrecht tackled the animal. Grabbed it around its barrel chest. Sprawled forward and drove the dog off of Karl.

"Just run!" Karl shouted.

Albrecht didn't answer. Now the dog had a mouthful of the sailor's jacket and was shaking him the way a terrier might shake a rat.

Just as Karl tried to get up to help Albrecht, a voice called out from a few feet away.

"Zeus, release. You pigs, do not move or I shoot!"

The dog let go of Albrecht. Karl looked up to see four German soldiers. Three of them pointed their Mausers in his direction. The fourth aimed a machine pistol at Albrecht. Karl couldn't identify the weapon, but it reminded him of a Thompson submachine gun. The dog trotted to the man with the machine pistol.

All four soldiers wore camo field uniforms. On one collar, the man with the pistol wore the rank of *hauptscharführer*, a senior NCO. On the other collar, he wore the runes of the SS. A *totenkopf* insignia gleamed on his field cap. The man's mouth was set in a thin, dark line. Salt-and-pepper hair trimmed close.

"Cowards," the *hauptscharführer* said. "We know how to deal with deserters."

With his good arm, Karl pressed himself up from the ground. Raised the other arm, fingers spread. Blood from the dog's bite trickled down his arm. He pretended not to understand what the soldiers were saying.

"Do any of you sprecken zee English?" Karl asked in mispronounced, gobbledygook German.

The *hauptscharführer* frowned. "Are you American?" he asked. His English was accented, but fluent. "You look more like deserters. Cowards and deserters."

"Yeah, I'm an American. I stole some clothes to blend in. But don't take my word for it. I got my identification—" Karl started to reach for the folio with his ID, but stopped himself. Good way to get shot. "I got my ID on me," he continued. "It's in the right hip pocket.

My weapon's in my pants pocket. I'm not going to reach for it—don't shoot me."

"Get up," the SS man said. "Slowly."

Karl rose to his feet. Winced from the pain in his thigh where the dog had bitten him. It hurt like hell, but he had no trouble standing up. Apparently, those razor teeth had ripped only skin and not muscle.

"Who are you?" the German demanded.

"I'm a U.S. pilot. We got shot down about a week ago."

Karl stood with his arms held high. Albrecht lay still and said nothing.

"Search him," the *hauptscharführer* ordered in German.

One of the other men, an SS corporal, slung his rifle over his shoulder and stepped forward. Patted down Karl's sleeves and pockets. Found the Colt, with the lanyard tied to Karl's wrist. The corporal drew a long-bladed knife, cut the lanyard, and stepped back to examine the pistol.

"United States issue," the soldier said in German.

"Give me that," the *hauptscharführer* said. Took the weapon from his underling and placed it in a deep pocket of his tunic.

The soldier continued frisking Karl. He found the ID folder, opened it, eyed the identification card, looked back at Karl. Held the card at such an angle that Karl could see its familiar wording: *WAR DEPARTMENT, The Adjutant General's Office, Karl Robert Hagan, First Lieutenant.* Photo with his tie tucked into his shirt.

"Seems to be him," the corporal said.

The *hauptscharführer* held out his hand for the ID, and the soldier handed it over. The head man examined the card, grunted. Placed it in his pocket with the Colt.

"You," the *hauptscharführer* barked in English at Albrecht. "Get up." Motioned with his pistol barrel for the corporal to search Albrecht.

"He's my navigator," Karl said. "Like I said, we were shot down—"

"Shut up," the *hauptscharführer* said.

The corporal began frisking Albrecht—who looked more pale than Karl had ever seen. The U-boat man looked at Karl, then down at the ground.

Don't lose it, Karl thought. *For both our sakes.*

Albrecht lifted his eyes and stared straight ahead. The corporal found Albrecht's .45 and handed over that weapon to his boss as well.

"What were you flying?" the *hauptscharführer* asked.

"I don't remember," Albrecht said. "Lemme think."

The corporal glared at Albrecht for a moment. Punched him in the stomach. Albrecht doubled over. Groaned, sank to his knees.

Good, Karl thought. *Now don't push your luck.*

"Does that refresh your memory?" the *hauptscharführer* asked.

Albrecht sucked in two ragged breaths, then looked up. "A B-17 Flying Fortress," he said.

The corporal grabbed him by the collar and hauled him back up to a standing position. Frisked some more until he found Albrecht's wallet. Found nothing but a family photo. The corporal examined the photo, flipped it over.

Karl felt his heart start to pound. What if Albrecht had written a date—or anything else—on the back of that picture in German?

Apparently, Albrecht had not. The corporal tossed away the photo and shook the wallet.

"Where is your identification?" the corporal asked.

"I lost it when I jumped out," Albrecht said in English.

Bailed *out,* Karl thought. *You mean you lost it when you* bailed *out. Didn't think to cover that.*

"But I got my dog tags," Albrecht added. Lame attempt at an American accent.

But apparently it was good enough. When Albrecht fished the tail gunner's dog tags from around his neck, the corporal seemed satisfied. Albrecht glanced over at Karl, met his eyes. Karl tried to remain expressionless.

The *Storch* growled overhead, waggled its wings. Flew so near that Karl could see black wisps of exhaust swirl from the cowling. Two of the SS men waved. *Yeah,* Karl fumed, *they found us, you bastard.*

"March them to the road," the *hauptscharführer* ordered. "We'll turn them over to the *Volkssturm.* They'll be in a stalag by nightfall." Then he turned toward Karl and Albrecht. "I do not need to tell you that if you try to run, we will cut you down."

One of the SS troopers moved around Karl and shoved him from behind. Pushed him back in the direction from which he'd just fled.

Karl couldn't quite judge the attitude of these goons. Were they elated to capture American airmen? Or were they disappointed not to arrest deserters? Had they wanted to satisfy their bloodlust with a summary execution? No matter. Karl decided not to waste time wondering what made an SS killer's day.

"Don't look so sad, Yank," the *hauptscharführer* said. "Your war is over. If it were up to me, I would shoot you right here, but Göring wants you fliers taken alive. Now move."

Karl began trudging through the forest. Looked at the boot prints and dog tracks in the snow, wondered if he could have done anything differently. *We should have left the cabin earlier,* he thought. *I was so tired, I wasn't thinking straight.*

In the end, though, maybe it didn't matter. It was a miracle to have evaded capture even this long. And at least the SS had bought Albrecht's story about being a navigator. For now.

But what would happen to Albrecht in the middle of a bunch of Allied aviators in an air prison? It would take a real B-17 crew dog about fifteen seconds to realize Albrecht's story didn't add up.

Can't do anything about that now, Karl thought. *We've lived through the last ten minutes. Just gotta take this one crisis at a time, make it up as we go along. Improvising on the verge of disaster.*

At the road, three trucks waited. Engines idled. Dogs growled. Troopers lit cigarettes. Some of the SS men sneered at Karl and Albrecht. With a loud clang, one of them dropped a tailgate.

"Get in," the *hauptscharführer* said. One of the goons prodded Karl between the shoulder blades with the barrel of a Mauser. Karl sighed and hauled himself aboard the truck. The truck smelled of gun oil and wet German shepherd. Karl wondered how many of *Hellstorm*'s crew had experienced a moment like this. He hoped most of them had. It was better than hitting the ground at a hundred miles an hour with a failed parachute—or getting beaten to death by a mob.

Albrecht climbed in behind Karl. Just after an SS trooper slammed the tailgate closed, Karl heard the *hauptscharführer* bark orders: "Call division. Tell them they weren't deserters. They were two American airmen, and we're bringing them in."

PART III

31

Kriegies

Wilhelm's gut still ached. The SS goon had knocked the wind out of him. The truck rumbled and vibrated, and every bump and pothole sent needles through his midsection. Pain radiated upward into his ribs, which remained tender from the bomb blast back at Bremen. The plan for him to playact as a Yank aviator had worked, but Wilhelm now believed it had bought him only a day or so of life.

I cannot possibly fool the SS for long, he thought, *and I will drag Hagan with me into doom.* He sat beside Hagan in the back of the truck and felt himself sinking into oblivion like a U-boat, powerless and darkened, descending to crush depth.

He lost track of time; one of the SS men had taken his watch. How long before the goon noticed it was a *Kriegsmarine* watch? Just one of a thousand things that could give away Wilhelm's identity at any moment.

After a long drive, the truck rolled to a stop. The *hauptschar-führer* opened the tailgate. One of the SS men prodded Wilhelm with a rifle barrel, and he and Hagan rose from their wooden seats. Wilhelm's eyes had become adjusted to the darkness inside the truck; he emerged blinking into daylight.

Perhaps, Wilhelm thought, *this is the scene of my execution.*

They had stopped at a crossroads in the middle of a forest. Pines with reddish bark lined the highways. A second military truck idled at the crossroads; four uniformed men stood beside it, milling about as if they had been waiting a long time. Wilhelm looked more closely, and he saw that two of them were boys in their teens. Acne and eiderdown on their cheeks. The other two were gray-haired pensioners more suited for retirement home chess games than military operations. These were the *Volkssturm,* a new militia made up of old men, children, and desperation.

Every sinew in Wilhelm's body released tension. So this was not an execution, but a prisoner transfer.

The *hauptscharführer* addressed the *Volkssturm* pensioner, who appeared to be in charge. The SS man spoke brief words Wilhelm couldn't quite hear. Waved his hand dismissively. Stalked back to his vehicle with a look on his face as if he'd just sipped sour milk. Everything about the *hauptscharführer*'s manner radiated contempt for the *Volkssturm.*

The old man angled his Mauser toward Wilhelm and Hagan. He pointed toward the *Volkssturm* truck. He seemed to assume neither of his prisoners spoke German, and Wilhelm did not wish to disabuse him of that notion.

Wilhelm and Hagan climbed into the truck. The two boys joined them in the back of the vehicle, and the old men took their seats in the cab. The engine clattered. The truck heaved and swayed onto the road. Wilhelm exchanged glances with Hagan, and the American shrugged. His manner suggested he felt relieved to be out of the hands of the SS.

Yes, Wilhelm thought, *better the* Volkssturm *than the SS.* But he knew his flimsy ruse as an American flier could still shatter at any moment.

The truck rumbled along for half an hour, and the two boys gaped in silence at Hagan and Wilhelm. One of them tried to look tough, pointing his rifle at Wilhelm's torso. Wilhelm noted the boy's trigger finger. Good—he held it across the trigger guard and not inside it.

The truck stopped, turned, and accelerated. The ride grew smoother. Wilhelm wondered if they had merged onto one of the new autobahns—and he wondered which direction they traveled. No matter. Navigation was no longer up to him. Nothing interrupted the trip except one urgently needed stop for urination along the shoulder of the road. They were indeed on an autobahn; a signpost read FRANKFURT 132 KM. Wilhelm recalled trips to Frankfurt with his parents for shopping or concerts. Now he moved as a stranger in his own land. Sunset reddened the tiled roofs of a distant village.

Darkness fell and the truck rumbled on. When it finally stopped, shouts and barks sounded from outside. Someone pulled open the tarp above the tailgate. Crisscrossing searchlights pierced the night. Guard towers loomed above coils of concertina wire. Rows of barracks stretched into the darkness; Wilhelm could not tell the size of the camp.

"Out," a man ordered in English. He wore the uniform of a *Luftwaffe* sergeant.

Wilhelm instinctively took offense. Part of him wanted to shout, "Is that how you address a naval officer, you cretin?" *But you're no longer a naval officer,* he reminded himself. *You are a fugitive, an outlier. And you had better start thinking like a Yankee flier.* This *instant.*

The two *Volkssturm* boys held the tarp aside for Hagan and Wilhelm to exit. The younger one nodded by way of good-bye, perhaps acknowledging some thin bond forged during their road trip. Hagan jumped from the tailgate. When Wilhelm hesitated a moment, the *Luftwaffe* sergeant grabbed him by the arm and pulled him down.

Trying best as he could to imitate Hagan's lazy vowels, Wilhelm said in English, "Get your hands off me."

Though Hagan made a deliberate effort not to look at Wilhelm, the Yank appeared to smile.

Wilhelm saw nothing to smile about. At any moment, he expected to feel a pistol barrel at the back of his neck. Somehow word of a deserting naval officer would have filtered through the system, and he would be discovered.

But instead of taking Wilhelm away for execution, the guards led him and Hagan to a holding cell.

The room looked little bigger than a boxing ring, with thirty men crowded inside. Some stood mutely. Many sat cross-legged on the floor. A few leaned against the walls. Most of them wore the winged

star sleeve insignia of the United States Army Air Forces, though a
few wore Royal Air Force badges. They ranged in rank from sergeant
to lieutenant colonel. Half were hurt, though none seriously.

Wilhelm saw bandaged hands, burned cheeks, scraped noses. Injuries from bailouts, presumably. Evidently, the fliers with broken
bones and worse injuries had been taken to hospitals. All of the inmates needed a shower; the holding cell smelled like a cattle pen.

"Are you boys Americans?" a man asked. He wore the silver bars of
an American captain.

"Yes, sir," Hagan said. "Air Force."

"Where are your uniforms?"

"We ditched 'em. Tried to blend in. It worked for a little while, but
not long enough."

"Nothing works long enough to keep you out of here."

"You ditched your uniforms?" another man said. "Bullshit." A
sergeant sitting on the floor. Hollow eyes. Stubble from days without
shaving.

"What?" Hagan asked.

"How do we know you ain't some kind of plant? Like a Nazi spy or
something?"

"Aw, shut up, Deke," a third voice called. "If they was spies, the
Nazis would give 'em American uniforms that looked better than
yours ever did."

"Hmph," the sergeant said, looking at Wilhelm. "Then who won
the World Series this year?"

"The Cardinals beat the Browns at Sportsman's Park," Hagan said.
"And I'm not wearing rank, but I'm a lieutenant. The next time you
talk to me, you start with 'sir.'"

The hollow-eyed sergeant did not respond. In the *Kriegsmarine*,
any petty officer would have bolted upright and barked apologies
upon learning he'd shown such insolence to an officer. But the
man's suspicion worried Wilhelm more than his insolence. Were all
these Yanks so attuned to those in their midst who might not belong? What if Hagan had not been so close with a ready answer about
American sporting events?

I'll be lucky to make it through the night, Wilhelm thought, *let
alone weeks or months of captivity.*

"Sir," Hagan asked the captain, "how long have you been here?"

"Couple days. This is what they call a *dulag luft*. A transit camp. I don't think anybody stays here long. They separate the officers from the enlisted and send us somewhere more permanent."

"They gonna feed us?"

"Yeah, they'll be along pretty soon with some grub. But it ain't exactly haute cuisine."

"Grub"? Food, apparently. "Ain't"? What kind of word was "ain't"? Not a contraction of "is not" or any other English phrase. Why couldn't I have fallen in with a British *pilot? Passing as an upper-class Brit would have been so much easier.* Wilhelm resolved to listen closely to this American slang—and to speak as little as possible.

He had another problem to consider as well: What should he do with the dog tags of Carlton Meade, the flier whose bones they'd found in the B-24 wreckage? The tags had served a purpose—they'd gotten him past the SS when first captured. But now that Wilhelm was in the stalag system, if he posed as Meade, that name would get reported through the system—and to the American command as well. Meade's wife would be told her husband was alive and well.

I cannot permit such a cruelty, Wilhelm told himself. *But when and where can I lose these identification tags? Mein Gott, we did not think this through.* No matter what course he steered, every bearing led to depth charges and mines.

After half an hour, the cell's steel door swung open and two *Luftwaffe* guards pushed in a pair of rolling carts. The carts carried sliced loaves of black bread, pitchers, and tin cups.

"Chow time," someone said.

"Ja, chow time, kriegies," one of the guards replied. Obviously, he'd dealt with Americans long enough to learn some of their banter.

But what did he call the prisoners? "Kriegies"? Ah, yes. Kriegsgefangenen. *Prisoners of war.*

The guards left the carts in the room. As the *Luftwaffe* men departed, Wilhelm heard the slide of a bolt as they locked the door. The prisoners passed around the bread and tin cups in a fairly orderly manner. To Wilhelm's relief, these Allied fliers retained enough discipline not to rush at the food and fight over it. When he received his portion, he found himself with two slices of stale bread and a cup of tea already cooled to room temperature.

Wilhelm sat down and ate while staring at the concrete floor, hoping to avoid talking. But a chatty Yank forced him into conversation.

"So, what's your story, Mac?" the Yank stranger asked.

Sweat began to pop from Wilhelm's pores. Here came the first test. He took a large bite of bread. He wanted to look hungry, and at the moment, that required no playacting. And he hoped that talking with his mouth full—something very American—might cover his accent.

"Not much to say," Wilhelm said, chewing. "Got blown up by the Krauts. Bad luck."

"You got that right. Me, I had only four missions to go before getting home to my dame."

What was it with these Yanks and their endless, yammering small talk? This man was worse than Hagan. Wilhelm examined his would-be friend. Red hair and freckles. Perhaps twenty years old. Forehead singed by fire: a raw, oozing streak. Wilhelm noted the man's insignia and tried to remember American ranks: This was a second lieutenant.

"How about you?" the lieutenant continued. "You got a girl at home?"

Wilhelm took a sip of tea and shook his head.

"Oh, I get it. You don't want to talk about it. Maybe she sent you a Dear John letter. Our radio operator's fiancée did that to him, too. Bitch. Shacking up with some draft dodger. She's gonna feel bad when she finds out he's dead."

The lieutenant did not seem suspicious like the insolent sergeant a few feet away. If there was no avoiding conversation with this babbling Yank, then perhaps it presented a training opportunity. *Listen to the slang,* Wilhelm thought, *and try to learn a little. Careful, now.*

"Yeah, she sent me a Dear John letter," Wilhelm said. *What in Neptune's name is a "Dear John" letter? Something bad, apparently.*

"Sorry about that, Mac. It happens."

Wilhelm looked at Hagan, who was following the conversation with great interest. Hagan nodded as if he approved.

The lieutenant babbled on about "dames" and their infidelities, his hard luck, the World Series and how those St. Louis Browns were a bunch of bums. Wilhelm managed one- or two-word answers to inane questions:

"Where are you from?"

"New York."

"What did you fly?"

"B-17."

"What's your name?"

"Ah, Meade. *Thomas* Meade."

That must have sounded American enough; the yammering lieutenant immediately began addressing Wilhelm as "Tommy."

"Good talking with you, Tommy," the lieutenant said. "Heck, maybe Patton will spring us out of here by Christmas."

Wilhelm decided to venture a question. Not just for practice; he really wanted to know.

"When will they let us out of this crowded room?"

The answer gave Wilhelm another threat to worry about.

"They say they'll let us into regular barracks after they take us to interrogation."

32

Hangar Flying

On Karl's third day at the *dulag luft,* a guard ushered him into a windowless room. The room contained only a steel desk, a desk chair, and a wooden stool. The guard motioned for Karl to sit on the stool. As Karl took his seat, the guard exited and locked the door from the outside.

Figures, Karl thought. *They want me to sweat. Shove me in here and plop me down on a low stool. Then give me time to imagine what kind of ogre might come in here to grind my bones to make his bread.*

If they wanted Karl to sweat, it worked. Though he recognized a psychological game when he saw it, he could not help but worry about what was coming. Would they use torture? He hadn't heard of that happening to American POWs, but he couldn't be sure.

Physically, Karl felt a little better than on the night of his arrival at the transit camp. His arm still hurt from the dog bite, but at least it hadn't become infected. A Kraut medic had cleaned and bandaged the wound. The Germans had let him shower and shave, and—to his surprise—they'd replaced his filthy welder's jumpsuit with a USAAF gabardine shirt and a set of G.I. trousers, all supplied by the Red Cross. Over the shirt, he wore an infantry field jacket. The shirt and jacket bore no insignia and hung a little too loose across his shoulders, but at least he looked like a soldier again.

Now, however, he was a soldier with much on his mind. How hard would the Krauts lean on him for information? Would they beat him up? Would they put a gun to his head, pull the trigger if he didn't talk? Thus far, he'd experienced no worse abuse than the occasional shove. But he was in enemy hands, and the enemy could always change tactics.

And what about Albrecht? Would his flimsy cover story hold up under a questioner who might have interrogated hundreds of downed airmen?

The jangling of keys interrupted Karl's worrying.

Name, rank, and serial number, he reminded himself. *Nothing else.*

A guard pushed open the door, then snapped to attention and saluted. The man who entered the room did, indeed, look like a disfigured ogre. Burn scars covered the right side of his face. Black patch over his right eye socket. The man wore a spotless *Luftwaffe* uniform with the insignia of a *hauptmann,* or captain. Karl noted a *Luftwaffe* pilot's badge: an eagle clutching a swastika. The captain was thin and carried himself with casual grace—or was it arrogance? He held a folder stuffed with papers. The man's youth surprised Karl; he looked to be in his middle twenties.

"Good afternoon, Lieutenant Hagan," the captain said. Fluent English, but with a distinct German accent. He offered his hand.

Karl wondered what to do. He had already decided he would not salute a German of any rank. But he'd not considered lesser courtesies. Before he'd had a chance to think it through, he stood, took the captain's hand, and gave it a firm shake.

He immediately regretted it. *Damn it,* he thought, *what if they're filming this from a hidden camera?*

Headline: AMERICAN PILOT MAKES FRIENDS WITH GERMAN CAPTORS.

Think, Karl, he ordered himself. *Think, think, think.*

The Kraut captain seemed to read his mind.

"Do not worry," the captain said. "We are not filming this. We do not seek to embarrass you. As I'm sure you know, we have bigger concerns."

Yeah, he's very fluent, Karl thought. *Smooth bastard, too.*

"I suppose you do," Karl said.

"Allow me to introduce myself," the captain continued. "I am *Hauptmann* Eric Kostler, and I flew 109s before I let one of your Mustangs get behind me for a fraction of a second. That was all it took."

"Do you expect me to feel sorry for you?"

"Not at all. This is purely a professional matter."

Yeah, Karl thought. *You're my pal. We're just a couple of pilots doing a little hangar flying. I might not be the sharpest knife in the drawer, but I ain't that stupid.*

Karl returned to his stool, and the captain took the desk chair. The captain opened the folder and said, "We have a few questions, just to make sure the Red Cross gets the right information and your family knows you are safe."

"Karl Hagan," Karl said. "First Lieutenant. Five-two-four-one-nine-eight-seven-three."

Kostler nodded. "Yes, yes, yes," he said. "Name, rank, and serial number. We have that already." He looked through his papers and glanced up at Karl. "We also know you were assigned to the 94th Bomb Group, 331st Squadron, based at Rougham Field in Bury St Edmunds, England. And that your home is in Pennsylvania, and that you come from a German family."

A twist of nausea churned through Karl's gut. *How could they know so much? Don't let him see you sweat,* Karl thought. *Act like it's no big deal.*

"If you know all about me," Karl said, "then why are we talking?"

"As I said, Lieutenant, it's merely for the benefit of the Red Cross. To make sure they get the right information to the right family. Your country has many people of German extraction. Surely, you are not the only Karl Hagan." Kostler reached into a pocket, withdrew a fountain pen, and unscrewed the cap.

Karl folded his arms. "Karl Hagan," he said. "First Lieutenant. Five-two-four-one-nine-eight-seven-three."

Kostler pushed his chair back and placed his feet on the desk, one boot over the other. He let several seconds pass in silence. Then he said, "You have no idea what I would give to fly again. When I was stationed outside Rome, I met this Italian girl. Ho-ho, what a beauty.

Talk about high performance. What about you? You have a girl back in England?"

"What's that got to do with anything?"

Kostler shrugged. "Relax, Lieutenant. We both know where this war is going. Your armies are closing in. Your bombers are crushing our cities. It's over. And for you and me, it is *really* over. You could not possibly betray your country now, even if you wanted to."

You are *a smooth one, aren't you?* Karl thought. "Well," he said, "since it's over, we might as well not waste each other's time."

Kostler shrugged. "I suppose you're right. But, tell me, what's it like to fly the heavies? I've always flown single-seat fighters, but I think it must be nice to bond with a crew."

Don't even think about steering me into that *subject,* Karl thought. *If you think I feel bad about my crew, you're right. But it won't get you a damned thing. Except maybe an ass-kicking. Might be worth taking a bullet just to put my fist against your jaw.*

When Karl answered with only a silent glare, Kostler again seemed to read his mind. "My apologies," he said. "I don't know if you lost any crewmates, and I didn't mean to bring up a painful topic."

The apology seemed almost genuine. *What the hell?*

"But tell me," the captain continued, "is it fun to fly something that big? I heard one of your colleagues say it's like sitting on your front porch and flying your house."

"Yeah," Karl replied, "it's big." *Not exactly classified information.*

Kostler put down his pen and steepled his fingers. "With all that multiengine time," he said, "you can probably get a good airline job after you get home." He pointed to his eye patch. "Sadly, I do not have that option anymore."

"Sorry about that."

"Yes, well, the fortunes of war."

Kostler picked up his fountain pen again and tapped it on the desk. He let the conversation pause for several seconds. Then he asked, "Did you ever fly one with a Mickey?"

Karl began to sweat. He hoped the captain didn't notice his reaction. No, he'd never flown a B-17 with a Mickey. But how did the Krauts even know about that? And how did they know the slang term? Probably from some dumbass who blabbed—maybe right here in this room.

"Don't know what you're talking about," Karl said. "Mickey Mouse?"

"You know very well what I am talking about," Kostler said. "Your H2X radar."

So that's what this was all about. Radar. The Krauts feared new Allied radar technology as much as the Allies feared new German rockets.

Karl shook his head. "Don't know a thing about it," he said. That was close to the truth. The Pathfinder ships carried the Mickey radar set to locate targets in bad weather and bomb through clouds. But Karl had never flown a Pathfinder.

"Come on, Lieutenant. You must have at least seen one somewhere."

Karl did not speak. He didn't blink. He didn't respond in any way.

Maybe now is when they get tough, Karl thought. He steeled himself for more questions. He steeled himself for a beating. But to Karl's surprise, Kostler changed the subject.

"Very well," the German said. "So that we do not, as you say, waste one another's time, I will tell you something about what's ahead of you."

What followed wasn't an interrogation. It sounded more like an in-briefing. Karl got the impression that somebody had told Kostler to ask about radar. Once he'd done that, he'd filled the square and just didn't care anymore. The gearshift in the conversation came so abruptly that at first, Karl wondered if it was another interrogation technique.

"The *Luftwaffe* runs the camps for downed airmen," Kostler said. "Or we did, in any case. The SS exerts more influence now, so be careful."

Kostler went on to explain that the *Luftwaffe* tried to follow treaties on handling prisoners of war: Officers were housed apart from enlisted men, and officers did not have to perform manual labor for the enemy.

"I would like to say we treat you as fellow airmen," Kostler added, "and officer camps *are* a little better than those for the enlisted. But supplies are growing short for all of us. You, me, everyone. And the camps are getting crowded."

The German flier seemed almost regretful. In some ways, he reminded Karl of Albrecht.

"This is no doubt an unpleasant experience for you," Kostler continued. "But be thankful you wear the insignia of an American officer and pilot. I hear rumors of other kinds of prisons for other kinds of prisoners. Certain guests of the Reich face far worse conditions."

This was no interrogation technique. It was damn near a confession.

"Why are you telling me all this?" Karl asked.

Kostler lifted both hands off the desk. The gesture looked nearly like . . . surrender. He opened his mouth to speak, but said nothing. Several seconds went by in silence.

"One more flight," Kostler said finally, pointing into the air with his index finger. "Do you know what I would give to pull back on the stick and lift into the sky one more time?"

"It gets in your blood," Karl said.

"Yes, it does. A very good way to put it." Kostler folded his arms. "And now, Lieutenant," he said, "I must apologize. You see, I have to follow the rules. I asked you about the H2X radar. You told me nothing. So you must go to the cooler."

"Cooler"?

Kostler must have noticed Karl's expression. "Solitary confinement, Lieutenant Hagan," he said. Then he shouted, "Guards, take this man away."

33

Length, Beam, and Draft

Wilhelm's fears had run wild ever since the guards had taken Hagan for questioning. He knew his turn would come soon, and he supposed this day would not end well for him. Surely, an interrogator familiar with Yank fliers and their ways would see right through him. How could one fake that flat accent, that swagger, that attitude? Yes, imitating a Brit would have been easier; even passing as a Frenchman would have seemed simple by comparison. Wilhelm had spent time in France, speaking the language, eating the food, bedding the women. But America might as well have been the moon.

On the other hand, who would think to look for a *Kriegsmarine* deserter in a transit prison for Allied aviators? Maybe Wilhelm had managed to find the one safe place for him in Germany.

The emotional pendulum reminded him of his first patrol. As the U-boat wolf pack headed to intercept the convoy, he expected to meet a painful death by drowning or suffocation. To spend eternity on the bottom of the Atlantic. But at other moments, he believed his training and the Reich's technology would prove more than adequate. Within a matter of hours, he swayed from cold-sweat terror to senior-cadet bravado. And back again. That day seemed a century ago, the history of someone else. But today, Wilhelm felt the same crests and troughs of fear.

Finally two *Luftwaffe* guards came for him—the same two guards who brought the food carts at each mealtime. Something about their manner seemed different. Whenever they brought food, they exchanged easy banter with the kriegies, perhaps enjoying the chance to perfect their English. Or their American English, to be precise. They seemed to bear these enemy prisoners no ill will. If they were thoughtful men, perhaps they actually felt grateful to the kriegies for giving them a job that didn't involve frozen death on the Eastern Front.

But when they called for "Thomas Meade" and beckoned for Wilhelm to come with them, they seemed . . . sad. Curiously, they had not appeared that way when they'd come for Hagan. What had changed? What did they know? Had Wilhelm's identity already caught up with him?

Yes, a dulag luft *is a highly unlikely place for a navy deserter,* Wilhelm thought. *But we Germans are nothing if not good record keepers. A place for everything, and everything in its place. And a ledger to track it. If an entry does not look right, a phone call or a telegram can clear the matter immediately.*

The guards led Wilhelm down a corridor in silence. He decided to try his act on them; he had precious little time left to practice, and surviving the next hour might depend on his limited thespian skills. In a low voice, concentrating on every syllable, Wilhelm called on new slang he'd learned during the past two days: "What's eating you boys?"

"Your interrogator, Major Treider, is a bastard," one of them said.

"Shh!" the other responded.

The news came like a ping from an American destroyer: Danger was closing in, and there was little Wilhelm could do about it. He resolved simply to hold on to his honor as he defined it. Wilhelm no longer had a country to betray, but he hoped he would not betray himself.

Sunlight burned Wilhelm's eyes when the guards opened the outer door. He squinted, held up his palm to block the glare as if opening a U-boat's hatch into a bright day. He'd not been outside since the night he and Hagan arrived, and the march to the interrogation afforded him his first real view of the camp. Twenty wooden barracks stood along either side of a muddy compound. Tangles of razor wire lined the outer fence, and a pine forest lay beyond the camp perimeter. Kriegies stood outside in knots, talking and smoking. Most wore various combinations of American uniforms; others appeared to be Brits or Canadians. Their eyes followed Wilhelm as he passed. From their expressions, he gleaned no hint about what lay ahead of him. Though they all looked thin, none looked as gaunt as the starving Jews he'd seen at Valentin.

He shivered as he walked across the prison grounds; his new American field jacket from the Red Cross failed to keep out the chill. But at least now he had the costume for his stage play.

On the other side of the compound, the guards made Wilhelm wipe the mud off his boots. They ushered him into a room and sat him on a stool before a desk. Then they locked the door and left.

No one entered the room for an hour. Wilhelm listened closely, like a U-boat's sound man at his station, waiting for any noise that might signal trouble. He heard nothing—no shouted questions, no screams of torture, not even a typewriter's clacking.

Finally footsteps came and the rattle of keys. The door swung open to admit two guards he'd not seen before, along with a heavy-set *Luftwaffe* major carrying a folder. Wilhelm presumed it was Treider. The major did not wear a pilot's badge, so Wilhelm had no idea of the man's training and background. Intelligence, perhaps? As a U-boat officer, Wilhelm knew more about the American and British Navies than the German Air Force.

"Stand up when I enter the room," Treider shouted.

Unsure how to respond, Wilhelm hesitated. How would an American react? Wilhelm rose to his feet, but he did it slowly while attempting a smirk.

The major crossed the room in two strides and stood with his nose just inches from Wilhelm's face. Or inches from his neck, to be exact. The *Luftwaffe* man stood a few inches shorter than Wilhelm. Up close, Wilhelm noticed beard stubble, angry gray eyes, bad breath.

"You had better show some respect, Lieutenant—or whatever your rank is," the major said, "or I will have my men teach you respect."

This major missed his calling, Wilhelm thought. Perhaps he failed at pilot training. In any case, he seemed more suited for the SS than the air force.

Treider sat at the desk and ordered Wilhelm to return to the stool. He opened the folder, which contained only one sheet of paper.

"Meade is your name, correct?" Treider asked.

"Correct. Lieutenant Thomas Meade."

"Give me your identification tags."

So this is how it ends, Wilhelm thought. *Do not betray yourself.*

"I, uh, lost them."

Treider stared at Wilhelm for several seconds. "You what?" he said.

"I lost them."

The major said nothing. He simply cut his eyes at one of the guards, then tipped his chin toward Wilhelm.

Instantly the guard fell upon Wilhelm. Grabbed him by the collar of the field jacket. Lifted him from the stool. Propelled him two meters across the room and slammed him into the wall. Wilhelm felt his head crack against the brickwork. The guard swung him away from the wall and threw him onto the floor. He landed on the ribs he'd cracked during the bombing at Valentin. Pain wracked Wilhelm. His vision grayed.

The guard stood over him, leering. The sight put Wilhelm in mind of the SS goon who had tormented the Jewish *eisenkommandos.* He wanted to leap to his feet and smash the man's face with a left jab and right hook. But he knew that would ultimately bring more pain on himself. When navigating a strait littered with sharp rocks, one needn't steer into trouble deliberately.

"How could you lose your identification tags, you imbecile?" Treider asked.

Wilhelm sat up, placed his hand on his side, winced. "I don't know," he said. "I had them when we were captured." *Careful about the accent,* he reminded himself. "Your SS boys beat us. My dog tags must have fallen off then."

"And well they might have beaten you *terrorfliegers,* the way you bomb our cities, our women, and our children."

Wilhelm shrugged. The guards grabbed him by the arms and dragged him back to the stool.

"Do you have an identification card, anything at all?" Treider asked.

Wilhelm shook his head. "Those SS boys took my, uh, wallet. And my watch."

The *Luftwaffe* officer seethed. Wilhelm understood why. Very German of him to want a card or a tag to match with a record. Here was something that could not be documented. Would this fat major accept the story, or would he make dangerous inquiries? No turning back now. The tide would sweep Wilhelm according to its will.

Treider scanned his file folder, then slammed it onto the desk. "Your case is very curious," he said. "Normally, by the time we interrogate a kriegie, we already know his base and unit, his hometown, his crew position, and more. On you, we have nothing."

"Thomas Meade is a common name." *Did I offer that too quickly?* Wilhelm asked himself. *Do not protest too much, as the English say.*

"I am aware of that, imbecile. How could you be so stupid, so lax in discipline, as to lose all manner of identification?"

Do not speak to me of military professionalism, you overweight file clerk, Wilhelm thought. But while his emotions raged, his intellect calculated. *Yes,* he decided, *I am a stupid, lax, undisciplined American. A dummkopf.*

"Well, just go ahead and yell at me for it," Wilhelm said. "It is—it's not like I, uh, ain't been yelled at before."

Again Treider glanced at his guards. One of them kicked the stool. It clattered from under Wilhelm, and he tumbled to the floor. He broke his fall with his arm and skinned the heel of his hand. Felt another jolt of pain through his ribs, but not as bad as before.

"Pick up the stool," the guard ordered.

Wilhelm got up onto his knees, rubbed his hand on his trousers, then stood and collected the stool from the corner where it had come to rest. Placed it in front of the desk and sat down again.

"So you are used to your superiors shouting at you," Treider said. "I gather that you are something of a failure as an officer."

Think, Wilhelm ordered himself. *The conversation is going in the right direction. Use this moment well if you want to live.*

"I got transferred around a lot," Wilhelm said. "It wasn't my fault. I just had, uh, bosses who didn't like me."

"What do you mean?"

"I was with the 94th when I got shot down, but I had been with other units."

"Other units?"

Wilhelm thought for a moment. *What is the terminology? "Bomb group"? You must get this right,* he told himself.

"Other bomb groups before the 94th. I'd get into trouble and they would transfer me."

"Perhaps this is why we have no file on you."

Yes, yes, exactly, Wilhelm thought. He looked at the major and shrugged.

"Then we will begin with the basics," Treider said. "What is your full name?"

"Thomas Meade."

"Your *full* name, idiot."

A middle name, Wilhelm thought. *What would be an American middle name? It could be anything. Just something you won't forget.*

"Slocum," Wilhelm said. "Thomas Slocum Meade."

The major scribbled onto the paper in his file folder. "Rank?" he asked.

"First Lieutenant."

"Service number?"

For this, at least, Wilhelm had prepared. From perusing Carlton Meade's dog tags, he knew he needed an eight-digit number. Not the real Meade's number, of course. That might have caused Meade's family to get a false report of his survival and capture. Wilhelm needed a different number. One he could easily recall.

"Six-seven-one-six-two-four-eight-eight."

Specifications of the *U-351:* Length of 67.1 meters. Beam, 6.2 meters. Draft, 4.8 meters, and she cruised submerged at eight knots. Where was she now? Still tied to the pier at Valentin, Wilhelm hoped. He prayed she had not taken her crew pointlessly to the ocean floor.

"Date of birth?"

Wilhelm had considered this question, too: What should he say beyond name, rank, and serial number? The more lies he told, the more he'd have to remember. Better to keep it simple and just look like an American who didn't want to talk.

"Name, rank, and service number," Wilhelm said. "That's all you get."

The major stopped writing and looked up from his paper. He glared with such hatred that Wilhelm almost thought him mad.

"Date. Of. Birth," Treider enunciated.

"Thomas Slocum Meade. First Lieutenant. Six-seven-one-six-two-four-eight-eight."

The *Luftwaffe* officer capped his pen and slapped it onto the desk. Waved a hand at the two guards. Sat back and folded his arms.

The guards rushed at Wilhelm like Dobermans unleashed. One came behind Wilhelm and grabbed him by his jacket collar. Hauled him up from the stool. The other came at him from the front and drove a fist underhand into his stomach.

The blow doubled him over and forced the air from his lungs. The guard behind him let go of his jacket and let him collapse to the floor. He lay gasping, but he could not take in air. For long seconds, he felt he might suffocate like an entombed submariner. Some part of his mind told him: *You deserve this. You should have died struggling for breath with your crew.*

But no, he decided. *My crewmates, those gallant souls, should not die for men such as these goons in this room. If my crewmates are still alive,* Wilhelm thought, *I am taking this beating for them.*

A boot caught Wilhelm in the small of his back. Pain shot through his whole body. He might have cried out if he'd had breath to do so. But he felt glad he hadn't given these cretins the satisfaction of hearing him scream. Now if he could only keep silent for a little longer.

The next blow landed on the back of his legs, behind the knees. Didn't hurt much, but forced his legs to fold nearly into the fetal position. Maybe the guards took that as a sign of weakness, because the beating and kicking intensified. A heel landed on the small of his back. That *did* hurt, like a dagger between his vertebrae. Wilhelm clenched his jaw to stifle a scream. By the time the sound emerged, it came out as a snarl through gritted teeth.

The guard who'd kicked him from behind came around in front of him. Raised a boot inches from his nose as if to smash his face. Wilhelm closed his eyes, waited for a crushing blow.

"Careful," Treider said.

What is this? Mercy?

If so, a twisted version.

Instead of stomping Wilhelm's face, the guard kicked him in the breastbone. The impact rattled his damaged ribs. This time, the pain overcame Wilhelm's willpower. He opened his mouth and let out a full-throated scream. His cry echoed off the walls.

The guards smirked, apparently satisfied. They stood over him, arms folded like tradesmen who'd just completed a task.

"Pick him up," Treider said. "Photograph him. Process him. In the unlikely event this fool knows anything useful, the cooler may loosen his tongue."

The guards yanked Wilhelm up by his jacket collar. He tried to stand on his own; he wanted no help from these goons. But when he put his weight on his left foot, pain radiated through his whole body.

Very well, he thought. *Let them do the work.*

They placed his arms over their shoulders. Treider opened the door and the guards carried him from the interrogation room, his boots dragging on the concrete floor. They dragged him down the hall, turned left, and dragged him down another hall. Stopped in front of an office door, opened it, and dragged him inside.

In the office, a woman in civilian clothing worked at a desk. She looked up and frowned, stared at Wilhelm and the guards who carried him. Wilhelm got the impression she'd seen this before, but didn't like it.

Across from the desk, an empty chair stood backdropped by a sheet of white cardboard nailed to the wall. The guards lowered Wilhelm into the chair. He took hold of the armrests and tried to steady himself.

So this is why the major stopped them from smashing my face, Wilhelm realized. *No evidence of misdeeds in the photograph.*

"Camera," one of the guards said. The woman opened a drawer, withdrew a Leica camera stamped with an eagle and swastika. Passed the Leica to the guard.

"Sit up straight," the guard snapped.

Wilhelm raised himself so that his spine did not touch the back of the chair. The guard aimed the camera, snapped a photograph.

"Stay there," the guard said.

Wilhelm sat in the office with the woman for an hour. When the guards returned, one handed him a new identification card.

"If you lose this," the guard said, "the beating we gave you this morning will seem like a holiday."

Wilhelm looked down at the card. The photograph showed a tired sailor with dark swells under his eyes, looking fifteen years older than his real age. The wording, in English and in German, identified him as Lieutenant Thomas Slocum Meade, U.S. Army Air Forces. Birthplace, birthdate, and religion remained blank. But under the entry for *Lager,* it read: *Stalag Luft XIV.* So they had already decided where to put him. And he would go there as: *Prisoner of War Number 8683-C.*

34

The New Europe

Three days in solitary confinement felt like light punishment for Karl's refusal to talk. During that time, he subsisted on black bread and water, along with some thin beef broth. But apart from the lousy food, he suffered no abuse, he had plenty of time to rest, and the wound on his arm from the dog bite was healing. At the very least, he no longer worried about getting pitchforked by every farmer in the countryside.

Still, he found other things to worry about—especially Albrecht. How was his story holding up? How was *he* holding up? Karl's thoughts also kept returning to his crew. What he wouldn't give now to be back in the cockpit all those days ago, to have one more chance to turn back. He saw the faces of his friends, and he wondered who had survived.

Maybe he'd learn more about their fate when he reached his next stop. The guards had told him—and his POW card confirmed—that he was bound for Stalag Luft XIV, one of the large prison camps in eastern Germany. With luck, perhaps he'd even meet some of his crew there.

On the morning of Karl's fourth day in solitary, the guards woke him before sunrise. They were the same two guys who had always brought the food around, and they seemed decent enough. One of them said, "I am sorry, Lieutenant, but you must remove your boots."

"What for?" Karl asked.

"You and your friends are getting on a train today. The commandant doesn't want you escaping."

"It's damned freezing outside."

"I know. You may keep your coat. But you must remove your boots. We will tag them, and you will get them back at your destination."

Karl muttered curses, untied his boots, and pulled them off. The guards opened his cell, collected his boots, and led him outdoors. The cold cut through his socks immediately, but all the activity outside kept his attention off his discomfort. In the cold, clear darkness, at least a couple hundred men began lining up in rows. All officers, all without boots. So the enlisted were going somewhere else. Guards moved among the POWs like sheepdogs, some pointing with their fingers, others snarling and prodding with their machine pistols.

Karl noticed his interrogator, Captain Kostler, standing with his hands on his hips, saying nothing. Kostler nodded to him in a manner that seemed almost friendly.

So long, Karl thought. He remembered what Kostler had said about the SS and the POW camps. Now he wished he'd asked for more details.

Another German officer, a lard-assed major, made his way through the kriegies and started shouting orders. "Line up," the major screamed. "Get in line or we will shoot you where you stand."

The prisoners shuffled into line more quickly. Karl looked around for Albrecht, but saw no sign of him. Was he already dead or in some Gestapo dungeon?

The major yelled more spittle-flecked orders, and the lines began moving. The prisoners were marched to a rail platform just outside the camp. Each man picked up a Red Cross parcel for the journey.

Though Karl felt eternally grateful to the Red Cross, whatever appetite he might have had left him as soon as he boarded the boxcar. The odor—something between a sewer and a barnyard—overpowered him. The kriegies began retching and complaining, and an American lieutenant colonel shouted something about this being unacceptable. The fat *Luftwaffe* major slapped him. When the American officer drew back as if to hit the major, a guard jammed the muzzle of a machine pistol into his chest.

The Germans shoved thirty men into the boxcar with Karl. Other prisoners filled boxcars on either side. Atop one of the cars, a guard sat behind a pintle-mounted machine gun; anyone who broke and ran from the train would make an easy target. Inside the boxcars, the men could only stand. No one had room to sit or lie down—and Karl wouldn't have wanted to lie down, anyway. He had no desire to get any closer to whatever filth mixed with the straw that covered the floor.

After an hour of waiting, the train finally began to move. The boxcar jolted and swayed, and the locomotive's smoke mingled with the general stink. The men stumbled and struggled for balance. Karl held on to his Red Cross box and tried not to fall into anyone.

As the train chugged along, his need to urinate became more urgent. Karl didn't want to push his way through the men to reach the single bucket at the rear of the boxcar, but he no longer had a choice. Muttering "sorry" and "excuse me," he weaved through the crowd. He stuck the Red Cross box under his arm, unzipped, and did his best to keep his urine stream within the half-full bucket.

When he finished, he looked up and saw Albrecht. The sailor leaned into a corner as if he could barely support himself. His Red Cross parcel lay at his feet, unopened. Eyes closed, he'd turned his head to place his nose between the boxcar's slats for slightly fresher air. Despite the discomfort and smell, Karl felt a rush of relief. If Albrecht was here, it meant his act had held up.

"Hey, uh, Meade," Karl said. "You okay?"

Albrecht opened his eyes, looked over at Karl. Gave a thin smile.

"Yep" was all he said. Sounded reasonably American, despite apparent pain.

"They work you over pretty good?"

Albrecht closed his eyes, turned his nose back to the slats. Inhaled slowly as if breathing hurt. Nodded.

"I bet you didn't give 'em nothing," Karl said. Because, of course, Albrecht had no information to give. At least nothing the *Luftwaffe* was looking for.

Albrecht shook his head.

"Make some room, fellas," Karl said. "This guy just took a beating from the Krauts."

Somehow, the men managed to open enough space for Albrecht to slide down the wall into a squatting position. Hardly comfortable, but maybe a little more restful than standing.

"Hang in there, pal," someone said.

"How bad are you hurt?" Karl asked. "You need a doctor?" As soon as he asked the question, Karl felt foolish. Where would they get a doctor today? And even if a German doctor were available, Albrecht wouldn't want to call attention to himself.

"No broken bones," Albrecht said. "Just very sore."

Karl puzzled over the sailor's rough treatment. During Karl's interrogation, Kostler hadn't laid a hand on him. Maybe Albrecht had gotten someone different. But whatever had happened, Albrecht must have kept his cool and stayed in character.

For hours, the train rolled through dark forests, shuttered villages, and fallow farmland: Karl caught glimpses between the slats. Someone stumbled and kicked over the urine bucket, and the smell worsened until he retched. At midmorning, the train slowed and groaned to a stop. Karl hoped the journey was over, but when the guards slid open the doors, he saw only a small village's railway station. Apparently, the train was just stopping for coal. Guards wielded their machine pistols and ordered the men out.

"Anyone running will shoot," one of the guards called out in broken English. Not exactly what he meant, but the message came through.

"Yeah, yeah, yeah," a kriegie responded. "Don't get your panties in a bunch."

The men tumbled from the boxcar, stretched out their arms, took deep gulps of fresh air. Karl held back and helped Albrecht down from the train. Albrecht winced and held his side, but he did not complain.

"Where do you think we are?" Karl asked.

Albrecht looked around. "I do not know this village," he whispered.

Townspeople waited on the platform, presumably with tickets for a more comfortable train. Old burghers in long wool coats glared at the prisoners. Small children gaped. Girls giggled and pointed at the men's feet, clad only in socks.

On the station's outside wall, a tattered poster read: *Das neue Europe ist unschlagbar.* The poster's weathered look suggested it had hung there for at least a couple of years. Above the lettering, a map depicted an expanded Reich encompassing most of the continent. Arrows pointed outward toward Britain, Iceland, and Greenland, and into the Soviet Union. One even pointed straight across the Atlantic. Karl noted that the slogan, like the map, now seemed a little out of date: *The new Europe is unbeatable.*

While the train took on coal, guards let the prisoners drink water, eat from their Red Cross boxes, and relieve themselves behind the station. Moving like a very old man, Albrecht lowered himself onto the platform floor and sat with his back to a wooden pillar that supported the roof. The guards positioned themselves at intervals along the platform, and the man on the machine gun swiveled his weapon left and right as he scanned the kriegies. His belt-fed cartridges glinted in the sunlight, and no one tried to bolt.

Karl opened his Red Cross parcel. He found crackers, a tin of Spam, two bars of soap, three packs of Lucky Strikes, four ounces of coffee, and cans of prunes, jam, and dried apples. Offered a cracker to Albrecht, who shook his head. Karl placed the cracker in his mouth and began crunching. The salty taste reminded him of home, and it depressed him a little.

The townspeople cast silent looks at Karl and his fellow prisoners. The stares made him uncomfortable; he felt like a zoo animal on display. But no one made threatening gestures. Though any encounter with German civilians worried Karl, it appeared this one would pass uneventfully.

Then a group of Hitler Youth appeared. They tromped up the plank steps to the platform in a column of twos.

The dozen boys looked younger than the *Volkssturm* kids who had guarded Karl and Albrecht at the start of their captivity. These were maybe twelve or thirteen, and they wore black trousers, khaki shirts, and black neckerchiefs. Each sported one little splash of color: their black, red, and white Nazi armbands. They carried knives in black sheaths on their belts. An old man led them; he wore the insignia of an honorary SS officer.

When the boys saw the POWs, it seemed something dark inside them awakened. The transformation put Karl in mind of an electrical contactor in the B-17 closing on a bad circuit. In an instant, they switched from red-cheeked children to snarling zealots, shouting phrases and catchwords they'd heard in classrooms and on the radio.

"*Terrorfliegers,*" one screamed. "*Luftgangsters!*"

"*Juden,*" shouted another.

"You die," a third called out in English.

One boy drew his knife and ran toward the kriegies. A guard caught him by the arm, spun him around, and shoved him back toward his friends. The boy offered no resistance. He probably never expected to stab a POW, Karl thought, but he'd been programmed to show hatred toward the enemy. The guard who caught him gave a shallow smile. Approval, apparently. Karl thought the guard looked like a coach chiding a favored linebacker for being a little *too* aggressive.

"Just kill them all," the boy said in German as he placed his knife back in its sheath.

Another leered at Karl, drew his finger across his throat in a slashing motion.

"In a way," Karl whispered to Albrecht, "that's the scariest thing I've seen here."

"We learned nothing like that as Sea Cadets," Albrecht muttered.

We better win this war, Karl thought. *What if all the young people in Europe got brainwashed like this?*

The old man in the SS uniform barked orders, and the boys formed up in two rows.

"As you can see with your own eyes," the man said in German, "the enemy is not ten feet tall. He is a man like any other—at best. Unlike us, some of them carry blood tainted by *untermenschen.* That means their minds are not as sharp, their vision not as clear, their coordination not as developed as our own."

Karl rolled his eyes. *So that's why the boys' leader had brought them here. This guy—what did you call a Hitler Youth leader, anyway? "Scoutmaster from Hell"?*

Whatever his title, somebody had told him when the POW train would stop in his little backwater town, and he had figured it for a training opportunity.

Karl tried to imagine what a training folder for Hitler Youth might look like: *Item 32: demonstrate acting like a hateful little son of a bitch.*

Check that box.

What a damnable crime to poison kids' minds like that. You could teach them so many useful things in youth groups like the Boy Scouts or the Four-H, Karl considered. *How to put up a tent or dress a wound or milk a cow. But instead they learned* this.

"Someday you will fight our enemies," the Scoutmaster from Hell continued. "Note their weakness. Look at them, milling about like drunkards. Now do you see why our victory is inevitable?"

"Yes, sir!" the boys shouted in unison.

Scoutmaster from Hell called the boys to attention, and they locked up with arched backs and stiffened arms. The man raised his index finger and conducted as the boys sang:

> *"Deutschland, Deutschland über alles,*
> *Über alles in der Welt."*

Some of the old folks beamed. One or two kriegies groaned, which earned them prods from the guards' rifles. The boys completed the anthem and continued their hit parade with "The Horst Wessel Song." When they finished, their leader snapped marching orders. The boys about-faced and filed off the platform, heels thumping in unison.

"Wasn't that precious?" one of the prisoners muttered.

This stop in the fresh air couldn't last long, Karl realized, so he opened his Red Cross box once more. He had little appetite, but he knew he'd feel even less like eating once he reboarded the stinking boxcar. He opened his tin of dried apples and ate with his fingers. He also opened a pack of crackers for Albrecht, who raised his hand as if to say *no thanks.*

"You need to eat," Karl said. "It will be easier here than on the train."

Albrecht's mouth twitched in a dismissive expression, but he accepted the crackers. When Karl finished his apples, he opened the Lucky Strikes. Tapped out a cigarette and lit it with matches from the Red Cross parcel. Took a deep drag and exhaled through his nose. At least for a few minutes, the smoke would clear his nostrils of the boxcar's odor.

As soon as the smoke wafted across the platform, a guard came over. He carried his Mauser with the muzzle down, so he didn't look particularly threatening. Karl hadn't noticed him before; unlike some of the guards who liked to scream, this guy had stayed pretty quiet.

With politeness that surprised Karl, the man said in accented English, "May I have a cigarette?"

Karl took another drag, held the smoke in his lungs, and eyed the guard. Exhaled and said, "You want a Lucky Strike?"

Albrecht, in character again as Meade, offered an explanation: "They like our cigarettes a lot better than theirs."

The guard nodded vigorously.

"You got a name?" Karl asked.

"Brunner. I am Private Brunner."

Karl fished a cigarette from the pack and offered it to Brunner.

"Danke," Brunner said as he took the Lucky. Placed it between his lips, withdrew a lighter from his pocket, and lit the cigarette. Savored the first puff as if it were a delicacy.

This Brunner doesn't seem like a bad sort, Karl thought. He remembered how he'd wished he'd asked Kostler more questions when he had the chance. Maybe here was another opportunity to learn something useful.

"What can you tell me about where we're going?" Karl asked.

Brunner twisted his face like a schoolboy puzzling over a tough math problem. Perhaps he was considering whether he'd get into trouble for talking to prisoners. After a few seconds, he said, "You are going to Stalag Luft XIV."

"Yeah, I know. What's it like there?"

"Prisoners back on the train," another guard shouted from across the platform. "All aboard now, now, now."

Grumbling and cursing, kriegies began to rise and shuffle toward the boxcars.

Brunner's expression darkened. He took his cigarette between thumb and forefinger. Squatted next to Karl and spoke in a low voice.

"When you get to Stalag Luft XIV," he said, gesturing with the Lucky, "please do nothing stupid. Do you know what happened at a camp near there in March?"

Karl shook his head.

"It was at Stalag Luft III. Some very foolish kriegies, most of them British, dug escape tunnels. Several dozen got out."

Karl gave a wide grin. He hadn't heard of this, but he liked it.

"Do not smile, Lieutenant," Brunner said. "This story does not have a happy ending. I tell it to save your life."

Karl's grin faded. "All right," he said. "Go on."

"We recaptured all but three. Fifty of them were executed."

Karl tapped ash from the end of his cigarette, looked over at Albrecht. "Son of a bitch," he whispered.

"The stalags have become very hard places," Brunner continued. His tone carried no hint of gloating. "Please watch yourself, and advise your countrymen to do the same."

35

Hell, Fenced Off

After two miserable days riding the boxcar, the kriegies' train trip finally ended. Wilhelm recognized the pine forests of Silesia, and he knew he must be somewhere near Germany's eastern border. The locomotive hissed to a stop in the early evening. Clouds heavy with moisture hung low like smoke left over the ocean after a tanker burns and sinks. Searchlights stabbed the gloom. The temperature hovered around freezing, and the wet air made it feel even colder. Wilhelm pulled his field jacket more tightly around him. Guards shouted. Dogs barked. Englishmen grumbled. Americans cursed.

Hagan and two other Yanks helped Wilhelm down from the boxcar. Pain radiated from Wilhelm's ribs and pelvis, though not with the same heat as yesterday. He nodded thanks to the kriegies who steadied him alongside the tracks. During the train trip, they'd treated him with deference as "the guy who took a thumping and didn't say nothing." Still, Wilhelm worried about maintaining his act in the longer term, especially among prisoners who had lost friends in the mass execution Private Brunner mentioned. Surely, such men would remain highly suspicious, always attuned to anyone they saw as a rat among their ranks. Brunner had called Stalag Luft XIV a hard place, but that wasn't the half of it. Both the Germans and the prisoners would consider Wilhelm a spy if they ever found reason to doubt his story. Both sides would want him dead.

The guards formed the POWs into four columns and marched them down a dirt road through the pines. The pines ended at a fence that encircled a dozen wood-frame buildings. The dirt between the buildings had been raked so thoroughly that no pine straw littered the ground. Wilhelm noted that no razor wire topped the fence and the only people behind it were Germans. This, then, was not the POW camp itself but the *Kommandantur,* the military compound for the commandant and his staff.

Farther down the road, coils of concertina wire appeared, and Wilhelm took his first glance at the prison. Double rows of razor-edged fence surrounded barracks that appeared far less maintained than the *Kommandantur.* Doors slanted off broken hinges. Newspaper covered broken windows. Prisoners wandered between the buildings; the men wore mismatched and tattered uniforms.

At the main entrance, guards unchained the gates and swung them open. Most of the new prisoners marched into the compound, but a few held back. Wilhelm could imagine what they were thinking because he felt it himself: *Once I cross that threshold, I am well and truly a prisoner of war. A mouse in a cage. A captive.*

But what is the alternative? Run for the woods and get cut down?

Eventually, to the shouting of guards, everyone shuffled through.

Hagan scanned the camp's inmates with such focus that he didn't look where he was going and nearly stumbled into the man in front of him.

"Watch where you're going, bub," the prisoner muttered.

"Sorry," Hagan said. "Just looking for friends."

"Do you see anyone you recognize?" Wilhelm whispered.

"Not yet."

Enlisted *Luftwaffe* men led the POWs into a receiving building. Wilhelm found himself inside an open bay nearly as large as a submarine pen. Electric lights hummed overhead and cast a harsh glare. The new kriegies remained there for hours, waiting their turn for processing. During the night, they were photographed, fingerprinted, and taken to a shower room. The shower lasted only a couple of minutes and it stung Wilhelm's scrapes and cuts, but it came as welcome relief after two days of living in the boxcar's filth. The water ran brown as it flowed down his legs, and the grime left sediment around the drains. After the shower, the prisoners were deloused and issued blankets, towels, and a mess kit. All the gear went into cotton duffel bags. As promised, the Germans also returned the boots that had been taken from them at the transit camp. The act of lacing his boots back on made Wilhelm feel slightly less vulnerable.

At the final stage of processing, the prisoners received barracks assignments. Wilhelm stood close to Hagan in hopes they'd get assigned to the same building. To his relief, they were. In the dark, early-morning hours, Wilhelm followed Hagan to Hut 4B in an area called the Center Compound.

What the guards called a "hut" was actually larger than a typical German village home—about forty meters long and a third as wide. Built from rough-hewn lumber, the structure looked like a lot of other wartime construction: featureless and boxy, identical in every way to the building on either side. Hagan mounted the plank steps and pulled open the door.

Inside, a single oil lamp burned above a coal-fired stove. A man sat next to the stove in a wobbly wooden chair apparently built by kriegies. The stove barely took the edge off the chill, and to ward off the cold, the man wore a leather flying jacket. The jacket bore the silver bars of an American captain. The captain sat with his legs crossed, apparently at ease with himself; these Americans somehow maintained that casual swagger even in captivity. The captain was a tall, thin man, a little too big for his makeshift chair. His lanky frame reminded Wilhelm of that nineteenth-century American president—what was his name? Lincoln? Yes, Lincoln, but without the beard. As soon as he saw Hagan and Wilhelm, he placed his index finger in front of his lips.

"Shh," he said. "Try not to wake anybody. They told us to expect some new guys. I'm the block commander here, Captain Drew McLendon."

In the lamp's yellow rays, Wilhelm discerned rows of bunks on either side of the stove. Men slumbered and snored under green blankets. Naked lightbulbs hung from electrical cord. *So the huts have electricity,* Wilhelm concluded. *McLendon must be using the dim oil lamp to keep from waking the other men.*

Whispering, Hagan introduced himself, and he introduced Wilhelm as Lieutenant Thomas Meade. Both men shook hands with McLendon.

McLendon pointed to his left. "There's a couple empty bunks down there at the end. They're all yours. Try to get some shut-eye, and we'll get you all briefed up in the morning."

"*Shut-eye*"? *Oh, yes,* Wilhelm realized, *sleep. Good heavens, any conversation could give me away.* A camp full of Yank fliers was a minefield of American slang and aviator lingo.

Working in pale light, Wilhelm and Hagan took the blankets from their duffel bags. They placed them over the thin layers of padding that served as mattresses. For Wilhelm, simply making his bed became an act of endurance. Every movement pulled at something sore and bruised. When he finished, he removed his boots and belt. Other than that, he remained fully clothed as he pulled a blanket over him.

Captain McLendon extinguished the oil lamp, and Wilhelm lay in the darkness with his eyes open. *Sailors have embarked on many a strange journey,* he thought, *but few strange as this. Masquerading as a captured enemy in my own country. Am I a fool or a genius? Perhaps neither. Maybe just a lost soul adrift in a sea of war, shadowed by towering waves that could crash over at any moment.*

Troubled by such thoughts, Wilhelm doubted he would sleep. But exhaustion overcame his anxieties, and he fell into deep slumber. It seemed only an instant later when commands, shouted in American-accented English, roused him.

"Fall out, boys," Captain McLendon called. "Time for morning *appell.*"

Roll call.

Some things about military life never changed, regardless of nationality, rank, or status as combatant or captive. Late-sleeping kriegies scrambled from their bunks. Wilhelm tossed aside his blanket. Answering all his military instincts, he tried to spring from his bed—and pain pulled him up short. Sore ribs, tender tendons, and bruised muscles protested. He winced, groaned, closed his eyes, then sat up and supported himself with the heels of his hands.

"Easy there, bud," Hagan said. "Lemme help you up."

Hagan offered his hand. Wilhelm grasped it and let Hagan pull him to a standing position and steer him into a chair. Hagan then brought his boots, and Wilhelm pulled them onto his feet, gritting his teeth against the pain.

Kriegies who were already up put down tin cups and buttoned their jackets. Wilhelm stood under his own power, though it hurt, and he followed Hagan outside to what amounted to a parade ground. The first breath of cold air burned going down.

McLendon formed his men into six rows of eight. Similar groupings stretched across the parade ground. At the front of the parade ground, a British officer called the men to attention, and the block commanders repeated the order. Then the Brit ordered the men at ease.

"For you new arrivals," McLendon said, "that's our senior-ranking officer, Group Captain Ian Timmersby, Royal Air Force. They usually keep the Brits over in the North Compound, but lately we have a few here with us in the Center Compound as well."

Timmersby wore baggy flier's overalls. His hair and moustache appeared neatly trimmed. Unlike the men he had ordered at ease, Timmersby remained at the position of attention. Perhaps it was a small act of defiance; German sergeants strode between the columns of prisoners, counting, and Timmersby glared at them with undisguised hatred.

"Old Ian looks like he's about to bust a gasket," an American voice muttered somewhere behind Wilhelm.

"A ruddy fire dog, that one," a British voice answered.

Wilhelm could understand the British officer's attitude, given the escape attempt from a nearby camp and the resulting executions. The incident would surely remain a raw wound.

The *Luftwaffe* sergeants argued among themselves, counted, then counted some more. Apparently, their count was off.

"Not again," someone whispered. "We're gonna freeze our asses off."

Indeed, the cold was already seeping through Wilhelm's jacket. The chill sapped his reserves and worsened the pain in sore muscles.

A German officer mounted a podium at the head of the parade ground.

"That's *Kommandant* Becker," McLendon whispered.

"If one of you is hiding or has escaped," Becker called out in English, "punishment will come swiftly and severely. We will all stand here in the cold until my guards have assessed the situation."

"Screw you, Fritz," someone whispered.

"Shh," another man responded.

"Perhaps we will do the afternoon *appell* without coats," the *kommandant* continued.

The guards continued scurrying and counting, comparing their figures. In a low voice, Captain McLendon offered an explanation to the new arrivals.

"The Gestapo and the SS have been all over this place since March," McLendon said. "The guards are scared shitless of losing track of one kriegie."

Mein Gott, Wilhelm thought. *Of all the places to run aground, I find a hotbed of Gestapo activity.*

The guards counted again, then recounted. Apparently satisfied that there had been an arithmetic error and not an escape, *Kommandant* Becker returned to his office. Timmersby dismissed the kriegies.

Back inside Hut 4B, Wilhelm warmed his hands over the stove and got his first good look at his new home. Triple bunks lined the walls. Rectangular tables stood between the bunks. Clotheslines stretched across the room, and from the lines hung field jackets, gloves, socks, shirts, and other laundry. A bookshelf held a row of ragged paperbacks. Other shelves contained tin plates, bowls, and assorted cookware. Above some of the bunks, men had pinned photos of women. *So,* Wilhelm surmised, *the prisoners get mail. Or at least they used to.* Given how the war was going, he doubted the Reich would put much effort into getting mail to POWs now.

McLendon lifted a coffeepot from the stove and poured into two cups. He carried the cups to one of the tables and called out, "New guys. Over here." Wilhelm and Hagan pulled up chairs and sat with the captain, who pushed the steaming cups across the table. "It's more chicory than coffee," McLendon said, "but at least it's hot."

"Thanks," Wilhelm said in his best American English.

"Appreciate it," Hagan said.

Wilhelm took a sip. The bitter liquid tasted nothing like good coffee, but, as the captain had said, at least it was hot. For now, that was enough.

"You guys know what happened at Stalag III back in March?"

Both men nodded.

"Well," McLendon continued, "what you saw in the roll call pretty much tells the story. They're so worried about another escape that they actually punch holes in our canned goods. You can still eat the food, but it won't keep—so you can't take it with you on the run. And the fact that they're losing the war isn't making the Krauts any easier to get along with."

Wilhelm wondered how the captain knew with such certainty that the Reich was losing. Surely, the guards kept news of the war from the prisoners. But most of these prisoners were aviators—highly trained, intelligent men with time on their hands. Who knew what capabilities they had?

"Some of the guards are decent. Don't get me wrong," the captain explained. "But a few of them are bastards, and every now and then, we get an inspection from the Gestapo or the SS. And, believe me, they're all sons of bitches."

McLendon outlined the camp's routine and command structure, and he told Wilhelm and Hagan where to find the washhouse, the cookhouse, the chapel, and the library. The kriegies kept a duty roster for chores such as cooking, washing, and sweeping.

In a low voice, McLendon turned to more serious matters. "Watch your mouth every minute of the day," he said. "A few of the guards are what we call 'ferrets.' They sneak around and hide outside the windows. Sometimes they'll throw a surprise inspection and tear up all the bunks. They even pull up floorboards."

When the captain asked about their backgrounds, Hagan said he was a pilot from the 94th Bomb Group. He repeated the story that Meade was his navigator.

"Either of you boys speak German?"

"Both of us," Hagan said. "My dad came from Germany after the last war."

"That's useful," McLendon said. "Keep your ears open, then. But don't let on you understand them."

"You bet," Wilhelm said. *That's it,* he told himself. *Short American sentences. The fewer syllables the better.*

"By the way," McLendon added, "if you ever think you got it bad, just take a look across the fence at the Russian camp. The Krauts hate the Russians because they think Slavs are an inferior race. You know the saying 'This ain't hell, but you can see it from here'? At this place, that's literally true."

The captain described starvation on the other side of the wire. The Russians, he said, walked around gaunt and stubbled, with arms like matchsticks. Occasionally a shot echoed from that side. Sometimes it was a prisoner executed for a minor infraction. At other times, it was a suicide by proxy: A Soviet kriegie would make a feeble show of escaping, placing his hands on the fence as if to climb. A shot from one of the guard towers, which McLendon called "goon boxes," would end the Russian's misery.

"I even heard they caught a dog and cooked and ate it," McLendon said. "Turned out to be the *kommandant*'s mutt. That got several of them shot."

"They value a dog more than a human being?" Hagan said. "Unbelievable."

Wilhelm believed it; he'd seen the evidence at Valentin. Military dogs got treated far better than those Jewish slave laborers at the U-boat base. McLendon was correct: You could see hell from here. And from many other places within the Reich.

36

Climb and Confess

Karl practically bounded from Hut 4B. At the end of McLendon's briefing, he'd asked about his crewmates. One name rang a bell for McLendon: "Pell? Yeah, maybe we have a William Pell."

Searching the compound, Karl stopped every kriegie he saw: "Billy Pell. Do you know that name? A bombardier from the 94th?"

Three times, Karl's question met with a blank stare and a shaking head. That didn't surprise Karl; this was a big POW camp, and Pell couldn't have been here long. Finally someone recognized the name. The prisoner took a last drag on a cigarette, exhaled the smoke. Dropped the butt and stepped on it.

"Yeah, Pell's over in Hut Six Able. Good fella."

"Where?"

The kriegie pointed. Karl took off at full sprint. Pounded on the door of 6A.

"Yeah, yeah, Fritz," a voice called from inside. "We're coming."

A POW opened the door. Perhaps the man expected to see ferrets bent on ransacking the hut, because his expression softened when he saw Karl.

"Billy Pell," Karl said. "He here?"

"Yep," the man said. Then he turned and called toward the back of the hut. "Hey, Pell. You got a visitor."

A familiar voice sounded from the back of the hut: "A visitor? Tell me it's Lana Turner."

"Nope. He ain't nearly that pretty."

Karl felt a warm turn in the pit of his stomach. He'd dreamed of this for days: finding at least one of his crew. He'd have preferred not to find him in a prison camp, but he'd take what he could get.

Boot steps sounded across the hut's plank floor. Sure enough, Billy Pell, *Hellstorm*'s crack bombardier, materialized in the doorway's shadows. He wore a woolen watch cap and his A-2 jacket. Karl felt as if he'd encountered the ghost of a long-lost friend. Pell must have felt the same way, because when he recognized Karl, his face changed instantly. The sallow cheeks of a downed airman gave way to the broad grin of a schoolboy reunited with an old chum.

"Ha-haa," Pell shouted, spreading his arms wide. "Look what the cat drug in. I thought for sure you got burned up with the airplane." He stepped outside with Karl, grabbed him in a tight bear hug, slapped him across the shoulders.

"I almost did," Karl said. "Damn, it's good to see you. Who else is here?"

At Karl's question, the bombardier's face fell. "Just me, I'm afraid. And now you, of course. I landed close to Conrad; I had his chute in sight all the way down. We landed in a residential area, and Conrad's canopy snagged in a tree."

Pell described how he touched down in a park, unclipped his parachute, and ran toward Conrad. He covered the few blocks that separated him from Conrad and discovered the navigator suspended six feet off the ground. Conrad hung from his parachute risers. The chute's shroud lines had tangled through the tree's branches, and Conrad tugged at his release clips, trying to free himself.

A mob had already found him. Townspeople hurled rocks, bricks, and bottles. Conrad tried to shield himself with his arms. Then he went limp, blood streaming down his face.

"Awfulest thing I ever seen in my life," Pell said. "It was old men, old women, boys, even a couple of pretty girls. I pulled my Colt and fired up in the air."

Everyone scattered, Pell explained, but it was too late. Conrad was dead. The mob had stoned him to death in a matter of seconds. One or two rocks to the head was all it took.

"I wanted to cut him down," Pell said, "but that mob started getting back together and coming for me."

"Sons of bitches," Karl muttered. "How did you make it out?"

"I wouldn't have, except the *Luftschutz* showed up. Pulled up in a truck. I guess they had orders to take us alive. They started yelling at the crowd. Made everybody go home, and they took me prisoner. Had to ride in the back of that truck with what was left of Conrad. I tell you, buddy, be glad you didn't have to see that."

"What about the rest of the crew?"

"Got no idea. I didn't see any other chutes. Did Adrian get out with you?"

Karl turned his gaze down to the ground, then up at the sky. A layer of high, thin cirrus slid overhead, with clear visibility beneath. Good bombing weather.

"He didn't get out at all," Karl said. Karl told Pell about the cannon round that tore through the copilot's chest.

Pell stared out beyond the camp perimeter, ground his boot heel into the dirt as if trying to tamp down emotions. "So he never even had a chance to get out of his seat?" Pell asked.

"No, it was quick." Karl snapped his fingers. "He was there one second and gone the next."

"Damn it."

Karl tried to push his thoughts from grief to more urgent matters. "Billy," he said, "you got time to take a walk? I got something important to tell you about."

Pell raised his eyebrows and cocked his head, obviously puzzled. "I got nothing *but* time," he said.

He was about to become even more puzzled, Karl knew.

How to tell him about Albrecht? How to explain how a German deserter shows up in Stalag Luft XIV pretending to be an American? Oh, yeah, and he's pretending to be from your *crew.*

Karl had no idea how to start, so as he and Pell began strolling across the compound, he lowered his voice and just started at the beginning.

"After we got shot down," Karl said, "I had a little help."

Karl explained how he'd met Albrecht in the bombed-out ruins of

Bremen, how they'd tried to blend in and evade capture. How their luck had eventually run out. Pell stopped walking and stared at Karl with an open mouth.

"You mean to tell me a Nazi deserter was with you all this time?"

"Well, I don't think he was ever a Nazi party member, but yeah."

"What happened to him? Where is this guy now?"

"He's here, Billy. And they think he's one of us."

Pell's eyes widened, and his jaw dropped even farther. Then he closed his eyes, shook his head, and held up his hands with fingers outstretched as if to ward off a swarm of wasps.

"Wait," Pell said. "Let me get this straight. You brought him *here*? Why in God's name would you do that? And why are you telling me?"

"Well, I didn't exactly bring him here, Billy. It's not like we joined this country club by choice. I'm telling you because I said he was one of our crew. And I need you to do the same."

Pell glared at Karl now, eyes flinted with anger. All feelings of joyful reunion clearly gone. Behind the anger, Karl sensed confusion and befuddlement—and he could understand. The bombardier had been trained to handle a lot of things, but nothing like this.

"You *vouched* for him?" Pell asked. "And you want me to vouch for him, too? Have you lost your mind? I just told you what these people did to Conrad. And now you ask me to help one of them?"

Karl wiped his mouth with the back of his hand, thinking. How could he get through to Pell? *Of course*, this made no sense to him.

Finally Karl said, "Listen, he helped me. He didn't have to do that. If he hadn't, they might have done to me what they did to Conrad. And if we still have some of our crew on the run, I hope somebody helps them."

"Do you have any idea how dangerous this is?" Pell asked. "For him? For you?" Pell placed his hand across his chest. "For me? We don't got enough problems as it is, and now we're harboring—"

"I understand, Billy, but keep your voice down."

Pell looked around and whispered, "And now we're harboring a German deserter?"

"I know, I know. The Gestapo or the SS would love to get their hands on him."

Pell's cheeks flushed red with frustration. "Yeah, but not just the Gestapo," he hissed. "We got an outfit in here called the X Committee. They decide when we try to bust out. They're also on the lookout for spies and plants. That's what they'll think he is." Pell jabbed Karl's shoulder with his index finger. "They'll think you're one, too. And now they'll think I'm one."

"Look," Karl said. "I don't blame you for being mad. This is a lot to take in at once, and if I were in your boots, I'd be pissed, too. But I didn't plan on coming here—none of us did. Least of all, him."

The bombardier clenched his fists. He seemed to struggle for words.

"You're not hearing me," Pell said. "I don't mean they won't pick us for the softball team. I mean you could wake up one night with a belt around your neck. That happened to a couple of guys over on the Russian side. The Russkies just thought they *might* have been plants, and they strangled both of them."

"Damn, what happened after that?"

"The Krauts shot ten Russians."

The possibilities, all of them bad, raced through Karl's mind faster than he could process them. The overload felt like trying to calculate a B-17's descent rate when he was too tired for mental math.

"Billy," Karl said, "I'm sorry you're mixed up in this, but I can't change that now. Here's all you need to know. The guy was our navigator. His name is Lieutenant Thomas Meade. You know him. You're glad to see him."

Pell shook his head and said, "Perfect, seeing as how I don't even know what he looks like."

"I'll have to figure out a time to introduce you. He's actually a hell of a guy."

"Yeah, you're going to have to figure out a whole lot more than that. This is beyond crazy."

"What else do I need to figure out?"

Pell massaged his brow with his thumb and forefinger as if suffering from a migraine. Pursed his lips in concentration.

"You need to tell your block commander," Pell said. "I mean, right now. Right the hell now. Don't let him think you've been hiding something. Who is your block commander, by the way?"

"Drew McLendon."

"Good. He's got a good head on his shoulders. But he ain't gonna like this any more than I do."

"What about Timmersby? Do I tell him, too?"

"Probably. But let McLendon make that call."

"Anything else I need to know?"

Pell clicked his tongue, pondered for a moment. From that familiar mannerism, Karl somehow knew his old bombardier was still on his side.

"For the first several days," Pell said, pointing, "everybody's gonna be watching you. Anything looks fishy, the X Committee is gonna hear about it. You tell your boy, Thomas Meade, or whatever the hell his real name is, he better watch himself. He better put on an Academy Award–winning performance. Mainly, he better just keep his mouth closed. Dear God, this is nuts."

"I know it, Billy. We were supposed to be home by now."

"Yeah, well, just about everybody here was supposed to be home by now."

Karl made his way back toward his hut. The aroma of cooking— boiled beets, maybe—wafted from the cookhouse, while less pleasant smells drifted from the latrines. Kriegies stacked wood, hauled coal, carried laundry. Others lounged and chatted, while still others strolled the perimeter. In contrast to Pell, who still looked well fed, many of them appeared thin, their faces hollowed out by weight loss. Karl guessed they had been here the longest, subsisting on meager rations for as long as two years. Not starving like the Russians, but probably hungry all the time. Karl wondered how long he'd have to stay here, and how long before he looked like the long-term kriegies.

At Hut 4B, Karl found McLendon outside, smoking. He didn't know how to begin except simply to spill his guts. The predicament reminded him of what instructors had told him to do if he got lost in an airplane: climb and confess.

"Captain," Karl said, "have you seen Lieutenant Meade since roll call?"

"Yeah," McLendon said. He ground out his cigarette butt with his boot. "Meade's sleeping. I suppose he got worked over pretty good."

"Yes, sir, he did. And I need to talk to you about him. In fact, I got a bombshell to drop, if you'll pardon the expression."

McLendon cut his eyes at Karl. His face gave away no reaction, and he fished another cigarette from his pocket.

"I don't think anything could surprise me in this place anymore," McLendon said, "but shoot." He lit his cigarette with a Ronson.

Karl told his story the same way he'd told it to Pell: in chronological order. The block commander did not interrupt, and he did not gape. But he stopped smoking. The ash grew long on his forgotten Chesterfield. He regarded Karl with professional detachment, as if he were scanning instruments during a foggy approach. When Karl finished, McLendon flicked away his cigarette and said, "Well, I was wrong. You *did* drop a bombshell."

For nearly a full minute, McLendon didn't say anything else. Karl waited for him to explode in shock and anger, to get mad like Pell. But it never happened. The block commander just seemed to . . . calculate.

McLendon finally said, "I'd assume all three of you were spies—you, Pell, and Meade, or whatever the hell his real name is. I might even have the boys do something drastic. Except no spy would come to me with a story like this."

"Believe me, sir. I sure didn't plan it this way."

"Nobody in here planned it this way."

"So, what now?" Karl asked. "Do we tell the men?"

"No, let's keep this quiet. If everybody knows, the Krauts will know sooner or later. I'll talk to Timmersby. Beyond that, the fewer people who know about this . . . the better."

Relieved, Karl let out a long breath. Now that someone in the POW chain of command knew about Albrecht, he felt a bit less isolated. But protecting the U-boat man still amounted to flying through a flak barrage: It would take a hell of a lot of luck to get through. Even if most kriegies bought Albrecht's story, eventually someone might ask a question he couldn't answer. Karl couldn't possibly teach him enough about American culture. Or about the USAAF or the B-17. Something as innocuous as baseball could trip him up. What would the guys think of an "American" who didn't know about Ted Williams or Stan Musial?

Karl had a hundred questions for McLendon—about how to play it from here, about the X Committee, about the camp itself. But he didn't get to ask them. Five guards strode toward Hut 4B. Two carried crowbars. The others carried clubs. All wore Lugers and scowls.

"Damn it to hell," McLendon said.

"What is it?" Karl asked.

"Another ferret raid."

37

Eric Sevareid, CBS News, London

Wilhelm startled awake when the guards flung open the door and charged inside. For about two seconds, he thought his life had ended; surely, the Gestapo had tracked him down. However, the guards all but ignored him. When he stood up, one shoved him out of the way, pushed him against the wall. They had come not to arrest, but to search and intimidate.

They turned over the tables; metal dishes crashed to the floor. POWs cursed under their breath. The guards kicked down book-cases, knocked over shelves, flipped mattresses. With their crowbars, they pried up floorboards. Planks groaned and cracked. Dust flew.

"Looking for your wife, Fritz?" one of the kriegies muttered. "She was here all last night." He said it a little too loudly, and a guard heard him. The guard slapped him, then turned back to the search.

They found nothing but an empty can for that processed meat the Americans called "Spam." They acted as if they'd found an arms cache.

"*Was ist das?*" one of them said, holding the can high.

"It's an empty can, dumbass," a kriegie said.

Some of these Americans displayed panache under pressure; Wilhelm had to give them that much.

"And perhaps you save it for a scoop?" the guard said, switching to English. "Scooping the dirt?"

By this time, McLendon and Hagan had entered the hut. Hagan looked a little frightened; the block commander looked disgusted. A guard with a crowbar pushed and shoved through the men to reach McLendon. He placed the crook of the crowbar under McLendon's chin.

"You like to dig?" the guard said. "Perhaps you dig your grave with this scoop."

McLendon glared at the guard, but did not react. The naval officer in Wilhelm wanted to call these simpletons to attention and dress them down for unprofessional behavior. But, of course, that part of him was no more. Here, he was only Thomas Meade. Kriegie. Flyboy. New guy from New York.

"Look at the can," McLendon said. "Do you see any dirt in it? It's just a piece of trash."

The guard pressed upward on McLendon's chin with the crowbar.

"I hope you do try to escape," the guard said. "I will personally beat you to death with this."

The guard lowered his crowbar and turned away from McLendon. He and his four colleagues began tossing sheets and blankets, scattering cookware. Now they seemed not even to search, but simply to try to make as big a mess as possible.

When they could find no more beds to rip up or shelves to dump, they gathered at the doorway. As they left, one of them called out in heavily accented English, "Your maid has now much work to do." The remark brought laughter from the other guards.

McLendon slammed the door behind them and muttered, "Bastards."

"You okay?" Hagan asked him.

"Yeah, I'm fine," McLendon said, rubbing his chin.

"All that, and they didn't find nothing," a kriegie said.

The comment made Wilhelm curious: What was there to find? And where could it be if not hidden under floorboards?

"These guards ain't exactly their best and brightest," another man said. "They put their high-speed guys on submarines and airplanes, and they send their morons here."

True enough, Wilhelm thought. *True enough.*

The kriegies went to work remaking their beds, picking up their books, gathering their cookware. Wilhelm made a point of helping the other men and not just picking up his own belongings. He couldn't tell whether the effort garnered him any goodwill; the men hardly spoke to him except for the occasional "Thanks, bud."

The cleanup took until suppertime. In the evening, some of the kriegies brought steaming pots from the cookhouse. They ladled out bowls of a soup made from beets and potatoes. It wasn't very good, but it was hot and filling. Wilhelm sat beside Hagan. He felt better now, a little less stiff and sore. They ate in silence and listened to the prisoners' conversations.

"Gave the place a good going-over today, didn't they?" a prisoner said.

"Yeah," McLendon responded, "and they'll just get meaner as they lose the war."

The block commander spoke as if confident of his prediction. Yes, the Reich was losing—and badly.

But how do these men know? Some have been prisoners of war for two years.

How much news do they get here? And by what means? Questions swirled in Wilhelm's mind.

"They might have had an inspection today," a third kriegie said. Gestured with his spoon as he spoke. "The little visit they paid us might have been part of that."

"Probably," McLendon said.

"What kind of inspection?" Hagan asked.

"Ever since the escape attempt over at Stalag Luft III," McLendon said, "the SS has been dropping surprise inspections on all the prisons. They think the *Luftwaffe*'s too soft on us."

The mention of the SS churned the acid in Wilhelm's gut. He slurped from his spoon and chewed a chunk of overcooked beet, but he had little appetite now.

"They'll have a lot more to bitch about pretty soon, now that the Russians have rolled into East Prussia," another prisoner offered.

"And when the Russkies get here and see how they've treated their boys on the other side of that fence, they'll be mightily pissed."

Good heavens, how does this man know such a thing?

Wilhelm believed prisoners of war should be treated decently, to be sure. But that didn't require giving them intelligence briefings. A *kommandant* would naturally want the POWs to know as little as possible about the war. Of course, fresh prisoners entering the camp would bring some news, but with this level of detail?

"You guys want another update tonight?" a kriegie asked. A small, thin man with a dark moustache. On his sleeve, he wore a patch that depicted a cartoon rabbit holding a carrot and riding a bomb.

"Thanks, Sparks," another man said. "But maybe we better hold off if the SS is sniffing around the camp."

"After the way they busted up the hut today," McLendon said, "I think they're through with us for now. Tonight's as safe as any night."

"All right," Sparks said. "Lemme finish eating, and I'll rig her up."

Rig up what? Wilhelm looked at Hagan, who simply shrugged.

The man they called "Sparks" wolfed down two pieces of black bread, wiped his hands on his trousers, and rose from the table. He went over to the stove, which sat on a brick base. Sparks removed a brick and withdrew a coil of wire and three other small objects. He moved down the row of bunks and lifted a mattress. Reached through some sort of opening in the mattress, and found a block of wood not much bigger than a cigarette pack. The block had what appeared to be electrical components attached to it—perhaps diodes or resistors.

Sparks moved to the bookshelf and selected a volume. Opened the book and, from a recess cut through the pages, took a tiny cylinder with wires wrapped around it. Then he found an empty Spam can, the same one the guards had discovered earlier. On the table, Sparks began assembling a makeshift radio.

What ingenuity these men had; they reminded him of his *U-351* crewmates. He was so impressed that he broke his usual silence. "Fantastic," he said, in his best American accent. "How did you learn to do that?"

"I was a radio operator before I went to pilot training," Sparks said.

"Old Sparks is our window on the world," McLendon said. He turned to another of his men. "Charlie," McLendon said, "ain't it your turn at lookout?"

"Yes, sir," Charlie said. "Let me know what I miss."

The man named Charlie got up from his seat and took a position by the door. Cracked the door open and peered out.

"Coast is clear," Charlie said. "I'll cough if I see somebody coming."

"That's the drill," McLendon said. "All right, Sparks. Do your stuff."

Sparks moved his tuning coil. Static and hum sounded from within the Spam can. Then came a faint warble of voices, first in German, then in English. The men leaned in, strained to listen. Sparks stopped moving the coil when he found the frequency he wanted. Wilhelm shut his eyes to listen more closely, the same way his own audio man used to listen for the screws of a U.S. destroyer. His ears adjusted to the cadence of a tinny Yank voice: ". . . direct from important overseas stations, reporters of the Columbia Broadcasting System present the latest political and war news, brought to you by Admiral appliances. Now, here's Douglas Edwards."

The newsman described Japanese attempts to regroup following their naval defeat at a place called Leyte Gulf. Wilhelm had scarcely followed news from the Pacific; the Philippines might as well have been on another planet. The Russians had crossed the Danube.

How in the name of Neptune had they moved so quickly?

Fierce fighting raged near the French town of Metz, close to the German border. Patton's Third Army surged against panzer attacks. Churchill called for Frenchmen to rally around de Gaulle.

Wilhelm had known for months the war was going badly for the Reich. He could tell that purely from the short life expectancy of a U-boat on the surface. But he'd never heard such foreboding details; this report stood in stark contrast with Nazi propaganda broadcasts. Berlin described a fantasy world with new superweapons in development, fresh reserves called up, unrest in Allied capitals.

For a few seconds, the broadcast drowned in static until it became unintelligible. Wilhelm feared the signal would not come back, but Sparks moved his tuning coil ever so slightly.

"We usually get the BBC," Sparks said. "But this sounds like an American broadcast skipping off the atmosphere." The signal returned more clearly than before, just in time for Wilhelm to hear: "We take you now to Eric Sevareid in London."

The newsman Sevareid reported on ministerial sessions about how the Allies would take over the German economy. He spoke in dispassionate terms about running the farms and factories of a defeated Reich. Skilled and unskilled labor would be mobilized; Germans up to age sixty would be compelled to rebuild their own nation. Some would go abroad to repair the countries their armies had smashed.

Mein Gott, Wilhelm thought. *In their zeal to make us gods, the Nazis have made us slaves.*

Inside these meetings, Sevareid implied, German defeat was taken as a given. No doubt the ministers were correct, given the headlines at the top of the broadcast.

Then why in God's name did the fighting continue? Every life lost from now on is a waste, Wilhelm believed. *Yes,* he thought, *I saved my honor by losing it. I did not squander the lives of the good men on my crew. Maybe the U-351 never departed on its suicide mission. Perhaps the crew, or at least some of them, would survive the war. If so, they might spend a few months digging potatoes for the Poles, but at least they would eventually go home.*

At the door, Charlie gave a thumbs-up signal. McLendon gestured for Sparks to let the radio continue playing.

The broadcast turned to U.S. domestic news. Franklin D. Roosevelt had recently won an unprecedented fourth term as president. Wilhelm looked around at the Americans. None appeared surprised; most seemed pleased. The newsman noted that Roosevelt would begin the new term with a new vice president: Harry S. Truman, a senator from the state of Missouri. Wilhelm had never heard this name.

When the broadcast ended, Sparks dismantled the radio. He placed the various components in their hiding places, and the kriegies turned in for the night.

Wilhelm lay awake considering all he'd learned. Russians across the Danube. Stalag Luft XIV was in eastern Germany; Soviet troops could crash the gates within weeks, if not days.

How would the German guards react? They could melt into the

forest and leave the prisoners to fend for themselves. They could evacuate the camp and force-march the POWs elsewhere. Or they could simply execute every single kriegie and be done with it. Everything depended on who was giving the orders at the time.

Even if the prisoners suddenly found themselves free, they could find themselves free amid lawlessness. They might wander a landscape filled with desperate Germans, Russian troops drunk on victory and schnapps, and common criminals unconcerned about consequences.

Wilhelm recalled a concept from his military studies, now more troubling than ever: For civilians and POWs, the *end* of a war could become its most dangerous time.

38

The X Committee

Dawn came with a hard freeze. At the morning roll call, kriegies stood with their hands stuffed in their pockets against the chill. Frost coated the few blades of grass in the compound. Men shivered and cursed in impatience as each name was called out. When roll call ended, Karl chatted briefly with bunkmates, their breath visible in the cold morning air. But the real reason he lingered outside despite the weather was to get a private word with Albrecht.

"You feel up for a walk?" Karl asked.

"Yes," Albrecht said. "I don't hurt so much now. I would like the exercise." The two men began strolling the camp perimeter.

If we're gonna die here, Karl thought, *we might as well do it on a first-name basis.* "It was all a test, Wilhelm," Karl whispered. "By the way, call me Karl."

"Very good, Karl," Wilhelm said. "But what do you mean about 'a test'?" He wrapped his field jacket tightly around himself.

"The radio. Now that we know they have it, they want to see if they get another raid. They want to see if we rat them out."

"'Rat them out'?"

"Sorry. I mean, they want to see if one of us is a spy and tells the Germans they have a radio."

"We would never do that," Wilhelm said. "But, of course, they don't know that. And yes, I wondered why they trusted me so soon with such a fact."

"It's because they don't trust you at all, buddy."

"But why would they risk losing the radio? Such a treasure."

"I don't know. Maybe they think we're so close to the end of the war that it doesn't matter. Or maybe this guy Sparks is such a scrounger, he can just make another radio from a shoestring and a nail."

"He's very resourceful. He would make a good U-boat officer."

Karl chortled. "Yeah, don't tell *him* that."

"Indeed not."

"Listen," Karl said, "here's the other thing. I gotta get you and Billy Pell together, since you're supposed to know each other."

"Yes. I don't even know what he looks like."

"Yeah, well, we'll fix that today. And remember—you got shot down with him and you haven't seen him since. You're really glad to see him. Ham it up like Cecil B. DeMille is directing."

"I'll try."

Karl noted that Wilhelm was using contractions, sounding more like an American. And it seemed to come more naturally. That was a good thing—their lives could depend on it. Karl decided to kick it up a notch. He dropped his voice to the quietest whisper he could manage. "When you meet Billy, let people hear you, and use some slang. You *ain't seen him in a dog's age*. Stuff like that."

"'A dog's age'? This makes no sense."

"Of course, it doesn't. Your being here doesn't, either."

For just an instant, Karl thought he saw a sparkle of mischief in Wilhelm's eyes. Closest thing to humor he'd ever seen from the guy.

"Well," Wilhelm said in pure, flat Yank, "you got me on that."

Karl chuckled. "Damn, that's good," he said. "Keep it up."

Wilhelm rolled his eyes. "Good heavens," he said.

Karl wanted to rush to find Billy Pell. He knew the meeting between Pell and Wilhelm would be an awkward little stage play, and he wanted it over as soon as possible. But Karl had chores assigned, and he did them first. He drew laundry duty, which he hated. For four hours, he scraped shirts, trousers, and sheets against a washboard. Wrung them out and hung them to dry inside the washhouse. His fingertips shriveled in the cold gray wash water. If he ever got married, he vowed, he'd make sure to buy his wife one of those fancy machine washers to spare her this god-awful drudgery.

He pulled laundry duty with three other men, all of whom had lived in Stalag Luft XIV for at least a year. They had learned to read the camp, to see the signs for what they were, and to notice everything.

"It's getting real bad over on the Russian side," one of the long-timers said. A navigator from the Bloody 100th, so named for its heavy losses. His leather flight jacket had dried and cracked with the passing of German seasons.

"How's that?" Karl asked.

"I watched them during their roll call this morning. I swear to God they were holding up dead men to be counted. Four or five, from what I could see."

Karl stared at the nav. "Why in the world would they do that?" he asked.

"For the food ration. They're all starving over there."

"How do you know they were dead?"

"In the cold, you could see everybody's breath. But not theirs."

"The Jerries don't view us as their natural enemies," another laundry kriegie said. A Brit from Coventry who had gone down in a Lancaster. "But they hate the Slavs as much as the Jews."

"Good Lord," Karl said.

All that separates us from those starving Russians, Karl thought, *is a few strands of razor wire and a few lines of policy. And that policy could change at the stroke of a pen! Especially as the war goes worse and worse for the Germans.*

Karl left the washhouse with his fingers desiccated and aching from the cold water. He cupped his hands and blew warm breath into them as he scoured the compound for Billy and Wilhelm. He discovered Wilhelm in front of the chapel, smoothing the dirt and stones with a rake.

"You done?" Karl asked.

"I was finished an hour ago," Wilhelm said. "I see little point to this task."

"Me neither. Let's go see if Billy's in his hut."

At Hut 6A, smoke curled from the stovepipe. Karl could hear men inside chatting and coughing. His heart thudded as he rapped on the door, thinking: *This little act better look convincing.* Wilhelm stood behind him on the steps. Pell answered the door, and Karl cocked his head toward Wilhelm. Met Pell's eyes as if to say: *You're on.*

"Tommy boy," Pell cried. He pushed past Karl and grabbed Wilhelm around the neck like a roughhousing schoolkid. "Damn, it's good to see you. Thought you were a goner." The two men stumbled together into the graveled compound.

Pell released Wilhelm from the headlock, and Wilhelm grabbed Pell's right hand. "Ain't seen you in a dog's age," Wilhelm said.

"Well, it sure feels like a dog's age," Pell said. "I lost sight of you when we bailed out. Didn't know if you'd even got out at all."

"I didn't see you, either," Wilhelm said. He cocked his thumb at Karl. "But I had this guy in sight all the way down, and we met up after we landed."

"I'm real glad you made it. But this sure ain't no way to finish a mission."

Wilhelm hesitated, perhaps searching his mind for some new Americanism he'd learned. Finally he said, "You got that right, pal."

Some of Pell's hut mates drifted through the doorway and stood outside, witnessing the "reunion." That pleased Karl; it was the whole point of the exercise. They made no comment or interruption. The kriegies simply stood around with their arms folded, smoking and talking among themselves.

One in particular, however, followed the conversation with apparent interest. The man eyed Wilhelm and Pell with a look like he had a bad taste in his mouth. Karl had met him briefly—a bombardier from New York by the name of Fox. Spoke with a strong Brooklyn accent.

Karl didn't especially like Fox, and he liked him even less when he butted in without introducing himself.

"McLendon tells me you speak German," Fox told Wilhelm. "Where did you learn it?"

"Ah, I had an aunt who came from Germany," Wilhelm said. "And I took it in college."

Very good, Karl thought. *A prepared answer.*

Fox turned to Pell. "You never mentioned a navigator who spoke German."

Pell shrugged. "I didn't know."

"I speak German, too," Karl said. "My family spoke it at home. But we didn't have much use for it in the B-17."

"But Pell at least told us about you," Fox said. "Soon as he got here, he started asking if you were here. He mentioned a Hagan and a copilot named Adrian Baum. Thought maybe I'd know Baum, since I'm Jewish, too." Fox rolled his eyes. "But Pell never asked once about a navigator."

He never asked, Karl thought, *because he knew our navigator was dead.*

"I didn't think he got out," Pell said. "I'm damned glad to see he did."

"Hmm," Fox said. He hooked his thumbs into his pockets. Regarded Wilhelm wordlessly, and for long enough to move from awkwardness to open rudeness. Walked away in a manner that put Karl in mind of a crime film detective who'd just found a clue. A few of the other kriegies trailed behind him.

Some sort of little clique, Karl supposed. *Bastards.*

Karl fumed as he and Wilhelm left Pell's hut. The whole thing would have gone down smoothly if Fox hadn't nosed in. But they couldn't do anything about it now—except stay off the radar until one army or another plowed through the front gates.

After the p.m. roll call, however, Karl realized staying off the radar was damned near impossible. As the kriegies filtered back to their huts, Karl noticed three of them standing in a knot around Wilhelm. In the dusk, with light from a lamppost washing over them, they looked like gangland loan sharks cornering a debtor. And one of them was Fox.

Not good.

Karl lingered in a pool of darkness at the end of Hut 7C. His hiding place put him within earshot of Wilhelm and his new acquaintances.

"So, Meade," Fox said, "where did you go to nav school?"

Karl's diaphragm tensed. Would Wilhelm remember the things he'd taught him?

"Mather Field in California," Wilhelm said.

Karl let out a sigh of relief, but Fox continued with the third degree.

"Uh-huh," Fox said. "You and your buds do a lot of partying in L.A.? Look for some starlets in Hollywood?"

"Nope. Mather's close to Sacramento. Never got as far south as Los Angeles."

Another of Wilhelm's three interrogators spoke up: a short guy in a black watch cap, with a neatly trimmed moustache. Karl could barely understand his Scottish brogue.

"I'm still not buying your story, mate. If we find out you're not who you say you are, you just might have a little accident. Aye, ye'd never goose-step again."

Wilhelm glared at the Scot. "Are you calling me some kind of Nazi?" he asked. He must have been angry because he dropped the American accent; the question sounded more like the British English he'd learned in school.

"We don't know what you are, bub," the third man drawled. Karl had met him, too. A pilot from Oklahoma, though the kriegies called him "Tex" because of his accent.

In character again, Wilhelm muttered, "I don't have to listen to this." Turned to leave.

"Don't you turn your back on us," Fox said. Grabbed Wilhelm by the elbow.

Bad move.

Wilhelm reacted like the boxer he was: with a right cross. The blow landed on Fox's jaw. The Brooklyn man crumpled. He would have fallen if Tex hadn't caught him. The Scotsman lunged at Wilhelm, caught him around the waist. The two men fell to the ground and began kicking and punching in the dust and gravel.

"Hey!" Karl shouted. He ran toward the fight. Figured to break it up, make a big scene of coming to the rescue of a crewmate.

But someone else got there first.

Group Captain Timmersby, the senior-ranking POW, strode into the lamppost's glow. "Stop this rubbish," he ordered. "MacDougal! Stop it now!"

The Scot stopped struggling with Wilhelm—which was probably lucky for him. Wilhelm had freed his right arm and was ready with one of those powerful punches; Karl knew firsthand how much they stung. The Scot stood up, brushed himself off. Timmersby offered a hand to help Wilhelm up, but Wilhelm rose without assistance.

"MacDougal, you should be ashamed of yourself," Timmersby said in the clipped tones of a highly educated Brit. "Getting into a street fight like a common ruffian. You're a British officer."

"Yes, sir," MacDougal said, eyes downcast.

By now, Fox had recovered from Wilhelm's blow. He stood on his own, wiped blood from his mouth with the back of his hand.

"Just trying to establish some bona fides, sir," Fox said.

Karl turned toward Fox. "You leave my navigator the hell alone," Karl said. "Let's hope he knocked some sense into you. A man can't get much more bona fide than getting a B-17 blown out from under him. Ain't that right, Tommy?"

"Yep," Wilhelm said. Cut his eyes at Fox, who stared back as if saying: *This isn't over.*

"Now listen," Timmersby said. "We all know the war's going rather badly for the Jerries. They've got their knickers in a twist, and there's no telling what's in store for us. We've got plenty to worry about without fighting amongst ourselves."

Karl took a close look at the senior kriegie. Timmersby's flight suit bore the embroidered wings of a British pilot, with a crown in the center and a wreath around the letters *RAF.* Some sort of scar on his left thumb—probably a burn. Crow's-feet around his eyes. Given his rank, he was probably in his thirties, but he looked a decade older.

"We're just trying to figure out who we can trust," Tex said.

"Let me worry about that," Timmersby said. "If I see another fight like this, I'll put the lot of you on permanent laundry duty."

Just put them on laundry duty now, Karl thought. *Why let them off so easy?*

"Sorry, sir," MacDougal said.

Tex and Fox said nothing. They exchanged a glance, and Karl couldn't quite read whatever alliance ran between them. But Fox's contempt for Wilhelm and Karl was unmistakable; his smirk made that plain enough.

"We'll talk more about this tomorrow," Timmersby said. "Come see me in my office in the morning."

MacDougal and Tex at least had the decency to say "yes, sir" before they departed. Fox stalked off without a word. That left Karl and Wilhelm alone with the senior kriegie. Timmersby frowned like a man facing a new problem he didn't understand. Folded his arms as he looked at Karl and Wilhelm.

"McLendon told me about you two," Timmersby said. "You are a complication we didn't need."

"I realize that, sir," Karl said. "But I—"

"I'm not finished," Timmersby said, spoken in a command voice much colder than the one he'd used on Fox and Tex. "McLendon believes you, but I'm not sure I do. It really doesn't matter, though." He turned to Wilhelm. "There are men here who would kill you for being a spy, as you've probably gathered. If you really are a German naval officer, there are men here who would kill you for that, too. They wouldn't care if you deserted or not. And there are Jewish fellows here who worry about the SS coming round to take them to a place worse than the Russian side."

Fox among them. Maybe that explained his attitude.

"I understand," Wilhelm said.

"No, I don't think you do," Timmersby snapped. "After the escape attempt—I suppose you know about that—the stalags have become powder kegs. And you two amount to a pair of lit matches."

"Yes, sir," Karl said. "But with all due respect, if you just could get your boys to leave us alone ..." Karl gestured in the direction where Fox, Tex, and MacDougal had walked off.

"They were doing their job," Timmersby said.

"Beg your pardon, sir?" Karl said.

"Their job," Timmersby said. "Security."

Karl remembered Pell's warning, and then he understood. Wilhelm had just received a visit from the X Committee.

39

The Biscay Cross

Weeks passed and winter hardened. Mud in the Center Compound froze into concrete. Snow dusted the pines, piled onto window ledges, and drifted against outside walls. Wilhelm settled into camp life as best he could, but Karl and Pell remained his only real friends. The X Committee didn't trust him, and they'd put out word that no one else should, either.

Forlorn Christmas decorations began to appear around the prison camp. Someone placed a pine seedling in a corner of Hut 4B. Makeshift ornaments adorned its branches: foil from a cigarette pack, a label from a tin of English biscuits, an Eighth Air Force patch ripped from a uniform, a star carved from a block of wood.

One crackling cold evening, the kriegies' chaplain gathered the men for Christmas caroling around a barrel of burning trash. He wasn't a real chaplain; he was a bomber pilot. But before the war, he'd been a divinity student at an American school Wilhelm had never heard of: Wake Forest College. That was enough for the men to call him "Padre." He spoke in a United States Southern dialect Wilhelm could barely understand.

"Y'all know the Bible tells us the Israelites waited a long time for their deliverance," Padre said. "And many of us have waited a long time, too. We don't know the hour of our deliverance, but tonight we praise the Good Lord that it does seem near."

Padre then led the men in singing "Silent Night." Wilhelm listened, noting multiple layers of irony: Allied POWs, some of them Jewish, singing a Christian hymn originally written in German. Men in guard towers above them wielded loaded Mausers, and Wilhelm thought he heard one guard giving voice to the carol's original words: *"Stille Nacht."* Low clouds hid the moon and darkened the night, save for a single fissure that revealed a glimpse of ice crystal stars. Cinders from the barrel fire rose to meet them.

Distant thunder rumbled as the last notes faded. Or Wilhelm let his wandering mind pretend it was thunder, if only to stretch out this little moment of peace.

This, of course, wasn't thunder. It was Allied ordnance. Wilhelm didn't know if it was British bombers or Soviet artillery, but it didn't matter. The war was drawing closer.

Some of the men exchanged glances and smiled. From the darkness across the razor wire on the Russian side, cheers erupted.

"Sounds like we got some bass accompaniment," Padre said. The men laughed. "Let's close with 'It Came Upon the Midnight Clear.'"

Wilhelm had never heard this carol's lyrics. One verse was unfamiliar even to many of the Americans. Their voices died away, leaving only Padre and three or four others carrying the music. Those few voices sang loud and clear, and the words brought tears to Wilhelm's eyes:

> *"And man, at war with man, hears not*
> *The love-song, which they bring;*
> *O hush the noise, ye men of strife,*
> *And hear the angels sing."*

Detonations punctuated the final verse. The kriegies retired to their bunks, speaking in excited tones about release within days.

The next evening, they gathered for another hour of clandestine radio listening. Wilhelm hoped news might take his mind off his hunger. Supper for the POWs had consisted of nothing but stale bread and boiled potatoes—many of them starting to rot. He let himself imagine reports of a quick end to the war. Perhaps a coup had toppled Hitler. Perhaps fuel-starved German mechanized units had groaned to a halt. Perhaps the Allies had launched another invasion front from the Baltic.

Sparks began tuning his contraption, which gave off a warm hum. The tuning coil blipped and popped with snatches of voices in the ether, each word interrupted by crackle. For a while, no clear signal emerged, not even from the BBC. But those brief tatters of human voices from over the horizon gave Wilhelm hope in a world beyond his present darkness.

Sparks finally pulled down from the night a complete sentence, followed by more. An American newsman by the name of Richard C. Hottelet spoke of an unexpected development, but not the kind Wilhelm had envisioned.

A German offensive in the Ardennes Forest threatened to split the front. Already the map of Allied lines showed a bulge in the wrong direction, Hottelet reported, and overcast skies prevented air support. American forces seemed taken by surprise.

Maybe Wilhelm imagined it, but he thought some of the POWs glared at him as if he'd engineered the whole thing from the barracks of Stalag Luft XIV. If they looked for any hint of jubilation on Wilhelm's face, however, they did not find it. His spirits sank as if lashed to an anchor. He wished he could, like old Captain Slocum, simply sail away and disappear from the world altogether. Now it appeared the war might bleed on until the 1950s. Perhaps longer. Had not the kingdoms of England and France fought a Hundred Years' War?

Days passed and the cold bit harder. Frost crept across the inside walls of Hut 4B. Some men's fingertips turned glassy with the onset of frostbite, then darkened to purple when warmed again. Christmas came and went with little joy. Nights dragged and tempers flared. Unending hunger shortened everyone's fuse. The kriegies weren't quite starving, but they never ate their fill; rancid potatoes and kohlrabi satisfied no one.

Wilhelm had experienced hunger pangs before: During his U-boat days, the crew had occasionally lived on short rations to extend a patrol. But it was hard on these flyboys. Karl looked like he'd lost twenty pounds.

During the secret radio sessions, Wilhelm learned that an armored division led by General George Patton had relieved Americans at Bastogne, ending what the Yanks called the Battle of the Bulge. The kriegies were too cold and discouraged to celebrate.

The ferrets never came for Sparks's radio, but that fact did not seem to exonerate Wilhelm in the eyes of the X Committee. One afternoon in the washhouse, Fox and Tex taunted him with questions he could not answer: If he was from New York, how many boroughs did it have? Who pitched for the Dodgers? Did a Buick Roadmaster have four doors or two?

With each question, Fox moved closer to Wilhelm. By the time he asked about the car, his nose nearly touched Wilhelm's.

Fox seemed to want a fight, and Wilhelm decided to give it to him. Wilhelm grabbed him by the lapels, shoved him against a drying rack, and used another new expression: "I don't have to take any guff from you, pal."

A vein bulged in Fox's temple. He hawked up phlegm as if to spit in Wilhelm's face. But he never got the chance.

Wilhelm threw his uppercut—the one his opponents never saw coming. The blow came with a satisfying crack, and it knocked the USAAF cap from Fox's head. Tex grabbed Wilhelm from behind. For his trouble, Tex caught an elbow in the nose. Blood streamed from both nostrils.

Men outside must have heard the commotion; Karl and McLendon burst into the washhouse. The two grabbed Fox and Tex by their shirt collars and broke up the fight.

"I'm gonna make you boys stay after school if you keep this up," McLendon said.

"I'm telling you, sir," Fox said as he rubbed his chin, "there's something not right about this guy. I'm just trying to do my job, here."

"You're a hardheaded son of a bitch, aren't you?" Karl said. "I told you, he's my navigator. I've known him for almost two years."

"If he's a navigator," Fox said, "I'm Joe DiMaggio."

"Shut up, all of you," McLendon shouted. "You stop this crap now. We got enough problems as it is. One of the guards let it slip, we're getting another inspection tomorrow. I got a feeling things are gonna get worse before they get better." McLendon shook his finger in Fox's face. "And I don't need any more barroom brawls."

"Sir," Fox said, "if the SS starts pulling some of us out of roll call tomorrow, we'll know where they got their information."

"You go to hell," Karl said.

"Enough," McLendon said. "Meade and Hagan, out of here. Fox and Tex, finish the wash and get back to your barracks."

"Yes, sir," Tex said.

"Yes, sir," Fox said. But he wasn't looking at McLendon. He stared at Wilhelm until Wilhelm turned to leave.

At the next morning roll call, Wilhelm stood in formation and tried to stop his teeth from chattering. Dirty, packed snow crunched under his boots. Men coughed and wheezed. Life in U-boats could be miserable, but at least the damned things got warm when the hatches were closed.

At the front of the formation, two strangers appeared with *Kommandant* Becker. One was an SS *standartenführer*. The other was a *Luftwaffe* major. Wilhelm craned his neck for a better look. When the major came into clear view, Wilhelm realized the major was no stranger. *Mein Gott!* It was Treider, who had interrogated him at the *dulag luft. Yes, the flightless bird.* The *Luftwaffe* man with the temperament of a Gestapo commander. Treider remained within two paces of the *standartenführer.* Perhaps he wanted to be SS. As these Americans would say, a man who missed his calling.

The guards reported all prisoners accounted for, and Becker mounted the podium. He looked no happier than Timmersby, who eyed the SS officer with undisguised hatred. The *kommandant* kept his words brief.

"We are joined by *Standartenführer* Keisinger and Major Treider of the *Luftwaffe*," Becker said. With no further words of introduction, he yielded the podium to Keisinger.

Keisinger clomped atop the wooden platform, his jackboots gleaming. A leather trench coat shielded him from the chill. His hat bore the SS skull insignia, purportedly signifying an SS man's willingness to die for the German people. Wilhelm saw a simpler meaning: the pointless carnage brought about by the ideology behind that black uniform.

"I see you are enjoying a life of leisure, courtesy of the *Luftwaffe*," Keisinger said. He emphasized the last word in a way that dripped contempt for the air force. "But the SS requires more than leisure from a few of you. While we are here for inspections, we will conduct interviews with select prisoners."

Timmersby, face reddened, strode toward the podium. "I protest this," he shouted. He tried to say more, but Keisinger cut him off.

"Silence," Keisinger ordered. "Guards, take him to my temporary office. The rest of you, we will come and get you if we need you. For now, you are dismissed."

The kriegies did not disassemble immediately. They stood in place and watched two SS noncoms lead away the senior POW. Timmersby kept up a defiant front, his back straight as a mast. As he passed, one of the RAF kriegies offered a two-finger *V*-for-Victory sign. For his effort, the RAF man received the butt of a Mauser in his stomach. He doubled over and fell. Two other POWs helped him to his feet.

What could the SS want with us now? Wilhelm wondered. He noted how thoroughly he had come to identify with the POWs. *Yes, us.* Despite the X Committee's suspicions, he felt more in common with Allied prisoners than with the Germans who guarded them. There were Jews among them, just as there were Lutherans and atheists. *And no one cared.*

He doubted the SS would kill Timmersby and the other "select prisoners" outright. Maybe Keisinger hoped to glean information from high-value POWs as a crumbling regime scrambled for whatever advantage it could find.

But who could the other "select prisoners" be?

By the middle of the afternoon, Wilhelm learned he was one.

Two SS guards burst through the doorway of Hut 4B. Wilhelm and Karl had just sat down to tin cups of weak coffee. Wilhelm had taken only one sip when the door banged open and cold air rushed in.

"Meade," one of the guards barked. "Thomas Meade."

Karl and Wilhelm locked eyes. What could they want with "Meade," who was just another junior officer? Had Wilhelm's real identity finally caught up with him?

It seemed likely. So many little threads might have unraveled Wilhelm's cover: His *Kriegsmarine* watch, stolen when they were first captured. A careless word spoken with a German accent. An alert clerk noting that a naval officer had gone missing in the same city on the same day as the downing of several American fliers.

So now it ends, Wilhelm thought. *By my wits and the kindness of an American, I have lived a few extra weeks. But my survival was never the point. My crew was the point. Maybe, just maybe, they didn't die on a useless suicide mission, because they couldn't patrol without an executive officer. And the navy didn't have a lot of spare execs to replace me.*

Just hold on to that thought, Wilhelm told himself. *It will carry you through until the firing squad chambers their rounds.*

The guards evidently spoke no English. They said nothing except "Thomas Meade," and they gestured mutely with their weapons. They marched Wilhelm across the frozen compound, through a side gate, and down the road to the *Kommandantur.*

There, in the camp headquarters complex, the guards ushered him into a small wooden office building. They placed him in a bare room furnished only with a table and straight-backed chairs. They shoved him into a chair, tied his arms behind him, and left.

Wilhelm noticed light patches on the wall where maps, diagrams, or pictures of the Führer had recently hung. Until this morning, perhaps, this had been just another office. Now it had become an interrogation room, much like the one he'd seen before.

So this is probably not my execution chamber, Wilhelm realized. *But why interrogate me, or "Meade," again?*

An hour passed. His arms grew cramped and his bladder grew full. Exactly the point of keeping him here, he supposed. Soften him up for questioning.

Stay alert and keep thinking, he told himself. *They may not intend to shoot you immediately, but you will need an agile mind to survive this day.*

Boots clomped on the plank stairs outside. A moment later, the door swung open. In waddled Treider. His clothing was wrinkled and, as before, he needed a shave. Behind him came Keisinger, whose uniform was as immaculate as Treider's was sloppy. Everything on the SS officer shone black and silver except the red armband with the swastika. Clearly, one man took pride in his branch of service, though God alone knew why. The other apparently did not relish his ground role in the *Luftwaffe. The flightless bird wants a black uniform, too.*

The two SS guards came in with Treider and Keisinger. Keisinger carried a file folder. He opened it and perused a sheet of paper.

"Good afternoon, Lieutenant Meade," Keisinger said. "A pleasure to meet you more directly than during *appell*."

Wilhelm did not reply. His arms hurt and he needed a restroom. Treider stepped forward and leaned so close, Wilhelm could see the red veins across the whites of his eyes.

"*Standartenführer* Keisinger feels we went too easily on you on your first interrogation at the *dulag luft*," Treider said. "I tend to agree. So we will talk again, and you will tell us more."

You're an American, Wilhelm reminded himself. *Act like one. Talk like one. For every syllable.*

"I already toldya," Wilhelm said. "I was a navigator. Not the best one, but that, uh, ain't my fault. They didn't tell me much."

Treider grabbed Wilhelm by the hair. Yanked his head back to force his eyes upward. Wilhelm glared, seethed. In the ring, he could have destroyed this fat man in seconds.

Don't get emotional, Wilhelm told himself. *A battle of fists would be glorious, but this is a battle of wits. This man's failed ambitions have curdled inside him to create a meanness of spirit. Use that,* Wilhelm thought. *Use everything you know.*

"Those of you who did not tell us much will tell us much today," Treider said. "We do not have time for your fanciful excuses anymore."

Time? What is their rush?

The booms in the distance are their rush, Wilhelm realized.

As the Russians advanced, the prisoners would either be moved or liquidated. This was a last effort to extract information from them.

"In some of our other facilities," Keisinger said, "we have a range of methods to loosen tongues. Not here. Hermann Göring sees you as worthy adversaries, though I will never understand why. Yet, he has the ear of the Führer, and we must follow his orders."

"If it were up to me," Treider said, "I would introduce you to those other methods. But I do not have a knife or a needle. I do not have poison gas or a blowtorch. I have only my pen, for writing."

With great ceremony, Treider pulled a fountain pen from his pocket and held it up. Issued by the Party, the cap featured an inlaid swastika. For a moment, Treider looked like some comical fat man about to perform a magic trick: *I will make this pen disappear.*

Treider passed the pen to one of the guards, who stepped behind Wilhelm. The guard placed one hand on the back of the chair. With the other hand, he slipped the pen between the fingers of Wilhelm's left hand. Positioned the pen across the main knuckle of his middle finger. Pressed hard.

Pain shot through Wilhelm's hand and all the way up his arm. He arched his back and clenched his jaw. His breath hissed between his teeth.

"I suppose that hurts," Treider said with a smirk. Wilhelm thought about what his ungloved left jab could do to that smirk.

The guard released pressure on the pen and Wilhelm's finger. Wilhelm relaxed the muscles of his back and settled into the chair.

"What do you want from me?" Wilhelm asked. He felt sweat popping out across his upper lip.

"We want to know about the radar on your bombers," Keisinger said. "Let us begin with the simple things. Where in the aircraft is the radar unit located?"

"I don't know," Wilhelm said. And, of course, that was the truth.

I could not give them this information if I wanted to, he thought. Mein Gott, *they will break all ten of my fingers.*

Treider nodded to the guard behind Wilhelm. The pen crushed against Wilhelm's knuckle once more. Pain seared through his hand again, only worse. He turned his eyes to the ceiling and stifled a scream. The sound that came out of him turned into a series of grunts and gasps.

"You will never fly again if we cripple your hand," Treider said.

Wilhelm glared at him. He thought of a rejoinder, and he could not resist voicing it.

"Kinda like you never flew at all?" Wilhelm said.

Treider's face flushed. He stepped forward and slapped Wilhelm. The stinging blow turned Wilhelm's head. Then he felt the pen grind into his knuckle again.

Despite himself, Wilhelm cried out. He cursed himself for giving Treider the satisfaction. His bladder throbbed as though it would burst. Wilhelm fought to control it, tightened his loin muscles. Sweat now beaded on his forehead and ran into his eyes.

"Let us dispense with insults and get down to business," Keisinger said. "Again, where is the radar located?"

Wilhelm considered his answer. Why shouldn't he just guess? That couldn't hurt the Allied cause, and if he kept silent, he might lose the use of his hands.

"Amidships," Wilhelm said. Scheisse, he thought. *That is not aviator language. Think, think, think.*

"Where, 'amidships'?" Keisinger said.

"Uh, near the radio operator." Another guess.

Keisinger scribbled notes. Treider watched him write, and he beamed as if he'd just made a breakthrough.

"So," Keisinger said, "the radio operator also operates the radar?"

"Uh, yeah." Yet another guess. But it made sense. Radar was a form of radio.

Keisinger made another note, then glanced up from his folder.

"Very good," he said. "And what is the manufacturer and model number of this radar?"

"I don't know."

The guard clamped down with the pen. Wilhelm cried out again. This time, it felt as if his fingers would break like dry twigs. When he arched his back, his shirt tightened across his shoulders as if to rip at the seams.

"Surely, you recognize a pattern here," Treider said. "'I don't know' is the wrong answer."

"I . . . I wouldn't know the model number. I'm not the guy who uses it."

Wilhelm sucked in long breaths, forced himself to concentrate. Primarily, he concentrated on not losing his water. Then he tried to think through the pain. Now his fingers hurt even when the guard released pressure. He blinked to clear the burning sweat from his eyes.

"The control panel for this radar," Keisinger continued, "what does it look like?"

"Switches and knobs," Wilhelm said.

Again came the crushing pressure. This time, the pain was too much. Wilhelm let out a full-throated scream. He felt a few drops of urine escape, but he tensed every muscle in his midsection and stopped it.

"We need you to be a bit more specific," Keisinger said.

Now they will break my fingers, Wilhelm thought. *I have nothing more to give them. They might as well ask me Roosevelt's telephone number.*

Think, he ordered himself. Mein Gott, *think. But I know nothing of American bombers, except what it's like on the receiving end.*

The receiving end. Yes, Wilhelm thought. *I do know about that. Turn it around and use what you know.*

"Look," Wilhelm said, "I don't operate the radar, so I can't tell you how it works. But I can tell you we use it against your U-boats."

Both Treider and Keisinger looked straight at Wilhelm. Keisinger began writing again.

"Now we are getting somewhere," Keisinger said. "Perhaps you are not so stupid, after all, Lieutenant. Please go on."

No, I am not stupid, Wilhelm thought. *But you two are probably ignorant of naval tactics. What I tell you will be news to you, but of no harm to Karl's colleagues still in the fight.*

"We think your U-boats can detect the radar," Wilhelm said. Of course, they could, for a time. Wilhelm's crew used to employ something called a Biscay Cross, named for the Bay of Biscay, where it was so often needed. The Biscay Cross consisted of two crossbeams strung with antenna wire. It received radar signals and warned of an attacking aircraft's approach. Wilhelm had stood many a watch on the bridge with the Biscay Cross affixed above him.

"Very good," Keisinger said. "Very good. But why do you believe the U-boats can do this?"

"We use the radar to find them on the surface. But sometimes, as soon as we turn it on, they dive."

Keisinger and Treider exchanged glances as if they'd just extracted major intelligence. *Such morons,* Wilhelm thought. He decided not to tell them the rest of the story: The Biscay Cross had become useless. The Allies learned simply to change the radar's wavelength, and U-boats recharging their batteries on the surface once again became sitting ducks.

"You have been most helpful, Lieutenant," Keisinger said. "Take heart, you have not betrayed your country. On the contrary, you have aided it by shortening the war."

No, I have not betrayed my country, Wilhelm thought. *But you have.*

40

Courage Is Contagious

After the SS came for Wilhelm, Karl spent the rest of the day worried sick. Worried that Wilhelm might never return. Worried about who else Keisinger and Treider would interrogate. Worried whether his own turn would come for questioning under torture.

They never came for Karl, but they pulled out McLendon, Fox, and several other kriegies. Karl could not begin to guess why they made those choices. When the guards marched Wilhelm back into the compound, Karl felt a weight lift from his shoulders. Wilhelm looked all right, except he was cradling his left hand. Karl met him outside Hut 4B. As soon as the guards left, Karl asked, "What did they do to your hand?"

"They almost broke my fingers, but I got them to stop."

"How did you manage that?"

"I told them something they thought they wanted to hear."

Karl's mouth dropped partly open, and he furrowed his eyebrows. "What could you possibly tell them that wouldn't get you killed?" he whispered.

"Long story. But I heard a Yank expression a while ago that sums it up quite well."

"What's that?"

"'If you can't dazzle them with diamonds, baffle them with bull-shit.'"

Karl laughed out loud. He couldn't remember the last time he'd done that. "All right," he said. "Someday I want to hear the whole story, if we get out of here alive."

When darkness fell, the booms sounded again. By now, the report of heavy guns had become a nightly occurrence. Karl knew little about ground weaponry, so he couldn't identify the shells by their sound. But sometimes a high-pitched whistle preceded the detona-tions, as if the sky itself were ripping apart. The explosions varied from piercing cracks to ground-rattling thuds.

After supper, the kriegies in 4B gathered around Sparks's radio with a sense of dread. McLendon, their block commander, still hadn't returned from interrogation. Sparks put together his radio and posted a man on watch. He tuned in the BBC, and the POWs learned the Red Army had taken Warsaw. As if to punctuate the broadcast, an ex-plosion vibrated the floor.

"Sounds like they're taking a lot more than Warsaw," Sparks said.

Before anyone else could comment, the kriegie on watch turned and hissed, "Somebody's coming."

In moves too quick to follow, Sparks took apart the radio. Three prisoners snatched up components, and in seconds, all the pieces had disappeared.

"Relax," the watchman said. "It's McLendon."

When the block commander appeared in the doorway, Karl drew in a sharp breath. McLendon cradled his hand like Wilhelm had done, except splints covered two fingers. Bruises discolored his cheeks, and his lower lip was split.

"What happened, Captain?" Sparks asked.

"They roughed us up pretty good," McLendon said. He spoke as if it hurt to talk. "Beat the hell out of Timmersby. Fox, too."

"Sons of bitches," Sparks said. "They broke your fingers?"

"Yeah."

"Did they ask about radar?" Wilhelm said. "That's what they wanted from me."

McLendon stumbled to the table and lowered himself painfully into a chair. Sparks got up, went to the stove, and poured him a cup of tea.

"Yeah," McLendon said. "They wanted to know if we used it on U-boats." He gave Wilhelm a hard look. "But mainly they wanted to know about the X Committee. Did they ask you about that?"

"No."

"Well, maybe they saved those questions for those of us who've been here the longest."

"Wait," Sparks said. "They know about the X Committee?"

"They didn't call it that, but they know we have an organization." McLendon sipped his tea, crossed his arms on the table, and rested his chin on them. Sighed hard. "If anybody had given up any names, we'd probably know it by now," he continued. "They'd have been dragged off and shot. I checked with Timmersby on the way back. He said everybody's accounted for."

"Thank God for that," Sparks said. "Did the boss say anything else?"

McLendon raised his head, rubbed his eyes with his good hand, and said, "Yeah, we talked about the Russians getting here. Bottom line is the Krauts will either move us or shoot us."

No one spoke for several seconds. Another boom shook the rafters.

"The boss says he hopes one or two of the decent guards will tip us off if the SS or Gestapo decides to kill everybody," McLendon continued.

Slim hope, Karl thought. *Sounds like Timmersby has an overly favorable view of human nature.*

"What, then?" Sparks asked.

"Mass breakout," McLendon said. "No tunnel, no hiding, no nothing. Just storm the gates like wild horses. They'll shoot a bunch of us, but maybe some will survive. If you're one of the lucky ones, make your way to Allied lines as best you can."

So there it was. Karl's life, Wilhelm's life, and the lives of all the other men hung on whim and chance. Karl thought of his cousin Gerhard, probably still on the run from the FBI because of his pro-Nazi leanings.

What would I say to him now? Karl considered. *This place is hell. Wish you were here.*

Having thought of Gerhard for the first time in days might have caused Karl to seethe for an hour. But he didn't get the chance. A fierce pounding on the door rattled him out of his funk. The blows struck hard and sharp—not knuckles rapping, but wood against wood.

"What the hell?" McLendon said.

Karl wondered the same thing. Kraut guards would just burst in; they wouldn't bother to knock. But there was no courtesy to this banging. What could be so urgent?

"Open up," a voice called from outside. An American accent.

"I got it," Sparks said. He rose and went to the door.

"Who do they think they are, pounding like that?" McLendon said.

Sparks opened the door to a cold and brittle night. From where Karl was sitting, he could see five men standing outside: Fox, Tex, and three kriegies Karl didn't know. Pale light from the low-wattage bulbs inside spilled through the doorway and cast flickering shadows. Fox held a two-by-four; he must have pounded on the door with that. Tex wielded a sawed-off broom handle. The other men carried bricks. The scene put Karl in mind of a lynch mob showing up at the jailhouse, demanding the sheriff turn over a suspect. They lacked only the ropes and shotguns.

Fox pointed with his two-by-four. "We need to have a little discussion with Herr Meade, or whatever the hell his name is," Fox said. A bandage covered the side of his chin. A deep scratch on his neck had begun to scab over. The dim light set a ghoulish cast to his injured face, and something about his left eye didn't look right. When Fox turned his head, Karl saw that the white of that eye had reddened from a burst blood vessel. The man had apparently paid a price for protecting names on the X Committee.

McLendon stood, in obvious pain. Stumbled to the doorway. "Lieutenant Fox," he said, "we've both had a rough day, and I'll write off your bad judgment to that. But don't you *ever* come to my hut like this again. And the next word out of your mouth better be 'sir.'"

Fox glared. Slapped the end of the two-by-four into his hand like a batter walking up to the plate. Finally he said, "*Sir,* they know about our little committee, and they've obviously sent somebody to sniff it out."

"Of course, they know we're organized," McLendon said. "They've suspected it at least since the breakout over at Stalag III. Every prison has some kind of X Committee."

"Captain," Tex said, "don't you think it's a little strange that Meade don't seem to know nothing about New York, and he claims he's from there. Don't seem to know much about airplanes, neither."

Karl looked over at Wilhelm, who remained quiet.

"They interrogated him today, too," Karl said.

"Yeah, and look at him," Fox said. "Not a mark on him."

"We need to do some interrogating, ourselves," Tex said. *"Him."* Tex leaned through the doorway and pointed his stick at Wilhelm. *"Him."* He pointed at Karl. "And that bombardier Billy Pell, too. I don't trust none of them."

"What you need to do," McLendon said, "is take your little pitchfork-and-torches act off my steps. You're getting real close to a court-martial, either here or whenever we get back Stateside."

Somebody needed to blink first, and Karl wondered who it would be. If McLendon and the other commanders lost control, the camp could descend into mob rule. That would be deadly for Wilhelm—and not a good thing for anyone, with Russian divisions practically right outside the gate.

"I'm not kidding," McLendon said. "This is misconduct before the enemy. Do you want that reputation when you get back home? You'll never get a job again."

McLendon might be overreaching with that, Karl thought.

Karl didn't like Fox. However, if these guys suspected a Kraut plant in their midst, of course they'd want to do something about it. A jury would have a hard time calling that "misconduct."

Overreaching or not, the block commander's statement took the fire out of their eyes. Tex lowered his stick, and one of his pals dropped the brick he'd carried. Fox held on to his two-by-four. He turned to leave, and McLendon slammed the door.

Inside Hut 4B, McLendon didn't say a word. But he gave Karl and Wilhelm a slicing glance, and Karl could imagine what he was thinking: *Look what you've done to us, bringing a Kraut deserter in here. Thanks for nothing.*

At the next morning roll call, something felt different. The guards rushed through their count without the usual precision. Treider and

Keisinger stood around, but said nothing. *Kommandant* Becker looked distracted when he mounted the podium.

"Gentlemen," the *kommandant* said, "you are about to embark on a little journey. You will be marched west to another camp. You have twenty-four hours to prepare your things. Needless to say, anyone attempting to escape will be shot."

Becker stepped down, and a buzz rose from the assembled kriegies. *Where are we going? Why so little notice? The Russians must be right on top of us.*

Karl felt relieved. *A long march will be no picnic,* he thought, *but it's better than machine guns opening up on all of us right now.*

Group Captain Timmersby took the podium. He walked with a limp, the result of his latest interrogation.

"Well, chaps," he said, "there it is. Not much we can do about it, so we might as well get cracking. Pack your warm clothing and blankets, of course, and whatever nonperishable food you have. Remain with your assigned groups. Outside these gates, your block commanders will become your squadron commanders, as it were."

Treider and Keisinger looked out over the ranks of prisoners. Keisinger whispered something to Treider. Treider nodded. Keisinger folded his arms across that black leather trench coat. Both men stood silently as the POWs were dismissed.

The prisoners went to work right away. Karl and Wilhelm gathered remnants of Red Cross packages: mainly nuts and moldy crackers. Other residents of Hut 4B packed cookware and blankets. From old bedsheets, they improvised haversacks. Prisoners of war were not normally expected to go on field marches, so neither the Germans nor the Red Cross had supplied them with backpacks.

As the men went about their chores, Karl began to worry about what might come next. Last night showed just how frayed the command and control had become among the prisoners. The disorder of a march might give Fox the perfect chance to slip a knife between Wilhelm's ribs. Yes, Wilhelm could handle himself in a fight; he'd shown that more than once. But what if he didn't see it coming?

Even without tension among the prisoners, Karl knew this march offered plenty of potential for trouble. How would the Germans react if they found the Red Army on their heels? What might happen to kriegies who weakened and fell behind?

By afternoon, the camp had been transformed. Drawings and photos had come down from walls. Shelves had been cleared. Laundry had been taken down from clotheslines, and the clotheslines packed away as survival rope. The men formed up for roll call, anxious about the road ahead.

As the guards counted the POWs, two black staff cars and a truck rolled through the gate and stopped at the front of the formation. Keisinger and Treider met the vehicles. SS officers Karl hadn't seen before emerged from the cars. Armed guards in SS uniforms piled from the truck and stationed themselves around the rows of prisoners. The guards carried a variety of weapons: Mausers, machine pistols, even an MG34. The SS officers conferred at length with *Kommandant* Becker.

What was this about? Certainly nothing good. Karl looked at the kriegies around him. Everyone appeared nervous. Fox stood in the same row with Karl, two men to the left. Wilhelm stood two rows in front, Sparks beside him. At the head of Karl's section, of course, was McLendon. Karl couldn't see Billy Pell; the bombardier would have formed up with his hut mates, somewhere behind Karl. Timmersby, as the senior-ranking POW, stood facing the formation.

Finally Keisinger mounted the podium. In the cold winter silence, his boot steps on the wooden platform echoed across the camp.

"As you know," Keisinger said, "you are about to march to another prison. Most of you will remain under the control of the *Luftwaffe.* However, the Jews among you will proceed to a different location."

Karl felt his pulse pounding through an artery in his temple. Was he about to witness some Allied POWs marched off to their deaths?

"What is the meaning of this?" Timmersby shouted.

A guard strode over to the group captain. Swung a Mauser stock against the side of Timmersby's head. Timmersby collapsed.

"Unfortunately," Keisinger continued, "this camp has not kept proper records with regard to racial hygiene. Therefore, during this *appell,* you will identify the Jews among yourselves."

A murmur rose from the formation. Karl glanced over at Fox, who was trembling. Karl knew of Fox and just a few other Jewish men; he wasn't sure exactly how many Jews there were, and he was glad he didn't know.

"Silence," Keisinger called out. "You will keep your military bearing during this process, and you will identify each Jew. Group Captain Timmersby, if you please."

Timmersby rose to his feet with the help of two other kriegies. He stood at attention. He remained silent.

"Very well," Keisinger said. He opened his trench coat and unholstered a Luger. Keisinger walked up to Timmersby. Pointed the pistol at the Brit's forehead. Timmersby said nothing. He simply stared straight ahead with an expression of pure defiance.

Kommandant Becker rushed to Keisinger's side and spoke words Karl could not hear. Keisinger looked annoyed. The *standartenführer* lowered his pistol and began walking among the rows of prisoners. "Your *kommandant* prefers that I not shoot your senior officer," Keisinger said. "The rest of you are more expendable."

He stopped in front of a man several rows in front of Karl. "You," the *standartenführer* said. "Which Jews do you know?"

"I, uh, I just got here," the man said.

Keisinger's eyes rolled as if the man had given a particularly stupid answer to a simple question. He motioned for two of the SS goons. They hustled over and beat the man to the ground.

Dear God, Karl thought, *he's probably gonna shoot the next guy.*

Keisinger stalked the ranks of kriegies, searching for his next victim. As he came closer to the men of Hut 4B, Karl's heart pounded. *What do we do? What do we say?*

The *standartenführer* scanned the men. His gaze fell upon Wilhelm.

Keisinger moved through the formation. He stopped directly in front of Wilhelm. Held the pistol low, ready either to smash someone's face with it or blow out someone's brains.

"Ah, Lieutenant Meade," Keisinger said. "We had a most pleasant conversation earlier. I know you are a reasonable man. You would not sacrifice your Aryan mates for a handful of Christ killers, would you?"

Karl tried to imagine what Wilhelm was thinking. The man had given up everything to avoid sacrificing his crew for a cause like this. Wilhelm had told Karl of the slave laborers he'd seen at the U-boat bunker—their emaciated bodies, the casual murder. Men like Keisinger had engineered such horrors.

Keisinger seemed ready to start executing POWs until someone named names. Karl felt like a pilot flying a plane that had just lost its wings: This would end badly no matter what anyone did. More than likely, Wilhelm would refuse to talk, and he would take a bullet. And Keisinger would move on to the next man.

But Wilhelm did speak. He uttered his words in a voice loud enough for all to hear.

"We are all Jews," Wilhelm said.

Keisinger's eyes widened. His lips pursed so tightly the blood went out of them and they flushed white. The *standartenführer* shook with barely contained fury.

"We are all Jews," Wilhelm repeated in his best American accent. "Every one of us."

"Brilliant," Timmersby called out. He coughed, spat, then said, "Bloody right. We're all Jews."

A flight instructor had once told Karl that in a crisis, panic was contagious. But so, too, was courage.

McLendon shouted, "We're all Jews. Right, men?"

"Yes, sir," several kriegies responded, not quite in unison.

In his loudest voice, McLendon bellowed, "I can't *heeeear youuuuu.*"

"Sir, yes, sir!" the men answered, this time as one. Karl sang out with them at full voice.

Keisinger placed the Luger to Wilhelm's nose. The muzzle bounced as Keisinger's hand quivered with rage.

Perhaps Keisinger decided there were too many *Luftwaffe* men present as witnesses. Perhaps he feared what *Kommandant* Becker might report. For whatever reason, Keisinger lowered his pistol.

Then he punched Wilhelm in the gut. Wilhelm doubled over. Kriegies caught him before he could hit the ground.

Keisinger pushed his way through the assembled prisoners. He waved a black-gloved hand for his guards to fall in and mount their truck. A driver opened the door to the first staff car. The *standartenführer* sat in the rear seat and glared at the POWs. Treider and the rest of the SS men entered the staff cars as well. The drivers took their places behind the wheels, and all three vehicles drove out through the main gate.

41

The Edge of Endurance

For the rest of the day and into the evening, kriegies offered Wilhelm backslaps and congratulations. Tex came to him with an entirely changed attitude and said, "You stared that fool down like he didn't have nothing but a cap pistol. You *owned* his ass." Laughter—rare in the prison—bubbled around Wilhelm.

Karl had a slightly different take. He seemed greatly relieved; from time to time, he glanced at Wilhelm and nodded—almost as if checking to make sure Wilhelm was still there. But Karl made only one comment. He smiled and said, "You got more balls than sense."

Wilhelm had to think about that for a moment to decipher its meaning. Then he whispered, "One could say the same about anyone who steps aboard a U-boat."

Fox came to Wilhelm's hut, offered his hand, and shook firmly.

"I still don't get your story, Meade," Fox said. "But you're all right." He continued the handshake for a long moment, and he repeated, "You're all right." When he released Wilhelm's hand, he said, "I'm sorry about how I acted. I worried about who you were and why you were here. I'm still confused. But you're a mensch, that's for sure. I'm not confused about that."

"You have no reason to apologize," Wilhelm said. "You were doing your job as you saw it. You only wanted to protect your mates. Believe me, I understand."

Fox folded his arms and said, "One day, I want to buy you a beer."

Despite the sudden goodwill from Fox and the other POWs who had shunned him, Wilhelm felt no triumph. Yes, he had done the right thing. For once. He believed the deed weighed little against the rest of his record: torpedoes and flames, sinking freighters and drowning sailors—all for a cause not worthy of his crew's dedication.

Wilhelm, Karl, and the rest of the prisoners spent the next day continuing to pack food and clothing. They expected the order to move out at any moment. But this operation lacked classic German precision; guards appeared disorganized and with little more knowledge than the kriegies about what to expect. Wilhelm went to bed fully dressed, attempting to sleep with the one blanket he had not yet packed.

Around midnight, shortly after Wilhelm had drifted off to sleep, the order finally came. Guards flung open the door. One shouted, "*Alles* roust! Up, up!" The kriegies fell out into a subfreezing January night. Shots cracked in the distance. Flames billowed from the North Compound; someone had set a hut afire.

Wilhelm stayed close to Karl and McLendon as the men marched out of the Center Compound. The prisoners walked in threes and fours, keeping more or less within their assigned blocks. Dry snow squeaked underfoot. In the clear night, stars like silver dust wheeled overhead. Wilhelm picked out Orion, noted the Hunter's orientation, and determined the column was heading southwest. Shellfire rumbled and thudded from the east.

Three hours into the march, Karl moved close and whispered, "Are you gonna take off? The war's all but over. This might be your chance."

Wilhelm had already considered this.

"Too dangerous now," he said. At this point, he was unlikely to face a court-martial from a navy that barely existed. But between Russian and American lines, he would find desperate Germans with guns, both soldiers and civilians. Panicked perhaps, maybe angry, possibly drunk. Quick to fire. Wilhelm explained that he'd even heard a friendly guard talk of "werewolves"—dead-enders who could not accept defeat and wanted only to kill as many Allied troops or prisoners as possible before taking a bullet for the doomed Fatherland.

"Bullshit," Karl said.

"What?" Wilhelm asked.

"Yeah, it's dangerous. But you could blend in. You're one of them, for Pete's sake. Don't feel like you gotta see me through. You don't owe me a thing."

Wilhelm walked in silence for several meters. *But I do owe you,* he thought. *You and McLendon, the other kriegies—even Fox—are now my only friends.*

"I'm serious," Karl pressed. "Don't push your luck."

"I will not. But for now, I'm safer here."

In Wilhelm's considered military analysis, that was true. Yet Karl had a point. Whenever the time came, leave-taking would bring pain. More than likely, there would be no time for a proper *auf Wiedersehen.*

Do not let your emotions cloud your judgment at a critical juncture, Wilhelm told himself.

Dawn revealed avenues of snow-shrouded pines along both sides of the road. The sight would have been beautiful if not for the cold. Wilhelm's fingers, toes, and lips grew numb. He balled his fists inside his Red Cross–issued gloves. Karl and the other prisoners suffered as well. Frost formed on the stubble of Karl's upper lip as he exhaled moisture-laden air. Timmersby walked with a limp, the result of the blows he'd taken at the hands of the SS. Karl and Sparks offered to carry his bundle of food and blankets.

"Not necessary, chaps," Timmersby said. "Really, I'm fine."

The pines gave way to hedgerows and open fields. At a crossroads, the column halted. The POWs yielded to let a group of civilians pass through the intersection.

They appeared to be a group of farm families, refugees fleeing the Russian advance. Twenty people—young mothers, small children, older men—trudged alongside three horse-drawn carts. The men had not shaved in days. The carts groaned with furniture and crates. Pitchforks, scythes, rakes, and hoes bristled from one of the carts.

Wilhelm was a city boy and did not know horses, but to him, the animals looked sick and exhausted. Ropes of mucus dangled from their noses.

Every adult had a weapon of some kind. A woman with an old rifle glared at the prisoners and spat on the ground. One man wielded a single-barreled shotgun. Those who lacked firearms carried a variety of sharp-edged farm tools: sickles, corn knives, and axes.

They spoke not a word as they passed through the crossroads. The only sound came from the horses: the clopping of hooves and the jangling of hardware on their tack. A rangy animal smell lingered behind them.

Wilhelm thought: *This is what my country has done to itself. Brought down the world's wrath and turned ourselves into refugees within our own borders.*

By the third day of the march, men began to falter. At one rest stop, two POWs stretched out in the snow and refused to get up. Guards prodded them with rifles. Wilhelm feared he was about to witness another murder. He had heard shots in the distance, and he assumed guards farther back in the column were executing prisoners who fell out. But this time, the men rose up onto their hands and knees, then stood and began taking small steps. Patches of packed snow fell from their trousers. The guards did not shoot.

The march resumed. Pell left his own group so he could rejoin Karl. The two erstwhile crewmates walked alongside Wilhelm, McLendon, and Fox. Several meters ahead, a man staggered and fell. It was Timmersby.

"Sir," McLendon said, "you have to let us carry your stuff."

Timmersby lay on the ground, lips blue from cold and eyes rheumy with pain. He held his side and said, "It's not just where they hit me. My feet are in bloody awful shape. You chaps go ahead. I'll rest and catch up."

"Hell no, sir," McLendon said.

"Let's take a look at your feet, sir," Pell said.

Timmersby protested, but they removed his boots and socks. Wilhelm winced when he saw the group captain's feet. Red and white blisters oozed fluid and pus.

Up ahead in the column, a guard noticed the commotion. Wilhelm hadn't seen this man before; perhaps he was a guard from a different compound. No telling whether he was kind or not. The guard turned and began striding back toward the knot of men around the commander.

"Roust!" the guard shouted. "*Schnell!*"

He looked tired and frightened. He held his Mauser ready across his chest.

"Hold your horses there, Fritz," McLendon said.

The guard did not seem to understand. "Roust!" he said. Raised his weapon and pointed it at Timmersby. Thumbed the safety.

"We will carry him on a sled," Wilhelm said in German. "We'll make a sled," he repeated in English. The prisoners nodded their assent. No one commented about Wilhelm speaking German.

"You have ten minutes," the guard said, also in German.

"I need a blanket, some rope, and three strong poles," Wilhelm said in English. "This son of a bitch is going to start shooting in ten minutes."

"I got your poles," Karl said. He began scrounging at the edge of the woods.

Fox slid his pack—improvised from a blanket—off his shoulder. Untied the drawstring and dumped out the contents. Soup cans and packages of crackers tumbled into the snow. Fox shook out the blanket and tossed it to Wilhelm.

McLendon began running along the road. "Rope," he called. "Anybody got rope? We need it right now."

Karl returned carrying three branches. The effort reminded Wilhelm of building the raft, which seemed a lifetime ago. The sled would be much simpler—but now he had only about five minutes left.

Wilhelm placed the branches on the ground to form a rough U. Didn't bother to remove the twigs and pine needles. Spread the blanket over the branches.

Somehow McLendon came up with a coil of old clothesline. He dropped the line beside Wilhelm. Wilhelm grabbed a handful of blanket, wrapped a corner of it around a branch, and tied it off with the line.

"Knife," Wilhelm said. "I need a knife."

No one had a knife. Karl's folding knife had been taken long ago.

A few kriegies had managed to hide little penknives during their captivity, but camp authorities usually confiscated any blade they found.

Wilhelm looked at the guard. "Please lend me your bayonet," he said in German.

The guard stared, looked down at his web belt. To Wilhelm's surprise, the man unsheathed the bayonet. Handed it to Wilhelm almost politely, with the handle foremost.

"*Danke,*" Wilhelm said. "What is your name, Sergeant?"

"Gunther."

Wilhelm took the bayonet, cut several short lengths of clothesline. Handed the blade back to the guard. In less than two minutes, Wilhelm lashed the branches together and attached the blanket with two pile hitches and two anchor hitches. He also created loops for handles.

"Where did you learn to do that?" Fox asked.

"I used to be a sailor."

Sparks and Karl picked up the commander and placed him on the cloth sled. Fox grabbed the rope handle on the right side. Wilhelm took the left side, and they began pulling Timmersby through the snow.

As the day wore on, two other POWs collapsed. In each case, Wilhelm persuaded guards not to shoot the men as stragglers, and he rigged up quick sleds as he'd done for Timmersby. In each case, someone asked him where he'd learned such skills, and he told them the same thing: He'd been a sailor. The answer seemed to satisfy the kriegies; they pressed him no further. Perhaps they assumed he'd been an avid leisure yachtsman before the war.

The column stopped for the night at an abandoned brick factory near the town of Muskau. Rounded kilns, long cold, stood next to large warehouses. Frost patterned rows of windows, except for the odd pane broken out like a missing tooth. The men unfolded their bedrolls across floors chalky with red dust. An earthy scent lingered in the air. The buildings were unheated, of course, but Wilhelm felt glad just to get out of the elements. McLendon and Sparks helped Timmersby sit down with his back to an oaken pillar. They removed his boots and socks. The group commander winced as they dabbed at his feet with tincture of iodine from a medical kit.

McLendon screwed the cap back on the iodine bottle. "Something just occurred to me, sir," he said to Timmersby. "I haven't seen any of the Russian prisoners since we left the camp. Do you know what happened to them?"

Wilhelm had wondered the same thing.

"No, I don't," Timmersby said. "If we knew, I don't think we'd like it."

At suppertime, Wilhelm, Karl, and Pell sat cross-legged in a circle on the concrete floor. They placed what remained of their Red Cross parcels on the floor among them. Wilhelm had thought most of the good items were already gone, but they came up with prunes, crackers, raisins, jam, peanut butter, and cheese. They took turns choosing from the packages and cans. Karl and Pell left the crackers and jam; Wilhelm suspected they were leaving the best for him.

"Do you not want some of this?" Wilhelm asked.

"Nah," Pell said. "I don't like strawberry."

Karl shook his head.

The act reminded Wilhelm of little gestures of kindness he had witnessed among his crewmates: Near the end of a long patrol, galley stores would get low and men would save the best treats for the wounded or sick, or for those who had performed with particular skill or gallantry.

"Good work today on those sleds," Karl said.

"It was a small matter," Wilhelm said.

"Not to Timmersby and those other two."

On this night of war in his broken country, for a couple of hours, Wilhelm felt among brothers. But the warmth brought an undercurrent of melancholy. He knew he must leave these friends for a future that promised little but chaos.

Wilhelm hated for the evening to end, but fatigue washed over him. When he could no longer stop his eyelids from fluttering, he brushed crumbs from his lap and bedded down, still in his field jacket and boots.

42

Train to the End of the World

On the last day of January, the guards marched the POWs out of the brick factory. At first, Karl felt encouraged when Wilhelm translated a promise from Gunther. "He says we have only sixteen miles to go," Wilhelm said. But later, Wilhelm added: "Now he says when we get to Spremberg, they will put us on a train."

"I'd rather walk, if it's like the last train they put us on," Karl said.

It was exactly like the last train.

Kriegies groaned and muttered curses when they saw the boxcars waiting at the rail station. The stench from inside the cars hit Karl from forty feet away. And the odor, awful as it was, presented the least problem. From the air, this train would look like any other German freight train. It might contain weapons.

If I saw this thing from the cockpit of a Mustang or a Thunderbolt, Karl asked himself, *what would I do? I'd dive low, roll out nose-to-nose with the locomotive. Hold down the firing button from engine to caboose. Rip every car to splinters. If I had ammo left, I'd pull up off the target, roll into a steep 180, come back and do it again.*

As before, the prisoners crowded into the boxcars until they had room only to stand. No food. No water. This time, not even a toilet bucket. Men simply urinated on the floor. The odor grew worse and men vomited, which made the odor still worse. Karl almost wished a fighter plane would come and put all of them out of their misery.

The train moved in fits and starts, short rolls and long runs. From time to time, Karl thought he heard distant blasts, but nothing close. At the end of the first day, the train stopped at some nameless rail-head, and the men piled out for a meal of thin gruel and black bread. Karl hardly felt like eating. He sat with Wilhelm and Pell on the sid-ing, and he forced down as much as he could, only because he knew he needed the fuel.

Pell lifted a chunk of bread. "Just shoot me now," he said. With thumb and middle finger, he flicked away a weevil.

Wilhelm seemed in even worse spirits. He ate little and said noth-ing. When Wilhelm turned his face toward the glow of the setting sun, Karl thought he saw tears.

If this were happening to my country and my only friends were former enemies, Karl thought, *I'd weep, too. To Wilhelm, this must feel like a train to world's end. His world's, anyway.*

After three days of agony, the train reached its final stop. The doors slid open to a scene from the farthest corner of Hades. At a marshaling yard outside a good-sized city, prisoners in ragged cloth-ing toiled with shovels. They were digging slit trenches at the edge of the yard. Black smoke billowed across the horizon, and ack-ack guns pounded the sky. Heavy bombers were obliterating a target a few miles away. Air raid sirens howled. A signpost beside the tracks re-vealed the location: NUREMBERG.

Karl, Wilhelm, and Pell clambered down from the boxcar. They found Timmersby, who had somehow survived the train ride in his weakened condition. Supported by McLendon, the group comman-der shouted at an English-speaking *Luftwaffe* officer.

"You cannot mean to keep us here," Timmersby yelled, his voice scratchy and hoarse. "This rail yard is an obvious target!"

"We have no other place," the officer said. "This will have to do."

With the ground vibrating from explosions, the kriegies filed from the boxcars into abandoned buildings beside the rail yard. The build-ings appeared to have housed POWs at some point in the past: Filthy mattresses lined the floor. The open bays smelled of mold and rat droppings. Discarded articles of clothing lay here and there.

"This is worse than the brick factory," Karl said.

"Smells worse, that's for sure," Pell said.

"Perhaps we will get bombed," Wilhelm noted. "But the werewolves will probably not come near this place." Karl recalled the refugees they'd seen at the crossroads—their cold expressions, their weapons outdated but deadly.

Just as they'd done at the brick factory, the kriegies combined their dwindling supplies to make supper. But this time, the Germans supplemented their rations with dehydrated peas and beans. The men heated water on camp stoves and made flavorless soups.

With guards posted outside the buildings, but none inside, Sparks judged it safe to reassemble his radio. The men gathered around him in the dark to hear the latest news. He found a signal from the BBC.

"Prime Minister Churchill, President Roosevelt, and General Secretary Stalin are meeting in Crimea to discuss postwar administration of Europe," the announcer said. "Allied officials say the Big Three leaders have agreed to demand Germany's unconditional surrender. Their agenda also includes establishing zones of occupation. Preliminary reports suggest Germany will be divided into regions administered separately by Britain, the United States, the Soviet Union, and France."

Men whooped at the mention of surrender, but other kriegies shushed them. No sense tipping off the guards about the radio. A few of the POWs seemed less enthusiastic about the news.

"If they think the war's over," Pell said, "they should come here and listen to those guns and bombs."

"Yeah," Fox said. "And how about they get us home while they're at it?"

Wilhelm said nothing. Karl left him alone. What could you say to a man who had just heard a matter-of-fact discussion about the end of his country? Carve it up like pie slices. Send diplomats from Washington, London, Paris, and Moscow to run it. Maybe not even call it Germany anymore. What would this mean for Karl's uncle Rainer and aunt Federica? Were they even still alive?

Later in the evening, bombers came again. The usual rotation,

Karl supposed: Fortresses and Liberators by day, Lancasters, Stirlings, and Halifaxes by night. The kriegies rushed for the slit trenches and kept their heads low. But there was really no point. If bombardiers began walking five-hundred-pounders across the marshaling yard, these trenches would amount to nothing but previously dug graves.

The sky convulsed with booms and flashes—and the bombs fell much closer than during the day. Searchlights swept the night. Prisoners shouted and cursed, called out differing wishes: "Let 'em have it!" "Give 'em hell!" "Let us sleep, you sons of bitches." A burnt odor drifted in the air—from bombs, ack-ack, burning buildings, or some combination.

Fire all around, and the smell of sulfur. Yeah, Karl had heard of such a place, but he'd thought you had to die to get there.

The kriegies remained at Nuremberg through the rest of February and into March. The bombing never ended. Sometimes it thundered close; sometimes it rumbled faint in the distance. Each day, Karl feared annihilation and hoped for liberation. He imagined American trucks and tanks clanking up the highway that ran alongside the rail yard. If the bigwigs were already talking about what to do *after* the war, how much longer could it last?

At the end of March, the POWs moved again. In the rail yard, Timmersby addressed the kriegies. He looked better now; he could stand without assistance. He told them they were bound for yet another stalag—this one in the town of Moosburg. Once more, they would travel by foot.

"Stay together, lads," Timmersby said. "Escape was always our goal, but the war is as good as over now. Don't strike off on your own and get shot by angry civilians."

The prisoners marched from the rail yard and hiked along a highway. After an hour of walking, bomb-scarred Nuremberg lay behind them. The countryside displayed the first signs of spring: Pastures were greening. Trees budded. Cattle grazed, chewed, and flicked their tails at flies.

Karl walked with Wilhelm, Pell, and McLendon. During the morning, Fox fell back from his own group and joined Karl and the others. He produced a pack of Camels.

"Anybody want a smoke?" he asked. "I think this is the last pack."

Karl declined, but Wilhelm took a cigarette. Fox lit it for him.

Wilhelm took a deep drag, exhaled through his nose, and said, "Very kind of you."

The men walked in silence for a few minutes. Eventually Fox said, "Anybody know where this Moosburg place is? I've never heard of it."

"It's north of Munich," Wilhelm said.

"You know your geography around here, don't you?" Fox said.

"Navigator," Wilhelm said. He smiled for the first time in days.

"Uh-huh," Fox replied. His tone suggested he still didn't believe that story, but he no longer cared.

"The Krauts are running out of places to put us," McLendon said, "because they're running out of real estate."

Two distant booms emphasized McLendon's point. And got Karl thinking: *Yeah, it'll be over pretty soon. What will happen to Wilhelm then? He's damned near transformed himself into an American. Why not make it official? When we get liberated, just find the highest-ranking officer on scene and tell him the whole story. Especially the part about Wilhelm refusing to identify Jewish POWs. Give him asylum in the United States. Hell, the navy would probably love to know what he knows about U-boats. Get him a job, too.*

Karl waited for a chance to speak to Wilhelm privately. When the kriegies spread out across a wide highway shoulder, Karl pulled Wilhelm aside.

"Buddy," Karl whispered, "I know you love your country. But like you've said yourself, your country may not love you right now. What do you think about coming home with us?" Karl explained how he thought it could be done, right down to the part about working for the U.S. Navy.

Wilhelm took the last drag from his Camel. He dropped the butt, crushed it out with his boot. Looked across the fields as if trying to focus on something barely within sight.

"I will think about this," he said.

A few days later, the kriegies entered Stalag VII-A in Moosburg. They found the camp overcrowded to suffocation. Prisoners from stalags all over Germany streamed into the place. Karl and Wilhelm bedded down in an open-bay barracks built for about a hundred men. Now it housed four times that many. Latrines filled. Food ran short. Men stood in line for hours to get to a water faucet. Karl could not guess how many POWs were in Stalag VII-A, but it was at least tens of thousands.

They found one silver lining: With so many men to watch, the guards couldn't keep a close eye on anyone. Guards seemed scarcer, too; Karl supposed some of them had just slipped away to go home. Listening to the news on Sparks's radio became almost a casual routine.

The kriegies learned that American forces had invaded Okinawa, part of Japan's home territory. The two sides joined a furious land and sea battle: Kamikaze pilots crashed into U.S. vessels, and American airplanes destroyed the Japanese battleship *Yamato*—one of the largest battleships ever built.

One evening near the middle of April, the radio brought news that stunned the men into silence:

"The Press Association has announced that President Franklin D. Roosevelt is dead. Initial reports say the president died of a cerebral hemorrhage at the Little White House in Warm Springs, Georgia. Harry S. Truman has taken the oath of office as president of the United States."

Some of the men wept. Karl felt only a cold emptiness. Roosevelt had been president for almost as long as he could remember. He'd always assumed FDR would continue leading the country at least through the end of the war.

Wilhelm placed his hand on Karl's arm and whispered, "My condolences. I wish I could admire my leaders the way you do."

Later in the week, Karl, Pell, and Fox ran across Padre—the bomber pilot and would-be minister from North Carolina. Padre wanted to hold a prayer service for the Roosevelt family and the United States. Kriegies—Christian, Jewish, and even the agnostic—gathered in the center of the compound.

As Padre finished his remarks, a faint buzz rose in the distance. Not the thunder of heavy bombers—more like the clatter of a lawn mower. Karl shaded his eyes and scanned the clouds. He spotted a speck that grew larger until it took the form of an L-4 Grasshopper, the military version of the Piper Cub. A little scout plane.

The Grasshopper descended and circled over the camp. It flew close enough for Karl to make out the white star on its fuselage. Kriegies shouted and waved.

The L-4 rolled into a steep bank. It dived low, skirted the treetops, and flew away.

"That means our boys are close," Pell said, "and now they know where we are."

43

Ivory-handled Pistols

The ground war came to Moosburg during the last week of April. One afternoon, kriegies spotted tanks on a hill a few kilometers from the prison. After dark, shellfire thumped in the distance and grew louder as the night deepened. The explosions made sleep impossible, but Wilhelm could not have slept, anyway. He faced a life-changing choice. Karl—God bless that crazy Yank aviator—had offered to help Wilhelm become an American. Not simply in accent or appearance, but in fact.

That could mean opportunities Wilhelm had never dreamed of, and quite possibly save his life. Who knew what a German deserter might face after the war from hateful German diehards? Who knew what any German might face from vengeful Allied victors? What if he wound up in a Russian zone of occupation? Wilhelm could well imagine how the Russians might treat German prisoners, after the carnage of the Eastern Front.

But leaving Germany would also mean wrenching himself away from everything he'd ever known and everyone he'd ever loved. What if he never saw his parents again?

Very soon, Wilhelm would have to decide. And he'd have to decide in a sleep-deprived state, with limited information, perhaps with firefights swirling outside the fence.

In the small hours before dawn, Wilhelm finally drifted off to sleep, still fully dressed. He got little more than a nap. At first light, shouts woke him from outside his hut.

"Look at that!" someone called. Pell's voice.

Prisoners cheered and laughed. Wilhelm sat up on his cot, rubbed at sleep in his eyes. Stumbled outside.

On the hill to the west, two panzers burned. Flames swathed both machines; only the muzzles of their main guns extended clear of the fire. Twin columns of smoke churned into the sky. The panzers rocked as their ammunition exploded.

An hour later, rifle fire crackled outside the camp. Some kriegies took cover from stray bullets. More adventurous souls climbed atop huts for a better view. The guards melted away. Some fled, and others might have gone outside the perimeter to surrender, Wilhelm supposed.

The POWs grew more excited by the minute. "Today's the day, buddy," Sparks told him. The men laughed, waited, watched. They sang "The Star-Spangled Banner" and "Rule, Britannia!"

Wilhelm, however, felt a forty-fathom sadness. Not for the defeat. Awful as it was, he believed defeat had to happen for Germany to enter any hopeful future.

But it would enter that future without him.

The clear light of morning washed away his doubts. He had started a journey back in Bremen that he would take all the way to its logical end. He would leave his home, his family, all of his old friends—what few may have survived. He wanted to go to America.

Having just taken such a momentous decision, Wilhelm wanted to be alone—in a place where that was impossible. He needed time to wrap his mind around what he was about to do, to let his resolve crystallize. The nearest thing he found to solitude was a corner of the camp's fence line, with kriegies crowded around him. He placed both hands on the chain link and stared out at the forest, the hills, the burning wreckage of the panzers.

Cheers from the other side of the compound interrupted his thoughts. Wilhelm turned to see men surge toward the main gate.

A tank clattered along the road just outside the camp. White star painted on its side. An American tank, Wilhelm noted. Smoke sputtered from its exhaust. Fire stains marred its turret. Hand-painted letters along its side read: *From Bastogne to Berlin.*

A new unit slogan, or a statement of intent.

The tank shuddered to a stop. The machine clanked and growled, turned toward the camp's main entrance. Kriegies lined the fence; they waved and cheered.

The tank's hatch opened, and a crewman emerged wearing a tanker's helmet and goggles. He pushed his goggles up onto the helmet, revealing grease-rimmed eyes. The man was chewing bubble gum.

"Any of you boys know the way to Newark?" the tanker asked.

The prisoners laughed and talked over one another. One POW called out in a loud voice, "Yeah, you start by busting right through here." He pointed at the main entrance, held shut by loops of chain.

"Not a problem," the tanker said.

He blew a bubble, popped it, and spat out his gum. Dropped beneath the hatch and closed the cover. The engine revved. The tank lurched forward and crashed through the gate. Chains popped, fence posts splintered, and wire mesh got crushed beneath the tank's tracks.

The men went wild. They shouted, threw hats, hugged one another. A stranger embraced Wilhelm and cried, "It's over, Mac. We're going home!"

Wilhelm moved with the crowd toward the front of the camp. He looked for Karl—and found him running among the men.

"There you are," Karl said. "I've been looking all over for you." The Yank pilot placed both palms on Wilhelm's shoulders. "My friend," he said, "it's time to decide."

Wilhelm's eyes welled. His throat clenched as he spoke. "I have," he said. "I would like to go with you."

A broad smile spread across Karl's face. He threw his arms around Wilhelm and laughed. Broke off the embrace and said, "I was hoping you'd say that. I can see it right now. Someday you'll bring your American wife over to my place for martinis and a game of bridge."

"We should not get too far ahead of ourselves."

"Yeah, yeah, you're right," Karl said. "This will take some doing, and we'll have to find the right guy to talk to."

Some of the troops on the tanks began throwing packs of cigarettes, gum, and other treats into the crowd. Kriegies shouted, laughed, and chased after the goodies. But Wilhelm and Karl simply watched—the Yank with obvious satisfaction, and Wilhelm with a storm of mixed emotions.

"Hey, guys," one of the tankers called out. "You're gonna get a special visitor pretty soon."

Wilhelm looked at Karl, who shrugged. They didn't have to wonder long. Less than an hour later, a well-polished Packard glided through the front gate. A flag with four stars decorated the front fender. The top was down; the general in the rear seat wore a polished combat helmet and a tightly knotted tie with his service coat. POWs parted to make way for the vehicle. Many snapped to attention and saluted. The Packard stopped, and the general stood on the running board. He wore a pair of ivory-handled pistols—which Wilhelm thought ridiculous.

"I bet you sons of bitches are happy to see me," the general called out. The crowd roared.

"Do you know who that is?" Karl shouted over the noise.

Wilhelm shook his head.

"George S. Patton."

Wilhelm knew the name: the man who had clashed with the *Afrika Korps* in Morocco, Tunisia, and Algeria. This general had bested some of Germany's most brilliant officers. *Eccentric in his dress*, Wilhelm thought, *but a truly formidable soldier.*

With the aid of a bullhorn, Patton spoke to the prisoners for a few minutes. He offered encouragement and thanked them for "helping me kick Kraut ass." Some of the kriegies took the general on a tour of the camp.

A retinue of officers trailed General Patton. Wilhelm and Karl watched them inspect barracks. Their boss shouted profane disapproval of the overcrowded conditions.

"I wish the *kommandant* hadn't already run off like a little bitch," Patton fumed. "I'd choke his ass right now." As the general spoke, he stabbed the air with his lit cigar.

"I'd love to meet him," Karl told Wilhelm, "but we got things to do. And the best thing we can do right now is catch one of his staff."

When Patton went inside the camp's administrative office, Karl addressed a major standing outside. Wilhelm's heart raced like a bilge pump. His fate might turn on this conversation. His fate might turn on the attitude of this major. Was this major the right man to trust? *We have to trust someone*, Wilhelm thought, *and we're running out of time*.

"Sir," Karl said, "if you have a few minutes, I have one helluva story to tell you."

"I'm all ears, Lieutenant," the major said. He extended his hand, and Karl shook it. "Name's Bill Neal, by the way."

"Karl Hagan. And this is Lieutenant Thomas Meade. Except that's not his real name. Or rank."

Major Neal folded his arms and gave Karl a dubious look. Yet, his manner still seemed friendly. His uniform was clean and neat, as Patton would have certainly demanded. But his boots were not polished and his sidearm was a standard-issue .45.

"Let me introduce you," Karl continued, "to *Oberleutnant* Wilhelm Albrecht. German Navy."

Neal placed his hands on his hips. His mouth dropped open and he started to say something. He checked himself and continued to listen in obvious confusion and amazement. Karl told how he'd met Wilhelm in Bremen, how they'd evaded capture for a time. How Wilhelm had defied the SS at Stalag Luft XIV.

"Sir," Karl said, "I might not be here if not for him. He deserves to come to America."

Neal opened a pocket flap and pulled out a field notebook and pen. "How's that last name spelled?" he asked. Wilhelm answered, and Neal scribbled as he spoke: "The French are processing German prisoners. He'll have to apply through them. I'll try to get word to them to expect a good guy."

"Can't he just stay with us?" Karl asked. "Process with us?"

Neal looked up from his pad. "Come on, Lieutenant," he said. "You know my boss. You think he'd just let me slip a Kraut in with you guys—no offense—even if he's a good Kraut?"

"But the French—"

"I know," Neal said. "Probably not real magnanimous with Germans right now." He glanced at Wilhelm. "Look, Albrecht," he continued, "I'm impressed as hell with your story, and the Frogs will be, too. Just tell it to them like you guys told it to me."

Wilhelm doubted "the Frogs" would be so easily impressed, but

Neal offered no alternative. "How do we find these French officers?" Wilhelm asked.

"Just stay right here and they'll come to you," Neal said. "We got three or four of the camp guards in custody. The French will be along in a day or two to pick them up."

Karl locked eyes with Wilhelm and sighed hard. Raised his arm and scratched the back of his head, his expression as if he'd taken a sip of vinegar. "All right," he said, "if that's the best we can do."

"I'm afraid it is, *Lieutenant,*" Neal said, emphasizing Karl's lower rank. "Really, I'd like to be more help. But the war's not over yet."

Wilhelm took the major's meaning. Patton's staff—and the Allied forces in general—did not have a lot of time for special cases.

The general and most of his entourage departed later in the day, leaving behind a few NCOs and junior officers to look after the kriegies. Technically, the POWs were free now. Yet, they had to remain behind barbed wire because there was no safer place to put them.

That afternoon, the kriegies threw the biggest celebration Wilhelm had ever seen. The American flag fluttered over the camp. Champagne, cognac, cigars, and candies appeared; Wilhelm supposed Patton's men had brought them all the way from France. Perhaps they'd been saving the treats for the fall of Berlin, but, in soldierly generosity, they shared them with POWs. Men puffed from *Romeo y Julieta* cigars, then passed them to the next kriegie. A stranger shoved an open box toward Wilhelm. He thanked the man, took a chocolate-covered cherry, and popped it into his mouth. The liquid sweetness nearly brought him to tears with memories of Christmas. The prisoners—or ex-prisoners—also took sips from bottles of Moët. Wilhelm marveled that the bottles had survived a long overland journey—not to mention tank combat.

Occasionally a man would take a deep drink too quickly, then nearly choke on foaming champagne. His buddies would laugh and clap his back as the embarrassed kriegie spat white suds.

"That's not your daddy's rotgut, dumbass," one POW remarked.

The loudest laughter came from a gaggle of men in the back of the compound. Wilhelm and Karl went to investigate; maybe Karl expected to share the joy of liberation with old friends. Goodwill and happiness.

They found something entirely different.

At the center of the group sat four men with their hands tied. Bruises marred their faces. One had a bloody lip. Another suffered a black eye. Dirt flecked their matted hair.

Four German guards. One of them was Gunther. Something, perhaps a boot sole, had left a deep abrasion across his cheek. Blood oozed from the scrape and dribbled onto the collar of his uniform.

A soldier lifted a bottle, took a swallow of champagne, and spat it onto Gunther's uncovered head.

"Hey, that's alcohol abuse," someone called. More laughter.

Gunther stared straight ahead and said nothing as foam and spittle streamed through his blond hair.

"Stop it," Karl said.

The soldiers and kriegies fixed their eyes on the Yank flier as if he'd spoken blasphemy. Finally one of the troops said, "We're just having a little fun with these Krauts, sir. Serves them right." The man wore the stripes of a U.S. sergeant and a patch that Wilhelm now recognized as that of a tank battalion.

Karl pointed to Gunther. "That one's all right," he said. "He treated us okay."

The sergeant shrugged. Swayed as if drunk—which he probably was. "He's a fucking goose-stepper," he said. Cleared his throat, brought up a gobbet of mucus, and spat at Gunther.

"I said *stop it,*" Karl called out.

The sergeant turned toward Karl. "You been sitting out the war while we been doing all the fighting," he said. "And you ain't in my chain of command."

Karl lunged at the sergeant. Grabbed him by the throat with both hands. The sergeant's eyes bulged. A vein throbbed across his temple. He fell back three steps, and Karl stayed on him.

"I'm in your chain of command now, asshole," Karl said through gritted teeth.

The sergeant dropped his hand toward the Colt holstered on his web belt. Karl tightened his grip.

"What?" Karl asked. "You gonna shoot me in front of a thousand witnesses?"

Karl released the sergeant's neck. He grabbed the man by the shirt and shoved him onto the ground. Then he turned toward the guards' other tormentors.

"Anybody else wanna talk to me about chain of command?" Karl yelled. Wilhelm had never seen him so angry. His blood was up, literally. Red splotches darkened his neck.

No one else dared challenge him. He pointed to the sergeant, still on the ground. "Get this idiot out of my sight," Karl said. "And somebody get a medic."

"Yes, sir," a soldier responded. He trotted away.

Karl extended a hand, helped Gunther to his feet. Wilhelm assisted the other three guards.

"Thank you for that," Wilhelm whispered to Karl.

A few minutes later, the soldier who had run to find a medic came back. He brought with him a man who wore a white armband with a red cross. The medic carried a musette bag.

"This is Doc Greeley," the soldier said.

Greeley nodded to Karl and said, "What you got, sir?"

Karl, his face still clouded with anger, waved a hand toward Gunther and snapped, "Fix him. Look at the others, too."

"Will do." Greeley opened his musette bag, dug around, and withdrew what appeared to be iodine swabs. "Anybody speak German?" he asked.

"I do," Wilhelm said.

"Tell him to hold still. I'm sorry about what happened to him."

Wilhelm translated. Gunther's expression softened from fear to gratitude—though he winced as Greeley began dabbing at the scrape. The iodine left ochery stains on the side of his face.

"I hate it when the guys act like this," Greeley said, "but in general they've been pretty professional. This could have been a whole lot worse."

"What do you mean?" Wilhelm asked.

Greeley related a scene he'd witnessed shortly after his company crossed the Rhine. Another unit had captured five German troops and couldn't figure out what to do with them. On a field telephone, the company commander called up to battalion. He received instructions to hold them for military police from the new French First Army.

The G.I.s waited for an hour. They passed the time chatting with one of the Germans, who spoke fluent English. The English speaker wore wire-rimmed glasses and looked no more than nineteen. He said he had been a mathematics student and wanted nothing more than to get back to school. His father had served in the Great War. "If the Americans come," his father had said, "the jig is up." The boy added, "Here you are. If that means the war is over, then I am not sorry to see you."

But if he'd known what was coming, Greeley said, he'd have been sorry to see the French. Three soldiers showed up, armed with Lend-Lease rifles—old bolt-action Enfields. The G.I.s mounted their vehicles and started moving out.

"I was in the last jeep," Greeley said. "Just before we rounded the curve, I saw the Frogs put the Krauts on their knees."

One by one, they shot each prisoner in the back of the head. Greeley described the bolts clacking, the brass tumbling, the boy's glasses flying in a spray of blood and brains.

"Stupid waste of labor, if you ask me," Greeley said.

"How's that?" Karl asked.

"From what I hear," Greeley said, "the ones they don't kill, they're putting to work clearing mines."

44

The Least Bad Option

At the end of that first day of freedom, sunset painted the hills be-yond the camp a red hue that bled out into purple as night ap-proached. The fighting had pushed east; Karl heard only the occasional snap of rifle fire in the distance. After the medic's story, he didn't care to speculate on the reason for the shots—which came singly, or sometimes in twos and threes. Sounded more like Pennsylvania in deer season than Europe in all-out war.

The celebrating died down. Men—tired, drunk, or both—lay in their bunks or on the floors, waiting for someone to tell them what to do. For now, everyone seemed content to stay put. After all, where would they go? The ex-POWs who remained alert and talkative swapped war stories, usually of the engagement that shot them down. In their leather A-2 jackets or cloth B-10 coats, they spoke of steel in the sky. Using their hands as imaginary airplanes, their palms and fingers banked and yawed until their fingers spread apart to de-pict explosion and flames.

Karl visited the cookhouse in search of coffee, though he ex-pected to find only the fake stuff. The same idea had occurred to Wil-helm. Karl found him heating water on a Nuremberg stove. Kriegies had stripped the shelves of instant coffee and nearly everything else. From the remnants of a Red Cross parcel, Karl made weak hot cocoa.

He and Wilhelm sat on the cookhouse steps with steaming tin cups. For a long time, Wilhelm said nothing and wore a face of stone.

"Don't let it get you down," Karl said. "Like I said, we just need to find the right guy and tell him your story. Next thing you know, you'll be driving your new Chevy in Pittsburgh."

Wilhelm's mouth twisted into a momentary and rare smile—which faded as quickly as it appeared. "And what if we find the wrong guy?" he asked.

"Then we keep working on it."

Wilhelm shook his head and cracked another ironic smile. One smile was rare; two within a single minute was unheard of. "How very American," he said.

"Huh?"

"You believe every problem has a solution. To be fair, your country's recent experience supports that notion. But mine does not."

Karl gave Wilhelm a gentle shove with his fist. "Come on, Lieutenant Meade," he said, "don't go getting all Germanic on me."

Wilhelm sipped from his cup and seemed to stare through the camp fence, across the hills, beyond Europe and into the North Atlantic. "I cannot let you risk it," he said.

"Risk what?"

"What is that American expression? *Ja*, don't play dumb with me."

"I'm not *playing* dumb," Karl said. "I'm really an idiot. Otherwise, I wouldn't have strapped on several tons of bombs and gasoline and flown them into Germany."

Wilhelm laughed out loud. Now they were truly in uncharted airspace. So uncharted that Karl didn't like seeing Wilhelm so at ease. Wilhelm had come to some new conclusion. One that Karl might not like.

"If we find the wrong guy—and it sounds like there are a lot of wrong guys out there—he may decide you are German, too," Wilhelm said. "He might blow my head off, and in the next instant turn his gun on you."

"Nah," Karl said. "That's a little far-fetched."

"Well, then, let's consider a more likely possibility. We don't get our heads blown off. But I find myself on my hands and knees in France, probing for mines with a spade."

Karl had no answer for that. He let the remark hang in the air for several seconds. Finally he said, "So, what do you want to do?"

Wilhelm put down his cup and looked at Karl. "You and your fellow Yanks have done much for me," Wilhelm said. "But I must ask one more favor."

"You did plenty for us, too. What do you need?"

"I would like you to help me get out of here. Tonight."

Karl sat up straight. He had hoped to sponsor Wilhelm's new life as an American. Now, if he honored Wilhelm's request, he'd probably never see him again.

"What will you do?" Karl asked.

"Exactly what you suggested when we left Stalag Luft XIV. Blend in. Go home. Try to stay out of the internment camps."

Karl sighed hard. Rubbed the knuckles of one hand into the palm of the other, thinking. He hated to discard the idea of Wilhelm going to the United States, but maybe this was the least bad option. The French were already on the way to collect the former guards. What if they didn't believe Wilhelm's story? What if they *did* believe it and just didn't care? Wilhelm could wind up in an internment camp for months while the Allies sorted war criminals from the relatively innocent—assuming he didn't get shot or sent to the minefields. Wilhelm was correct: Not every problem had a good solution.

"All right," Karl said. "I hate it, but all right."

"I will find my parents, whatever family I have left. We will start over from nothing. People have suffered far worse fates."

"No doubt about that."

They sat in silence for a few minutes, and Karl appreciated the quiet. *No sense yammering on and getting sentimental. Decision made, and that was that. Very German,* Karl thought. *Of both of us.*

Wilhelm began unlacing his right boot. Karl wondered why—until Wilhelm slid off the boot, tipped it over, and caught a pair of dog tags.

"That's how you hid them all this time?" Karl asked.

"Yes, except when they took away our boots for the train ride. Then I kept them in my socks." Wilhelm passed the tags to Karl. "Please see that Mrs. Meade receives these."

"You bet." Karl pocketed the dog tags. "Good of you to keep them. I thought maybe you'd just ditched them."

"No, the widow deserves something more tangible than a tele-gram."

"Yeah, she does." Karl let a few moments go by, then changed the subject. "Let's think about how we'll get you out of here. Hey, here's an Americanism for you, 'how are you gonna blow this Popsicle stand'?"

"'Blow this Popsicle stand'?" Wilhelm said. "That makes no sense."

"I suppose not."

Before now, Karl might have believed the easiest thing in the world would be walking out of a liberated POW camp. But when he and Wilhelm started talking about it, he realized it wasn't so simple. Sure, the electric fence had been turned off. And there was nobody in the goon boxes waiting to shoot escapees. But Patton's men had left sentries—not guards, but sentries—for the kriegies' own protection. All kinds of dangers lurked outside the wire. Wandering outside at night would be so crazy, the sentries might assume Wilhelm was an escaping guard.

But Wilhelm couldn't just sit around, either. By tomorrow, the French could show up looking for him, thanks to the story they'd told the major.

"What might we do, then?" Wilhelm asked.

"Cut a hole in the fence," Karl said. Razor wire topped the inner fence, which made climbing it dangerous. Better to go through it rather than over it. The outer fence—which had been electrified—presented no cutting edges. Once through the first barrier, Wilhelm could climb the outer fence and make his getaway.

"Cut the fence with what?"

"Whatever we can find. Let's check the offices and storage build-ings. With all this wire around us, the Germans must have had wire cutters."

Wilhelm considered that for a moment. "If we find wire cutters," he said, "how will we use them without looking suspicious?"

"I don't know. Lemme think."

For several seconds, Karl brainstormed. Cutting the fence might take a while, even with the right tool. If he could get a few guys to stand around and block the view, he could work unobserved. How many guys would he need? Only Pell, McLendon, and Timmersby knew Wilhelm's true identity. Better to have a couple more than that, to remain safely out of sight. How many guys could he trust? Karl explained his idea for using a screen of bodies, then asked, "Who do you think might help us?"

Wilhelm took in a long, slow breath and stared into the middle distance—a bit like a man doing math in his head. "I have an idea," he said. "But before we approach anyone, we should see what tools we can find."

"Yeah, first things first."

They searched every building. In the cookhouse, they found pots, pans, and ladles. In the offices, they found pens, scissors, and paper clips. In the guards' break room, they found cigarette lighters and broken glasses. The guards' armory was padlocked; they kicked at the hasp until it gave way—and they found one broken Mauser and swabs for cleaning rifle barrels.

The last storage building they checked turned out to be a toolhouse, also locked. They broke down the door. The room gave off the oil and metal smell of every tool shop in the world. When the door gave way, Karl smiled because there had to be wire cutters somewhere in there.

There were no wire cutters.

Various tools rested on shelves or hung from nails on the wall: There were hammers, screwdrivers, drills, wrenches, even a lathe. Nut drivers and chisels. Handsaws and coping saws—but, of course, no hacksaw for cutting metal.

"You gotta be kidding me," Karl said aloud to no one. "You have just got to be kidding me."

Wilhelm picked up a pipe wrench. "What about this?" he said.

"What about it? It's a pipe wrench."

"Yes, it cannot cut," Wilhelm said. "But we can use it to twist wire back and forth until it breaks."

"That'll take forever."

"We have all night. And we need to make only a small opening. I am a U-boat man, remember. I'm used to climbing through a narrow hatch."

Karl chuckled. "Yeah," he said. "I guess you are."

They left the pipe wrench in the toolhouse and turned to the next task: finding accomplices. They tracked down Pell, McLendon, and Timmersby—all of whom whispered their regret at Wilhelm's leave-taking. They all understood the reasons, though, after Karl related what he'd heard from the medic.

"Yeah," McLendon said to Wilhelm, "it ain't fair. You should get to come home with us if that's what you want. But it sounds like you better just disappear."

"If you were a Brit, I'd recommend you for the Victoria Cross," Timmersby said.

"Thank you, sir," Wilhelm said. "I will have to make do with my Iron Cross."

"What time do you need us?" Pell asked.

"Twenty-three hundred," Karl said. "Rear fence, as far from the lights as you can get."

At nightfall, the searchlights mounted along the camp's perimeter flickered on. Now their beams tilted upward, perhaps to identify the camp to Allied bombers and prevent it being mistaken for a target of opportunity. The intersecting rays lent a granular quality to the darkness beyond their range.

"You said you thought of someone else who might help," Karl said to Wilhelm.

"Lieutenant Fox."

Karl nodded. Yes, the bombardier and former X Committee security man—who now owed his life to Wilhelm. They found Fox in his overcrowded hut, finishing a dinner of Spam and crackers. Fox looked up and smiled when he saw Karl and Wilhelm. He brushed crumbs from his lap, stood up, and offered his hand. Wilhelm shook it.

"Evening, boys," Fox said. "Why do you look so serious? We're about to go home."

"Can we talk to you alone?" Karl asked.

"Sure."

Fox took the single remaining cracker from his plate and followed Karl and Wilhelm outside. He looked puzzled, but happy. Of course, he was happy. He was going home.

"You always did see something fishy about Meade, here, didn't you?" Karl asked.

"I did," Fox said, "but he came through when the chips were down. Hey, I'm sorry about—"

Karl held up his hand to cut Fox off. "It's okay. Your instincts were right. His name isn't Meade and he's not a navigator. I don't have time to explain it all, but right now, he just needs to get out of here."

No surprise registered on Fox's face. He paused only for a second before responding. "What do you need?" he said.

Karl explained his plan to cut the fence, how he wanted two or three more bodies to stand around and block the view. Fox placed his cracker between his teeth, crunched it, and chewed slowly. With food in his mouth, he said, "Don't worry about asking more guys. I got this."

"Thanks," Karl said. "Twenty-three hundred. Back of the camp."

"See you then."

While waiting for eleven p.m., Karl and Wilhelm strolled the camp. They walked mainly to work off nervousness. Karl felt he had one last mission to accomplish—to get his friend away safely, and he worried about pulling it off. Few words passed between them; little remained to be said. Radial engines rumbled overhead: fighters and bombers on the way to targets so distant the explosions were not heard in Moosburg. What remained of the Reich lay to the east.

At a quarter to eleven, they returned to the toolshed and Karl grabbed the pipe wrench. He felt that same knot underneath his breastbone that had formed on every bomb run. When they rounded the corner of the last hut, they found at least a dozen men standing at the edge of the fence. Chatting, smoking, looking nonchalant.

Karl glanced over at Wilhelm, who once more broke into that rare smile.

"That's more than we need," Karl said. "They came to wish you well."

"Crewmates," Wilhelm said.

"Yeah."

As expected, Karl saw Pell, McLendon, Timmersby, and Fox. Fox had also rounded up Tex, the Oklahoman on the X Committee—as well as MacDougal, Sparks, Padre, and several men Karl had never met.

"Thanks for turning out, fellas," Karl said. "Let's get this done."

Without another word, he set about his task. He kneeled beside the fence and placed the jaws of the pipe wrench across a length of wire mesh. Twisted the adjustment until the jaws closed down. Wilhelm stood next to him, and the rest of the kriegies arranged themselves to hide Karl from view. An observer forty yards away might have concluded they were sharing a bottle of hooch or watching a friendly wrestling match.

Karl yanked the wrench, bending the wire this way and that. After he bent the wire about forty times, it finally broke. To open a hole large enough for Wilhelm to get through, he'd need to part the mesh in at least twenty other places. And his arms were already tired. He put down the pipe wrench and stretched.

"Let me spell you for a little bit," Pell said. The bombardier picked up the wrench and went to work. After ten minutes, he made a second break in the wire.

Wilhelm appeared moved by the team effort. "Gentlemen," he said, making no attempt to sound American, "I wish you peace."

"You too, bud," Pell said.

"Maybe we'll see one another again in better circumstances," Padre offered. Karl wondered if Padre meant this world or the next. Karl had given Wilhelm his home address, but who knew when Wilhelm could get out a letter? For that matter, Wilhelm's very survival over the next days and weeks looked dicey.

But I can't do anything about it, Karl thought, *except to get him out of here.*

McLendon took a turn at the wrench and eventually broke the wire again. Timmersby reached for the wrench, and McLendon tried to stop him.

"Sir," McLendon said, "you're in no shape for this."

"Poppycock."

Timmersby took the pipe wrench and broke open another square of the mesh.

After the kriegies cut the wire in eight places, Karl took hold of the partially severed section of fence. He bent it inward. That opened a gap big enough only for a man's leg.

"Still got a ways to go, boys," Karl said.

Wilhelm took the pipe wrench and eventually made two cuts. "Save your strength," Karl said. "Once we spring you, you still got a long night ahead."

Sparks took the pipe wrench. While he worked, some sort of commotion began across the camp. Karl stood for a better view and saw headlights at the front entrance. The sentries opened the gate.

"Hey, Pell," Karl said. "Go see what's happening."

"You got it."

Pell strode toward the front gate. He disappeared amid the glare and shadows of headlights and searchlights. While he was gone, Sparks finished a cut and Fox took a turn. Karl's curiosity curdled into worry: Had Patton returned for some reason? Had another general come to visit? Or was this something else?

At a full sprint, Pell came back, panting. "It's the French," he said. "Military police. They've come for the guards."

Now Karl's worry hardened into dread. "At this hour?" he said. "Damn it all. Look, get back there and stall them. Let them go anywhere but here."

"Sure thing."

As Pell turned to leave, Karl added one other instruction: "Tell 'em Gunther's all right. Make sure they know he helped us."

"Will do."

Tex stepped forward and reached for the pipe wrench. "We better double-time this rodeo," he said. He placed the wrench on the wire and cranked as if he were pumping water from a well. After several minutes, the wire broke. "My daddy always said make sure you use the right tool," Tex said. "Right now. he'd be saying, 'Boy, I taught you better'n that.'"

Other kriegies attacked the fence, one by one. While they worked, Karl eyed the goings-on across the compound. The French truck had stopped and turned off its lights. Men moved around in groups and gaggles. Karl heard lots of chatter, but nothing he could make out. No shouts or gunfire, thank God. The Frogs appeared to be touring the prison.

After a few more cuts, Karl again pulled at the freed section of fence. Not quite there yet: The hole remained too small for a man's shoulders. Karl grabbed the wrench and started cranking. He broke the wire, and the hole widened by a few inches.

An engine clattered to life. Karl turned to see the truck's lights come on. The vehicle began moving. Toward the back fence.

"They're coming," Karl said. "Can you get out?"

Wilhelm placed his boot at the edge of the opening and stretched the wire as far as he could. Placed his arms through the hole and began pulling himself through. Karl grabbed him by the legs and pushed.

Sharp ends of broken wire dug into Wilhelm's shoulders. The wire left deep scratches. Wilhelm groaned in pain. And he cleared the inner fence.

The truck rolled along the rows of barracks. Now Karl could hear soldiers speaking French.

"Go," he hissed.

Wilhelm crouched by the hole in the fence. He reached back through the opening and extended his right hand. Karl gripped it and nodded to his friend. He wished for appropriate words of parting, but there wasn't time. "Get out of here" was all he said.

Electric insulators studded the posts of the outer fence. Experimentally, Wilhelm touched the fence with the tip of his boot. Apparently satisfied that the electricity was off, he placed his hands on the wire and started climbing. He scaled the fence in two seconds. Reached the top and thudded to the ground on the other side.

Without looking back, he disappeared into the night. Wilhelm vanished with such speed and silence that Karl thought of a U-boat submerging into a black sea.

Five days later, Karl and Pell boarded a C-47 at a newly built dirt airstrip outside the prison camp. The steel-and-sweat smell of the military aircraft instantly shifted the cogs in Karl's psyche. Climbing into an airplane returned him to a world where he made his own decisions, exercised at least some degree of control.

Kriegies packed into the plane. Karl and Pell perched shoulder to shoulder on seats of canvas webbing. The left engine coughed, barked, and sputtered to life. Exhaust smoke wafted into the cabin. The fumes smelled good to Karl. The right engine fired up, and Pell grinned and offered a thumbs-up.

The C-47 bounced along the runway scraped only yesterday by bulldozers. The tail came up as the aircraft gathered speed, and Karl felt himself lifted into smooth air, an untroubled sky. Some of the former prisoners clapped and broke into song:

> *"Off we go into the wild blue yonder,*
> *Climbing high into the sun,*

Here they come zooming to meet our thunder,
At 'em boys, give 'er the gun!"

The pilots turned onto a heading for Le Havre, France. An army reception center near Le Havre, Camp Lucky Strike, had become a processing station for liberated POWs. Home lay just days away: family and friends, school and a job, a place in a wide-open future to which Karl had earned every right.

He scanned the faces of fellow passengers. They all looked happy, and well they might. The uncaring hand of randomness had spared them; everyone knew crewmates who hadn't survived. Karl still didn't know how many of his own crew remained among the living. He hoped to learn more at Lucky Strike.

The C-47 climbed, and the air turned cooler. Through a cabin window, Karl looked down at the fields and forests of Germany flowing beneath him. *So beautiful in this spring of 1945. How could horrors have unfolded in such a picturesque setting?*

In the last broadcast Karl had heard on Sparks's radio, Edward R. Murrow reported from a place called Buchenwald. The descriptions suggested something eternally damned within the German soul—or maybe within human nature itself.

Yet Karl knew shreds of decency remained. The proof hid somewhere in the landscape below, a sailor making his way home.

AUTHOR'S NOTE

Did Wilhelm survive? I like to think he did. By the time he escaped, the SS would no longer have been looking for him, and the Allies would have focused on catching war criminals. I imagine Wilhelm a couple of decades on as a West German diplomat, perhaps Bonn's ambassador to Britain or France.

Once Karl got back to the States, he would have contacted Janet Meade as soon as possible and sent her the dog tags. Perhaps she'd have taken a small measure of comfort in knowing her husband's fate. Many families never received closure: To this day, more than 72,000 Americans remain missing from World War II, according to the Defense POW/MIA Accounting Agency.

At home, Karl would have gone right back to business school. The G.I. Bill would have made that easier for him. I picture Karl becoming a Bethlehem Steel executive, and perhaps a lieutenant colonel in the Pennsylvania Air National Guard. We might find him in the VIP section during a salute to veterans at a Steelers game. A natural leader, he may have become commander of his local American Legion post.

Sooner or later, he probably looked up surviving crewmates. Various World War II units formed memorial associations. I can see Karl joining a gray-haired Fairburn and Pell at a Marriott bar, clinking tumblers of Maker's Mark in honor of Adrian. No doubt Karl would have visited Adrian's parents and told them of their son's courage and dedication.

Karl and Wilhelm might have exchanged letters. During their journey together, they transitioned from enemies to uneasy allies, and from allies to friends. Robbed of his airplane, his weapon, Karl also went through another kind of metamorphosis: He transitioned from a team leader and warrior motivated by duty to an individual motivated by conscience. Though he agonized about bombing Bremen, where some of his relatives lived, he really had no choice. He had his orders, and part of him knew all along he would do his soldierly duty. But when he bailed out of *Hellstorm,* that part of his war ended. As a downed airman and then a prisoner, he found freedom to make human choices.

Maybe Karl and Wilhelm would have visited each other. Karl might have flown to Bonn to meet Wilhelm in better times. They might have introduced their wives, toured the Rhineland, visited Beethoven's birthplace.

Or maybe not. Veterans of that generation moved immediately into building careers and families, and a lot of them wanted to put the war behind them. Many of their descendants say their fathers or grandfathers never talked about the war until late in life. Some never talked at all. Even now, new stories from World War II continue to emerge, and some of them are extraordinary. I can't help but wonder about the stories never told.

HISTORICAL NOTES

My fictional lieutenant Karl Hagan endured an experience shared by tens of thousands of American aviators in World War II. At the end of the war, Germany held 95,000 American prisoners, including 38,000 airmen, according to Donald L. Miller's *Masters of the Air,* a definitive history of the U.S. air campaign in Europe.

A number of POW memoirs served as valuable source material for this novel: *Shootdown: A World War II Bomber Pilot's Experience as a Prisoner of War in Germany* by William H. Wheeler; *Red Tail Captured, Red Tail Free: Memoirs of a Tuskegee Airman and POW* by Alexander Jefferson, with Lewis H. Carlson; and *The Flame Keepers: The True Story of an American Soldier's Survival Inside Stalag 17* by Ned Handy and Kemp Battle.

The Stalag Luft XIV of this novel is fictional, but the Stalag Luft III mentioned in these pages is real. In 1944, seventy-six prisoners escaped Stalag Luft III through a tunnel. Nearly all were recaptured, and fifty were executed. The incident became known as "The Great Escape," described in a 1950 book of that same name by Paul Brickhill and a 1963 film.

Readers may note that conditions in the stalags depicted herein seem mild compared to Germany's infamous concentration camps. POW accounts bear this out: Nazi Germany maintained different types of prisons for different types of inmates. Survivability inside the prisons depended on how the Nazis viewed the prisoners. American and British POWs faced food shortages, while some Russian prisoners starved outright. And, as history has noted, the concentration camps built for Jews amounted to death factories.

After Karl reunites with bombardier Billy Pell in Stalag Luft XIV, Pell describes how their navigator, Conrad, was killed by a mob. Sadly, this is also based on veterans' accounts. In *Masters of the Air,* an Eighth Air Force flier describes seeing the body of a fellow aviator hanging from a lamppost. Miller's book also includes an account of six fliers beaten and stoned to death in the town of Rüsselsheim.

To research Wilhelm's life as a U-boat officer, I drew on *Iron Coffins: A Personal Account of the German U-boat Battles of World War II* by Herbert Werner. After the war, Commander Werner escaped Allied captivity and eventually moved to the United States and became an American citizen. He died in Vero Beach, Florida, in 2013 at the age of ninety-two.

In *Iron Coffins,* Werner writes of a suicide order that went to fifteen U-boat commanders just before the D-Day invasion of Normandy in June 1944. Here I have taken a bit of artistic license: Wilhelm's crew receives the suicide order in November of that year.

Other valuable background information came from *Bitter Ocean: The Battle of the Atlantic, 1939–1945* by David Fairbank White. *Bitter Ocean* mentions Otto Kretschmer, the U-boat ace recalled by Wilhelm for his decent conduct toward crews of torpedoed freighters. Kretschmer was Germany's most effective U-boat captain: He sank forty-seven Allied ships before he was captured in 1941. Kretschmer spent several years as a prisoner of war in Canada, then returned home and eventually became an admiral in West Germany's navy.

Chapter 2 of this novel includes a reference to Wilhelm's suspicions that the Allies could read messages from U-boat headquarters. They could, indeed. Codebreakers at Britain's Bletchley Park, led by Alan Turing, had cracked the Enigma code—including the particularly difficult naval version.

My interest in U-boats began during my college days at the University of North Carolina at Chapel Hill. As a member of the UNC Scuba Club, I dived on several World War II shipwrecks off the Outer Banks. One of them was the *U-352,* sunk by depth charges from the Coast Guard cutter *Icarus* on May 9, 1942. The *U-352* lies off Cape Lookout at a depth of 110 feet, listing at a 45-degree angle. She is a Type VII, like Wilhelm's boat, and her oceanic grave is now on the National Register of Historic Places. By the way, if you'd like to see a U-boat up close, you don't have to strap on scuba tanks. The Museum of Science and Industry in Chicago hosts the *U-505,* a Type IX-C submarine captured in 1944.

To check out Karl's aircraft, the B-17 Flying Fortress, a number of opportunities exist. The Texas-based Commemorative Air Force flies B-17s and other World War II aircraft in nationwide tours. Museums with excellent exhibits include The National Museum of the United States Air Force in Dayton, Ohio; the National Museum of the Mighty Eighth Air Force in Pooler, Georgia; and the Palm Springs (California) Air Museum, just to name a few.

The refusal by Wilhelm and other kriegies to identify Jewish prisoners is based on an actual event. In January 1945, Master Sergeant Roddie Edmonds, of the U.S. Army, was the senior noncommissioned officer in Stalag IX-A near Ziegenhain, Germany. When told to point out Jews in the camp, he ordered every American to step forward. According to witnesses, a German officer said to Edmonds, "They cannot all be Jews." At gunpoint, Edmonds insisted they were. The German officer backed down.

In 2015, Edmonds posthumously received Israel's highest honor for non-Jews who risked their lives to save Jews during the Holocaust. The Knoxville, Tennessee, native was designated "Righteous Among the Nations" by the Yad Vashem Holocaust memorial in Jerusalem. Edmonds died in 1985.

On a personal note, my interest in the air war over Europe began with stories from my grandfather Thomas Morgan Daniel, who served as a B-17 mechanic. When I was ten or twelve years old, I found a softcover booklet in my grandparents' attic. It was titled *Target: Germany—The U.S. Army Air Forces' official story of the VII Bomber Command's first year over Europe.* The wartime publication described in great detail the men and machines and the dangers they faced. I had a thousand questions for my grandfather—then and over the next couple of decades.

After *Target: Germany,* I read anything else I could get my hands on about the Eighth. Excellent memoirs by veterans of the Eighth are too numerous to list, but an especially good one is *The Lucky Bas-*

tard Club: A B-17 Pilot in Training and in Combat, 1943–1945 by Eugene Fletcher.

By the way, my fictional creation, Lieutenant Hagan, flies with the 94th Bomb Group. That was my grandfather's unit. When my grandfather got out of the service, he could have continued in aviation; he said the airlines offered good pay for experienced mechanics.

But he would have none of it. After the war, he came home to the farm in North Carolina and never touched an airplane again.

Tom Young
Alexandria, Virginia
June 2019

ACKNOWLEDGMENTS

Researching and writing a historical novel can become a team effort. You bounce ideas off fellow history buffs. You visit museums and libraries, where guides and docents point you in the right direction. You receive input from a circle of trusted manuscript readers. And as with most books, nothing comes to print without the hard work of editors and literary agents.

My circle of support begins at home. My wife, Kristen, is not a professional writer or editor. But as a lifelong reader, she has a natural instinct for flaws in a story or in a turn of phrase. Her red pen knows no mercy. Her mother, retired UNC-Chapel Hill professor Laurel Files, also provided a practiced eye for proofreading.

Speaking of ruthless red pens, some of the best writing instruction I ever received came from Professor Richard Elam, who taught me at the University of North Carolina at Chapel Hill in the 1980s. Our friendship, grounded in shared love for the English language, continues to this day. He helped me polish this book, and he still doesn't cut me any breaks. I'm sure he'd say the first sentence of this paragraph is too long. Sorry, Dick.

Valuable input also came from an old squadron mate in the West Virginia Air National Guard. Many thousands of miles passed under our wings as I flew with Lieutenant Colonel Joe Myers. Joe loves books, and he loves history, and his suggestions made this a better story.

When I retired from the military, the decision came hard. It's tough to break bonds forged in harm's way. But someone gave me good advice: Get involved with veterans' groups. American Legion Post 20, affiliated with the National Press Club in Washington, has become my new unit. Its former commander, Vietnam veteran Ken Dalecki, worked for *Kiplinger Washington Editors* and *Congressional Quarterly*. Ken can spot an unnecessary word at a thousand yards, and he eliminated more than a few from this manuscript.

Novelist and writing instructor Barbara Esstman has helped sharpen all my novels, and this was no exception. My partnership with Barbara goes back years, to when I first took one of her workshops at The Writer's Center in Bethesda, Maryland. Thanks also to Robert Siegfried, for his review of the manuscript.

If you follow news on the radio, more than likely you've heard news from Camille Bohannon. During my years with the broadcast division of the Associated Press, Camille became a dear friend and colleague. She knows how to tell stories and paint pictures with words—and she helped me tell the story you hold in your hands.

Other valuable input came from fellow Tar Heel and novelist Jodie Tighe—as with all my novels. Thanks, Jodie, for a writing friendship now in its fourth decade. Thanks also to my parents, Bobby and Harriett Young, for their unflagging support—and close read of the manuscript.

While writing this book, I enjoyed a pleasant visit to the Palm Springs Air Museum in Riverside County, California. Volunteers there fielded my questions and let Kristen and me climb through their B-17, *Miss Angela*.

My dauntless literary agent, Michael Carlisle, believed in this project and saw it through to success. As a result, I now have the great pleasure of working with editorial director Wendy McCurdy and the team at Kensington Publishing.

Perhaps you noted the name on the dedication page of this book. Brigadier General V. Wayne "Speedy" Lloyd led my old unit, the 167th Airlift Wing, West Virginia Air National Guard. Before his retirement, he became commander of the entire WVANG, overseeing operations at both of the state's airlift wings.

When 9/11 came along and the call went out, we were ready, thanks to General Lloyd. He now serves a higher command. Good tailwinds, sir.